Daniel Applegate

A Novel of the American Revolution
based on a true story

Daniel Applegate

Terry Applegate

Brief Candle
Press

Cover and book design: Brief Candle Press.
Cover image based on "View on the Catskill—Early Autumn," Thomas Cole, 1837.
Map reproduction courtesy of Library of Congress, Geography and Map Division.
Fonts: Doves Type and IM FELL English.

First Brief Candle Press edition published 2025.
www.briefcandlepress.com

ISBN: 978-1-942319-88-7

Dedication

For my family.

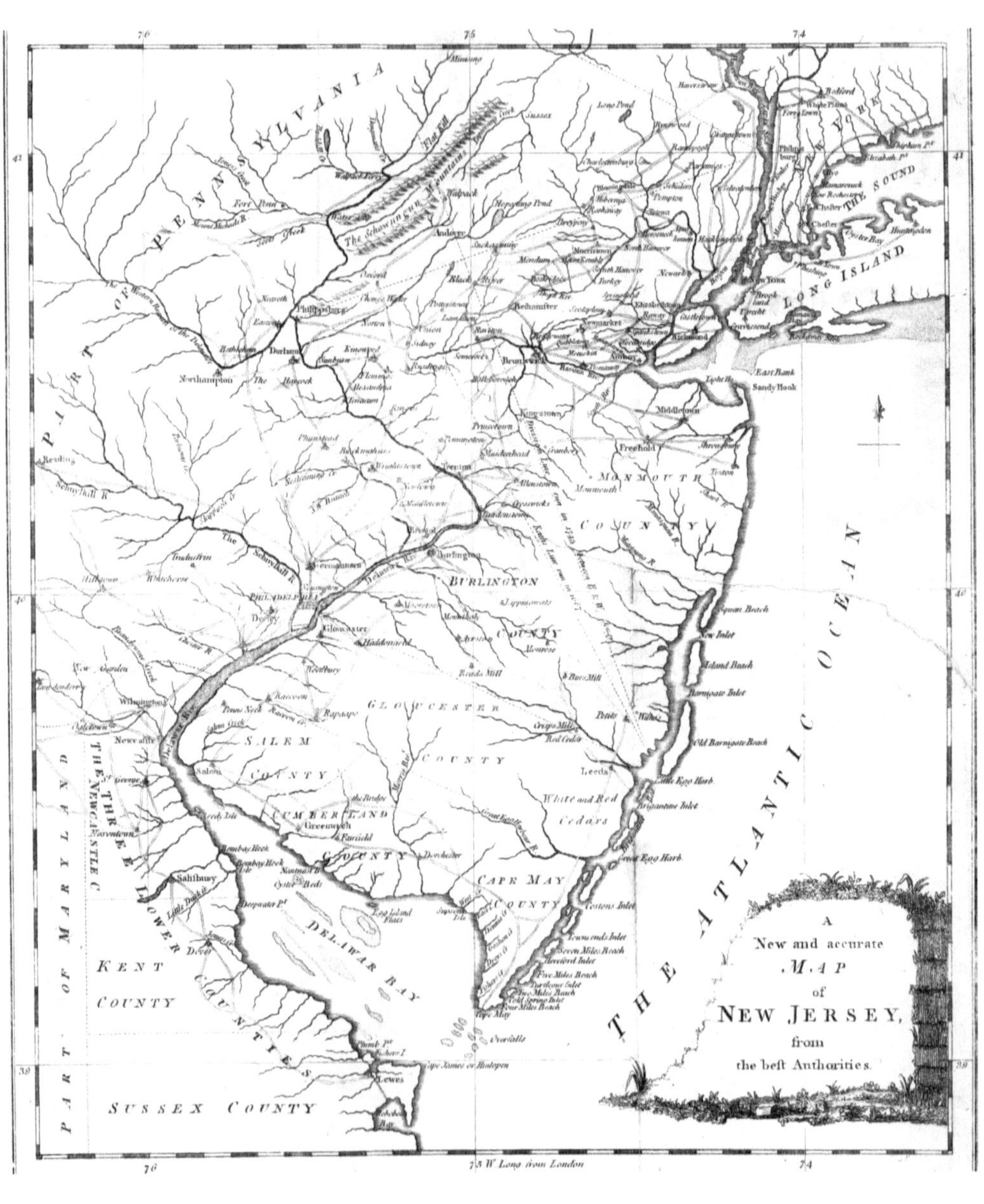

A
New and accurate
MAP
of
NEW JERSEY,
from
the beft Authorities.
THE ATLANTIC OCEAN
PENNSYLVANIA
NEW YORK
LONG ISLAND
THE SOUND
PART OF MARYLAND
THE THREE LOWER COUNTIES or NEWCASTLE C.
MONMOUTH COUNTY
BURLINGTON COUNTY
GLOUCESTER COUNTY
SALEM COUNTY
CUMBERLAND COUNTY
CAPE MAY COUNTY
KENT COUNTY
SUSSEX COUNTY
DELAWAR BAY
Sandy Hook
Sussex
Long Pond
Walpack
Andover
Black River
Philipsburg
Northampton
Bethlehem
Durham
Reading
Schuylkill R.
Trenton
Burlington
PHILADELPHIA
Gloucester
Haddonfield
Wilmington
Newcastle
Salem
Greenwich
Fairfield
Dover
Lewis
Freehold
Middletown
Brunswick
Princetown
Kingstown
New York
Richmond
Amboy
White and Red Cedars
Leeds
Little Egg Harb.
Great Egg Harb.
Brigantine Inlet
Old Barnigate Beach
Barnigate Inlet
Island Beach
New Inlet
Squan Beach
Cape May
Five Miles Beach
Cape James or Hinlopen
Overfalls
76 W Long from London
41
40
39
76
75
74

Table of Contents

Prologue

The flight to Portland was five hours, then after that was the long trip to the village of Yoncalla with a total travel time of about eight hours. I was tired. The three-hour time difference was catching up with me as I drove the rented Yaris through mountain valleys and passes that made up the Cascades. The mountains were impressive, covered in yellow tamarack; we certainly had nothing this tall and golden in the east. The air was hot and dry. It was a hundred degrees outside and took my breath away, literally. I had thought Oregon was supposed to be cooler, a lot cooler.

I went to meet my father's family, a group of people that I never really knew existed until a few years ago. He had told us he had no family, but then he was never one to tell much of the truth anyway, and then he was gone by the time I was two.

Suffering through the heat was just a small part of this adventure. The real worry started when I drove through the smoke of several forest fires in my going back and forth between family homes and to the reunion. This was all kinds of crazy, I thought, as the miles ticked away to my destinations; I had never seen this much smoke in my entire life.

What prompted this quest was my emotional reaction to a battle sequence in a book written by one of my favorite authors. I thought for sure the author would mention my three times great grandfather in this scene that she had written, and I desperately wanted her to, but like the talented writer and teacher that she was, she didn't. It was then that realized my curiosity about that grandfather got the best of me, which lead me to

Oregon looking for a family and a history I did not know.

I arrived at Susan's home, my second cousin, by late afternoon. She was an artist, internationally known for some of her water-color paintings. The paintings were beautiful, haunting in some ways, but I loved them all. We made an early night of it, because the next day I was going to spend time with Shannon, another second cousin, who was one of the family historians and an author/lecturer on the history of Oregon and its first families.

The next morning Susan took me to the "old house", our family's home that was built prior to Oregon's statehood. It was a mansion of white clapboard, reminiscent of New England saltbox homes. Great-great-Grandpa Charlie needed a home that size, since he had fifteen children that grew into adulthood there. The home was in disrepair in the 1980s, but loving care from the local family made it livable again. We entered through the back porch and passed Grandma Melinda's herb garden; Grandma was an herbalist/midwife and the only doctor for a thousand miles in any direction prior to 1860.

Around the corner, Shannon sat at the dining table with notepad and pencil in hand, wanting to record as much as I could remember about my father and his immediate family; those that were my stories. I had thought it strange that there was no computer at her fingertips, but then there are folks who really like the feel of pencil and paper in their hands, and I couldn't object to that. To this day, I love the smell of a number two Ticonderoga pencil.

Shannon listened with the intensity of a researcher, writing and asking questions in between as I recited what I knew. After a time, her visage softened, and she became the kindly professor that she was. As we were winding down with the flow of information, she suddenly locked those blue-green eyes of hers with mine and said in a commanding whisper, "You will write a book one day". I didn't know what to think of that, except that she thought my sad story was good enough to put to paper—or Microsoft Word—as the case might be. But that project would be for another day, another time.

My interview done, and a new sistership made, I walked through the home that was my family's inheritance. I touched the treasured items of the souls that had lived there in a time long before mine, breathing life into my imagination. Daniel's drum was there, and letters too from children who wrote to Grandpa Daniel, giving their thanks for the sacrifices he made during the Revolutionary War. Most of Daniel's things had been destroyed with the first trip down the rapids of the Columbia River nearly 180 years ago. The drum was the only item left.

I turned a corner and there were several paintings done by Susan, representations of the family's pioneer life on this farm. One painting held my attention, and that is where Susan found me at the end of the day when she came to bring me back to her home.

"This looks like a Christmas party," I said as she came up behind me. The painting depicted a rather large gathering of people all wearing clothing from different time periods and dancing to the music of a flute and fiddle. The scene was lit by a roaring fire in the hearth and the golden glow from it spread warmth through the rest of the room. The party was complete with a table full of turkey, beef, a variety of vegetables, and fruit pies. Susan and Shannon were sitting at the corner of the buffet table and involved in a serious conversation.

"It is. It is a seven - generation painting. This house was the place to be for all sorts of celebrations in the county at one time, with the parties lasting way into the wee hours. Here, read the poem written by Grandpa Charlie. We found the poem buried in one of the trunks," she said as she pulled the painting from the wall and flipped it over. Taped on the back side was a set of verses that had been copied from the original document:

"Now my young people think of a plan,

To celebrate Christmas the best way you can.

Get up your jellies, your pies, and good meat

And ask all your kinfolk, to come help you eat;

And all other young folks that you wish to see
Make them perfectly welcome, jolly and free.
And when all are together, you'll have a good chance
To make Buck get his fiddle and have a good dance
And go on until morning without any fear
Or as long as you please!
Your Daddy don't care!" (Grandpa Charlie, circa 1870)

"Not bad for a blacksmith; what a treasure," I said as I re-read the writing and touched it to make it real. It was a message retrieved from a bottle long lost in the great sea of time, containing a small bit of wisdom given for future generations, a real treasure indeed. "So, where's Grandpa Daniel in the picture?"

"There, just there," she said as she pointed and smiled. Daniel was depicted as a boy of about three or four, dressed in a homespun shirt and pulling on his aged granddaughter's skirts, trying to get her attention as she was holding a serving platter of beef for an older gentleman. "I'll be in the kitchen when you're ready."

"All right, I'll be there in a few." I stood there for a few more moments, staring at Daniel. He was the watershed, the thing that sets in motion all things after it. I wasn't sure I could think of him as this young, but he had to be at one time.

My voice betrayed my thoughts, and I whispered, "Tell me your story, Grandpa."

Pennsylvania Harvest

"Daniel! What are ye doing all the way up here?" Annabelle said as she pulled her golden tresses from her eyes to see him better. Her hair spilled out of her cap and the entire headdress was about to fall to the ground.

"Thinking." It was a perfect time to be doing just that, with the bustle of the wheat and hay harvests finished. I stole a few moments to be alone and watched the sun creep slowly down, bringing with it the gloaming in hues of gold and pink to the early twilight sky. "Ever thought of going to the Ohio Country?"

"Na, too many Indians there wanting to fight us. Might as well stay here with the sort we know. Don't need to purposefully walk into it. On second thought maybe, if I got married to a big strong man that could handle them."

"So, what are ye doing up here, Annabelle? Shouldn't ye be helping with the feast?" The little girl was like a puppy. She followed me everywhere when she was visiting, bringing a smile with her. I pinched off a stem of the orchard grass missed by the scythe and handed it up to her as she stood beside me. The air was fragrant with it: a light spicy and fruity aroma, like cinnamon and lemons, that made everything feel clean and fresh.

"Yer sister said to find ye. She needed ye to help with some things, I guess. Hey, what happened to yer left eye?" she said as she plopped down beside me, sucking on the long piece of orchard grass. I had made the mistake of turning my head to look at her as she spoke.

"Nothing. Just ran into a tree limb, that's all."

"No tree limb did that. It's all swollen and going purple."

"Are ye calling me a liar, Annabelle?"

"Ye got a handprint on yer face too! Did the tree limb do that? Ye need to lie better, Daniel."

"Hmmph. Guess I can come up with something else. I don't think anyone will notice."

"I noticed. Yer sister won't be happy 'bout it either."

"Well, it'll be dark soon. No one will see it then. Really, I am not that badly hurt, save my pride."

"Boer hit ye again, didn't he?"

"We gotta go Annabelle, they'll come looking for us," I said as I reached out to pull her up.

"Well, if ye don't tell Aletta by tomorrow, I will."

"All right. I'll mention it to her. I certainly don't need yer help, though."

We separated at the bottom of the hill; Annabelle to the kitchen and me, unfortunately, towards Master Boer, the factor of the farm. It was time for me to make my appearance before him. If I didn't go see him, he'd make me pay later. I made my way through the running children and diverted myself past the fire pit to catch the aroma of the roasted pork — it smelled wonderful — then on to where Boer had stationed himself with the beer keg.

He filled each mug to the brim with our home brew, all the while joking, teasing, and laughing with the men in line. He was certainly civil with them. I wasn't sure he'd be with me.

"What are you doing here, boy? You finished with your chores?" he said when he finally looked up at me. He was a short grizzly haired man with a temper meaner than a wild boar that he resembled.

"Yes sir, I am," I said without hesitation, looking into his eyes without malice, hoping that I didn't rouse the beast within.

"All right then. Mistress Aletta will be calling for the evening prayer soon. Go on then, get you some dinner. I'll check on your work later."

"Thank ye, Sir." I left the area quickly, not giving him time to change his mind.

ᴑᴑ ᴑᴑ ᴑᴑ

The sun had drifted below the horizon, leaving the clouds covered in dark pinks and golds draped in a field of darkening blue. A slight chill tinged the air. It was fall after all, and soon winter would be here.

"Daniel?"

I turned to the sound of my sister's voice as and saw her near the fire pit, talking to one of the men there. She looked so much like Mama standing in the firelight, and once again the longing to see my mother welled up from the deepness of my heart. "*Ja* , coming, sis," I responded as I gently closed the door to feelings that I could ill afford on this night.

"Help me by rounding up the children and get them in a circle near the fire. Oh, and get them to wash their hands, please."

"*Ja,* sure." Washing their hands wasn't the problem, it was keeping them from throwing water and snapping towels at each other. "Annabelle!" I hollered as she walked past us, her arms loaded with trays of warm bread that smelled wonderful. "I need yer help!"

"I'll be there in a minute." She unloaded the trays at the tables and made her way to me and the little miscreants. "Ye do have yer hands full," she said as she came to stand beside me. "Watch this: *Children!*". Well, that got their attention. They stopped throwing the water in very short order. "Ladies and gentlemen, if ye want to eat yer dinner and have dessert, ye will wash yer hands without dousing each other with water. Understand?"

"Yes 'um Annabelle," they said as one, all looking at their feet in guilt.

"All right then dry yer hands and go with Daniel to make a circle near the fire, and try not to fall into it."

"Yes, ma'am."

"Show them no fear, Daniel." Annabelle told me in my ear as she left in a flurry of petticoats to bring more food to the tables.

We arrived at the fire pit, made a decent circle, and complete silence ensued as the adults moved into the circle with the children grasping small and large hands alike. Jacob Lanterman, Aletta's brother-in-law, slowly turned his head, acknowledging each of us with a smile and a twinkle in his eye. He then closed his eyes, lowered his head and we began our prayer, saying as one:

"The eyes of all wait upon You, O Lord, and You give them their food at the proper time. You open Your hand and gratify everything that lives with satisfaction.

"Our father which art in heaven, hallowed be thy Name, Thy kingdom come, Thy will be done as in heaven, so in earth. Give us day by day our daily bread. And forgive us our sins: for we also forgive everyone that is indebted to us. And lead us not into temptation, but deliver us from evil ."

Then, Jacob alone repeated, "Lord God, heavenly Father, bless us and these gifts you have given us, which we enjoy from Your bountiful goodness, through Jesus Christ, our Lord."

"*Amen!*" we all said.

The children quickly scrambled to the tables with their mothers in tow, and the men followed them. I sat beside my sister at the table nearest the kitchen door, so that I might help her bring out more food when it was needed. Master Boer kept his distance and sat conveniently at another table to mind the beer keg and keep the pitchers full throughout dinner.

The tables were heavily laden with the roast pork, cooked vegetables, mashed potatoes, bread, cheeses, and pitchers of cold milk straight from the springhouse. I had just poured some milk into my cup when Aletta brought two mugs of beer and handed me one with a grin. "Ye deserve it, Daniel."

"Really, ye think so?"

"Ye worked as hard as any of the men here today. But mind ye, there will be no more for ye tonight, little brother." She ruffled my hair with her hand and then drew it slowly across my cheek. "Ye so look like Papa, Danny. I am sorry that he is missing this."

"I miss him too," I whispered into her ear as I hugged her. "Thank ye for the beer, sis." I turned my focus to my plate and ate like I hadn't eaten in a year. The chatter at dinner was as plentiful as the food, but then I heard part of a conversation about the loss at Savannah earlier in the month.

"Hey, sis, Savannah's in the colony of Georgia, right?" I whispered so not to disturb the conversation.

"*Ja,* it is, and don't ye go thinking that the Revolution is something glorious with all this talk from them. It's not. Savannah was a disaster."

"Na, not thinking, just curious, that's all." I left it at that and listened to Master Jacob and Aaron, a local man that had just returned from business in the south.

"Seems General Washington was right. Losing Savannah has left the Brits in complete possession of Georgia. My guess is South Carolina will be their next foothold. Damn d'Estaing! Damn his honor! Giving Prevost twenty-four hours to respond to his demand of surrender!"

"*Master Lanterman!* The children if ye please!" Mistress Lanterman exclaimed while covering her youngest's ears. Tiny giggles escaped from the rest of Jacob's children, and it was obvious to the rest of us that by their reaction, the children had seen similar by-play between their parents before. The rest of us sat a little bewildered at the situation, paused our conversations to watch what would happen next.

To his wife's discomfort, Jacob stood with his head bowed in a manner of a man looking for the right words. The children's giggles stopped as they watched their father, and quiet settled around all the tables. He slowly raised his head. His face was remorseful, save a bit of mischief in his eyes when he looked directly at his wife. The look lasted only for a second, and his wife drew her face into a worried frown. He then lowered his head a fraction, with his eyes to the ground.

"Your servant, Madam, always and forever," he said as he made a very low stiff bow to his wife. He then un-bent his torso slowly, looking at his wife lovingly first and then each of his children, saying, "Please accept my apology, Dear Wife and children. I apologize for the vulgarity of my tongue." He nodded his head and grinned at Mistress Lanterman and, with a flourish of moving aside invisible coattails, sat down, returning his attention to Aaron. Mistress Lanterman just sat there and stared at him for a minute in a sort of a state of shock, then cracked a slight smile at Jacob and shook her head. She then took her leave of him, leading their youngest child into the house.

"Do ye know how many men were lost, Aaron?"

"From what I heard, somewhere between a thousand and twelve hundred dead and wounded. All because of d'Estaing's honor and the two traitors that had alerted the Prevost of the attack. I heard that the battle didn't last an hour. May God rest their souls," Aaron whispered the last as he contemplated the food on his fork. "That is more men than General Washington has lost in any other battle," he said a little louder.

"Then all is lost, ye think?"

"No, the Brits have Georgia, for sure, but I think they have been misled. The Redcoats believe most of the people in the southern colonies are Loyalists. They are wrong. There are stories of the British and the Loyalists committing atrocities against several of the backwoods families. Men hanged, women ravished, crops and homes burned to the ground. Those actions are not going unnoticed by our Patriots and those who, until now, have been undecided.

"No, I truly believe all is not lost, Jacob. General Washington is certainly not ready to give up. Neither are his generals and even if they wanted to, they cannot. As ye know, they all have bounties on their heads."

"General Washington is keeping his bodyguards close, I hope?"

"He's not keeping them; they are keeping him. They don't like it if he is out of their sight for too long," Aaron said with a chuckle.

"The north has been active with small skirmishes as of late—outside of the Indian activity in the recent months. Is there any chance of a large battle anytime soon?" Jacob asked as he reached for his tankard.

"I don't know. I fully expect those skirmishes to continue during the winter. The real goal will be to keep the Patriots and their homes safe. The Loyalists are famous for rooting out the 'disloyal' citizens from their beds in the dead of night in nothing but sleeping clothes and walking them barefoot to the Sugar House, that prison in New York. Very few live to walk back out its doors, once they are pushed in," Aaron said as he drained the last drop of beer from his mug and reached for the pitcher, pouring more into it.

"So, ye will be headed back to the New Jersey Line soon, then?"

"*Ja.* I've signed on for another three years."

With that, their conversation on the Revolution ended and a new one started, about business in the Pennsylvania, New Jersey area and the signs of the coming weather. I had heard all I needed to hear and quickly finished the last of my dinner as I asked Aletta if I could be excused from the table.

"What, ye don't want thirds?" Aletta asked.

"Na, I am stuffed. I'll stay, help clean up, and pack leftovers for those leaving tomorrow, if ye want."

"Are ye catching a fever?" Aletta asked as she mockingly laid a hand on my forehead. "This is not like ye."

"I am fine. Let me help, and then I'll be off to the barn and bed." I had been sleeping in the barn the last week to make room in the house for the Lantermans.

"All right, but let's wait a few more minutes. There is to be some music and dancing. We can work on moving the food after that starts. Ye sure ye don't want to play with the other musicians? Ye've not had much chance to practice that fife this week."

"That would be fun for sure, but really, sis, I am just tired. It's been a long day. I'll help ye with the food and then head off to bed, unless ye'll be needing me for something else."

"Sure. In that case, I'll go ahead and start cleaning up the dirty plates left on the tables, now anyway. The ladies will be in soon enough to work on washing the dishes. Ye get the kettles of water to the fire to heat up?"

"I can do that." I said with a smile.

Once the water kettles were set for warming, I went back to help carry the scraped dishes to the makeshift table set beside the wash basins that were outside the kitchen door. "The pigs are going to enjoy their dinner tonight. It has been a while since they've seen this many scraps," I said, passing up Aletta with my stack of dishes. I turned back to help with hers, which were about to topple over.

"Oh, thank ye, Daniel. How 'bout ye take those scraps to them now?" Aletta said with a nod of her head toward the pigs' food trough. "Don't let yer guard down with that boar, ye know how he is. He'll take yer hand off with no thought at all."

"Ye warn me of him every night, sis!"

"*Ja,* and so far, every night ye come back undamaged. Take the lantern so ye can see."

Ahab, our boar, was just a mean animal. With a personality like his namesake, that wicked old king of Israel. He would maim or kill anything, given half a chance. Aletta had asked Master Boer to put him down as his behavior had become more aggressive and erratic of late, but Boer was disinclined to do so. He claimed that Ahab was good breeding stock, and that he really wasn't that bad after all.

When I got back, Aletta had already begun to package some of the leftovers in the empty flour sacks. "Sis?"

"Hmmm? How were the pigs? Did Ahab accost ye?" she asked

as she covered a small crock full of some roasted pork and tied burlap cover to the top.

"I'm unmolested," I said as I snitched a piece of the pork from the platter in front of her. She turned to look at me, then to see the truth for herself.

"Not molested! What happened to yer eye?"

"Oh, that's nothing." Apparently, the candlelight was better than I had thought.

"Nothing, nothing! It's black and blue! He did get ye."

"Sort of. The fence door didn't hit me that hard. Ahab got a bit aggravated and butted his head against it as I was latching it back down. My face just happened to be in the way." I hated lying to her, but if I told her the truth, the plan that I had made for later this evening would fall apart.

"That boar is going to be the death of one of us. All right, I'll tell Master Boer in the morning. He certainly is in no condition to deal with Ahab tonight. He refills his mug when he refills a guests'," she said as she went back to packing the meals.

She was exhausted. The dark circles around her eyes were more prominent and her face sallow. She hadn't even bothered to corral her dark blonde hair back under her cap, as was her constant habit. The week had taken its toll on her, and yet she kept a smile on her face for me.

"Ye so look like Mama, Leta," I said as I hugged her from her back and laid my chin on the hair that covered her shoulder and smelled of orchard grass, roasted pork, smoke and sugar, the mark of her long day.

"Aww, thank ye, Danny. I've not heard anything so nice in a while," she whispered as she turned and hugged me back. We rested there for a few more moments and then she let me go to continue with the wrapping of the leftovers.

"Sis, may I have a plate to take to the barn with me tonight to snack on?" I asked as I helped her with covering another crock with a cloth.

"I knew ye were going to be hungry later. Sure, get a clean plate and a fork from the cupboard. Take what ye want. Wait . . . before ye do that, please take these leftovers to the springhouse for me."

"Should I put them on any specific shelf?"

"No, wherever they'll fit. I'll get them tomorrow for the Lantermans' trip back to New Jersey. Thank ye, Danny."

It was just a short walk up a gentle slope to where the house was buried into the side of the hill. A spring ran under the wooden floor of the house, keeping the house cold enough to store fresh fruits, meats, and vegetables for a time.

I hung the lantern on its hook on the wall and surveyed the interior for the best place to set the packaged food. There was some space left on a shelf above the burlap bags full of potatoes. The fall had been good to us; there were multiple sacks of apples, pears, potatoes, carrots, turnips, and beets all from this year's harvest, occupying just about every inch of space in the house, save the corner that was inhabited by the cheeses and butter that was put up for the winter. No one living at the farm this year would go hungry, and there was enough for an itinerant visitor.

I pulled out a small flour sack of my own out of my shirt and loaded it with some carrots and a couple of potatoes, and threw in a small round of cheese. I moved across to the other wall where the fruits were stored, picking out a couple of apples and pears and then smelled the hanging grapes, the last of the season.

I plopped the first one into my mouth, and heard a popping noise just as I bit through the tight skin. A sweet and tart flavor sprung loose on my tongue, making my mouth water. With the first grape gone, I decided to add a small bunch to the flour sack to take with me, since no one would notice anyway. After I left home tonight, it would be quite a while before I had anything that would taste this good.

I grabbed the lantern, latched the door, and blew out the candle in the lantern, navigating the path to the barn by starlight. Once there, I'd hide the sack under my blankets and then return to the kitchen to get my plate.

I would have enough food for a while until I could safely hunt. If all worked well, Annabelle would tell the family that I was headed west. That short conversation about the Ohio Country would get them looking for me in that direction, while I was really traveling east towards Easton.

⚬◯⚬ ⚬◯⚬ ⚬◯⚬

"That took ye some time," Aletta said, looking up at me from drying off a rather large tray.

"When I was leaving the spring house, I heard Hiram squawk and thought I'd better find out why," I said as I set the lantern down and re-lit it for more light. "Turns out two of Daniel Lanterman's sons were up to some mischief. I found them teasing Hiram with an apple, dangling it in front of him so that he followed them out of his stall, and to the outside of the barn. Hiram didn't want to go beyond the fence, though. Don't blame him, it usually means he has to work."

"Oh, my! Hiram's is a draft horse and weighs nearly two thousand pounds. They could have been killed if they he got his ire up. I've seen him when he isn't happy 'bout something."

"*Ja.* I gave them a talking to and shooed them out, got Hiram settled and let him have two apples for the trouble. He's no worse for the wear. Oh, and I took another blanket from the closet and took it up to the loft. It was a bit cool last night up there."

"That's a blessing that no one was stomped or chomped on. Just bring all the blankets down in the morning and I'll shake them out," she said, wrapping a loaf of bread in a cloth. I watched where she put it, thinking I might come back for it later.

"Yer plate is over there, if ye want it," Aletta said, nodding in the direction of the plate on the sideboard as she dried another tray. I hesitated, thinking about how I was going to pack all that food in the sack.

"Ye look so tired. Why don't ye take the plate and head back to

15

the loft? Just bring it all back in the morning when ye come to help with breakfast, Danny. Now shoo!"

"Ye're the one that needs rest. Make sure ye get to bed soon." I said with a yawn.

"Just gonna finish up these last few dishes and then I am ta bed."

"I love ye, sis," I said and gave her one last hug. She pulled a curl behind my ear, kissed my cheek, and physically turned me toward the door. I left and didn't look back.

Runaway

I awoke long before dawn, startled by an owl screeching like a banshee outside of the barn. It had disturbed the horses just enough that they were shifting their feet and making little woofing noises in their stalls below me. I heard nothing amiss, once all the animals quieted down and then I listened to see if any of the men that shared the loft with me had awakened. They hadn't; a good omen for sure.

I dressed as quietly as I could, so as not to wake anyone or thing in the loft or barn. I needed to be unseen and unheard to even have half of a chance of leaving this place. I climbed quietly down the ladder from the loft and landed softly in the hay. It was chilly, and the temperature had dropped considerably since going to bed last evening. Now, it was cold enough that I could see my breath in the light of the gibbous moon and its starry companions as I left the barn.

This was it, *freedom!* No more belittling, whippings, no more fighting with Boer. I was irrevocably on my own, until I found either Papa, or my brother Ben who was with Spencer's Additional Regiment somewhere east of the Delaware River, maybe near Morristown.

I walked stealthily, listening within the silence of the dark for any human noises that could keep me from this adventure. The chill in the air lessened as I quickened my pace on the packed dirt road that led away from the farm. Soon I would go off the road using the cover of the forest and a deer path to hide my footsteps from all except an expert tracker.

Cornplanter

It was Cornplanter who had shown me how to hide my tracks. I said a silent prayer of thanks for him, and chuckled afterword, knowing full well that he would think that very strange.

Cornplanter was half Seneca and half Dutch by blood, and he never let the Dutch get in the way of his life as a warrior of the Seneca. He taught me many things over the last few years: bits of his language, hunting with a bow, the best roots to eat in the wilderness. He was a second father, a teacher, and a friend. I was nine when I first met him three years ago.

He had passed through our farmlands on his way back to his home during midsummer. When I first saw him, he looked every bit like the Indian I imagined from the stories I had heard. He was dressed in a breechcloth with leggings and moccasins, holding in one hand a rather large dead rabbit dripping blood, and in the other a huge hunting knife he had used to gut it.

He stood very still and stared at me, trying to judge if I planned to scream or run. I did neither, but held his eyes and slowly walked towards him, greeting him with open hands and an open mind. He relaxed his stance, said nothing while cleaning the blood from the knife on the grass in front of him, and motioned me to come closer. He mimicked eating and rubbed his belly, beckoning me to sit at his fire.

"Do you speak this language?" he asked me in Dutch as he skewered the rabbit for roasting on fire and stuffed a few vegetables under its coals.

"*Ja,* a little."

"You are hungry?"

"A little."

"For such a tall young man, I would think you would be very hungry." Both were true. I was shoulder height to my Indian friend, and I was very hungry.

"I am a guest at your table. I don't want to be ill-mannered to one who is also a guest on our farm."

"So, I am a guest?"

"*Ja*, as far as I am concerned."

"Your sister and the master of the house may think otherwise."

"They may, but they are not here, and I am."

He chuckled at that as he rotated the rabbit on the fire.

"You are alone?" he asked as he stabbed his knife into the vegetables to turn them as well.

"Not quite. The hired hands are back at the house." He looked at me and then stood quickly and scanned all four horizons. "They won't come looking for me. Your safe here."

"And your father, where is he?" he asked, squatting back on his heels.

"I don't know. I've not seen him in a few months. He travels a lot for his employer."

That evening, while we shared the roasted rabbit, he told a story of his people and then asked me for one of mine. The exchange of stories continued into the wee hours of the night until I could no longer keep my eyes open. We slept near the fire and when I woke in the morning, he had already gone.

Into the Wilds

Easton, at the very least, was a two-day walk from my sister's house. From there, I'd cross the Delaware by ferry and then pick up the road to Morristown. Getting through Easton, though, might be a bit tricky; folks watch out for one another and their children, especially a child that has run from home more than once.

If I made it through the Easton crossing without being noticed, I figured I'd be in Morristown in four days with good weather and eight days if it wasn't. Once my food ran out, I would bow hunt in the woods. I would sleep under the shelter of a large pine tree or in a barn. It would be better still if I could find a fellow traveler with a wagon, then I could ride most of the way, and sleep in, or under the wagon at night. If it got much colder, though, there would be no one on the road to ride with.

I kept my eyes on the deer path for most of the walk, out of fear of tripping on a root or falling in a hole, but with the coming dawn, I stopped for a rest and watched the sun rise through the frosted trees, coloring their edges in shimmering gold. As the sun rose higher, it turned the sky above from a vast dark expanse into azure, with streaks of purple and crimson. *Red sky in morning, shepherd's warning,* Papa had said when he saw the morning sky like this. I shook off the foreboding feeling and moved on; I couldn't let fear get a foothold on my soul.

By noon, the air seemed a little chillier than in the morning, but no matter; I was at a good pace and had changed direction ever so slightly so to be heading directly towards Easton. I had a small meal then, after finding a boulder relatively clear of lichen to sit on. My tummy had been growling a little for a while and rumbled in earnest as I pulled out some bread and a little of the pork from last night's harvest celebration.

The bread had not dried out and the pork was still very edible. Both tasted better than last night's dinner. Strange how eating outdoors does that. I ate slowly, savoring each bite, and watched the cloud mottled sky. It smelled very good here, crisp with the scent of pine mixed in with the musty scent of soil.

I washed the bread and pork down with water left in my canteen. I would need to find clean water soon and a place to sleep, before the thick clouds above me decided to release their load of snow or rain, or maybe both.

A few hours or so after the meal, a wet, heavy snow began to fall, making it clear that I needed to find a place to camp, and soon. I reached the top of a hill and found the perfect spot under and between the branches of a large pine tree. It would offer more comfort and safety than sleeping out under the clouded sky.

Safety, though, was more of a priority. I had heard the throaty growl of a mountain lion earlier at the boulder, but hadn't heard him since. I didn't need to encourage him to visit, and I figured resting under a pine tree laden with snow would cover my scent. I crawled in, placing my back against the cold thick trunk of the tree, in between two branches, and thanked it for its protection from the weather and everything two footed or more.

Slowly, the warmth returned to my hands as I rubbed them together. As soon as I could move them, I pulled a biscuit from my pack and stuffed it in my mouth, quelling the rumbling in my belly. They were as good as they were at yesterday's breakfast. Aletta did know how to make a good biscuit.

Taking a quick inventory, I found that the bread was nearly gone, and the pork would be gone shortly. There were no more grapes, but I still had four apples, eleven biscuits and the small round of cheese from the springhouse. That might get me through most of tomorrow. The day after that, I would have to hunt.

I finished my cold dinner as the light disappeared under my tree, and my last thoughts before sleep turned back to Papa. He first left us when he was conscripted into the Pennsylvania militia in the late spring, just before I met Cornplanter. I didn't want him to go; we had just lost Mama and I was afraid he'd not come back. However, if he didn't go, by all rights they could hang him, since he had no money to pay the fine that would keep him from service.

I remembered I had cried silently as he hugged me, then wiped the tears from my eyes and kissed the top of my head.

"Ye know, son, I have done this before, years ago, during the French and Indian War, and I made it back safe and sound. I must go. Freedom never comes free," he said quietly in my ear as he hugged me one last time.

He hugged Aletta and Ben then, and smiled. "I'll be back as soon as I can. Ye take care of each other, now," he said at the last, then he turned to catch up with the rest of the militia as they marched out of Easton.

I drifted into sleep, resting long and deep through most of the night until the sounds outside of the pine tree woke me in the wee hours. The blowing wind that lulled me to sleep had stopped, leaving in its wake a muted silence created by the fallen snow, until I heard the first crunch.

Something large and sure-footed was breaking a thin layer of ice that had formed on top of the snow. The animal was close enough that I could hear it breathe as I imagined the air around its snout clouded with mist from its breath. The beast began to sniff and root around the tree, and I froze in place, refusing my body's desire to run.

I reached under my blanket for my hunting knife and quietly slid it out of the sheath. The knife that stayed tucked in my shirt all night was warm and comforting in my hands. Time was moving much too slowly for me, but patience in the hunt always proved its worth, as both Papa and Cornplanter had reminded me so many times. So I waited, calming the urge to move, and listened, not making a sound.

Not quite satisfied, the creature walked with heavy footfalls around the pine, pawing at the icy snow from the tree's limbs, trying to find a good place to burrow in and under. The sound of the footfalls was telling. He was large, maybe as big as me. That meant I was going to have one chance at survival when the right time came, but it was not yet.

The pawing continued for a few more seconds right in front of me and then he changed tactics by trying to nudge the pine boughs out of his way. My fear coiled like a snake seeking release and I stilled myself as best I could, planning anticipated movements each of us might make in battle, eventually deciding that I had to strike first. Suddenly he stopped, turned away from me, as he listened to a triumphant howl coming from the southwest. He returned the call to his friends and bounded off after the ruckus.

I took a deep breath, relaxed my back against the tree, said a prayer of thanks and waited an eternity to make sure the animal and his friends stayed gone in that southwest direction. Finally, I left the tree with the coming dawn and ran stiff legged upwind, in the opposite direction of the beasts, making my trip to Easton and the ferry a little longer. No matter, I would still get there alive.

Papa had told me stories of wolves and mountain lions when I was younger. I had heard both very near our farm once when I was very young, maybe one or two years old. I remember sitting outside on the porch one day when Mama came and pulled me back into the cabin at the sound of the call of a catamount. Papa left in a rush with his long rifle then. Not too long after, we heard gunshots, and then we heard it no more.

Cornplanter drew me pictures of both in the dirt and then howled like each one of them during one of his lessons. "Wolves and panthers still roam the lands to the north and west, but here, they are very few," he said, raising his hands to the woods with great sadness in his eyes. "The whites have hunted and killed most of them. They say they do it to protect people and their livestock, but they've killed too many of these animals and we will all suffer for it."

The wolves and the mountain lion weren't supposed to be here, and I wondered what had pushed them so far south. Cornplanter and Papa both taught that both animals and birds move with the seasons. Geese fly to the south in the winter, and elk, deer, and panthers would come down from the cold north of the mountains to find food. The predators that I encountered must have come from the far north, where the cold of winter made hunting food very difficult. It must be frigid up there.

I reached a small meadow on the downslope of a hill that sparkled like diamonds in the rising sun. It was cold, with my breath hanging heavy in the air, but bearable out on the field as I headed back into the woods.

All Saints' Day

I sat on a rock at the top of a Pennsylvania mountain, chewing on the last of the biscuits I had taken from my sister's larder two days ago, and studied the deer path below me. The climb up could have been much worse, given the melting snow, ice and resulting muck from the warming midday temperatures, but going down the steep, curved muddy trail in front of me was not what I would choose, if I had a choice.

Thorny bushes that topped the down curve on the left side of the trace would block any fall if I slipped near that side, but I certainly didn't want to find out. The right side was rock, with few handholds. Sliding on the mud, catching a root with my foot tripping, or any other misstep could be deadly. Papa and Ben would never forgive me for being so foolhardy.

Then there was that final bend that I could not see beyond, save a few of the thorny bushes. All I could imagine was a narrow ledge and a fifty-foot drop continuing around the rock corner. "Nothing for it," I muttered to myself, and took the first slippery steps on the twisting downward slope and prayed that there was still a rock wall on the right side of the path as I made the turn.

Within a few minutes of careful footwork, my prayer was answered; I was still bounded by a sturdy corridor of rock and bushes with a mud floor. Eventually, the path straightened, giving way to dryer ground. Within half an hour, I was back walking on the spongy leaf mold at the bottom of the trail, feeling much relieved that I would live for another day.

Closing my eyes, I listened to the deep wood, and I gave thanks for the safe passage down. The Delaware River was close; I could hear water gently running over and around the rocks near the shallows. The squirrels here were taking advantage of the warmer weather this early evening, still rooting under fallen leaves for the nuts they had missed earlier in the season. Surprisingly, the crows were oddly silent—usually they made a racket this time of day.

Then I opened my eyes to a vast dim place of grey and black trees asleep for winter, with intermittent golden sunlight seeping around tree trunks and limbs. A cool, moist wind blew in from the river and touched my cheek, bringing with it the scent of a campfire and the sound of muffled male voices.

As I turned into the breeze, I saw the campfire and hunkered down immediately, trying to make myself as small as I could behind a tree trunk, and hoping they hadn't heard or seen me. The voices belonged to the men of an Indian war party. I caught a glimpse of their faces as I squatted to the ground. They had colored themselves with red and black paint and looked more like demons from hell than men; but then I guess that was the purpose of the paint—to scare their enemies first.

An arrow whizzed past my chest, missing me by an inch, and I fell to the ground. It was followed by a small axe that struck the tree where my head had been. "*Dang!*" I cried as I got my feet under me and ran like a hunted deer as the war whoops sounded behind me.

I tried to focus on what was ahead of me, watching for foot traps, but I looked backwards anyway, and my heart sank. There were four grown men charging towards me all screaming, with a desire to murder me before I escaped from them.

I turned back and there was a fifth Indian in front of me, streaked with red and black paint, just like his fellows. I plowed into him, knocking him to the ground, and put my hunting knife to his throat, daring him to move. The man did not resist, but calmly spoke "Jo'ä:ka'?". The name was mine, a name he gave me.

"Cornplanter? Is that *you?*" I asked in Seneca.

"*Get off! Get off me before you get dead!*" he screamed abruptly.

I was too slow, so he threw me off to the side and to the ground. Cornplanter stepped in front of me and yelled at a warrior who had his tomahawk raised, aiming for my skull. I didn't understand what Cornplanter hollered at him; his Seneca was spoken too fast, but whatever it was, the warrior stopped mid swing and lowered the axe.

Just when I thought it was safe to get up, Cornplanter saw me from the corner of his eye and backhanded me to the ground. "Stay down, Jo'ä:ka!" he said, much slower than before, and keeping his eyes entirely on the man in front of him.

"There is no honor in taking his scalp, Nyakwai'. He is but one child in the wilderness. Have you not had enough of blood and death to last a lifetime?" Cornplanter asked.

"Gaiänt'wakê, look at him! He is of age and can die like any man. You know too the English will pay good money for that head of red hair," he said, nodding in my direction.

"Yes, and how many have we laid dead already, helping the English? This boy is no threat to us. He is Jo'ä:ka', so named by me. He has been as a son to me in this land of the Lenape. I have taught him many of the ways of our people. I will not have him harmed," Cornplanter warned the warriors. He was still crouched in a fighting stance holding a knife in one hand and tomahawk in the other; staring fiercely at each of them. He would not be disobeyed.

"Jo'ä:ka'? Good name, Raccoon," the warrior Nyakwai' chuckled, as he walked slowly toward us and stopped in front of Cornplanter. "I see it in the dark around his green eyes." Then the other four looked at each other, nodding one at a time and without a word spoken between them, they backed away from us, re-sleeving all weapons.

"Jo'ä:ka' will leave in the morning," Cornplanter said at the last. The four shrugged and turned back towards their camp.

◗◯◖ ◗◯◖ ◗◯◖

Cornplanter watched them as they sauntered back to their camp, making sure they hadn't changed their minds to come for us. "What on earth are you doing out here?" Cornplanter asked, switching from Seneca to Dutch in the middle of his question.

"I left my sister's house."

"And where is your father, your brother, Jo'ä:ka'?"

"Papa has not come back from the back country and should have long ago. Ben is with the New Jersey Brigade, I think. Thought I'd go look for both."

"You need to return to your sister's house. It is too dangerous for you to be out in this wilderness."

"I cannot go back, Father. Boer gave me this black eye; he attacked me with his fists this time. I hit him back, and I figured that if I stayed with Aletta, he would continue to beat me. He thinks of me as a beast of burden that needs to be broken." Cornplanter turned my head to see the eye better in the light.

"You hit him back hard?"

"I did, and he has the bruises to prove it."

"Good."

"What happened that he thought he needed to give you that black eye?"

"Nothing. He was frustrated with the harvesting and the people that came to help. His plans had been changed by the elder Lanterman brother. I just happened to be the closest thing to him."

"Did you tell your sister?"

"No, it wouldn't have done any good if I had, you know this. He would make amends and then it would start all over again, only worse. You've seen how he is. After I hit him back, I felt it best to leave."

"All right. There, see that outcropping of rock? It will shelter us from the cold tonight. We'll start our fire there. Is your sister safe with him?"

"He is fond of her, and he won't harm her. Besides, she is not alone. Abraham Lanterman and the hired hands are there until her husband returns and that should be within the next week. Now all I need do to is locate Papa and Ben," I responded as I laid my belongings underneath the rock shelf that Cornplanter had pointed out earlier for our rest.

"What of them?" I asked, nodding towards the warriors. "Are they something I should worry about tonight?"

"No, Little Coon. You are with me. They will not harm you. Being chief allows me to follow certain whims within reason."

"So, now I am whim?"

"In a way," he said as he chuckled.

"How so?"

"You know we cherish our children. My people would never think of hitting them with our fists or whipping them with a leather strap because we were angry. Come here, let me tend to that eye. Although this is a little late, it still may help with the healing. Ah, here it is," he said as pulled out a small bag from his satchel that he carried. He dabbed a bit of a salve that smelled of sage and pine around my eye.

"I remember this smell. You used this salve once before when I got hurt with the stag that nearly gored us."

"I did. Tell me what plant this comes from," he said as he looked to the other bruises on my arms and chest, dabbing the salve here and there.

"A little yellow flower, like a daisy and all yellow with little red seeds in the middle."

"Good. I hope you remember a lot more than just this. You'll need all that I and your Papa have taught you for this long journey. Are you hungry, Little Coon?"

"*Ja.* Not had much more than biscuits the last couple of days."

"Well, you will feast tonight. Just have the fire ready when I return." With that, he went back the way we came, toward the campsite of the four warriors.

⊙⊙⊙ ⊙⊙⊙ ⊙⊙⊙

"Good hot fire, Little Coon, and those green sticks for cooking will do fine." As promised, Cornplanter returned with a small side of red meat wrapped in a deerskin that he laid on a slab of stone that I had placed beside the campfire.

"Cut the venison into smaller pieces, Jo'ä:ka' so that they'll cook easily on the sticks over the coals," he said with a nod of his head and a smile on his lips.

"Here, rub a little of this into it before you put it on the fire," handing me the little pouch that he kept in a pocket of his buckskins. "Oh, and grease the meat a bit with the fat in this bag before you rub in the seasoning."

I opened the small leather pouch of spices and stuck my nose in it, smelling the aroma of dried onion, garlic, salt, and something else that smelled a lot like pine trees, but different from the pine scent in the salve he just used. I pulled my nose out and shook my head. "You added pine needles?"

Cornplanter grinned. "No, Little Coon. It comes from a little plant grown way in the south. I got it at a trading post. It does smell a little like pine needles. The whites there call it rosemary. Trust me, it won't make you sick."

I did as he told me and settled the venison pieces over the coals. Cornplanter busied himself pulling another object out of another pouch in his pack.

"We might need this before the night is done," he said as he set the object on another flat rock nearby. It was a small silver container, a gentleman's whiskey flask with some filigree work near the top of the lip. The letters J and A were engraved in the middle of the bottle.

"Where did you get this?" I asked as I picked up the flask. He just raised an eyebrow at me, then took the flask and set it back down.

"Ahhh, there are a great many things I will tell you tonight, Daniel

Applegate, the least of which is how I came to have that. Give me a moment to gather my thoughts and I will tell you," he said as he pulled out some turnips that he had carried with him in his satchel. I waited patiently as he buried the vegetables under the coals of the fire.

I had not seen Cornplanter for more than a year, and he had changed. He seemed smaller, but I reasoned this was because I had grown slightly taller than him. His war paint had settled in the wrinkles of his face and body, making him look more like a dried-out painting, and traces of gray ran through his still very dark hair on the crown of his head. Like all Iroquois, he had kept his head bare except for the very top, leaving a scrap of hair to drape down the back of the neck. The gentleness of his dark brown eyes was etched with tiredness.

His buckskins, shirt, blanket, and moccasin boots had seen better days. There were rips and tears in various places of his clothing, and no attempt had been made to repair them. It wasn't like him to be in such tatters. I thought he must have been traveling for some time without respite.

The aroma of sizzling meat pulled me out of the revery and as I made to check on that part of our dinner, Cornplanter turned his head to the side, as if listening closely to someone or something, he sighed, slumping his shoulders, and nodded once. "Daniel, I have a long and sad story to tell you. When I am done, you may think much less of me."

"No, I won't."

"You speak too quickly, son. That you should not do with anyone. You've not seen me or heard from me this past year to make that judgement. All I ask is that you be quick to listen and slow to anger. I believe you are old enough to understand all that I will tell you, but first, let us give thanks to the Creator for our dinner." After our prayer, he wrapped his back in his blanket and made himself comfortable to sit and eat near the fire.

The smell of the roasted meat did not compare to the taste of it as it settled on my tongue. "Mmmmm, this is so good, Father," I said with my eyes closed, focusing on slowly chewing what was in my mouth.

"Ah, it must be the pine needles," he teased between bites. I laughed under my breath in agreement and speared another piece with my knife.

"That heap over there. Is there something buried over on the side of the fire, Daniel?"

"Sweet potatoes. I forgot about them. I found them over there in the small meadow while I was gathering the wood for the fire," I said as I pointed and shrugged my shoulders. "Got some salt? I'll see if they're done." They were, and I handed Cornplanter one on a stick and took the other.

"A lucky and welcome find, Daniel. Thank you. The Lenape planted these a while ago and just left them here, maybe for weary travelers like us," he said with a smile. "They have lived all along this river and farmed the land nearby since the beginning of time."

"That so? If you see them, please give them my thanks for the potatoes. Your venison was a pleasant surprise too, Father," I said as I held a piece of the savory meat between my fingers and promptly laid it on my tongue.

"Hmmph, you're welcome. You know I have brothers, Daniel?"

I shook my head yes, as I had stuffed my mouth with more food and was busy chewing.

"One of the brothers, Handsome Lake is his name, is both a great warrior and leader, but he also is a seer, a prophet—a dreamer to our people. He told me four or five years ago that I would find a young white boy with red hair, whose father had left him living among the Dutch. He said that when I met him, I needed to befriend him and teach him our ways. He seemed to think that this white boy would save a tribe of people beyond our Western Door, and far into the west and past the Great River. When I saw you in that field by yourself, and how you reacted to me when I first met you, I knew you were the boy that Handsome Lake spoke of. Any other young white boy would have cowered and run from me. You did not. "So that night long ago, I began to show you the way of the Seneca; how we hunt, live, pray, and stand up for what is right and true."

Frowning in confusion, I asked, "Why did you tell me this? I am no hero."

"You know why, son. It is not by accident that I am here looking like I am running for my life, which is truly what I am doing. My warriors and I are searching for our people that have not yet returned to us, to bring them to safety and to home. Enough damage has already been done between us, the British, and the colonists. It needs to stop for our survival. I am asking no more of you in the future than I do today of myself. Handsome Lake believed that the boy he spoke of would grow to manhood long before these people in the west would be in harm's way."

I objected, "Handsome Lake is wrong. I am not the one. I have no wisdom or learning to save anyone, and little to save myself."

"Have you not learned some medicine from what I have shown you? What of the wisdom in the stories I told you over these three years? Has not the father that gave you life, given you his wisdom as well? You have learned much from both of us. I have faith in you, Daniel. You will do all that you want to do, if you set your mind to it and heed our lessons as well as those of the Great Father as he guides you." He said no more and ate the last of his dinner, washing it down with the water from his waterskin.

He offered me the bladder as well. The water was thoroughly chilled, and it would be frozen by morning if we left it in the open. I drank deeply of the water a second time, giving me a moment to find words for a reply. I handed the waterskin back to Cornplanter and said, "I hear you, Father. I am sorry to doubt. I will do what I am able when the time comes," as I felt the heavy weight of an oath laid across my shoulders.

"That is all I can ask, son of my heart." I hung my head for a few moments after he called me son of his heart. It was an honor to be called this.

"Thank you, Father," I replied as I looked into his eyes. "So, tell me, where is this Great River?"

"It runs from the north to the south, just past the *Ohi:yo* Country. A journey of about thirty days from here if you walk from sunup to sundown in good weather."

"From there, how far is it to this people that Handsome Lake mentioned?" I was not afraid of traveling, but I wanted to know how far I should expect to go.

"Maybe one hundred twenty days. I've never ventured that far, but I have heard stories. It is a very beautiful place, where the mountains are at least three times as high as ours. There's a vast grassland covered in buffalo that rests below those mountains too, and the water in the lakes and ponds is as blue as the sky."

"Buffalo?"

"They look almost like beef cattle, only much, much bigger. Their backs are taller than you. Their hair is thick like lamb's wool, only brown and they graze on the vast fields in the west.

There have been no buffalo here in a while, but I have seen them south of the *Ohi:yo'* River in *Ken-tah-the*. You know these places as the Ohio River and Kentucky.

"I don't think I want to run into buffalo even if they are grass eaters. The land though sounds a little like heaven," I said as I pulled out the berries that I had gathered earlier in the day. I offered one to Cornplanter first. He bit into the berry and grimaced, spitting it out of his mouth.

I looked over the berries in my hand to make sure that they weren't fuzzy with mold. They weren't; they were just exceptionally sour. I offered another to Cornplanter. He smiled and shook his head. He gulped down more of the water instead, then passed it back to me. By silent agreement, I threw the berries back into the forest, while Cornplanter pulled more wood into the fire. He watched the fire burn for a few minutes more and, with another heavy sigh, started his narrative again.

"What have you heard of war, Daniel?"

"Not much. Papa didn't talk about it at all, except to say that wars give us a glimpse of hell and that if anyone thinks that war is glorious, they will be severely disappointed. He also said that *if* we fight in a war, it should only be after all other peaceful solutions have failed, and then war is only justified for the defense of the lives of our family, our property, and our freedoms, as men accountable to the Creator."

"I hold to that same truth, Little Coon. Handsome Lake and I argued to remain neutral between the British and all the colonists, feeling that our fate, if tied to the Red Coats, would be nothing but hardship and pain. We lost that argument at the Grand Council, a council of all the chiefs of the Iroquois Confederation," he said as he reached for the metal flask he had set aside earlier and took a swig.

"Joseph Brant, chief of the Mohawk and friend to the British, persuaded all the others. He said that we had sacrificed enough land and game for the whites, that if we didn't put a stop to it, our way of life would end, and we would be no more. He also believed that the British would leave us be afterwards. I and Handsome Lake weren't so sure.

"We had little choice but to join Brant because of our clan family relationship. To us, a clan brother is like a brother that is born to your mother and father, like Handsome Lake or like your brother Ben. I could not let my brothers fight alone. I think you may understand this?"

"Yes."

He took another sip of the whiskey and handed it off to me. "It'll warm you a bit."

"Thank you. Ahh, the whiskey is good, Father. How did you come by it?"

"It came from a trading post at a fort up north. Sadly, there will be no more for sometime."

"I'm sorry for that," I said as I handed the flask back to him and watched him as he gazed into the fire.

"You have heard of the Indian attacks on the villages of the white settlers in the north last year?"

"Yes. We heard the stories," I said as I remembered the tales of homesteads being burned to the ground, and settlers tortured and killed. Some were able to escape, but those that did not were made slaves for the tribes. All the while, the British watched and did nothing to stop the horror.

"I was there, fighting alongside Brant and the British. I have done many things for the survival of my people over the years, but what I did this year past has torn my soul. We fought the battles in the north to protect our families, our lands, but what we did went too far. I was right there with the rest of my brothers. I am not who you think I am, Daniel," he told me, as he looked into my eyes.

"I am not afraid of you, Father, but I do not like what has been done by the whites or the Indians. What I can tell you is that you saved me this day from the others who disagreed with you on the worth of my life.

"I do not understand all the particulars of how the whites came to live on Indian lands, but your people have a right to survive, just as we do. I have no answers, save to leave the British behind, for they are a wily people."

"True, but in the beginning, we thought it was the right strategy. The enemy of my enemy is my friend. That is the game the Iroquois Confederacy has been playing for as long as I have been alive. First with the French, and now with the English, in the hope that we could take back all that was originally ours. It is time for a change, a new strategy. I am tired of all this death," he said, as he grabbed a log and added it to the fire.

"Early tomorrow morning, I'll take you to a ferry that will bring you across the river. We will say our goodbyes then. Get some rest."

ꙮ ꙮ ꙮ

I woke before dawn to the sound of a hissing fire and a cloud of smoke that made me cough. Cornplanter had dumped the contents of his water canteen on the fire.

"Up, Little Coon," he said as he shook me fully awake. "Time to wake. Here, eat." He laid some jerky on the slab next to the drowned campfire. "Chew while we break camp. We need to move before there is too much light."

"But, I, I . . . "

"*Move, I said!*"

"All all right," I answered with a yawn, rubbing the sleep from my eyes as I began to rise. I was ensconced in an ice leaf cocoon; I had buried myself in the leaf mold for warmth the night before and the top layer made small crackling noises with my every move. I broke free and walked a few steps to relieve myself. It was bone cold, and I thought my parts would freeze in the open air. I grabbed the jerky off the stone and shoved it in my mouth. It tasted of too much salt and smoke, but it would quell the growling in my belly. I had a few things to gather and was ready to go before Cornplanter.

"Father, there is no need for you to go with me. You risk much by walking with me. I can find my way." We walked on frosty ground that crunched under our feet as we followed the river heading to the northeast, nearly the same direction he and his warriors had come from yesterday.

"And if I don't go with you, I may live to regret it. Don't forget about my companions. They are trailing us—you know this?"

"Ah, no, I didn't." I turned my head, hoping to see them behind me, but saw nothing.

"Stop looking, Daniel, you won't see them," he said as he pulled a thorny bush out of our way. "I will see you safe across the river."

"Thank you, Father, but it is not necessary." He rolled his eyes at me in response, and I just smiled back. "You never did tell me last night about how you came by the flask."

"It belonged to my blood father, John Abeel. He traded iron goods, pots, pans, and the like for our furs when he met my mother in her village. Remember I told you that the Seneca women choose their husbands. Later, if they decide they don't like them for some reason, they set the husband out of the home with his possessions?"

"*Ja*, I remember."

"Mother took a liking to John, and so I am here. Yet, he decided not to live with us and left for his own people when I was very young. Handsome Lake and I are half-brothers, as the whites say."

"That had to be hard on you."

"Not really. The other men in our village made sure I was raised in the way of the Seneca, and Handsome Lake's father made me his own.

"Not too long ago, we raided a village and my father, John, happened to be trading with the village that day. He and many other whites were taken prisoner. I had no part in the raid and only found out about it when I came back to my village and heard from my mother that he was one of the prisoners.

"It took some talking with the chief and the elders, but I freed him. Mother and I asked him to stay with us, but he thought there would be too many difficulties making a home with us. So, we sent him back to his people. Just before he left, though, he handed me the flask and told me to keep it. It was the only possession he had besides the clothing he wore. He was an old man, with few summers left."

"I am sorry, Father. That had to be hard to see him leave."

"It was, but what was done cannot be undone. What is past is gone, and only memories exist. Make good memories with your life, Daniel."

"I will try, Father."

We walked in silence for a while, as talking felt cumbersome. The sun continued its slow movement skyward, warming everything in its path and slowly lifting the fog from the Delaware River. The ice-encrusted mud began to melt under our feet and soon our trail would be a slushy mess.

"This way, Daniel," Cornplanter said, holding another tree branch out of my way and moving us back into the forest to drier land.

"How is your son? Is he any better?"

"Not yet. He is still slow to learn, and his speech is jumbled. He still cannot do things or understand things I would expect for a child of his age. His time is getting late. I worry that he will not be able to hunt for himself when I am no longer here, when I die. It is breaking my heart." I wanted to tell him that I would be there for his son as he was for me, but I knew given the circumstances between our peoples that might be more than I could promise an impossible task .

"I know this might not mean much to you for the moment, but I will keep you and him in my prayers."

"That is enough, and it will be more than you know, Daniel," he said in gratefulness. "Handsome Lake says I will have more children and they will help care for their brother."

We were close to the ferry station; I could smell smoke mingled with the scent of bacon in the cold breeze. For the first time, I heard the footfalls of the warriors behind me, catching up to Cornplanter to make their journey home together.

"There's the station, Daniel. This is as far as I go with you." I looked at him, memorizing his face, seeing the sadness in his eyes. "Do you have money for the crossing?"

"A few shillings, nothing more."

"Take these coins. I have no need for them now. Here's my wampum belt. It will give you safe passage, should you meet any more warriors. Show it to them. They will know it is mine and that you are my friend. It will save your life. Stay on the road and out of the woods. Now go, Daniel Applegate, son of my heart, and do not look back. You will not see us standing here in the brush."

The wind had grown colder in the last few minutes, and he held his blanket closer to his body as he spoke. In this light, he looked ancient, frail, and my sadness at leaving him was overwhelming. "Too soon, too fast," I said as I reached out my hand for him. I felt lost and knew that without a doubt that this was the last time I would see him for a long time, if ever again.

He pulled me into a bear hug, thumped my back, and then pushed me away. "You must leave now, before we are seen. Go!" .

I kept my watering eyes forward, knowing full well Cornplanter was behind me in the woods. It would be treasonous to give away his location by turning to look even if I could not see him, so I did not. I wiped my eyes and reached for the bell hanging from a tree limb that would call the ferryman.

Dutch Ferryman

"What are you doing out here at this time of day, son?" the owner asked in his Dutch accented English, as I climbed into his canoe.

"I am headed to see my family in New Jersey, sir," I replied in the Dutch that I knew how to speak. "My name is Daniel. Daniel Morford." I had given him my grandmother's maiden name, so that if someone from my sister's farm came looking for me, they wouldn't know that I had been there. Only Aletta would know that name, and by the time she found out, I would be long gone.

"You have the Dutch!" giving me a nearly toothless smile. "I am Johann Hochstetler, and my wife's name is Saskia." Johann was a slightly bent old man with wisps of white hair that escaped from under his cap and curled up at the brim, but his sky-blue eyes were young and full of mirth. His cheeks were red though from the cold, and I regretted getting him out of his warm cabin to bring me across the river at this early hour.

"How much for the ferry and a meal?"

"Two shillings will do."

"Just enough, I think," I said, smiling back and handing him the money. "Here, let me pull the boat ashore."

"All right there, son. Good enough. Head on into the house. Mistress Hochstetler will get you a warm plate and a hot cup."

The bacon I smelled down river was even better indoors, and my mouth watered as I entered their little kitchen. Mistress Hochstetler motioned me to the table and brought a cup of coffee that warmed my soul, particularly since coffee was a hard thing to find these days. It was more milk than coffee, and pleasantly sweetened with honey.

I took a sip while she stood there and smiled up at her. I was in heaven. "Thank you, Mistress Hochstetler. I have not had coffee in a very long time." She grinned in response and headed back to the hearth to check on breakfast.

"You speak the Dutch very well, young man. What is your name and where are you headed?" she asked, as she cut thick slices of bread on a table near the fire.

"I am sorry. I should have introduced myself first. My name is Daniel Morford, mistress. I am headed to Perth Amboy." I said and then took another swallow of the coffee, letting it warm me from the inside out, as I watched her work at the hearth.

She was pleasantly chubby — a mark of a good cook—and dressed in a dark green woolen petticoat and jacket that had been carefully mended in several places. Strands of her unrestrained grey hair draped the sides of her face, easing the sternness of will that was marked there.

"What is in Perth Amboy for you?" Saskia asked as she loaded some bacon, eggs, and two slices of the warm buttered bread on a wooden plate, then set it and a fork in front of me.

"Smells wonderful, Mistress Hochstetler, thank you. My family. They sent a letter requesting that I come as soon as possible, because my uncle is gravely ill." I replied, raising my fork full of scrambled eggs to my mouth. "I have not seen any of them in some time."

She seemed satisfied with my response and returned to her duties at the hearth. The bacon, eggs, and bread were every bit as good as they smelled, and I relished every bite.

"There you are, husband! Just in time. I'm not sure I could keep the food much longer without burning it." She carried a cup of coffee and set it on the table for him. On the way back to the hearth, she briefly brushed the top of his forearm and squeezed his hand in affection, while he took his cap and coat off at the coat tree.

"I went to the barn to check on the cow. She's doing fine. No calf yet," Johann said as he sat down at the table. "Oooo, that smells wonderful, wife!" Mistress Hochstetler had filled his plate and set it before him, only to return with bowls of more food and her own breakfast plate.

"So, young man, what is your plan for today? Are you moving on or taking a day of rest?" he asked while taking a sip of the steaming, dark coffee. "We have a few rooms here that you could rent should you decide to stay. Resting might help that black eye a bit." His blue eyes were filled with mirth, and a bit of a challenge.

"The black eye I got from fencing in a rather cantankerous hog. He pushed the fence door into my face. I hope they turn him into a ham roast before long. As for staying the night, I would like that very much, but I do not have enough money. Is there something I could do to help you today in exchange? I could use a restful night's sleep before I take my leave."

"Daniel, there's plenty of food here. Get more if you are still hungry."

"Thank you, Mistress Hochstetler," I said as I added more eggs and bacon to my plate.

"What do you say, husband? You know it will be very cold tonight."

"*Ja*, the cold is coming. I feel it too, *Schatje*."

"Well, Daniel, you certainly don't look like you have an aversion to work. You're built like an ox. I could use those long strong arms around here today. We've got some cows to milk, and cattle to bring in from the field before tonight and maybe a calf to birth. There's a fence and some roof shingles that need mending, not to mention cleaning out the barn and laying fresh hay, bringing in some vegetables that the mistress put up in the cellar that's near our spring, and chopping more wood. Think you could handle some of that?" he inquired as he scooped up more of the scrambled eggs and put them into his mouth.

I took another sip of my coffee and looked him in the eye. "I can. Where do you want me to start?" I asked, smiling.

"You hear the cows?"

"*Ja*, they're getting a little impatient."

"I think I would be impatient too if I had an udder full of milk. We had best start there. The mistress will show you where the buckets are, once you're done, bring them back to her and we can get started on tidying the barn a bit, and get ready for the new calf," he said, grabbing a few more pieces of bacon.

⚙⚙⚙

All through the morning, we worked companionably, checking off the chores as we talked about General Washington and the general state of the military. Johann had mentioned that he didn't think The Battle of Monmouth in June of '78 was a win for anyone, but we did hold our ground and that was something.

He said that the best thing to happen in '78 had been signing the alliance with the French, even though Admiral d'Estaing had destroyed some of his faith in the French by losing a thousand men in the battle in Savannah. "*Ja*, He needs to have his rank taken away, never to lead again. The cost of his bravado was paid with the lives of the men under his command.

"Then there was the burning of New Haven, Fairfield, Norwalk, and New London this past summer by the British and the resistance of the Patriots. When Major General Tryon was done with his raid, the homes, warehouses, barns full of grain and other food stores, schoolhouses and other public buildings in those villages were all in ashes."

"Lunch is ready!" Saskia hollered out the door, pausing our discussion.

"Be there as soon as we put some tools back in the barn, wife!"

Johann opened a side door to the cabin and the aroma of smokey ham and onions enveloped us. My stomach growled in response, and

Johann heard it. "Guess you're hungry?" he chuckled.

"*Ja,* a bit."

"Saskia will be pleased. Take your boots off before you go in. Mistress Hochstetler gets a little testy if we dirty up a floor she's just cleaned. Oh, and use the washbasin there to wash your hands. The pitcher is full of warm water. See it there?"

"I do." I waited as Johann wiggled his feet out of his boots and then followed him to the washstand.

"We managed to get quite a bit done, already didn't we, Daniel?" Johann said as he walked in his stocking feet and sat down at the table behind his bowl of ham and bean soup.

"*Ja,* we did." I said as I took the chair to the right of him and breathed in the steam from my bowl while waiting for Saskia to join us. Johanne smiled at Saskia as she settled in her chair, and we grasped hands as Johann led the prayer blessing the food and George Washington.

"Mmmm, the soup is very good, Ma'am. Tastes just like my mother's," I said as I shoveled another spoonful in my mouth.

"I am pleased that you like it, Daniel. Thank you."

"I told you Daniel, that's why I married her. She is a good cook."

"Well then sir, you best behave yourself or you'll be missing one cook real soon, if that is your only reason for marrying me." she said, smiling sweetly as she buttered a thick slice of the warm bread and handed it to me.

"Thank you, Mistress Hochstetler. May I have another bowl?"

"I think we may have starved the boy this morning, Johann. *Ja,* I'll get you another," she said, as she made to stand up.

"No, I just worked him hard, and he's still growing. He's just hungry."

"No, no, you stay and enjoy your lunch, ma'am. I can ladle it out myself."

"Thank you, Daniel."

"I think we'll start on the roof after we eat. Sound good, Daniel?"

"*Ja.* The sun melted the ice on the shingles two hours ago and they should be dry enough for us to climb on. We shouldn't slip on that steep slope."

"Are the shingles that you made last fall still good?" Saskia asked.

"I checked before I came in, and they're fine. We only need to use ten of them to replace the bad ones, from what I can tell."

"Good. You two be careful up there—and Daniel, don't let Master Hochstetler do anything foolish."

"I'll try."

◦◯◦ ◦◯◦ ◦◯◦

"How 'bout I go up on the roof and fix the shingles and you stay on the ground holding the ladder, Master Hochstetler?" I asked as we walked back to the front of the cabin with the shingles, nails, and hammers.

"I am not so old yet that I can't climb a ladder and shingle a roof," he told me, smiling as he handed me a hammer and a satchel of shingles and nails. "I'll be fine. You go up first and I'll follow."

I made my way to the sharply sloped rooftop and waited as he climbed up. He got to the rung just below the roof edge and gave me his right hand to steady his next step on to the roof.

"Not so bad for an old man," I said, smiling as I let his hand go.

"I've had a lot of practice, unfortunately," he replied, bending at the waist to catch his breath.

"Now I just need not look down at the ground," he said as he unbent himself and looked at the rows of shingles above where we stood. "See the shingles on the left side third row from the top? Those shingles have warped a bit and are in the process of breaking apart. I'll remove the old ones and replace them with new ones. Look to the second row on the right side, and you'll see a few shingles in the same condition there. They too need to be removed and replaced with new ones. Do you think you can fix those up there?"

"Sure, I can do that."

"Good. Then the sooner we are done, the better. I don't want to be up here any longer than I must."

After slinging the hammer and nailing a few shingles down, I turned to check on Johann, since I hadn't heard any hammering in a few minutes. He had completed his side and had moved closer to the middle of the roof, sitting on his backside with his head bent and eyes closed. "Master Hochstetler, are you well?"

"What me? I am fine, just fine," he said without looking up. "Are you done up there? I'd like not to be up here much longer if possible. I take issue with anything that keeps my feet off the ground. Don't tell Saskia though. She'll laugh at me."

"Don't worry, she'll not hear anything from me." I flashed a quick smile and turned back to finish the repairs.

"Let's keep talking then. It'll help me until you're done."

"All right with me. Heights are not my favorite thing either."

"*Ja,* but you didn't swoon. You know about the Wyoming and Cherry Valley massacres?"

"I heard about them from our factor back home. He and a neighbor talked endlessly of both massacres. I don't believe all that they said, though. Both happened some distance from our home, and you know how stories change when they are passed by word of mouth."

"*Ja,* I do, but I got the stories from two men that had been there, that first week of November '78."

"So, what did they say?"

"Well, it was an early morning ambush on the fort and town's people at Cherry Valley. They said that it was a group of Loyalist militia, British regulars, and the Seneca that carried out the slaughter. A British general by the name of Butler, and a Seneca chief named Joseph Brant carried out the deadly raid.

"The General and the Chief's men are responsible for the deaths of thirty people, mostly women and children. Some had their heads smashed in by rifle butts or cleaved apart by tomahawks. Others were scalped or burned to death by fires started by the attackers. Those fires raged through the town, leaving over two hundred homeless."

"The stories I heard about the Wyoming massacre were just as gruesome," I said between nailing shingles. "Men, women, and children burned at the stake; others tomahawked. Sometimes stories about battles have a way of growing more terrifying with each telling. Most times anyway."

Speaking of this made me feel the wrongness in my heart. "*We fought the battles in the north to protect our families, our lands, but what we did went too far. I am not the man you think I am,*" Cornplanter had told me yesterday, as he felt the pain of remorse in his soul. There was hope for him then. Papa had told me long ago that war can make men lose their humanity in vile ways, but a man who expresses grief over the loss of his humanity may once more find it again. I prayed this would be so for Cornplanter.

"I am sorry Master Hochstetler, I didn't catch what you just said."

"I said that I believe them. General Washington did too. He sent Generals Sullivan and Clinton to quell any further uprising of the Iroquois Confederation in northern New York. That ended with a battle with the Iroquois at Newtown in New York last August. Why would he send them to do this if it wasn't true?" Johann responded in agitation.

"Sullivan didn't leave a single village untouched in the country of the Six Nations, burning homes, crop fields, and taking livestock for our troops. The village warriors were gone, leaving the defense to women, children, and old men. I did not hear that any of the villagers were killed, but they will go hungry, and may even starve to death this winter given that their hunting grounds are not as abundant as they once were. I have a hard time seeing how this action is honorable," I said as I pounded a nail into the roof and then turned to walk down to Johann to sit beside him to talk.

"It sure wasn't honorable killing and burning out the colonists, either. Some of those that survived the raid starved to death, and others died from the cold last year," Johann added.

"No, it certainly wasn't honorable to kill and maim the white women and children, by our standards. I have no doubt that some of the colonists that survived the Iroquois raids did not make it through the winter.

"What is disagreeable to me is that the British and Loyalist militia were involved in both massacres and did nothing to reign in the violence against the colonists. The Iroquois protected their people and hunting grounds in the way that they have for thousands of years. No more or no less than we've done in as many years."

"Think of it this way, Daniel. General Washington doesn't have much of a choice. If he hadn't sent Sullivan, he would be fighting wars on two fronts. One against the British and Loyalist militia in the colonies back east, and the other with the Iroquois as a proxy for the British and the Loyalist militia in the wilderness. This fledgling country of ours simply doesn't have the men or the money to fight two wars at once. Washington needed to remove the threat from the back country. If I were the Iroquois, I would live on vengeance now," he said as he moved to the edge of the roof and to the ladder. "Daniel, it is not safe for you to travel alone to Perth Amboy. I hear the British are still paying for white scalps."

"I know," I said in a soft, husky voice. It was the only answer I had to give him. He looked at me, reading the turmoil in my face, then turned and stepped down onto the ladder.

"Dinner will be on the table soon. My wife is usually very timely about it. Don't dally up there much longer," he said when he was half-way to the ground. Then I heard him drop the rest of the distance to the thick turf below and walk into the cabin. I walked the few paces back up to the line of shingles, picked up the hammer and nailed the last three into place. Working with my hands always felt good, especially when I knew that what I had done was nearly perfect. This repair should last them a long while.

I looked at the sky as I stood back up. The blue was deepening with the sun just a golden shimmer on the western horizon, and wispy clouds colored in deep pinks welcomed the coming night. I watched as I sat on the roof and felt the cold descend again as the sun made its way to the other side of the world.

ɘ◯ɵ ɘ◯ɵ ɘ◯ɵ

I smelled the stew when I came through the door to take my shoes off. It was rich with the scent of onions, thyme, and hickory, and my tummy growled in response.

"That you Daniel? I think you just might be as hungry as a bear. I've refilled the wash basin near the door. Make use of it," Saskia said to me, as my mother would have, were she alive. I smiled at the memory and hung up my coat.

"Thank you, ma'am. I will scrub very hard." I heard a chortle from her as she stirred the pot hanging above the coals of the hearth.

"What about you, Johann? Your hands clean?"

"I guess it wouldn't hurt to wash them again. I just checked on Strudel, no calf yet. Maybe tomorrow," he responded, with a peck of a kiss to the side of her head, where her cap had slipped a bit. He placed a pitcher of fresh milk from the evening's milking on the sideboard.

Hands washed, the stew pronounced ready and placed on the table with warm golden biscuits. We sat down and bowed our heads in prayer as Master Hochstetler spoke the words of thanksgiving and gratefulness. Midway between, my tummy decided enough was enough and rumbled louder than before. "Better end the prayer quick, husband. He just might eat his fingers off with the waiting," Saskia said, giggling.

"Thank you, Lord, for the reminder to keep my words heartfelt but short. We are truly blessed!" Johann finished, chuckling to himself.

"And thank you, Daniel, for all you've done here today. You have been a great help to my husband, and saved me from all that worry of him

50

up on the roof by himself, that is for sure," Saskia said, as she passed the crock of butter for the biscuits to me.

"You are welcome, ma'am. It was a good day of work. I think we truly have the roof fixed for now, and hopefully there will be no problems with it for a while."

"Daniel, Saskia and I were talking, and we were wondering if you would like to stay with us for a couple more days. There are plenty of things I could use help with here at the inn. What do you think?"

"It is a gracious and tempting offer, Master Hochstetler. I will sleep on it and give you an answer by morning, if I may?"

"Take as long as you like, son."

ᴥ◯ᴥ ᴥ◯ᴥ ᴥ◯ᴥ

After dinner, I was so tired I just wanted to crawl into bed. It was all I could do to keep my head upright.

"Ah, no Daniel, you must wash before you sleep," Saskia said as she cupped my face, gently lifted my chin, and excused me from dinner. "Take him and his things to a guest room, Johann. I'll be along with some hot water for him to wash up."

Johann guided me to the small bedroom and laid my pack and bow against one wall. "Mistress has a large breakfast planned, so don't be sleeping in," he said as he made his way to the door. "Good night, Daniel."

"Good night, sir."

It was nearly as cold in the room as it was outside as there was no brazier for a fire, but the bed with several quilts and a pillow looked welcoming. Saskia poured the steaming pitcher of water into the washbowl on the dresser as her husband was leaving. "Do wash behind your ears and get your feet. Hang the washcloth and towel on the quilt rack when you are done. Sleep well, Daniel."

"I will and thank you, ma'am."

ᴥ◯ᴥ ᴥ◯ᴥ ᴥ◯ᴥ

I woke in an abyss of a dream covered in blood, with the sound of

51

cannons and screaming men behind me. I fought my way out, grasping the walls near me for hand and footholds to climb out. It was pointless. I pulled the hand and foot holds loose from the wall and slid back down onto flat black ground. I was alone, afraid, helpless to alleviate the pain of screaming friends losing their life's blood on a dark field.

God help me. Slowly, I felt pulled to the surface and, finding it, woke to this world that was a warm, safe bed under layers of quilts and unclouded with moonlight. *A nightmare, just a nightmare.*

I dressed quickly and quietly in the frigid cold of the room, made the bed, and put on my coat, but carried my boots, knapsack, and bow. The hallway was a little warmer, but not by much. Through all my moving around, I heard no sounds from the Hochstetlers. They were sound asleep.

The hearth was still alive with coals that had deepened to a soft glowing red. I stirred them just a bit and added a small log to the right side of the hearth, knowing that it would quickly catch. On the other side, I placed a pot of water for coffee.

Mistress Hochstetler had left out a cloth-covered plate full of biscuits from last night's dinner, and there were some blackberry preserves and butter beside it on the table. I went on a search for a plate, found one, and sat blissfully eating the biscuit I smeared with butter and preserves.

Halfway through the second biscuit, the coffee was done, the aroma permeating through the miasma of a slightly smoky hearth. I savored the breakfast, eating more slowly in between the sips of hot creamed coffee because I knew it would be the last good breakfast I would have for some time.

After finishing all the biscuits I could eat, I sipped my coffee, thinking about the offer made to me the night before. I didn't doubt that staying with the Hochstetlers would be better than being on the road, but my father and brother tugged on my heart. I needed to find them.

That decided again, I wrapped several more of the biscuits in a cloth I had brought with me, stuffing it and a couple of apples on the table into

my pack I wrote a short thank you note for the food and a restful night —
well, almost restful, anyway—and laid a few shillings on the table to pay
for the food I took.

Departing in the wee hours just before dawn had its benefits,
one of them being not having another discussion with the Hochstetlers
about traveling in the cold with wild savages and animals running about.
Admittedly, they were good people, and they reminded me of my father
and mother in much happier times. Yet, time for travel was running short.
We all felt the coming weather, and it had been getting colder by the day.

I gently closed the door and breathed deep, filling my lungs with
very cold crisp air while I listened to the small waves of the Delaware
gently slap its shores behind me. The water sounded thicker, likely because
everything was slowing down with the cold. All else was silent, including
the animals in the barn. I stepped down to the ground and let the dark
envelop me, walking into the woods towards where the sun would rise and
hoped that the Hochstetlers would not try to follow me into the forest.

The Bully

The forest is a place like no other, filled with wonder and ruthless beauty. It is a dangerous place for those who do not have a healthy respect for it. That respect was drilled into me, first by my father and then by Cornplanter. My experiences of the last few days only etched their warnings deeper into my heart and mind.

I had found a deer path that meandered to northeast for some distance until it turned north around midday. Within a hundred feet of the northerly turn, another larger path forked off the deer trail to the right and continued in an eastern direction. A huge log had fallen on the side of the eastern trail, and it seemed as good a place as any to eat lunch before I cooled down too much. I sat down on the dead tree trunk under the warming sun, pulled a couple of biscuits and an apple from my knapsack, and studied the new trail.

This eastern path was likely made by the Lenape Indians long ago, and not been recently used. The trail was covered in leaf mold, with bits of grass stems poking through as far as I could see. It looked safe enough though, and if I was lucky, the path would soon cross a wagon road, where I might be to find a barn to rest in for the night.

Chewing on the biscuits, I couldn't help but think of Saskia and smile. I prayed that the Hochstetlers would be warm and safe this winter. They reminded me of better times when I was young, and my family whole, with Papa at home and Mama healthy.

Memories sometimes are soft, fuzzy things made indistinct by time. I had no clarity, no real picture of Mama in my mind now, and what we had said and done together. Yet, I *knew* I had been loved.

I picked up my backpack and started walking again as I pressed slowly into my mind and this phantom world of recollection to grasp hold of a single memory. I saw her sewing the torn pieces of quilted blanket that had been mine since I was born. By the time I was five years old, Mama had tried to get me to give up the blanket. The fabric was worn and patched, and the edges had frayed almost beyond repair, but I wouldn't have any of it. So, she repaired it as best she could and returned it to me clean and dry, with my promise it would stay on my bed.

In the early spring of my eighth year my cousin, Josiah, was visiting us with his family. He took the blanket from my bed and wrestled me to the ground as I tried to take it from him. In the process, he dropped the blanket, and I quickly picked it off the ground and started to run. He chased me, caught up with me and grabbed the blanket and pulled on it with all his weight. The blanket was keenly ripped into two pieces, with parts shredded on both sides. It was ruined, and I was in tears and furious.

With no word of warning, I punched Josiah hard in the gut. He fell unceremoniously into a great heap on to the ground and I continued to punch and kick him. Josiah was no small boy, he was three years older than me and at least twice my size. Papa pulled me off Josiah, and made me apologize to him after our mothers checked him to make sure he was not hurt, then I was sent to bed for the rest of the day and without dinner.

Later that evening, when everyone had gone, and Papa was out doing chores, I came down the steps partly out of boredom, but mostly because I was hungry. I sat on the steps, my head resting in my hands with my elbows on my knees, and waited for Mama to say something. She sat on a kitchen chair in the light of the fireplace, sewing my quilt back together with as much skill as she possessed. The dark circles under her eyes were more pronounced now than a few weeks before, but I thought nothing of it then. She looked exhausted in the candlelight as she sewed. She was seemingly driven to continue to sew rather than talk to me. She knew I was there.

Mama was dressed in her favorite dark blue petticoat and apron, and her hair was no longer held tight by the cap that framed her head. Wild curls of gold and silver sprouted beneath it. She pulled the hat off her head, letting her hair fall down her back, and brushed the obstinate curls away from her face almost simultaneously as she sewed. She then looked up at me with her forest green eyes full of love and said, "Daniel, come sit beside me".

I did as she bid me, staying silent while she worked, and I watched. The kitchen was still thick with the aroma of chicken stewed with carrots, celery and onions, and yeast bread that had been made for our dinner. My tummy rumbled. Mama smiled in reply to the sounds my belly made, but said nothing.

"Where's Papa?" I hoped that if he were gone long enough, I might just be able to talk her into a small plate of food.

"He has gone to see Lilly, to make sure she is well. Her time is soon. Perhaps we will have a new calf tonight." We all loved Lilly. Lilly had been made part of our family long ago.

Papa came through the door a little sooner than I wanted, as I had no real time to sweet talk Mama into some dinner. He hung up his coat, totally ignoring the fact that I was there, and rubbed his hands together over the hearth to warm them. "She is well. Nothing seems amiss," he said as he turned to Mama with a smile.

"Good, we'll have fresh milk for a while then." Papa walked towards her, and she lifted her cheek to him for a kiss.

"There's a toddy for ye by the fire, Richard. Test it first to make sure the pot's not too hot to pick up." Papa found the temperature acceptable and poured himself a cup of the fragrant tea. Cinnamon, cloves, and nutmeg with a hint of whiskey wafted near my nose as he sat between me and my mother.

"Hmmm, this is good, my treasure," he had said to Mama, putting his arm around her and kissing the top of her head as she leaned into him, resting her head on his shoulder. In that moment, his eyes were only for her.

I got up to return upstairs but wasn't quite quick enough and the hand that had held the mug now clutched my knee in warning. I heeded him and moved no further, sitting back down. Mama seemed not to notice that I had moved at all. Her entire being was focused only on Papa, and then as she rose from the embrace, with love in her eyes and a slow smile, she kissed his rough cheek and went back to the sewing.

Papa continued to look at her, as if memorizing her face, every line, every eyelash, every freckle while she worked. For an instant, I glimpsed a great sadness in his countenance, but in the next, the fierce father reappeared, and his eyes were on me. I immediately lowered my head and gazed at the floor.

"What are ye doing downstairs?" he asked in a quiet but stern voice. I knew that pleading any kind of innocence would likely make my punishment much worse. "I sent ye to bed without dinner, so ye would have time to think about why ye fought with Josiah. Have ye thought about it these past few hours?"

"Yes, Papa," I managed to say quietly, with my eyes still glued to the floor. I wasn't completely prepared to answer, although I had pondered the event several times. I really thought I would have until morning to sort it all out, but it was not to be, because I was hungry and came downstairs. The truth was always best. That is what Papa had told us many times over as a warning.

"Well, speak up, son. What happened?"

I opened my mouth to talk about the whole horrid story when he held his hand up again. "I hope out of all this ye've learned something and won't give me another heartache with the tell'n of the story." At that, I looked up and saw the full weight of his eyes on me. I swallowed deeply and began to tell the tale.

"Josiah called me a big baby because I wanted my blanket back. He wouldn't give it back to me, so I tried to take it from him. He yelled 'baby, baby, baby, nothing but a dirty little baby,' and threw it away from me. That's when he tripped me, and I fell.

"I got up and grabbed my quilt and walked away from him. That's when he punched me in the back, knocking me down again. Then we were on the ground wrestling for it. I managed to keep it tucked underneath me, and I think my fist connected with his stomach once or twice. After that, I got up and started to run back inside the house with the blanket. Then he shoved me and tried to take it from me again. That's when it ripped in two.

"My anger got the best of me, Papa. I bowled him over, slamming him flat to the ground and started kicking him. I shouldn't have done that," I said in a whisper, hanging my head and looking at the floor again. I had no more to say at that point and waited for Papa's pronouncement, getting myself mentally prepared for walking to the fence and the spanking that was sure to come.

"No, ye shouldn't be kicking a man when he's down. Anger out of control is very dangerous even when something precious is taken from ye."

"I am sorry, Papa; I'll try to be better next time."

"All right then. That is a good start. Was there any way to avoid the fight, Daniel?"

"No, Papa, at least I don't think so. Ask Ben. He stopped his chores to stand beside me when Josiah started to pick a fight earlier in this morning. Ben just looked at him, daring him to start the fight. That seemed to be enough to change Josiah's mind. But then Ben was gone to do chores and Josiah started in again later in the morning. I tried to avoid Josiah, but then he went and took the blanket Mama made for me off my bed. That was just too much."

"I see. Would it have been better to just let him have it all, to save ye from the fight?"

"No, it is *mine*. Mama made it for *me*, and no one else," I said, speaking much louder than I intended. Lone possessions were very hard to come by and this one item was not a hand-me-down. It was made brand new just for me and I didn't have to share it with anyone in the family. It was the only thing I could call all my own.

"Mama worked very hard and long to make that blanket. It's like love made real. Do ye know what I mean? It just belongs with me."

Mama laid her hand gently on Papa's arm, getting his attention. Her head barely turned signaling no and he, with a slight nod and the briefest smile given back to her, turned to face me again.

"Daniel, ye know how we feel about senseless arguing and fighting—it does no one any good, but I don't think this was senseless. Josiah is a bully, always wanting that which he cannot have and once gotten will tear it apart only to throw it in a hole to be buried. I assure ye, though, that he'll think twice about attacking ye again.

"We always want ye to share what ye have. It is the brotherly thing to do, and yet there are some things that are not to be shared. Yer quilt is one thing that should be held close for safe keeping. It does hold the love of your mama for ye, as ye said. Those things and other good people are worth fighting for."

"I, I'm not getting a whipping then?"

"No, not tonight or tomorrow or the next day. Ye learned a valuable lesson today. Take it to heart, when ye get older and choices are not so clear, this experience may help ye through a tough decision.

"When Mama has finished yer blanket, ye must keep it on yer bed and under yer pillow, only to be pulled out before ye go to bed. Under no circumstances should it be off yer bed, unless for washing.

"Yer dinner awaits, Son. By the time yer done, I should think Mama will have the quilt whole again."

"Thank ye, Papa," I said as I stood up to hug him. "I am hungry."

"I have no doubt. I am very aware of how much ye and yer brother eat around here," he said as I left for the kitchen hearth and the chicken stew.

"Catherine, I am going to check on Lilly one more time, then I'll be in for the night."

"All right. Don't be too long."

I came out of my recollection rather abruptly as I tripped on a tree root and fell to the damp cold ground cross-legged. I was unhurt, but I sat there for a while, staring at nothing but the woods, letting the warm tears flow over and down my cheeks until they were spent. Within a few months of the incident with Josiah, Mama was dead and buried. All I had left of her was the blanket I brought with me.

After a time, there was nothing but a feeling of peace, like when ye go to church and no one from the congregation is there, but then ye really aren't the only one there. I raised my face to the sky, finding a little warmth in the low sunlight, and listened to the quiet of the woods. A soft breeze tenderly caressed my cheek. "Thank ye," I whispered. I got to my feet and looked for a suitable place to rest for the night.

Last Call

My eyes opened to the golden light of dawn that streaked between evergreen limbs and into my sanctuary. I stretched leisurely, wiggled my toes in my boots and half sat up when I felt something bat at my feet. I jerked both legs back, but not fast enough; a hand had seized my right ankle, boot and all, yanking and pulling it to drag me out from under the white pine. I kicked with both legs at my attacker, but it did no good. He just grabbed the ankle tighter and pulled harder, sliding me across the ground, out from under the tree.

He stopped to catch his breath, and that's when I slammed my left foot into his shin. He roared a profanity that I recognized and let go of my right ankle. With my knife in hand, I got to my feet and had started to turn to run when I was confronted with two Indian braves. One had a bow and arrow pointed at my chest, while the other was behind me with his arm curled around my neck and his knife at my throat. I let mine drop to the ground.

The Indian with the bow came forward and picked up my knife, then returned to his spot in the clearing as he kept his eyes on me. The Indian with the knife at my neck kicked me behind my knees, and forced me back to the ground. He grabbed my hair and bowed me backwards so that I had to rest my head on his chest, leaving my throat completely exposed to his knife.

He reeked of sweat and smoke, with patches of his hair sprouting on the sides of his head where it should have been shaved off. Like Cornplanter, he and the others had been on the run for some time. They were Mohawk by the language they spoke, and likely doing what Cornplanter was doing when I ran into him—gathering the people back to safety in one last check before winter.

I saw five other Mohawk, including the one who had my knife. Four of them were all yammering away in loud voices, encouraging my captor. The fifth, an old warrior, perhaps their leader, was busy rummaging through my pack that had been pulled out from under the pine tree. My bow sat at his feet.

The knife wielder shouted more profanities at me, and for no other reason than he could do it, he pushed me forward, bashing my head on a granite boulder. I slid sideways off the boulder and onto the ground, ending back side up, face to the ground and splayed like one of my sisters' old rag dolls. The warriors all thought it was funny and laughed raucously at me.

I was dazed and now bleeding from my forehead, and my captor jerked me upright on my knees, turned to face me, and screamed. His fists found my jaw, and my torso became his punching bag for several long minutes. All the while, his friends watched and encouraged him in a taunting, sing-song way.

Floundering on my knees, I got a small respite while he pulled his tomahawk from its sleeve on his hip. He circled behind me, whispering some of the same words his friends were chanting, and then yanked all my hair to the rear of my head, wrenching my neck back in the process.

He placed the worn, chipped axe at the very edge of my hairline and looked me in the eyes to make sure I knew what he was going to do and how it was to be done. As I looked at him, I manage to squeak out the word "no!" but closed my eyes anyway. I had little hope of fighting any one of them, let alone six.

The chanting stopped suddenly, and all was quiet. I held my breath, bracing for the rough slicing, scraping movement of the tomahawk against my head. A gentle breeze stirred, brushing my arms and face, and then I heard the clacking of seashells.

My abductor let out an ominous bellow in his language and I thought that this was it. I was going to die. When nothing happened immediately, I opened my eyes — well, one anyway, as the other had swollen shut.

The old warrior, the chief, came into view. With a nod of the chief's head, my kidnapper let my hair go, but hesitated to remove his tomahawk from my forehead, his eyes full of hate. After a minute that seemed like an hour to me, the chief then laid his left hand on the younger man's forearm, and he returned the tomahawk to its sheath.

The old warrior held his right hand high, showing me and the others as well, why my abductor bellowed. In the palm of his hand, and dangling down his forearm was Cornplanter's wampum. The chief carefully put the wampum into his belt, then reached for me.

Uncaring about the blood dripping down my face and soaking my shirt, the old warrior latched on to my shoulder, holding me still to keep me from tumbling over. I was more than dizzy, and my stomach confirmed it. I was aware enough, though, to realize it certainly would not do to vomit on the man or fall over at this moment.

He then looked into my good eye. I had a hard time keeping it open with the swirling trees and just wanted not to see anything until it stopped. For good or worse, I decided to close my working eye to shut out the swirling and focus on not throwing up. He had the grace not to pull my eye back open and instead began to speak in a soft semi-comforting tone, just touching me with feather-like movements. It is what I would have done with a startled horse.

I had no understanding of what he was saying, but at some point, he sounded as if he had asked me who I was to Cornplanter. It took several breaths through aching ribs to force my wits back together to respond to him. With a prayer in my mind for salvation, I answered with the words, "friend . . . of Father . . . Cornplanter," in the tongue of the Seneca. After that, I quickly bent over to the side and puked my guts out.

Then the yelling began again. My captor didn't even let me wipe the spittle from my mouth with my sleeve before he had me on my knees with my hair again in his hand and pulling my head back for the perfect scalping position. He was kind enough to switch his language to Seneca, which was polite of him, I thought.

He directed his barking cries to the old warrior. "*Lies! He lies, Rohahes! You cannot trust what he says—they've killed Cornplanter, and this white has taken his wampum as a trophy!*"

Rohahes, the old chief yelled right back. "*Who are 'they,' Akwirarion? He is alone. Where are his people? Look at him—he truly is just a boy, likely no older than your son was.*"

Calmly, he added, "Let him go, Akwirarion. He is not the one that harmed your family. Let us speak to him."

It took a few minutes for Akwirarion to work through his rage to hear all these words from Rohahes, but he eventually reasoned them out and removed the axe from my forehead. I had hoped that he would just put the dang thing away, and I had the thought to suggest such, but managed to grab hold of a bit of sanity and not say a word.

The other five warriors were focused on the three of us in front of them. Their lack of movement in our direction seemed to tell me they were waiting to see how this situation would play out and, at the very least, wanted to hear my story.

"Can you speak now, boy? Can you tell me how you came by this?" asked Rohahes, showing me the wampum again.

"Water . . . may I have some water?" I asked. Rohahes brought me his water skin from his satchel and put it to my lips. I cleaned my mouth of vomit residue, spit it out, and then took a large gulp of water.

"Yes, that's good. Now drink. Here, peppermint leaf—chew this, it will make you feel better," Rohahes said. He was right. My head hurt, but the dizziness began to subside, and my tummy stopped its somersaults.

I crumpled to the ground, waited a few seconds, and untwisted my legs so to sit cross-legged while I gathered thoughts. I prayed that I'd get the Seneca correct because there would be no second chances with these men like there would have been with Cornplanter.

I took a deep breath, still feeling some pain from my expanding ribs, and began with my Seneca name. "I am Little Coon. It is the name Cornplanter gave me, himself." I purposely hesitated after that sentence, looking at each of them in turn, daring them to say otherwise.

"Cornplanter also called me a son of his heart. My Seneca father taught me much of the way of the Seneca. I met up with him just west of the river two days ago and there he gave me the wampum for safe passage to the east. When I saw him, he was well, and looking for any of his people that were this far south; to bring them to safety in the north.

"I travel east to find the father of my body. He has not returned home for the winter. My mother is long dead. There is no one else with me. I am alone." At that, the Rohahes nodded his head and gave me a little more water to sip.

"From which direction did you come, Little Coon?"

I pointed and showed them the path. Rohahes looked at one of the other five warriors and moved his head in the direction I had pointed. The warrior took off immediately.

"And how long have you been walking?" he asked, as he handed me his water skin, nodding that I should drink more. I drank deeply again, feeling the cool, clean rush of water down my throat.

"I have been traveling almost a week, Father Rohahes," I said as I wiped my mouth with my hand and tried to hand the water skin back to him. He motioned for me to keep it and to keep drinking.

We sat there quietly for a few minutes, while the others were watching the deer path for the return of their brother. "Tehawehron, the warrior that left, is looking to see if you are telling the truth, Little Coon. He is the best tracker out of all of us. If you are lying about being alone, we will know."

I thought it would be a while before Tehawehron returned and little would happen to me until he did. I was extremely tired and knew that I should stay awake at all costs, but could not, because my skull hurt so badly. So, I let my head droop to my chest, closed my eyes, and slept while the others kept the watch.

ᕗ ᕗ ᕗ

"Little Coon, Little Coon, wake up, Tehawehron is back." Rohahes said, shaking my arm to wake me. I awoke curled up on my side again. I opened my eyes and shut them quickly. The light made my head hurt. I had to get up, to face Tehawehron and what he would say to the others. I had to show respect and courage.

I slowly tested my ability to sit upright with my eyes closed. That worked fine. There was no dizziness. Gingerly I opened my uninjured eyelid, a quarter, then half, then full open. That made the light just tolerable. The swollen eye objected and remained closed. It was mid-morning, by my best guess. I had slept maybe two hours. Rohahes must have stayed with me all that time, and I was grateful for that.

Tehawehron stood in the makeshift semi-circle between me and Rohahes and the other warriors to announce his findings. "Little Coon tells the truth. There is only one set of footmarks on the deer trail, and they are his. There were no other footprints on or near the path. He is alone," he confirmed. In unison, I heard a sigh of relief from the group.

"Then we will rest here for the day and the night since Karontase, Shakohahiiostha, and Tehawehron have found no danger nearby." Rohahes said as he looked intentionally at each of his men. They all seemed to relax and turned to focus on clearing a little of the brush for a camp. Rohahes must have sent Karontase and Shakohahiiostha out in the other directions while I was sleeping.

Akwirarion sheathed his tomahawk, finally. He put his head in his hands and said nothing. The others left him be with his thoughts and they started a small campfire. No one was concerned with me so, I laid back down and slept a little more.

When I next woke, I felt a cold wet cloth on my face. I wasn't startled at all but laid there for a while, trying to understand why it had been put on my face. Memories of the early morning came back to me, which I suppose was a good sign, so my head hadn't been too badly injured by the beating. But I hurt—a lot.

Rohahes had cleaned my face of the blood and dirt, and had started to gently rub a lavender scented salve into the cuts.

"You can open your eyes now, Little Coon." He knew I had been playing possum, and when I opened both my eyes to my surprise, he showed me a broad, toothy smile. I cracked a small smile at him, as it hurt too much to do more.

"Do you think you can sip on some broth from the venison stew that was made? I hope you can, as I am getting tired of hearing that belly of yours growl."

I sat up slowly. Trees and people seemed to stay in one place and did not spin when I turned my head.

The small fire that had been started earlier was stronger, larger, and the warmth radiating from it did my bones some good. I would likely not be too cold sleeping this evening. There was an aroma of roasting meat along with the venison stew, an indication that the hunters had been more than successful.

My mouth watered in expectation and my tummy groaned loudly again. "Sure, I think I can without getting sick. It all smells so good."

"I better get you some food then before the grumbling gets much worse," he said, chuckling. "Mind you, just the broth. If you hold that down, then maybe I'll give you some heavier food."

He turned and called out, "Akwirarion, bring the broth you saved for Little Coon. He is ready to try it."

Fear stabbed through my heart, and my survival instincts kicked into overdrive. I stood up too quickly and nearly swooned. Rohahes snatched my arm and steadied me. "Sit," he said, as he moved his hands to my shoulders, pushing me down to the ground. He then squatted beside me and laid his hand on my leg to make sure I knew that I was to stay. Akwirarion watched all of this with a wry smile on his face.

Akwirarion brought the steaming bowl to me with my spoon in it. Apparently, they had gone through the rest of the contents of the backpack while I was sleeping. Not much in there really, just my blanket, my fife, the wampum, and a handful of Saskia's biscuits.

I brought my nose to the bowl. The venison broth spiced with onions steamed in my face as I slowly sipped on the warm liquid.

"Thank you," I said to Akwirarion as I managed a painful smile. He gave me a nod of acknowledgement and walked back to the fire.

Rohahes left me to the broth while he claimed part of the roasted meat and cooked roots for his dinner. He commented appreciatively to the cook and returned to sit by me. He handed me one of my biscuits, mimicked dipping it in the broth, and continued to eat. I touched my tongue to my teeth and found several of them loose, but none of them missing. Dunking the biscuit was sound advice.

I finished my broth and biscuit and waited patiently for Rohahes to do the same. He had been joking around with some of the other warriors during his meal, while I was contemplating my fate. I was getting anxious about what their plan for me was going to be. They hadn't killed me yet, though they could have easily done so, so it seemed unlikely I would face that possibility.

Rohahes' funny stories had worked their magic. The warriors were at ease with each other and paid little attention to me, which, in turn, made me feel safer. I certainly was in no shape to run from them, and likely wouldn't be for a few more days. The best I could hope for was that they would leave me be and continue their journey in the morning. Otherwise, they would likely take me with them, and I would end up a slave to the tribe.

"How's your belly now, Little Coon?" Rohahes asked after the laughter had died down. "You think you can eat some of the stew, instead of just broth? You've kept the broth down; maybe you'll keep the stew down as well. It just might be tender enough by now."

"Thank you. May be just a little of the stew? The broth was very good." To refuse would have been in bad taste and an insult to the cook. To ask for a large bowl would have been just as bad, so even though I was famished, I asked only for a little.

Rohahes looked at me, and I could tell he was in a bit of a tussle with his thoughts. "Do you feel up to getting it yourself, Little Coon? I want to see you walk."

"Sure," I said, thinking that this was strange. He seemed intent upon helping me get over my bumps and bruises, regardless. My best guess was he wanted to make sure I could walk without a mishap.

"Then go to Akwirarion. He made the stew and would be honored if you asked for more." Ill-fortuned, I thought, the guy who wanted to kill me a few hours ago just because I was one of the whites. Akwirarion looked up at the mention of his name and watched me with a scowl as I stood. There was no getting out of this, and I didn't quite understand why Rohahes was trying to create an opportunity for us to be around each other.

I was a bit shaky on my feet at first, but everything seemed to improve as I walked. It did hurt to breathe a bit, but it was manageable. Akwirarion watched me as I walked toward him with my bowl.

"The broth you made for the stew was delicious. Is there any of the stew left that I could have, please?" I said as I held my bowl out to him.

He stood there frowning at me as if I were a stray dog. He then took the bowl from my hand and added some stew. He held on to the bowl longer than customary and looked as if he wanted or needed to say something, but was just looking for words.

"Little Coon, friend of Cornplanter, I am sorry I hurt you. I thought to have my revenge on any white man that had a son for the loss of my son.

He was not much older than you when he died by a white man's musket ball.

"The pain of my son's death is a knife in my heart, but taking another life will not remove it. You have not done me any harm. I hope that you will forgive me." With that, he handed the bowl to me and walked away.

I said nothing. I was stunned by Akwirarion's apology, and I made to return to my place near Rohahes. I stopped midway, reversed my course, and walked slowly back towards Akwirarion and the others.

They were all sitting near the fire, involved in another conversation, when Karontase acknowledged my presence by raising his head to look at me. The others noticed as well and became quiet. Akwirarion stood up and turned around to find me behind him.

I looked at him and held his eyes and said, "I forgive you." Then I left to sit closer to Rohahes. I sat down with my bowl and stirred the stew, thinking about the whole surprising encounter when Rohahes pulled me out of my thoughts.

"How did the walk feel?" he asked. "Do you think you can make it out of the woods and on to a road that is near here?"

"Yes probably, after a night's rest," I responded, as I chewed a bit of venison. Then it dawned on me that they were going to let me go. "I am not going with you?"

"No, not if you think you can make it to the road that is southeast of here. It is at least another day's walk from this place. When we leave tomorrow, we will go north, and you will depart to the southeast and stay in that direction until you reach the road. Can you do it?"

"Yes, I can do it. I'll get to that road."

"Good. Then we will pack food for you from today's hunt and send you on your way. But for now, finish the stew and rest the night with us. We leave at dawn, and you must as well."

ꙨꙨ ꙨꙨ ꙨꙨ

"Little Coon, time to get up. We leave soon. Open your hand,"

70

Rohahes said. I did, and he handed me a handful of nuts and some dried berries.

"What's this?"

"Breakfast, eat quick. Here's some of the cooked venison. Eat it today and tomorrow, after that throw it away," he said as he added it to my pack. "Ready, Little Coon? Any message for Cornplanter that you'd like me to give to him? I am sure we will see him at Oswego," he said.

"No. Yes. Tell him that I am well, and that I said thank you. He said the wampum would protect me. He was right," I said with a hint of a smile and a little sadness in my heart. "Thank you as well. Had you not looked in my pack and found the wampum, I don't think I would be here talking to you. I pray Akwirarion finds peace."

"Thank you, Little Coon. I think he may have found some after last evening. Here's your hunting knife and bow. There is also some medicine for the cuts and scratches and bruises you have. Use it sparingly.

"Go quickly, go safely, Little Coon. Be on that south road tonight or first thing tomorrow. No later." With that, Rohahes turned his back to me and followed his comrades out of the clearing.

Raccoons

Walking wasn't easy. Every part of my body hurt, even where I had not been punched or kicked, and any missteps made it worse. Most worrisome, though, was the pain I felt breathing. I think I couple of my ribs were broken. The beating felt much worse than the punches given to my face and torso by Master Boer over a week ago. I just barely managed to keep the pace I set. My thoughts drifted back to Rohahes and his insistence that I be on the road by late today or very early tomorrow. The only reason that made sense to me is that he thought other Iroquois might also be using the trail, and he wanted me out of their way.

By mid-morning I had tired of sucking on the dried berries Rohahes gave me and decided to take a respite to gnaw on a biscuit that I had to dunk in water. My teeth were loose, and I couldn't eat the nuts or the meat he gave me, so I left them at the bottom of my pack. Maybe in a day or two I'd be able to eat solid food.

I wrapped my coat tighter around me, tying it with the belt, as I prepared to walk again. It was notably colder now; my breath was visible in the air and the sky had begun to cloud over. I had no concerns about the meat spoiling. With this weather, it would just freeze, but so would I if I stopped for the night. I needed to keep going.

The forest was unusually quiet, as if all the wildlife had simultaneously decided to seek their homes and shelter themselves from the cold. There was no rustling under the leaves, no chirping from squirrels, or birds, for that matter. The woods had decided to pause all activities of life. I was the trespasser in this dreary world, witnessed only by the black hardwood trees silhouetted against the thick grey sky.

By early evening, light snow began to fall from the sky in the diminishing light. I stopped to pull a biscuit from the knapsack to suck on as I continued to walk southeast. My best guess was that it was near eight o'clock when I found a road going due south that bordered the woodland on either side. I had hoped this was the wagon trail Rohahes had wanted me to be on. It was near ten when I found a ramshackle empty barn just off the road to sleep in for the night. I looked for a home near the barn and saw none in the dark.

Morning came when the sunlight pierced the seams of the slatted wall of the old barn and ran across my face, into my eyes, waking me gradually and allowing me to take stock of my surroundings. The barn had not been cared for in some time; it smelled old and musty with natural decay. There were broken wallboards and holes chewed in the bottoms of all four walls as well. The hay loft door was off its hinge, but still blocking much of the door opening, keeping some of the weather out. Empty birds' nests graced the rafters above, providing much of the musty smell and dust motes that were now visible in the air. There was no scent of cows, horses or other homey beasts left in the barn at all.

I moved slowly, grimacing here and there in pain, judged that I was doing better than I had been two days ago, and moved to get on my feet. Getting up was not too bad, so I walked to the rickety barn door and unlatched it. I needed to relieve myself and for whatever reason, it didn't seem right to do my business in the barn. I was alone on this farm, and there were no human noises to be heard.

The dusting of snow from last night had become heavier and there was now a layer of sparkling white in front of me, at least two inches of it. It was a little wetter than it looked and dressed the tree limbs, outlining them in white. The wagon path was also covered, and some snow had blown with the wind, creating small undulating drifts along the sides of the dirt road.

The day was much colder than the day before had been, and I was thankful for my warm clothes. I looked up at the thick layer of cloud cover and thought it was likely that more snow would fall tonight. I had no footwear other than my boots; my feet would be cold and wet before a day's walk was done.

I looked past the back corner of the barn and found the cabin. It was partially hidden by overgrown trees, brush and leafless vines that entombed the rest. I could just barely see the doorway lintel through the vines. .

The cabin reminded me of an old vine covered crypt that sat between four very old and crooked trees at Nut Swamp. We were visiting our cousins, and they offered to take us to the crypt to pay our respects to our relatives lying there. The door screeched when Cousin Jacob opened it, giving us a view of a dark, damp place that was full of small insects and other unseen creatures. I couldn't see them, but could hear them. It was best not to dwell on the house and its one-time occupants, just as I tried not to dwell on that crypt after we left.

I returned to my spot in the barn and pulled a biscuit from my pack, tested it against a molar and decided that chewing would be best left for tomorrow, along with the meat. If I had a pot, I could almost make a broth of the meat and dribble it over a biscuit. Better yet, if I had a pot, I could make snowshoes and keep my feet warm.

I stood back up, with a watered biscuit in hand and walked back outside to look at the cabin. It was made with all the familiar things in all the right places, including the now moldering shingles, some of which had been torn off by weather. I felt that something terrible must have happened here and I looked for small humps in the snow that would mark recent graves, but didn't see any. Maybe the family just up and left. I heard that happened a lot out in the wilderness.

I watched the house for some time, to see if there was any movement inside, but there was none. A hooting owl distracted me from my grim thoughts about the house for a moment. He was in the tree line just beyond the cabin. He seemed rather put out by the snow that had graced his roost, shooing it out of the way with his feet and chastising it loudly for being there in the first place. I knew exactly how he felt and smiled with the knowing.

There was nothing more on the outside of the cabin that could tell me about the inside. Surely the racket that the owl made would wake someone in the house and make them race to a window to see what the kerfuffle was about, but no one came to any of the windows. I waited a few more minutes watching the owl until it struck me that Papa would tell me I was dawdling over the matter. He would have been right this time, at least.

Back in the barn, I grabbed a board laying on the ground to use for protection. It seemed to fit my hand and arm well. I got my knife and walked to the cabin, making as much noise as possible. Once there, I walked around to the back.

As I rounded the back corner of the house, I saw a gaping hole the size of a wagon reaching from the cabin floor to its loft above. All the remaining logs surrounding the opening were charred and blackened from a blazing fire that had burned through ten-inch-thick logs. There was no remnant of a door left, but it certainly looked as if one may have been there. The destruction couldn't have been caused by an over-fired hearth, as the hearth was intact. It sat in the far corner of the gaping hole with no scorch marks across the loft ceiling to the wall opposite. My gut told me that the fire had been set by someone, but who and why?

Turning my head to look further behind the back of the cabin, I saw the snow-covered mounds I had not seen from the front. There were two of them. The mounding wasn't high, so they had been there at least since last spring, and maybe longer than that.

Perhaps they died in the fire and some kind soul buried them. I decided not to get closer to find out if they had actually been buried or left above ground. I asked God to grant their souls peace, though, and turned back to the task at hand.

I didn't want to be in the cabin any longer than I had to be, but I still waited a minute or so for my eyes to adjust to the lower light inside the building. The light from the entrance now seemed plenty, enough so that I could see a child's moth-eaten rag doll akimbo on the slatted floor to the left of me, along with broken chairs and an overturned table along the back wall. There was an old rusting hunting knife protruding from the table, which was odd because folks generally keep them sheathed to protect the blade.

A shelf on the wall near the overturned table had been pushed askew. The rails that held one side of it were pulled away from the wall and broken in two. All the wooden plates and cups from the shelf were scattered in all directions underneath it.

A reek of animal urine and scat hit my nose, making me gag as I walked farther into the room. I stood very still for a moment and heard nothing but Papa's voice in my head urging me to leave. Ignoring his voice, I was sure that the animal that created the mess was long gone after all the noise I made getting up here.

Then, as quickly as I silenced Papa's warnings, I heard rustling noises coming up from under the bed that rested against the wall directly ahead of me. There was nothing under the bed that I could see from where I stood, likely just mice scurrying across the floorboards. The bed's pillows had been tossed about and shredded by something sharp—maybe that hunting knife had been used. The quilt, too, had been ruffled up and had a large brownish stain on it. I didn't want to think about that.

There was little else in the room. A spinning wheel had been thrown on its side and was resting between the hearth and the front door of the cabin. Over the hearth, there were hooks for many pots, pans, tongs, and large spoons. But not a single pot, pan, or spoon still hung on the hooks, nor were they on either side of the hearth floor. They were just gone. My heart sank after not finding anything useful.

As I turned to make my way out, I caught sight of something just under the molded ash in the fireplace. It looked like a long iron rod, likely just a fireplace poker, but curiosity had me and so I turned back to investigate it further.

Crouching down, I grabbed the iron rod and pulled a bit of it out from under the pile of debris. Then it got stuck and would no longer move. I tugged harder, using both hands and heard the sound of metal scraping the stone floor. As I sprung the rod completely loose, I fell into a heap, with ash billowing in front of my face and half-burned logs pushed on either side of me. The pot that I so desperately wanted, sat upside down in my lap. It was perfect for my needs.

As I rested there in disbelief, I heard the pounding of four heavy feet, running on the floorboards at a full gallop straight at me. I moved quickly out of the way, clutching the rod, I faced the onslaught of five creatures, a mother and four of her babes.

The animals were scared out of their minds as much as I was. Ears pushed back, teeth barred, hackles up, both growling and hissing, all five ran like lightning to get away from me.

I watched as the last tail bounced through the burned-out wall and veered left out of my sight. I had never been that close to a raccoon without a real weapon, let alone five simultaneously. Laughter bubbled out of me with the knowledge that I was unharmed and safe.

I got up and brushed the ash off my clothes as best as I could and moved back away from the hearth to make my exit. I looked up past where the loft floor met the back wall and there, about four feet up from the loft floor, was an Indian arrow that had been forgotten. It had missed its mark and remained in the wall since the day it was loosed. I backed up further, so I could see more of the loft. There were two child size sleeping cots, but no clothing, blankets, or toys left on the beds or the floor. All memory of them was gone.

The children must have been taken and their parents killed, as the two mounds out back were too large for children. I knew the little ones would likely be adopted into a tribal family, just as they would if white settlers had found them alone in this place. I made one last prayer for the babes of the family and left the cabin to its present occupants.

It was then I realized I was caught in the middle of this strife between the whites of the backwoods and the peoples of the Iroquois Confederation; understanding both, but not able to commit to a side.

I recovered the pot and took one last look around the inside of the cabin. There was nothing more there that I could use. I walked back toward the barn, but made a little side trip to the woods near the cabin. There, I found two young pliable hickory trees with limbs that looked promising for making snowshoes. With the pot, not only would I be able to reheat the meat, tenderizing it a bit, but I could steam the hickory, bending the wood to make some serviceable snowshoes.

For the last three years, when Boer would leave the farm for supplies, I would make my excuses to my sister after the morning chores were done, to spend the hot afternoons "fishing". That is when I would meet up with Cornplanter. We did fish, but he also taught the Seneca way of life and language. It was Cornplanter that showed me how to make snowshoes the summer before last.

He said birch trees were the sturdiest and the best to bend into shape, but said hickory would work if a healthy birch tree could not be found. After finding the right trees, it took us about two days to steam and bend the wood into an oval, like a spoon, and then weave and space the leather lacings on the new snowshoe frames. If made correctly, the shoe would allow me to walk on snow without sinking into it, keeping my boots dryer than they would have been otherwise.

Last winter, I used those snowshoes for the first time, while Boer was gone for the day. I grabbed them from their hiding place in the barn and snuck off in the early afternoon after most of the chores were done, to try them on newly fallen snow. It would be a very short try out, as I needed to be back before twilight to finish feeding and bedding down the animals. The snowshoes took a bit of getting used too. I had to place my feet a little farther apart than normal as I walked. They worked fine and kept my boots mostly dry.

The sun was at about the four o'clock mark when Master Boer saw me walking on the snowshoes as I returned from the woods to the barn. He waited at the barn door for me, wearing his dour face, holding his hand out and palm up. I stopped and debated walking back the way I came, leaving for the woods, but he would follow me and hunt me, anyway.

"Turn them over to me now, Daniel," he said roughly. "If you make me work to get them, you'll suffer another lashing and lose the racquets." Staring defiantly at him and with no backtalk, I took them off, handing him the snowshoes. I watched as he broke them in half in front of me, realizing I would find no peace to escape to that winter, even if I had the chance. I would be his prisoner for a while, yet.

He turned toward the house, carrying the ruined snowshoes, and burned them in the fireplace later that evening. It didn't matter. I would be able to make five hundred of them if I wanted to once I was free of him.

Dutton Farm

I was healthy enough, as the old bruises were fading, and the new ones didn't hurt as much as they had. My breathing was less painful, and I had finished the snowshoes the day before. It was time to put distance between myself and this sad place. I shut the door to the barn and replaced the rough wooden plank over it, saying a short prayer of thanks for the shelter of the last couple of days.

Winter had set in for sure. The clouds were a thick gray and the air damp with spitting snow and sleet. It wasn't yet time for the new snowshoes, but at this rate, I would need to use them soon. At least my feet were warm. I had properly sealed the leather of my boots by melting and rubbing quite a lot of candle wax into them. I had dared my fate by going back into the cabin a second time and had found candles that had not melted in the fire. The old wax was no guarantee that the boots wouldn't get soggy and wet, but it was worth the try.

My teeth had healed enough for soft foods by the second day at the barn. I had turned the venison broth into a stew by cooking the rest of the meat chunks long and slow, then adding some of the carrots and potatoes I had scavenged from the family garden behind the cabin. Between the stew and Rohahes' mix of herbs, I felt almost as good as I had before I met him and his warriors.

Buried under the dried herbs, I found Cornplanter's wampum belt neatly wrapped in a piece of cloth and placed in the bottom of my knapsack for safe keeping. The wampum belt told the story of Cornplanter's life, his accomplishments and disappointments. It was a treasure I was glad not to have lost in the confusion with the Mohawk. Rohahes must have felt it was necessary to return it to me, but he had done so inconspicuously so that the others could not know that he had given it back. After the altercation with the warriors and what I surmised had happened at the cabin, I was more than happy to carry the wampum the whole way to Morristown.

I walked a little faster after testing my legs and ribs for a while, and watched out for the nearly invisible ruts left by wagons on an otherwise mostly flattened dirt road that had solidified with the cold. The forest on either side of the path was uncomfortably silent. There were no crows or other birds calling out in the dull morning light. It was as if I was in *the time between times* when a dead man's soul walks the earth in a thick cotton of semi-darkness until he sees light. There was no other sound but my own breathing and footsteps as I made my way down the road.

The spitting snow and sleet had stopped by mid-morning, and I was gifted with a slight breeze, tickling my nose with small flakes and bringing the clean scent of pine from the woods. I kept my eyes constantly roving between the trail and the forest on either side, watching for any movement, be it man or animal. Finding a small critter for the cooking pot would be most helpful for this evening's dinner. Rohahes was right, though. If there were Iroquois here, they would be unseen in the forest, and I didn't like the idea of entering the woods again, knowing that some might be there. I had learned my lesson.

Just a little before noon, the scent of a fire drifted through the trees and as I rounded a curve in the road, the source of that smoke was in sight. Just like the farm I walked from, there was another farm with a barn and a much larger cabin, all sitting right in the middle of nowhere. A sign had been nailed in a very visible place over the barn door that read "Norton". I wondered if this was one of the new postal or coach stops Papa had told us about.

The cabin was well cared for and even had some rockers sitting on the porch. I was relieved that I wouldn't be walking into another tomb if

I ventured within. The owner had iron hinges attached to the door frame and an actual iron door latch. That was unusual, in that iron hinges and latches were expensive, so most were made of leather.

I rapped at the door in the hopes that I might buy some food; Rohahes had seen fit to leave Cornplanter's money in a pocket in my knapsack. A man answered with his musket cocked and aimed right at me, with his wife peeking around the door. "Oh, my goodness! What has bedeviled ye? Can't ye see he's just a boy?" the wife said to her husband as she shoved him out of the way and came through the door in a swish of her frock.

"Bessie! Ye need to stay put when I tell ye!" Bessie's husband came immediately from behind and stepped in front of her, simultaneously releasing the cock and setting the barrel pointing at the floor. He continued to scowl at me, daring me to move. Bessie pulled on her husband's shoulder to get his attention, but he ignored her.

"Abe, I . . . " she started to say.

"Doesn't matter what ye want at the moment, Bessie." At that, Bessie moved silently beside her husband and waited for him to speak next.

"What's yer business, young man?"

"My business is my father, sir. I am traveling to Morristown, hoping I might find him. I thought maybe I might buy some food from ye to eat on my way. The food I brought with me is nearly gone and though I had planned to hunt as I traveled, but because of the cold, there are very few beasts that are leaving their nests."

Abe relaxed his stance a bit. He was still staring at me, but with less intensity than before. "Ye've been in a pretty bad fight from the looks of yer face. What happened?"

"Yes, sir, I was. I was waylaid by some Iroquois in the forest ten—fifteen miles after crossing the Delaware River. Lucky for me, that they had a leader who had enough of killing. It was one of his warriors who did this to me before the leader stopped him. He, the leader, provided me with some medicines and venison, then sent me on my way the next day. Those provisions are now gone."

"What's yer name, son?"

It took me just a few seconds to think about this. At the time it didn't feel right using another name at the Hochstetler's, but it seemed necessary. This time I was far enough away from the river, and with the snow on the ground I doubted anyone would come looking for me at all. "Daniel. Daniel Applegate, sir." At that, Abe eased a little more and his demeanor changed.

"I am Abraham Dutton, and my wife's name is Elizabeth. I call her Bessie," he said, smiling directly at her.

"Are ye one of Richard's sons, perchance?"

"Yes sir, I am, his youngest."

"I know yer father. What would he be doing in Morristown? No, wait," he said, holding up his left hand. "Let's go inside, then ye can answer me, Daniel, as it's cold out here. And Bessie, if ye still feel the need to do something more for him, best be starting on it." They moved away from the cabin entrance and let me walk in first, with Bessie following, and Abe close behind her. He shut the heavy door with a thud and put an iron rod back in its place across the door. Abe placed his musket in a rack between the hearth and the door, where kept his other musket.

The cabin was lit primarily by the hearth. The windows let in some light as well, but as it was dreary out, there was little but muted light coming from them. I noticed that Abe had made indoor shutters which were as thick as the door and latched them with a similar rod system used on the door. He had built himself a fortress within the cabin, and he could withstand an isolated attack for some time, though not forever. Yet, maybe it would be long enough for help to come.

"Take yer coat off and let's have a look at ye," Bessie said. "I've got some ointment that might help with the bruising and some of the pain." She came closer to look at me, lifting my chin, moving my arms, and touching my ribs. "It is good that the swelling has gone down. On second thought, maybe an herbal tea would be better. Those bruises look to be healing nicely and from yer wincing, the ribs are still a bit sore, but I don't think they're broken.

"Go set yerself at the table by the fire, Daniel. Have ye eaten? Can I bring ye a bowl?" Without waiting for my response, she went to a pot hung over the fire in the hearth and ladled a large helping of stew into a wooden bowl. With her free hand, she set the teakettle to the fire to heat up. I could not help but smile. "Thank ye, ma'am. It smells wonderful!"

"Ye're welcome, Daniel. Now let me go put the leaves together for the tea. Abe, would ye like some tea as well? I am going to brew some for myself."

Abe had decided to join me with his own bowl of stew, and brought a small loaf of round bread to the table with him.

"Here, ye'll need that to mop up the gravy. Won't want to miss a single drop," he said as he handed me a chunk of the bread ripped in half for us. "My Bessie is the best cook within a hundred miles of here, I dare say," he added, with a wink of his eye.

"I heard that, Abraham! It's just because I am the only woman within a hundred miles of here that would put up with ye," she said with a smile, as she re-entered the room.

"Begging yer pardon, Mistress Dutton, yer husband is correct. This is the best stew I've had in a long time. It is food for a sore soul and a hungry body." I hadn't realized just how hungry I really was until I had walked into the cabin and smelled the stew right off.

"Eat it all then, son. It will help heal those sore muscles and if ye want more, just say so," she said with a grin, then turned to break up the leaves for the tea.

"So, Daniel, tell me about yer father. What news?" Abe asked between bites.

"Papa was called up with the 6th Battalion of the Northampton

County Militia in early July to do another term of service. He should have been home by now and he isn't. There is no one back home to go look for him but me," I said, taking another bite.

"I take it ye checked the hospital at Easton?"

"Well, no. I have it on good authority, though, that he is not there. I thought perhaps he may have been called up to the Continental army and sent to Morristown. That does happen sometimes. Or he could be with Ben, my brother. Visiting, maybe? Ben is with Spencer's Regiment."

"I see. Obviously, I can't tell ye how dangerous traveling is at the moment, because ye already know," Abe said, gesturing at my face. "It is truly miraculous that ye haven't been badly maimed or killed. The angels are certainly watching over ye."

I nodded at that, but I couldn't tell him that the angel was a Seneca Chief; Abe might know of someone that would be very interested in Cornplanter's whereabouts. "I don't suppose there is more to that story that ye want to tell me, is there?" he asked. I had a mouthful of food, so I shook my head and shrugged my shoulders and continued to eat.

"Would ye like any more, Daniel?"

"I am pretty full, ma'am, but I thank ye, though."

"Here's yer tea, son. Sip it slowly," Bessie said as she handed Abe his tea and sat at the table with us and her own bowl of stew in her hands. Abe handed her the chunk of bread he had saved from his half of the bread loaf.

"I don't suppose it will do me any good to try and talk ye out of journeying any further? At this point, though, going back might be more dangerous than going forward to Morristown."

I shook my head 'no' as I slowly sipped on Mistress Dutton's tea.

He was right, though. It was likely that Iroquois in this area had already left the Jersey area, but Pennsylvania might be another matter. The band that I had run into had been the last and had said as much, but Rohahes had told me to stick to the dirt roads, knowing that if there were any stragglers from the exodus, they would avoid the settlers completely by staying in the backwoods and off those roads.

"Oh my, this is tea is wonderfully good, Mistress Dutton. Thank ye so much."

"Yer most welcome, Daniel. If ye want more, just let me know. We have plenty," she replied with a smile.

"Thank ye. How do ye know my father, Master Dutton?"

Abe had finished his tea and got up from the table to reach for his pipe over the hearth, giving himself some time for a response. "Umm, let's see," he replied, standing still in thought with one hand in his tobacco pouch and the other holding his pipe. "I've known Richard going on about 25 years, since the Battle of the Monongahela. Has he talked to ye of it?"

"Not much, Sir. Papa rarely spoke about what he did prior to marrying Mama."

"Well, it's a bit of a long story. Ye got time for it?"

"I do. Especially when I am resting where it is nice and warm." That drew a chuckle out of both of them. I felt at ease for the first time in a long time and with the cold outside, I wasn't particularly excited about leaving immediately.

"All right then. The French had taken over William Trent's trading post at the fork of the Monongahela and Allegheny rivers. That didn't set well with George Washington, his Ohio Company, or the English. The French renamed the trading post Fort Duquesne and shortly thereafter, with their Indian friends, they started a campaign of harassment of the folk that settled there. Homes were burned, crops destroyed, and there were reports of scalpings too. It was an extremely dangerous time for those of us living in the wilderness, much like it has been this past year."

Abe went silent for a moment, reaching for his chair and moving it closer to the hearth, then sat down to light his pipe. I left Abe collect his thoughts a bit more and helped Mistress Dutton with the dirty dishes by, carrying them to the sideboard.

"Thank ye, Daniel. Go now, ye'll want to hear the rest of the story," she said, nodding her head toward her husband. I pulled my chair near to the fireplace as well and relaxed as I waited for Abe to start again.

"As apprentices in two separate merchant businesses, yer father and I were friendly competitors. Always trying to get the best deal for goods from the same seller and constantly bidding against each other for those goods at the traders' warehouses. Boy, would we get into it, shouting and yelling at each other over the price of a bolt of cotton or a load of apples. By the end of the day, we'd find each other at the Kings Arms Tavern in Perth Amboy and eat dinner, drink, tell our stories of the day's lost pursuits and bidding wins, drink more and at the last, carouse with the barmaids." Abe's eyes were closed, and a faint shimmer of a smile appeared on his face as he remembered this part of his youth with my father.

"*Abraham Dutton!* We don't want to hear about yer liaisons with the barmaids," Bessie said in exasperation. Master Dutton lost the shimmer of his smile quickly, and his eyes popped open, forcing him into the present time with a jump start. "Bessie, I'm . . . "

"It's all right Master Dutton, ye're married, not dead and those *ladies* are nothing to me; they are in the past."

"They've been nothing to me since I met ye darlin'," he said, holding an arm out to her, wanting her to be close.

"I know, ye big oaf." She came over to where he was sitting and planted a kiss on the top of his head. His arm found its way around her waist, giving her a gentle hug. "Now get on with the story and forget the barmaids," she said with a chuckle, and gently pushed him away.

"Richard and I both were acquainted with another merchant, James Burd. Master Burd had a nice size trading business and a plantation in Pennsylvania. We would buy furs and fresh produce from him, and he would take our pots, bolts of cotton, sugar, China, and the like to trade with those in the local towns and the frontier.

"In the late spring of 1755 we had gotten word that Master Burd needed a little help with a road that he was building through the mountains. We didn't really know why he was building a road at the time, but had an idea it might have something to do with Fort Duquesne and the suffering of the settlers there. We both were a bit perturbed over the incident with Fort Duquesne.

"Richard had also wanted to scout out the western frontier for himself and his brothers. He decided to go help Master Burd, figuring that scouting might be safer with a small contingent of men nearby. Ye know, the idea of safety in numbers?" he asked, boring those light blue eyes directly into mine.

I nodded my head, 'yes' that I understood—and got the underlying message that I would be safer if I had a companion with me.

"I came along because I couldn't let yer father be the only one with a tale to tell when he got back," Abe said with a twinkle in his eye while drawing on his pipe, enjoying the taste of the tobacco smoke. He let out his breath and the smell of a refined tobacco mixed with the wood smoke from the hearth filled the air. It was not unpleasant and between the warmth of the fireplace, the rather large lunch, and the tea, I was feeling very comfortable for the first time in over a week.

"We knew it would be dangerous. The stories we heard laid out the danger in no uncertain terms. But when ye are young—and we were in our 20s, not nearly as young as ye—danger is really something that happens to someone else. So, we packed our horses, muskets, musket balls, powder, knives, and my sword, thinking nothing more about how dangerous it might be. Our saddle bags carried a bit of food as well. According to what we heard, if we signed up, which we were determined to do, we would only be required to work two weeks and then we could go home. It all seemed simple enough.

"When we reached Shippensburg in Pennsylvania, we signed the contract for the two weeks of work just as we heard. Our horses had to be stabled there in town, as they could not be taken with us. We didn't understand why we had to leave them until we got to the encampment and learned of the plans and the strategy for building the road.

"It was a warm and muggy day in May when we walked from the town to the entrance of Burd's Road that would take us through the wilderness. The day promised to be a real scorcher by afternoon. We were in a group of fifteen men, including the two of us, who were up before dawn and walking towards the road at first light. Everyone was somber after a full night of revelry, so yer father and I just stayed together, leaving the other men to their thoughts.

"We reached Burd's Road in a short span of 15 minutes or so and stood in awe at the breadth of the road. It was nearly thirty feet wide and bordered by a forest that was so thick with trees that the dawn sun shown as mere beams of light. It was cooler in there and with the familiar morning bird song, everyone moved at a steady walking pace. Before long, quiet conversations broke out, spattered with soft laughter from jokes told and the young men teased.

"In the rear of this cavalcade was the supply wagon that held new saws, shovels, hammers, axes, medicines, food, tents, muskets, swords, and our packs. Richard and I would not part with our muskets or my sword, so we carried these and our hunting knives as well.

"At midday, we stopped at a creek, drew fresh water, ate a little lunch, and rested for a bit before continuing. The heat began to pour into the forest and with it came great clouds of flies, gnats, and mosquitos, all looking to dine on us. Napping was impossible, but we were grateful to sit still for a moment. It was then that yer father went to the wagon to pull out a brown earthenware jar from his pack. He opened it, and rubbed the contents all over his arms, face, and neck, just anywhere the little vampires could bite. Immediately, the scent of peppermint saturated the air surrounding us.

"Richard then handed it off to me to try. Said he got the receipt from an old Indian that had come to trade with him. The Indian used bear grease. Nasty stuff, bear grease. Richard made it from pomatum, purchased at the apothecary's, and he mixed in the peppermint. The smell was overpowering. I thought that it would burn the hairs off my face and skin!

"I told him no and handed it quickly back to him." Master Dutton took a moment to smile a bit at the memory, then added a tad more tobacco to the unlit pipe and reignited it with a bristle that he pulled from the broom sitting beside the hearth.

"I suppose that because the pomatum was made from lard and mutton suet, Richard seemed to think that the concoction would be more agreeable to me. He told me to quit being a baby. Well, that drew the attention of the other men and within a matter of two seconds, we had all their eyes on us.

"So, I had to try it. I grabbed the stuff back from him and slathered it all over, glaring at him all the while. 'Dandies Dutton and Applegate!' one of the men shouted. We turned to see the men laughing at both of us, but when yer father held his pot of peppermint salve for them to use, they all shook their heads and ignored us.

"So, we sat on the ground with our backs against a fallen tree and slept for maybe fifteen or twenty minutes without being disturbed by anything crawling or buzzing. When I woke, I found that the stuff worked. I had no bites of any kind. We started back on the road, with all the other men slapping themselves silly over the flying bugs, but yer father and I just sauntered by them smelling like peppermint sticks. We paid no mind to the little beasties as they buzzed by us in a fever to get at our friends.

"Within a half an hour of watching us walk in a rather relaxed manner, the caravan stopped, and all the men came humbly to us to ask if we would share a bit of the ointment. Yer father did, and everyone walked away with a dab of the salve to work into their bare skin.

"The forest had gotten quieter as the morning moved to the afternoon, bringing the heat that was foreseen when we first left. We walked the rest of the day in the sweltering heat, with the whole column smelling of sweat and peppermint rock candy, until the trail boss settled us near a stream for the night. We all waded into the water to cool down, sloughing off the dirt, the sweat, and some of the peppermint pomatum while the trail cook built a fire to fix our dinner.

"After dinner, there were a few stories told at the fire, but most of us were so tired, we just laid near the cool stream and fell asleep on the spot. About midnight, Richard quietly nudged me awake to tell me that something large was moving in the woods. 'Get yer sword and the knives while I prime the flintlock,' he said to me. We waited in the dark, listening for more movement, but we heard nothing else. It sure did feel like something was out there. In the end, we took turns keeping watch the rest of the night.

"The next day at breakfast we were promised that by late afternoon or early evening, we would meet up with the rest of the road crew. We broke camp and started on our way, passing around the earthenware pot of peppermint pomatum and walking. Richard and I kept a lookout on either side of the road. The feeling from the night before had never left us. When we stopped to break, we spoke to the trail boss about what Richard had heard and the feeling that we were being watched. The trail boss had the same thoughts. He told us to keep it to ourselves, and he set up watches with us taking the north side of the road and him and the cook taking the south side.

"We had stopped at several streams and refilled our water bladders several times that morning, moving just a bit faster each time, so by the time we stopped for an afternoon break, we had been at near a double time march. The trail boss decided to distribute what weapons and powder we had, and whoever didn't get a gun got shovels, saws, and hammers. By this time, the road crew were fully aware of what was within a quarter mile of them.

"The Mohawk had been popping in and out of sight, using the

shadow of the woods to keep us guessing where they were. Their faces were colored in streaks of black and red—war paint. There was no mistaking what the warriors were up to. Every now and then, one would shout catcalls, toying with us. It unnerved us all, and we managed to pick up the pace a bit more. Finally, we made it to the road crew's encampment, exhausted, overheated, and very hungry. The Mohawk melted back into the forest, but we knew they were watching and waiting.

"That night, Colonel Burd posted additional lookouts. Even through the exhaustion, we slept fitfully. The next day, we started the work we had come to do, the cutting and clearing of trees and moving earth and stone away for the road. Everything seemed normal from then on, but yer father and the other men with long rifles still took turns on guard duty.

"There were about a hundred and twenty of us working from sunup to sundown. We were required to clear about a mile of road a day. We were able to clear seven miles in ten days. The air was hot and thick with the damp. The afternoon rain showers only made it worse. Sweat ran off us in streams, attracting swarms of biting black flies and mosquitos. The peppermint pomatum was gone on our third day, and there was nothing to do but constantly swat at them.

"As the days went on and we traveled further in, fresh water right near us was harder to find. So, a small scouting group was organized and sent ahead of the work gang to locate water and bring back what they could carry. Yer father volunteered to go with them, and they were happy to have him, his gun, and his backwoods skills. After the first excursion, seeing that several of the men lacked weapons of any kind, he suggested they make bows and arrows for defense should the Mohawk return. Most of the group, though, was made up of Quakers and they objected to making weapons for this purpose. Quakers do not believe in violence, and besides, they figured the Mohawk had moved on. But Richard knew better.

"Two days later, the water group was attacked as they began filling the water pouches. Yer father and two other men, who had not been opposed to the use of bows, defended the others, but not without peril. One of the Quakers was hit by an arrow, clean through his chest. He managed to live long enough to be carried out of the woods and back to camp. He was the first of several men we left there. Another man, Jethro, was his name, ran off further into the woods and was lost."

Abe sat quietly in the shadows of the room for several minutes after his last words. I waited patiently for him to start again and finish his story. An occasional flash of orange-yellow light from the hearth fire would illuminate him and I could see that his pupils were large, and his eyes were black. The darkness had opened them, yet he was seeing little. His vision turned inward, intent only on looking for something far, far away, remembering the past, reliving what he could see clearly in his memory.

Then he got up and shivered. It wasn't cold in the room at all. The logs that he and his wife added to the hearth had not yet been burned down to stubs. Mamma used to say that shivering for no reason meant that someone was walking over your grave. I kind of think maybe for Master Dutton he was shaking off a memory he would prefer not to have had. He walked over to the teakettle and raised it in question, asking me if I wanted any. I shook my head no, not wanting to break the mood entirely, and waited for him to fill his teacup. Sticking his nose in the lavender and mint steam, he inhaled deeply, then pursed his lips, carefully sipping the hot tea, and he began again.

"It was the new moon and two days before our departure when hell broke free of its confines. The last work team made it back when the campfires were twinkling like beacons. There was still food left in the chow wagon and now that this group had come in, we would be able to get seconds. Others had begun the nightly ritual of storytelling and singing, all helped along with a little whiskey brought in later in the afternoon with the re-provisioning of the chow wagon. Richard and I sat by ourselves around our fire talking of our day and savoring every morsel of the chicken stew while pointing out the occasional streak of light made by a falling star sailing across the heavens.

"We washed up our dishes by the stream and settled ourselves in for the night. Between the work, food, and the welcome coolness of the evening, we could barely keep our eyes open. We laid down and were done.

"It seemed as if we had just gotten to sleep, when I heard yer father pull his gun from its resting place. He looked at me and laid a finger over his lips to keep me quiet. The forest was silent, and so was the camp. I sat up slowly and looked around, seeing several of the men alert and listening, with weapons in their hands at the ready. I unsheathed my sword from its leather binding and sat with Richard, waiting for an unseen enemy.

"After an eternity, we heard howls that would curdle the blood of the bravest of men. They came from between and behind the trees, at a distance, and then right in front of us. Our fires were low and the forest black without the moon, so we couldn't see who or what was out there. There was no need to wake the rest of the camp, as the screeches from the forest woke them in a matter of seconds.

"Then all went dead quiet again. Whatever was in the woods lay quiet, observing us like a hunter to his prey. We all moved in closer together, with our backs to the campfires, watching the woods for any movement that would give them away.

"The waiting was unbearable. We were trapped in the clearing with nowhere to run but the woods. The woodsmen, like yer father, encouraged us to stay put, as they knew better. Richard forcibly prevented several of the men from entering the forest, and he was thanked for it by being called a coward. Those men would have run only to die a brutal death.

"The older men among us understood what was beginning to happen to the camp and decided that the appearance of routine, calm work would help settle the men down. They pulled out the sharpening stones to hone axes, knives, and swords. If they didn't have those, they worked on mending their clothing, all while teasing and joking with each other. They were doing anything they could to control their fear of what lingered just past the tree line.

"The howling began again a little more than an hour later. But this time it was different, as we heard screams of agony over the howling. Only something from hell could cause a creature to experience such pain, such terror. Then, just as suddenly, the screams and the howling would stop, and silence would reign again in the forest.

"It was then that there was a good deal more talk of entering the woods to find the bastards who were doing this. There was also those that felt we should leave—start down the road and not come back. The gang bosses and the colonel were opposed to any kind of movement, as were the woodsmen. Richard was sure either way we would die regardless, but a chance, a slim chance for survival, existed if we kept our heads on and stayed put.

"I remember exactly what he told me. He said, 'That is their desire, Abe, to make us try to find them, so that they can pick us off one at a time. That and they are testing us, to see what we are made of—if we will give into our fears. If we go, they will believe us weak and they will kill most of us. If we stay, we have a chance that they will see strength in us and leave us be. The man that we heard tortured is already dead—and if he isn't, he will be, and there is little we can do about it. We must stay put.' I listened to yer father, and I am here today, Daniel. Others did not, and they died.

"The third time it was closer to two hours before the screaming began again and then we heard nothing at all." Abe whispered as he got up to look out the window, staring at the gray and the snow that was falling from the sky. Giving him some time for his thoughts, I grabbed a log from the side of the hearth and added it to the fire, thinking the warmth would help him. He was a little stiff getting up and out of the chair.

"Yer father and I saw the morning light at dawn. We were rather frayed at the edges, but for the most part whole. Not so for the ten men that left quietly that night to try their chances on the road. We found their scalps hanging in the trees first, and then we found the rest of them. All had been killed keenly by arrows and in quiet. As for the individual that had been tortured, we found his scalp in a tree, as well and what was left of his body. It was Jethro–the man that ran into the woods while Richard led the first water gang.

Not only was Jethro's scalp gone, but he was missing a foot and hand. Much of the rest of him had been badly burned as if he had been set afire by torch. They had not touched his face with the flame. That is how we knew it was himWe gathered Jethro's body and the bodies of the other ten, and buried them in a large grave near our camp."

I looked at Abe. He was still gazing at the falling snow, and then he let his head sink to his chest. His lips moved, but I heard nothing. My guess was that he was praying for those who had died and those that had seen and survived. I moved to the window with him and laid my hand on his shoulder and prayed quietly with him. He grabbed my hand on his shoulder, squeezed it, and let go, raising his head to the window and the snowflakes. "Stay this night Daniel, help me with the bedding down of the animals and I'll give ye supper and a warm fire this evening. Then we'll see what tomorrow brings. For now, ye are safe."

I woke early next morning, drowsy from a deep slumber and still feeling the warmth from the coals in the hearth. Master Dutton was awake, moving around me, grabbing both the pot and the teakettle. He opened the door quickly and swooshed out into the dark with the wind blowing in cold and snow. I sat up, rubbed my eyes, yawned while pushing my hair out of my eyes. For a moment, I thought about just curling back up into the blankets, but knew that I shouldn't, as it would be impolite and disrespectful. Getting to my feet, I pulled a log out of the stack near the hearth and put it on the fire.

"Whew! the wind's a gusting and we have at least six inches of snow out there," Abe said as he came in like a whirlwind through the door bringing in both the cold and snow, while carrying the teakettle full of cold water topped with chunks of ice. "Daniel, the missus will be out shortly.

I need to see to the animals. They are a grumpy lot if not fed on time, that is for sure."

"I'll come help. It should only take half the time with both of us," I said as I rushed to get my breeches on and stuff my woolen shirt into them before my coat and boots. By the time we were out the door to look to the animals, Mistress Dutton was up, working on breakfast. I shut the door and looked at the landscape, all covered in snow, and had an urge to get the snowshoes to try them. Abe was already grabbing the shovels, but he promptly put them down after having a second thought. He grabbed the corn broom and pulled out two straws.

"Whoever gets the short straw gets to shovel his way to the pond. Are ye up to it, Master Applegate?" I just smiled, showing all my white teeth, and reached for a straw. I was feeling the best I had felt in days and thought nothing of the hard work. Sure enough, I got the short one and the shoveling would be twice as much as Master Dutton's. But I kind of figured we were even, given the fact that he was much older than me.

The snow was light and fluffy, requiring little effort, and I made it to the pond shortly after Abe made it to the barn. Turning around to make my way back to him, I stopped by the chicken coop and cleared the snow around it, fed the hens, and then headed back. "There ye are, I thought maybe we lost ye in a snow drift back there," Abe said teasingly while patting down one of his three horses.

"Ah, no, not yet. I think it would have to be a very tall snow drift for all that."

"True, ye're nearly as tall as yer father, and taller than me." I came over beside him to attend to another horse, a red roan mare he told me was named Abby. She was a sweet girl and leaned into my warm hand as I massaged her neck muscles. They were a friendly bunch and the other one came over for the same attention. "Ye want to muck out Abby's stall for me, Daniel, and I'll get the last one?"

"Sure!" As I was working, Abby came to supervise the cleaning, using her muzzle to move me in different spaces of the stall, as if to tell me, 'Pick up this pile of dirty straw, and oh maybe ye could move that clean pile over just two more feet.' Before long, I was talking to her about how picky she was, but did what I thought she wanted, and she did seem happier.

"She likes ye, Daniel." At that, Abby whinnied and nuzzled my neck, woofing her steaming breath around my face. I turned and kissed her on the forehead in return, smiling into her eyes and patting her down. "She's a deary, Master Dutton."

"Don't suppose I can change yer mind about leaving today, can I?" Abe asked.

He stood there with his slouch hat covering much of his forehead and ears. His face was red from the cold, and he was leaning on his shovel ever so slightly, holding his breath, waiting for the answer I would give him. "No, sir. I need to find my father. If he is not in Morristown, maybe my brother Ben is. Maybe then Ben and I could go look for Papa together, when Ben's not soldiering."

"All right then; I see that ye're determined. Let's get some food into us and that'll give me some time to think on what I am able to do to help ye," he said as he latched the barn door and headed back to the house. "Can ye get a couple buckets full of water from the pond to put into the barrel on the porch while I help Bessie with breakfast? Ye might need to take that axe."

"Sure. I noticed the pond looked as if it were frozen solid in places while I was shoveling." I grabbed the hand axe and the buckets and headed off to the pond, just as the door shut behind Master Dutton.

ɞＯ੧ ɞＯ੧ ɞＯ੧

Doing chores was really the only thing I could offer them in payment for the food I ate and the shelter they gave me through the night. I had not yet been called for breakfast, so I filled the barrel on the porch with more water than Master Dutton asked for, mainly to save him the chore for a day or two and on one of the trips back to the pond, I noticed that the trough near the barn was almost empty too, and decided to fill it. As I brought the last buckets to the cabin porch, I overheard Abe and Bessie talking about me through the cracked door as they were making our breakfast. I slowly dumped the rest of the water and listened.

"Did ye try to get him to understand how dangerous it is for him to leave right now? If not the Indians, the weather alone might just take him," Bessie said.

"No. I said nothing. He knows. He has already been in one confrontation with the Iroquois and has survived it. He's lived in the backcountry all his life. I am positive that his father has shown him how to survive in the woods and in the cold. Not only that, last night he also let it slip that he had befriended an Indian warrior three summers ago, and he taught him their ways. Nay, I think he'll make it just fine. He's got about thirty-four more miles to go, with villages spaced about eleven miles apart.

"I'll send him with letters to John Taylor in Potterstown, and Jacobus Vanderveer in Bedminister. They will make sure he gets a meal and a night's rest, and they will take care of Abby. One of those two will know who he must see in Morristown to find Richard or Ben."

"Ben?"

"Ben—Benjamin—is Daniel's brother. He has been assigned to Spencer's Regiment. They went with the 2nd New Jersey with General Sullivan to northwest New York. I am sure they've already returned to New Jersey. They may very well be in Morristown or at least somewhere nearby, as Daniel thinks."

"Can we afford to let Abby go?"

"Can our hearts afford not to, Bessie?"

"No, ye're right. I couldn't bear the sorrow if there was something we could do to help and didn't."

"Abby will be a loan, and I fully expect him to return the horse when he is able. She'll protect him to some extent from the wild, by giving him warning of a wayward wolf, bear, or human, and she'll get him there much faster than him walking alone. She knows the trail to Potterstown and Bedminister. Daniel could sleep in the saddle, and she would still get him there safely without his direction.

"With Abby, he'll make it to Morristown for sure in three days with this snow, if not sooner. Likely, sooner. I'd prefer sooner. If the weather holds today and we see no more snow, he might be there by tomorrow, late. I've got a feeling that some bad winter weather is headed here though, and soon. That more than anything worries me."

"No, ye're right." Bessie replied It will make his chances of getting there in one piece a bit better. All right. I'll pack up some meat, potatoes, and anything else that'll keep for the journey after breakfast. I'll make sure he has enough if he decides to push through. I just pray no more harm will come to the child. Abe, he'll need a letter for Abby, too. We don't want anyone thinking he was a horse thief; Abby will be recognized."

I wasn't quite sure what to think or feel about their discussion, but I was deeply grateful for the help. I had no idea how I was going to provide for Abby, but because of who they were, I was sure they would work that out as well. I stomped my feet loudly, mostly to announce my presence and secondly to get the snow off my boots. I opened the cabin door completely, blowing in with the wind and snow, only to catch Abe and Bessie in an embrace. I made a deep throaty noise to announce my presence, and they immediately disentangled themselves, both made self-conscious by my presence. "Papa used to say hugs were definitely a good way to get warm and stay warm, especially on days like this." I smiled as I thought about Mama and Papa often being caught doing the same. Near the end, they never worried about being found hugging or kissing in front of any of us.

"Ah, well, that sounds like Richard. Mind ye, son there is nothing better than hugging the love of yer life on a cold winter's day."

"Well gentlemen, now that we have thoroughly decided when hugs are best, let's be getting breakfast on the table before it gets cold," Bessie said briskly, with her cheeks crimson with embarrassment.

⚬◯⚬ ⚬◯⚬ ⚬◯⚬

"Thank ye for praying for my journey, Master Dutton." I grabbed another of the warm golden colored biscuits, split it in two and slathered it in butter. The butter drizzled down the sides of the biscuit and into my hand, as I scooped up the last of the scrambled eggs on my plate.

"Ye need it. There are a lot of things out in the wilderness older, more cunning, and bigger than ye. If it were just a matter of size alone, ye might have a better-than-average chance." Abe took his time adding a dollop of honey to his second biscuit and bit into it, savoring it as if it were his last. Bessie just looked at me and winked, then turned back to her eggs and bacon on the plate in front of her.

"If, I tried to hold ye here, ye would just run, right?"

"Master Dutton, it has been a pleasure getting to know ye, and no disrespect to ye or yer wife, but yes, I would find a way to leave."

"All right then, I thought I would ask one more time—can't blame me for trying. Since ye don't have it in mind to listen to the advice of yer elders, we are going to help ye a bit with yer quest," he said as he passed the plate of bacon to me, questioning with his raised eyebrows in expectation that I wanted more. I took it as it was offered and with my fork, scraped about a third of what was left on the plate to mine and passed it back, waiting for him to explain how he might be able to help.

"Bessie, these fried potatoes are some of the best we've had recently. Do we have more?"

"We do. I'll get some."

"No, stay where ye are, girl. I'll get it." With that, Abe got up and not only put some on his plate but offered more to me and Bessie.

"So, as I was saying, I think we can help. I'll write letters of introduction for ye to both John Taylor in Potterstown and Jacobus Vanderveer in Bedminister. John has a grist mill a mile or two out of town and Jacobus might not be home, but he will have some people there that should be able to help—they know me. I helped to organize the transport and receipt of supplies into the Pluckemin Cantonment last winter for our soldiers."

"The Pluckemin Cantonment? Could Papa be there?" The last question came out cracking at the end with a high-pitched croak. I had been having a little trouble with my voice lately and was not sure exactly why. Bessie giggled beside me as I stared at Abe in horror, and I am sure my eyes had to be as big as the breakfast plates in front of us. Instead of getting any sympathy—which is not what I wanted anyway—he laughed, causing his whole body to rumble in waves of merriment at my predicament.

"Yer voice is changing, Daniel. It happens," he said between breaths, still laughing at my discomfiture.

"It always seems to happen at the wrong times, that is for sure."

Abe caught his breath momentarily and sipped on more tea and eased back into our conversation. "No. Your Papa is not there, not now anyway. The Pluckemin Cantonment was a place for the men to rest during last winter and part of the summer. General Knox lived in Jacobus' house until General Washington called them all to Morristown." Bessie took the break in the conversation to add more tea to everyone's cup and then began to pick up the dishes. Abe got up to help her, but she waved him off, and he stayed in his chair.

"So, did General Knox bring his cannon there? I remember hearing that he brought disassembled cannons on ox sleds from Fort Ticonderoga, through the cold of the wilderness over frozen lakes and streams, rough ground and through Indian territory, and settled them in Boston and right under British noses. There were fifty of them! Did ye get to meet Knox?"

"There were fifty-eight cannons when assembled and all pointed at Boston from Dorchester Heights. I guess the size of Knox's artillery line was a bit too frightful for the Brits because they retreated to their ships; withdrawing all the way to Halifax, Nova Scotia," he said, grinning.

"No, I didn't get to meet General Knox, but I saw him several times. He is a stocky sort of man shorter than ye or me, graying a bit at the sides of his head. He always had a bit of frown and a serious demeanor. War has a way of stealing youth and laughter. He was responsible for many lives. I am sure it took a toll on him."

Abe scooted his chair out from the table and made towards the hearth that was still crackling with a small fire and took the heated kettle of water to Bessie for washing dishes. I moved away as well and hesitated a bit about what to do next. I didn't want to leave the confines of this warm place, but I must go before I'd lose any daylight.

"If ye want to pack up yer things and get the saddle on Abby, I'll get to the letter writing and the map I promised," Abe said as he poured some of the hot steaming water into a small washtub and the rest into a similar tub that was used for rinsing.

"Yer letting me take Abby? Sir, I cannot. If I did take her with me, I don't know when I could get her back to ye."

"Daniel, we are more worried about ye getting to Morristown in one piece than we about not getting Abby back. Abby is a good horse; she'll keep ye safe and she knows the way that I am sending ye - she has traveled it enough with me. With Abby, even in this snow, ye are about three days from Morristown."

"But I can't feed her!"

"Don't worry about that. She'll eat when ye arrive at either John or Jacobus' homes. I'll send ye with some coin for the feed."

, "We have some carrots we can spare as treats for Abby. I'll add them to the other food that I'll pack for him, Abe, Bessie added "It will be all right, Daniel. The Taylors and Vanderveers are good people. They will feed Abby and ye, with or without any money, so need for worry." As she spoke, her hands remained busy, moving our dishes into the steaming soapy tub to soak.

"Ye are sure, both of ye?"

"Yes, we are sure. Now just say thank ye and get a move on. Ye're losing the sun with every moment we talk about this," Abe replied as he pulled three pieces of paper, quill, and a small pot of ink from a side cabinet.

"Thank ye, Master and Mistress Dutton," I said, bowing at the waist in formal reply and then rushing out the door to get Abby ready for the journey.

❧❧❧

I was hesitant to take my leave. I had been comfortable with the Duttons and knew not what I would find when I reached the Morristown encampment. Abe had told me before I left that food was hard to come by, and Congress was not in the habit of supplying the army with regular victuals, decent clothing, or shelter. One thing I knew for sure was that the weather would be unpredictable, and I could only pray that it would not get much colder than it was.

We said our goodbyes on the porch not long after loading up Abby. "Be careful and mind where ye are Daniel," Bessie said with tears in her eyes while giving me a very solid hug.

"Heed yer conscience, Daniel, and find yer father," Abe said straight-faced, and pulling me into a bear hug. "Make me and yer father proud," he whispered in my ear, just before releasing me.

"I will try, sir," I whispered back. "Thank ye both for yer help and for Abby," I said, while making a bow. "I will send her back as soon as I am able." With that, I climbed onto Abby, adding my weight to the nearly thirty pounds of salt pork, and several pounds of oats, sweet potatoes, apples, carrots, cheese, and bread that Mistress Dutton had packed into the saddlebags.

The temperature dropped hourly as I rode along the road that was shown on Master Dutton's map, and by early afternoon, it was much colder than the morning. We had made fairly good time, though, given that I mostly walked with Abby instead of riding her out of fear of injuring her. The snow on the trail hid ankle breaking ruts and holes that had been worn into the path over long years of use. So, when I could not see the road for the snow, I walked beside her. I stayed warmer that way for sure.

The real blessing was that the small creeks that we had to cross had frozen solid, so we did not get wet as we crossed them. We just had to be careful of slipping on the ice.

We stopped for a few short minutes just after Potterstown for a bit of a cold lunch. Then we were back on the road, but not before I patted my coat to make sure I could feel the letters still tucked away safe inside. True to his word, Master Dutton sent me not with just three letters, but four. Besides the Vanderveer and Taylor letters, I had the letter stating that I had his permission to borrow Abby, and the fourth was a letter for Papa when I met up with him.

I didn't need the Taylor letter. We passed the road to the Taylors' just after lunch. According to the map, the Vanderveers' was about eleven miles from the Taylors'. If we could keep the same pace, we would be there just before nightfall. I had no intention for me or Abby to sleep out in this cold.

The sun managed to make a brief appearance during the afternoon, which we both welcomed. Between the warmth of the sun, Abby's body heat and the gentle rocking from sitting in a saddle, I dozed off, only to wake up in the front yard of the Vanderveers. Master Dutton was right— Abby had found her way to the Vanderveers while I was sleeping. We arrived in the late afternoon with the sun hidden behind the clouds and snow falling again.

Vanderveer Farm

"Good afternoon, young sir!   Welcome to Vanderveer House." the man said as he walked towards me through the snow.

"Thank ye, sir. Is Master Vanderveer at home?" I asked as I finished tying Abby to the post at the front of the brown clapboard home.

"He is, and bids you welcome. When you're ready, please follow me. My name is Aaron. My goodness, is it cold out here."

"Daniel, Daniel Applegate, sir," I said as I made a quick bow. "That it is, sir, and my horse is just as cold. May I stable her in yer barn before meeting Master Vanderveer?"

"Don't worry about that, Master Applegate." He turned to the young man that had followed him out to the post. "Andrew, take Master Applegate's horse to the barn and feed her, then bring his bags to the house when you return."

"Yes, sir," he responded as he untied Abby's leader from the post.

"Master Aaron, I can take my own bags and Abby to the stable," I said, reaching for her reins as Andrew walked past. I didn't need someone to take care of me and do my chores when I was healthy and able.

"No, Master Applegate,"

"Daniel, please."

"Andrew will take Abby back to the stable and bring your bags into the house," Aaron said as he turned to walk to the front door, expecting me to follow.

"Those saddle bags need to be left in the cold. There's some meat in them for the Continental army when I find them," I said.

"All right, Master Applegate. I'll leave them in our winter spring house and bring them back to you when you are ready to leave."

"Thank ye, Master Andrew."

I ran to catch up to Aaron, who was not waiting for me but was making his way back to the manor house. The entry was crafted with a fan window over a six paneled red oak door that had been oiled to bring out the rich grains of red and gold colors of the wood. I hadn't seen a door like this since visiting my cousins in Perth Amboy.

A brass knocker and strike plate were attached as well, with outside edges of the plate all finely etched in swirls of thick vines that ended in oak leaves. The knocker was expertly crafted. It was smooth, soft to my touch, and did not detract from the plate underneath.

Master Aaron opened the ornate door, and I followed him into the vestibule, noting with dismay the state of my boots. They were full of mud and dirt, and I had no desire to walk on the floor depositing those bits and pieces on to the oak planking. I asked Master Aaron to wait a minute while I took them off.

Master Aaron grimaced in distaste as I carefully removed them, trying to limit the amount of caked mud on the carpet beside the door. For a moment, I thought maybe the smell of my feet caused his disdain. I sniffed and reached the conclusion that it was not my feet, because Bessie insisted that I wash before laying my head for sleep. It was just the state of my boots.

Aaron turned to pull a tassel on a rope beside the door, and I heard a bill ring down the hallway to the right. A lady came running down the hallway and curtsied in front of Aaron and then stood waiting patiently for Aaron to speak. "Ruth, please take Master Applegate's boots and clean them. Return them when you are done to the second bedroom on the left upstairs."

Ruth was a small lady, maybe five years older than me, creamy skin and long dark eyelashes that graced the deep pool of chocolate that were her eyes. "Yes, Master Aaron," she said as she bent to pick up my boots.

"Thank ye, ma'am, but ye don't need to do that," I responded as I picked up the boots. I didn't want a fuss made over me, and it seemed wrong to have someone else tidy up my mess. "I'll clean them after I've talked to Master Vanderveer."

"Master Applegate,

"Please, just call me Daniel."

"It is her job as housekeeper to make sure our guests are comfortable while staying at Vanderveer house. She will make . . . "

"Aaron, did I hear you say Master Applegate?" said the man, walking quickly into the vestibule in his stocking feet. He was dressed in rich dark blue woolen britches, a vest made with the same material and a linen bell sleeved shirt. His wig was slightly cockeyed on his head, making me think he had the wig off before coming to see what the racket was about.

"Yes, Master Vanderveer, this is Master Daniel Applegate," he said, waving a hand in my direction.

"At yer service, sir," I said, making a leg.

"You are Richard's son?"

"Yes, sir, I am one of them."

"How did you come to be here?"

"It is a long story."

"I look forward to hearing it. You will stay, won't you?"

"If it is no bother, Master Vanderveer. I won't turn down a warm bed and food."

"Aaron, please prepare a room for Daniel."

"Yes, sir. I have already asked Ruth to prepare one."

"Good, Thank you, Aaron. Daniel, please give your hat, coat, and boots to Ruth. She will have them cleaned and ready to wear by breakfast in the morning."

"Sir, please, there is no need."

"Well, there is a need now. You're holding everything so close that your boots have soiled your coat. Don't worry, Ruth will do a fine job cleaning them."

"But I don't want to overstep yer hospitality, sir."

"Nonsense. This is what we do for our guests."

"All right then, sir. Ma'am, I thank ye," I said as I handed off the heavy woolen coat and muddy boots to Mistress Ruth.

"Aaron, please do have some hot tea brought to my study for both me and Daniel. Maybe a couple of sweet biscuits, too. Thank you."

"Wait, Mistress Ruth! I have letters in the coat for Master Vanderveer," I said as I walked quickly to catch up with her. She stopped mid-stride, turned, and held the coat out to me to find the letters. "Thank ye, again Mistress Ruth," I said as I bowed. She smiled back at me with nearly perfect white teeth and curtsied again.

"A woman of few words is our Ruth, very unusual. What are these letters that I need to read, Daniel?"

"Master Dutton wrote ye a letter, mainly about me, I think, and then there is the one that says that Abby has been loaned to me for the duration of my trip and that I am not a horse thief," I said as I handed him the letters at his desk.

"I didn't think you were, Daniel. Please sit while I read these," he said as he motioned me to a chair that was in front of his desk.

"I hope Abby's doing all right in the stable. I am responsible for her care. It was very cold out there today and I hope she didn't get frostbitten."

"I understand, Daniel. Don't worry, Andrew is the best groom I've ever had. He'll make sure she is unhurt and warm.

"Thank ye, sir. I appreciate it."

"There you are, Jacobus! I went to the barns looking for you and got caught up with Wilbur," a lady exclaimed as she came in from the door behind Master Vanderveer's desk. He turned his head and smiled at her, reaching behind his chair for her hand.

She was a bit of a sight, dressed in a dark grey kirtle and apron, puffy with innumerable petticoats that looked as if they all had been dragged through mud and snow. Holding the sides of the dress up, away from her ankles and walking in her stocking feet, had saved much of the floor. In her wake, she dropped bits of hay like an enormous golden maple tree just beginning to shed its autumn leaves.

Once behind Jacobus' desk chair, she let the petticoats drop and reached for his hand.

"Where is your escort, my sweet?" he said as he took her hand and planted a kiss on it and then let it go.

"I tell you no lie. I escaped—but you know it will only be for a few moments. She will be here soon."

"Who do we have here?" she asked.

"Daniel Applegate, and Daniel, this lovely lady is Mariah Hardenburgh, my betrothed."

"At yer service, Mistress Hardenburgh," I said, standing and making another leg, while wishing these formalities would end soon.

"Thank you and welcome, Daniel," she said with a warm smile. It was a rare sight to see a grown woman without a cap. Her curly blond hair had formed a red nimbus around her head from the firelight, and as she came around Jacobus' chair, I could see that her bonnet was secured safely under the belt that she wore. "What has made you come so far in this weather? Your father told us that you were in Pennsylvania staying with your sister and brother-in-law. Is your father all right?"

"Well, ma'am, I really don't know. He should have arrived at the farm late September or early October, but he's not come, nor have we had word of his whereabouts. I did hear that he was not in the hospital at Easton or anywhere else nearby. It is likely, though, he is with my brother and the Continental army, but I do not know. I just want to make sure that he is all right."

"You mean you walked all that way to here? No child should

travel the country with heathens running around and in weather like this!" "Mistress Hardenburgh exclaimed, lifting her hand to the large window behind Jacobus' desk, and the weather outside. "How old are you, eleven years?"

"No, I am twelve."

"Well, that makes me feel a whole lot better, then," she said, rolling her eyes. "And what happened to your face?" She came closer and reached for my jaw, turning my head. "The bruising is healing. I bet your jaw and teeth hurt for a bit."

"*Ja,* they did, and they were loose, too. But I managed to make some broth with some meat to keep my strength up. Mistress Dutton gave me a cream for the soreness, and it has helped. As for the walking, yes, I walked all the way, except for riding Master Dutton's horse a bit to get here today. The healing is taking a little longer than I'd like, but I am mending. I slept part of the way on Abby's back."

"Who beat you?" she asked directly.

"I fell down a small ridge earlier this week, and that's what happened to my face. That's all. I am fine."

Mistress Hardenburgh looked at Jacobus in disbelief.

"Mariah, some people would think he has reached the age of maturity," Master Vanderveer said as he shrugged his shoulders.

"May I ask ye a question?" I ventured.

"We will answer, Daniel. If it is within our power, please ask."

"There is much my father has not told me. I was not aware that ye were an acquaintance of his. How did ye become so?"

"I have known your father awhile. He and I have been partners in a few business ventures. A few years ago, I provided goods for barter with the Iroquois and, in return, the Iroquois traded their furs and the like for those goods. On several occasions, your father was my representative with the tribes. Your father is a good man, Daniel, and he treated both me and the Indians fairly."

"Thank ye for saying so. He had often talked of the business and visiting the Indian towns, but never mentioned his business partners. It wasn't really my place to ask, and maybe it still isn't. After Mama died, he said very little of his trips to the frontier."

"I am sorry to hear that."

Mistress Hardenburgh moved to Jacobus' side and grasped his arm. He reached over with the free one and patted her hand and then kissed it again, then let it go. "I am off to the kitchen to see what I can do to help Ruth with dinner and let Mistress Van Meter find me there. Aaron, there you are! Don't eat too many of the cookies, Daniel, you'll spoil your dinner." Then she was out the back door in a flurry, with her petticoats pulled up to her ankles and still dropping bits of hay as she walked quickly out of the room.

"She must of have fallen in the hay, chasing after Wilbur. It is all over back here," he said as he opened the door to a cabinet behind his desk and pulled out a corked bottle of whiskey. He smiled and shook his head again as he stepped over the hay to return to his seat. "Oorlam?" he asked as he lifted it to view. "It will make the tea better and warm you a bit, I think."

"Yes, thank ye," I said as I held my cup out to him to add the dollop. Who is Wilbur?"

"Wilbur is a young ram who thinks he is a person and is in love with Mariah because she feeds him warm milk out of a bladder. His mother refused to suckle him when he was a babe."

He looked me over appraisingly. "So, you've come nearly seventy miles on your own two feet. You've done well in getting yourself here in one piece."

"Thank ye, sir. I've had good backwoods teachers, including Papa," I replied, taking a sip of the whiskey tea and feeling it warm me as it slid down my throat.

"Make sure you eat a cookie, otherwise Ruth will think that you absolutely hate them. As for traveling to Morristown, I think you might want to head towards Scotch Plains. The 2nd New Jersey and Spencer's Additional Regiment made camp there a little more than a week ago. We had the 2nd New Jersey's colonel here for dinner a couple of days ago and he mentioned where they were."

ᎾᏊᎾ ᎾᏊᎾ ᎾᏊᎾ

I awoke to a world covered in ice and cold. The Vanderveers' house, barns and trees were ensconced by it, and when Andrew went to check in on the animals at dawn, I could hear his feet crunch on the ice topped snow. Breakfast was laid promptly at seven and soon after, with full belly, I said my farewells to the Vanderveers and wished them well. Before I left, they packed up as much food as Abby could haul, and still left me room to ride her if need be. I had so much that it was a struggle to tie down the tops of the bags and my knapsack. Finding food for Abby on the trail wasn't going to be easy, but I still had carrots and the Vanderveers packed some dried apples for her. It helped that Andrew made sure she had her fill of hay the day before and this morning.

Scotch Plains

There were long thick icicles hanging from the tree limbs on either side of the snow-covered wagon road. As the wind blew against the trees, the limbs would bump up against each other, making clanking sounds and causing some of the long spikes to fall, cracking the ice encrusted snow ground below.

Once, I had heard a story that a man had died because of one of these frozen spears had pierced him clean through as he was hunting in the woods with friends. They had to drag his body all the way back to his home, while fending off wolves. The tale was likely not true — just one of those strange stories my cousins and I would tell each other around the hearth fire when we or they were visiting. Still, I thought it best to avoid being under trees at all costs.

The day grew colder as we walked. I could see ice crystals forming from my breath and my nose hairs felt as if they, too, were coated in ice. Abby, though, was still comfortably warm beneath me. I moved the knitted scarf given to me by Mistress Dutton over my cheeks and nose, to just under my eyes, and pulled the woolen cap from the Vanderveers farther down around my ears. Master Vanderveer's heavy woolen coat was just a bit short but kept most of me warm. I wore it over my own wool coat.

There was a winter I remember when we had all dressed like this - doubling up on coats, hats, and gloves to do chores outside for short periods of time. We kept the hearth roaring day and night, sleeping by it to stay warm on those long, dark, and cold nights.

On those nights, after our lessons and our Bible reading, Papa would make the evening special by telling the old stories that his father passed down to him, and his before him, and so on. Sitting on the floor near the hearth, sipping cups of hot apple cinnamon tea and honey, munching on popcorn that Mama had made, we would listen to Papa tell of princes and princesses, fairies, giants, trolls, and dragons, of battles fought, and loves lost. When we had gone through all the stories he knew, he would pull out a book he treasured and read it to us. Robinson Crusoe and Gulliver's Travels were favorites.

I could have used some of that hot apple cinnamon and honey tea with my lunch earlier. I found a large rock outcrop that blocked a good portion of the wind while we ate. Abby got her share of near frozen carrots and dried apples. Then I was back on my feet again, walking rather than riding. I figured if I sat for too long, my blood would freeze.

We arrived at a crossroads near Scotch Plains by late afternoon. I was bone cold, exhausted, and all I wanted to do was lay down, get warm and sleep. My eyes had begun to play tricks on me, blurring in and out so much that I wasn't quite sure what I was seeing. Squeezing my eyes closed and then opening them quickly, I saw two men come into view, not trees as I first thought, and I directed Abby toward them.

The men looked miserable themselves. I don't think that their fraying, patched blue coats kept them warm at all. I had dropped Abby's reins when I saw them. Then things all went gray, and I found myself on the snow-covered ground with Abby whoofing in my face. Rag covered boots were coming towards me and talking to me, but I just wanted to drift off, so I did.

"Ye can't sleep now. Stay with us, boy. We've got a fire, just over yonder. Can ye see it?" one of them asked.

They set me up, then got me to my feet so they could half carry and mostly drag me through the snowdrifts to the fire. They kept poking me and talking to me, saying things that made no sense and just wouldn't let me sleep. I so wanted rest, so I slumped lower and was nearly bent over to the ground again. I would be warm if I slept.

"Help us out here, child. You're a bigg'n and we canna do it by ourselves," another voice cried urgently. I wasn't at all sure why he should care whether or not I fell. I would be fine in the morning. With all the insistent pushing and pulling, I gave in, deciding it would be best to pull my legs back under me before they did tear me apart. I got control of my legs and succeeded in putting one foot in front of the other and reached the little fire. They let go, and I collapsed into a heap.

Abby was right with me, nuzzling my face to make sure I was all right. She was shivering just a bit herself. I stroked her leg and ankle. She was cold, colder than I should have let her become. The soldier that told me to help them took his dirty thread-bare blanket that was on his shoulders and laid it on Abby's back to warm her.

I moved up on my knees, steadying myself by holding on to Abby's leg, and we both moved closer to the fire. The heat seeped into all my cold parts. I closed my eyes, luxuriating in the warmth, and found that even the slightly smoky air was a comfort to me.

I awoke from this heavenly bliss by a god-awful screech and a very large flat hand bashing into my chest, knocking the breath out of me and sending me sufficiently backward that I ended up sprawled with the back of my head thumping against the frozen ground. A long, dark shadow reached out to grab my hand. It was the second time the man had tried to keep me upright. "I'm sorry child, can't have ye falling in the fire, either," he said. "Wouldn't be good on my record, being a father myself and t'all. What's yer name, son?"

"Daniel Applegate, sir."

"Good. My name's Hugh Barr and that is Joseph Carrington. Looks like yer brain's a begin'n ta work agin," he said with a broken toothed smile. "Would ye like someth'n warm ta drink? 'Tisn't much but it'll set ye straight," he said, patting my shoulder with an old blue woolen mitten that had been resewn several times and could use a few stitches even now.

Still gasping for breath, I nodded yes and watched as Hugh went to the fire to ladle a murky, brown-colored liquid into a cup and then brought it back to me. "Ah, ye look like yer breath'n better. Here, now careful there, Dan'l. You got the cup? Good. Yer still look'n a bit peak-ed."

I held the cup tight out of fear that I'd spill it and make everything an icy mess, as cold as it was. The warmth from the cup seeped through to my mittens. It felt nearly as good as putting my hands to the fire as I did a few minutes before. The tea, if that was what it was, was full of bits and pieces of something that looked like bark. Staring at the particles swimming aimlessly through the light brown liquid had a calming effect, and my breathing finally slowed back to normal. "I'm sorry son, that's all we'ins have, but it will do ye some good," Hugh said, thinking that I had disapproved.

I looked up at him, nodded and smiled in thanks, raised the cup to him and took a rather large gulp of the warm swill and immediately ejected it, spitting out the contents of my mouth on the white frozen ground beside me. I coughed so heartily I thought I had done some permanent damage to my lungs. Hugh grabbed the cup back before I splashed the rest of the contents on either of us. He reached over and patted my back between coughing spasms, cooing some words of encouragement, while Joseph stood laughing at my predicament.

"Enough Joe! No reason ta be a laugh'n at 'im. He's sick with the cold, that's all."

It took a few moments to catch my breath again, but when the coughing ended, I was in possession of my wits again. "I'm fine now, sir, it's all right. Master Carrington, I probably did look pretty funny," I said, as I grinned back at him.

"I'm a guess'n ye've not had applejack that strong, before, have ye Dan'l?"

"Ah, no sir, Master Barr, can't say that I have. Pa always watered it down a bit for us. It's good though. I'll just sip the rest if that's all right."

I hadn't been expecting the alcohol at all, and that large gulp nearly burned a hole from the inside out, but I wasn't about to tell either of them that. "May I get a bit closer to the fire, and sit on that log?" I asked.

"Sure, just don't be a fall'n into it like ye almost did a minute ago. Dan'l, take yer time sipp'n the tea. Nothing happin'n here for the moment, anyway. It will warm ye nicely if ye let it. Joe, come on. Might as well warm yerself, too. That crossroads isn't go'n anywhere and we can watch from here," he said, as we both walked to the fire and the log seats.

"So where exactly are ye from, son, and why'd ye end up here, of all places, in the middle of this winter?"

"He's a runaway, Hugh, can't ye tell? He needs to go home, and soon. Like we all should be doing."

"That is called desertion, Joe, and I'll not have ye talk about it in front of me or ta boy. If yer gonna go, go. Just don't talk ta me about it. I'm that tired of it." Joe did go, turning back to the crossroads and stomping with every foot that touched the ground. "Look, Joseph." Master Barr shouted, "I'm gonna take 'im to the encampment as soon as he's done wit ta tea and able ta walk the couple of miles. I'll be back. If ye are not here, I'll report ye as deserted, understand?"

"I understand," Joseph replied with no more words, but huffed off in the early twilight to his post.

"Make no mind of 'im. He's been grumpy ever since we ins got back. So, yer were gonna tell me where yer from and why yer here?"

❧ ❧ ❧

The encampment was settled in a gently rolling, snow-covered field encircled by the woods on three sides. The snow there was no longer pristine but marked with many footprints of men going to and fro.

We were stopped at the entrance to a tent village by guards who asked about our business. At that point, Master Barr pulled his scarf away from his face so that they could see him. "Just me, Robby, and this young'n. Me and Joseph caught 'im at the crossroads we was a watch'n. Dan'l is his name, says he's got family here. Thought I'd head over to Corporal Johnson's tent to see if he knows of Dan'l's kin."

"Well, I think the corporal is camped around about the twentieth tent down," Robby said as he turned and pointed down a row of tents just to the left of us. "Not sure it's exactly the twentieth, ye'll have to keep a lookout for him."

"Thank ye, Robby."

"At your service, Master Barr," Robby replied, bowing ever so slightly.

We had made our way with Abby in tow, through and around the soldiers, their tents, and campfires, on a frozen mud foot path to find Corporal Johnson's tent. The tents, many of them dirty, well used, and haphazardly patched with mismatched pieces of cloth, had been set up in rows facing each other to take advantage of community campfires between them. Master Barr had told me that there were nearly seven hundred men camped here, some from the 2nd New Jersey and others from Spencer's Regiment, all under a Colonel Israel Shreve.

The soldiers were a were a motley crew. There was no uniformity in dress between any of them. Many of them were in their own tattered garments they had brought with them from home. A few others had complete uniforms, including shoes and stockings, but they were only a handful at most. None of the men or their clothing had seen a washing in an age.

Their shoes and boots were in the same condition as their clothing. Most of them had holes where the toes peeked out, or seams that had been torn apart. They were no better than the sandals that some of the other men wore. Tied rags were used to hold the shoes together, like Master Barr's, but that would not last long for them. A good many of the troops were barefoot altogether, and that was worrisome. Many would lose toes if foot gear wasn't found for them soon.

Coats, hats, and mittens were missing from the men, as well. Most of them had wrapped themselves in their blankets to stay warm while they milled about the fire. Many of those blankets were dirty and in disrepair.

Finally, we had gotten free of that small mass of humanity and moved closer to the officer's quarters, where I could see that some of the campfires had a stew pot setting over hot coals. Given the state of the clothing and shoes, I gathered that there was little expectation of feeling stuffed after their dinner as well.

The aroma of onions and what I thought might have been beef from one campfire did make my mouth water, but when I got closer to look, what was in the pot was mostly broth with small pieces of shredded meat bubbling to the top. Sitting beside the pot were some sort of round flat bread pieces with specks of yellow corn in it. I overheard one man call them "fire cakes". They didn't look appealing at all.

At this point, I was grateful for the additional food supplies in the bags that Abby was carrying. I just wanted to make sure they got to my brother first, then I needed to get Abby home so that she wouldn't become someone's dinner anytime soon. Master Dutton and Master Vanderveer were right. These men, if not starving, would be soon, and if that didn't kill them, then the cold might.

Although troops lacked suitable clothing, shoes, and food, the general mood in the camp was lighthearted. As we walked amongst the men, we heard a lot of joking and resulting laughter. Somewhere farther down the path, we could hear musicians and singing all to the tune of "Banks of the Dee."

"Ah, there he is," Master Barr said under his breath.

"Corporal Johnson? Where the singing is?"

"Yes. They've had their supper already. We'ins sing, tell stories, talk of politics, battles, loves lost, and stay warm by the fires. Looks like the corporal's joined in."

Corporal Johnson was a man in his twenties at most, quite a bit younger than Master Barr. There was no gray in his dark greasy hair or crows-feet surrounding his eyes. He laughed easily with his troops at the fire, teasing several of them simultaneously into singing a rather ribald song, while they teased him back with no fear of being seen as disrespectful to his station. Master Barr caught the corporal's eyes, and by the wave of Master Barr's hand, Corporal Johnson gracefully disentangled himself from the joviality and came to meet us.

"Master Barr, is there a problem?"

"Well, not really, sir, but I don't know what else ta do with the boy here. I can't send 'im back the way he came. Tis not safe, and the last thing we'ins need is another runaway ta keep an eye on. He says he's here ta find his brother and his father. His name is Dan'l Applegate, late of Easton." He held his open, upturned hand in my direction.

"At yer service, sir," I said as I made a slight bow in the Corporal's direction.

"Are you now, young man?" he asked, looking me over. "Can you shoot and hit what you aim at?"

"Sir?"

"Well, can you? If you can, you might be of service," he said with the grin on his face.

"Yes, I can hit what I aim at, whether be it rifle, arrow or knife, sir. Muskets are a little harder to be accurate with, though."

"Good, you just might be able to keep yourself and a few others fed. You do look a little like Benjamin Applegate, even with all those yellowing bruises. Is he your brother?"

"Yes, I have a brother named Benjamin, but I also have a cousin by that name that could be here too."

"Yes, well, I'll have to walk you to his tent to be sure, then. Master Barr, thank you. I'll take Daniel and his horse to Benjamin, and we'll see if he is his cousin or brother. Before you go back to your post, though, sit by the fire, get what food and warm drink is left. Might take what's left of the bread to the other guard at the crossroads, too."

"Thank ye corporal, sir."

"Master Barr, it was good to meet ye and thank ye for yer help and the applejack tea. I will have that memory forever, and safe travels to ye, sir," I said, smiling as I bowed to him.

"For yer'in sake, I hope yer family is here. Take care young'n" and with that Master Barr was off after his dinner. I hoped it would be more filling than what I had seen earlier.

"So, tell me about the bruises, Daniel. Looks like your face got trampled by a very large deer. The swelling is gone," he said, turning my chin carefully from side to side to look at the damage. "Nothing broken?"

"No, nothing's broken. Really, I do feel better now."

"All right. So, tell me, did ye get any of your own punches in?" he asked as we began our walk to see Ben.

"I did, but they were on me before I could do much of anything. I got lucky that they let me go after a bit."

"Who were they? Do ye think they will be a problem for other folk nearby? Should we send someone to find them?"

"Na. I was first hit by the factor at my sister's house, then on my way here I ran into some Indians who did some more damage. They're long gone by now and were in a bit of a hurry to be gone. I came upon them after I crossed into New Jersey, maybe five miles from the Delaware River. They were just a small band of Mohawk, returning to their winter villages. They were headed north-west, I think."

"You're lucky to be alive, then."

"I am. Their leader talked the warriors out of murdering me. I was truly thankful for that."

"No doubt. The horse, is she yours?"

"No, sir. Abby belongs to Master Dutton. He lives in Norton, a place just inside the New Jersey border. He lent her to me out of concern of the weather and thought I'd be safer with her even if I ran into more Iroquois. Master Dutton tried to talk me out of coming, but I was determined to find my father and brother.   I have papers from him giving Abby into my care, if ye need to see them.   I need to send her back to Master Dutton as soon as I can."

"All right, we'll see what we can do about getting her back.   You came all the way from Easton by yourself?"

"Yes.   Well, north of Easton, anyway.   I did have some help though, from some folks like the Duttons along the way.   But yes, by myself."

"You're bloody lucky to be alive, son.   Let's get you to your brother. He's another couple of tents down.   See what he says."

Benjamin

"*What the hell are ye doing here? This is no place for ye!*" Ben roared when he caught sight of me, launching himself like a lithe cat after a mouse, to put his face within five inches of mine. "*Papa is going to whip yer arse until ye have none left, but I might do it for him, right now!*" He bellowed at me again, making sure the entire camp had heard him. They must have, because several soldiers from the closest camps came running to see what the fuss was about.

Before I could say anything to him to explain, the biggest black man I'd ever seen walked over and stood beside Ben. He was taller than Ben by at least four inches and much broader than Ben through the shoulders. Ben was not a small man either, standing six foot two inches in his bare feet. The black man sauntered right into the middle of the uproar with no hesitation. He briefly took notice of me, winked, and then turned to Ben.

"Everything all right, Ben? Heard ye loud and clear down at the camp. Got here fast as I could. I didn't want to miss the fun. This the little brother ye were talking about the other day?" he asked, cocking his capped covered head in my direction.

"*Ja,* Oliver, this is the little scoundrel. He's run from home, again," Ben replied, lowering his wrath filled voice so that only those near us could hear. "Oliver Cromwell, this is Daniel Applegate."

"At yer service, Master Cromwell," I said as I bowed.

"And yer's, Master Applegate," Oliver answered in the same manner. "Well then, perhaps we should be finding out why? I'm curious anyway," Oliver responded calmly.

"Yes, I'd like to hear this too, Ben, if you don't mind," Corporal Johnson said from behind me. Apparently, several others thought the same, as they nodded their heads at Corporal Johnson's request. This was sure to be the better story at the campfires tonight.

Ben turned to me again, his face still red with the force of his anger. "Ye had better have a good explanation, little brother," he hissed just above a whisper, still just managing to keep himself in check.

"Papa did not come to the farm the second week of September, as he promised. He still did not arrive four weeks after that, so I left to find him thinking ye two might be together," I said as I tried to keep any sort of boyish whine out of my voice. "It is not like Papa to be this late."

"True, but Daniel, ye need to go back. This is no place for boys," he said with a frown of resolve that bode no more discussion. "Papa will turn up, eventually. He always does. I am sure he is fine. He was with us for a bit before we got here and then left for Peter and Aletta's. Ye will leave for there tomorrow."

Ben was an extremely stubborn individual. I could say nothing that would change his mind on the matter, and I didn't make the attempt. Somewhat defeated, I lowered my head, mumbling through some thoughts of my own, and came to a decision. Nothing for it. I would have to show him. I took off my coats and shirt, staring at him as I did so.

"What in all Hades are ye doing? Have ye lost yer mind? It is cold out here."

"Ye need to see this." I turned and displayed my chest, sides, and back to him and his friends. "See the striped marks on my back, Ben?"

He was quiet for some time, tracing the few healed scars I had gotten from a horsewhip with his cold fingers. "What happened here, little brother?" he asked compassionately, the same voice I heard him use many times when I was little and had hurt myself with scrapes, bumps, and bruises.

"Boers took a horsewhip to me in August and for no good reason. Aletta and the other hands managed to stop him before he did worse. He gets very angry when he drinks too much. Some of the bruises on my back, sides and face are from the band of Mohawk that found me under a pine tree while I was sleeping. The rest are Boer's near the same places the Mohawk got me; from several days ago.

"I came through the fire to get here, Ben. I am not going back, unless it is to stay with ye or Papa," I said as I pulled my shirt over my head and put the coats back on.

"Excuse us, gentlemen. My brother and I need to talk a bit more alone. Can ye share another campfire for a little bit?" Ben asked his friends.

"Sure, Ben. I need to get back to my company, anyway. Come on boys, give them a bit of privacy. I've got a nice little fire over there to warm yerselves," Oliver replied, and then ushered the men out for us.

"We won't have long before everyone comes back, Daniel. I think I can figure out why the Mohawk hurt ye. Just in the wrong place at the wrong time, right?"

"*Ja,* there was no other reason, outside of retaliation for the events of the summer, the Sullivan Expedition and Newtown, that I heard about on the way. They were in a hurry to keep moving, that's for sure, or it could have been much worse."

"Ask me later and I'll tell ye the *real* story about the Sullivan Expedition. And Boers?"

"The whipping was because a horse got out of his stall and wandered into the fields beyond the house and near the woods. I had latched its gate at dinner. I know I did because I checked it, along with all the latches, before I went to bed. I've done that since the cows got out of the barn gates a while back. I think the horse used its nose to lift the plank and got out. Anyway, Boers didn't believe me and let his anger get the better of him.

"Early in the afternoon of the harvest feast, Boers was drunk again, but not overly. He was angry about something and took it out on me because I was the closest thing to him at the time, and there was no one around to stop him. I just had enough, and laid him flat to the ground with my fists."

"Good. He deserved to be pummeled. What of Aletta? Has Boers ever mistreated or threatened her?"

"No. He likes Aletta, and he's not done anything to her as far as I know. Boers understands who it is that feeds and clothes him and is not about to bungle that up.

"Abraham Lanterman is at the farm. He said he'd was gonna stay until Peter returned and the other hands are there, too. Peter should be home by now. He wrote to her and said his militia duty was ending, and he'd be home the first week of November.

"I would not have left if I thought she was not safe. I'm sorry. I don't mean to be crying like a baby," I said as I wiped away tears that had started to fall.

"It's all right, little brother," he said as he pulled me into a hug. I let him wrap his arms around me, sagging in relief. "Yer safe now, as safe as ye can be. Shh, shh, we'll talk more later. corporal, is it all right for me to keep him with me? Make sure he's all right?"

"Well, only if you take that horse to the picket line. She's making a mess of the path here. And oh, there's food in those bags, isn't there, Daniel?"

"Yes sir," I answered, wiping away some of the last tears. "Between the provisions provided by Masters Dutton and Vanderveer, there's enough to feed maybe five men for a week. They both begged me to bring it here. Abby, Master Dutton's horse, was all he could spare to carry the victuals, or they would have sent me with more, I am sure. I do need to get her returned to Master Dutton, though."

"I'll work on getting Abby home. In the meantime Ben, distribute the food amongst your messmates, and if there is enough to share with others, do so."

"Yes, sir. Thanks for letting him stay with me, Corporal Johnson."

"One more thing, Daniel . . . "

"Yes, Corporal Johnson?"

"Did you really come eighty miles by yourself to get here?"

"More like eighty-three miles, give or take, sir. I had to backtrack mebbe a mile, and I rode Abby for about two miles, and so *ja*, I probably walked a little more than eighty miles. My intent was to go to Morristown, but Master Vanderveer sent me here instead."

"It is true, Corporal Johnson. The farm he came from is about thirty miles from Easton, sir. It is about eighty miles in a straight line between there and here." Ben chimed in, grinning and patting me on the back. "Quite an effort for so young a man, don't ye think, sir?"

"He's just very lucky to be alive. Must be those guardian angels I've been hearing about. I'll see you in the morning, private," the corporal said as he turned back to his camp.

"Good evening, to ye, corporal," Ben replied.

"Let's get ye and the packs settled in the tent. The boys will be back very soon. Oooo, is that salt pork? I think we may be able to make some stew with that tomorrow. We'll bring some water back to let it soak overnight."

"*Ja*, sure, Ben. All right if I make my bed over here for the night?" I asked as we entered the tent. There wasn't much space, and I didn't want to take away anyone else's.

"That's fine. Ye had dinner yet?"

"No."

"Well then, grab my bowl and spoon over there and get a ladle full of what's left. Then we'll go take Abby to the fence after we unload her."

⊗⊗⊗ ⊗⊗⊗ ⊗⊗⊗

"It's good to be here with ye Ben, it feels like home. Believe it or not, I really missed all the teasing ye gave me before ye left. Never thought I'd say so, though," I said as we walked to a spring after securing Abby to the picket line. It was past seven in the evening and getting colder by the minute. The sun set an hour or so earlier, but there was no dark. The snow reflected the light of the crescent moon and filled the landscape with an ethereal glimmer.

"Really, little brother? I can certainly it start in again if it will make ye feel better."

"Ah, no. I prefer not to be annoyed by ye, at least for a little bit."

"Ye know, I mostly vexed ye to get ye to leave me alone. Didn't work all the time. Ye'd be right back being bothersome," he replied with a wide grin. "Ye know I do love ye, anyway?"

"I do. Just don't say it so loudly. Someone might hear us and think us peculiar," I said the last with a whisper.

Ben chuckled at that. "Well, little brother, we are a peculiar sort of family. Some are educated, others not; some are churchgoers, and others are not; and some believe and fight for the Revolution while a very few still want an earthly king," he said, kicking a stone out of our path and taking a deep breath.

"What will ye do if ye see a cousin of ours with the British, Ben?"

"My duty, but I will not shoot family."

We hadn't lost sight of the encampment when the wolves began howling not too far from us and I about jumped out of my skin. "Don't worry, little brother, they won't harm ye, not while I am here," he said as he bumped into me on purpose. "Strange that they've come this far south." I was glad Ben had shouldered his musket before we left camp for the picket line. "Wolves never used to shake ye so much."

"I've had an up-close encounter with one and his friends on my way here."

"Daniel, I am so sorry. If Papa had known that Boers was capable of such violence on a child, he would have taken ye away from there the first time ye ran. If I had known this time, I would have requested leave and brought ye back with me."

"I know. I had thought of just sending ye a letter, but ye can no longer count on the post to take or bring letters. They've stopped running altogether. We've had few visitors in the last few months that have passed our letters on to others to be delivered. Besides, even if I had written a letter, Boers wouldn't let me send it. He searched my room regularly for 'heathen' trash and would have found the letter if I had written one. There would have been the devil to pay then, for sure."

"I don't think I would have put up with Boers as well as ye have at your age. *Ja,* ye did the right thing, little brother. I would have preferred that ye had not come alone, though.

"Have ye heard of camp followers? There are all sorts of camp followers here. I think it will be all right if ye are added to the lot. Mind ye though, ye'd need to earn yer keep. Can ye do that?"

"Really Ben? Ye'd let me stay?"

"Well, Corporal Johnson will have to approve it and likely we will need to go all the way to Colonel Shreve to get permission. It's not like I can send ye back to Boers or risk ye to the roaming bands of Iroquois. Yer right about that. Mebbe we can convince the corporal and the colonel that it is just temporary, until Papa returns."

"It is temporary. So, when do we talk to them, tomorrow?"

"*Ja,* tomorrow. Johnson will be expecting me to come see him about ye, anyway. Hear that?"

To the northeast of us and fairly close, I heard running water even through the sound of crunching the freezing snow, turf and mud under our feet. "*Ja,* there's an artesian spring just there," I pointed.

"Still good with the ears, little brother. How far, ye think?" Ben turned us toward the sound.

"Maybe three hundred feet, near that hill."

"Good. Ye've not lost it. Let's count and see how far."

It was about three hundred and twenty-five feet, to be exact. The spring erupted about ten feet up from the base of the hill and fell over some rocks. Someone had stuck a hollowed-out tree limb the size of Ben's fist and inserted it between some of the rocks at the base of the spring. The tree limb diverted water coming from the hillside to a rectangular piece of limestone laid across the creek where a bucket could be placed until it was filled. When not filling buckets, the spring would still splash into the creek but by way of the limestone table. We just had to be careful not to slip on ice and fall into the creek.

Buckets full and both of us dry, we headed back to camp. "Ye know, I tried to tell both ye and Papa about Boer when I was younger, but I don't think I had the right words for ye all to understand," I continued after several minutes of walking in comfortable silence. "I didn't know how to describe what exactly I saw in Boers. I know now that Papa thought Boers' punishments were just, and maybe some were, but there was something odd about the whole of them.

"Something in me changed last winter when I began to understand the reason for my fears. For one thing, it didn't matter what I did, I could do nothing right and for another, he whipped me regardless, because he enjoyed it and would find any reason to do so. The last time Papa spanked me, he was hurting as much as I was. Remember?"

"*Ja,* Papa was not right with himself for several days after spanking either one of us. He didn't like doing it at all."

"Boers always took glee in punishing me. He always smiled in a cruel sort of way. This lashing in early August with the horsewhip was a new form of discipline that seemed to amuse him even more. He's evil, just pure evil."

"Once he found the horse that got out of the fence, he called me into the horse barn on a ruse and hit me with the whip from behind before I knew what was happening."

"Did ye hit him back then?" Ben asked as turned his face back to me.

"Well, no. Kind of hard to do when ye've got that whip flying at ye. 'Sides, we were taught not to hit our elders; I just couldn't bring myself to do it. Anyways, the most I could do was curl up in the hay to protect the rest of me.

"I gave some thought to it on my way here. What if I had hit back? I think it would have made the whole situation much worse. Although I am his size, he was still stronger pound for pound than me.

"I don't remember screaming, I tried not too because I knew it would make him angrier and he would enjoy it more, but I must have because Aletta and others were there and pulled him off me before he could hit me a sixth time. As Aletta helped me up, I looked at Boers. He was dripping in sweat with his face in that gruesome smile, nearly a snarl, while the rest of him shook as if he were having a fit of a sort. Aletta didn't see his face, only mine and her concern was for me. She got me on my feet and out of the barn very quickly.

"I knew then that if I did not leave at the earliest opportunity, I might not be alive to have another. The night of the harvest party was my one chance, and it was not without incident. He gave me a black eye the afternoon before I left. That's when I punched him to the ground. I had had enough.

"He didn't do this to anyone else, just me."

Ben stopped walking, put the bucket down and stood still as stone as he stared into the west. "One of us should have been there."

I moved closer behind him and laid my hand on his shoulder. "Neither of ye could be. I am whole and safe, brother."

Ben placed his hand on mine. "Safer than ye are out there for sure," he said, lifting his chin to the west, "but I cannot assure ye safety even within the confines of this regiment. Ye know this? Ye're directly in harm's way, Daniel."

"I know. I did not make this decision to come here lightly either, knowing that I'd likely have to stay a bit in this . . . this, confusion," I said, raising a hand towards the encampment.

He turned and glared back at me. "Don't ye get yerself killed, Daniel. I won't have ye to annoy and I will miss it," he said at the last with his countenance softening.

"I'll try not to. I'd like to think I am a little wiser about such matters, though, at this point, maybe?"

Ben turned his head to an angle and studied me, looking at me from head to toe and then deeply into my eyes. "Almost, little brother. Ye got a little way to go," he said, chuckling back at me, ruffling my hair and releasing the tension of the mood. "Regardless, ye're much bigger than when I last saw ye, but I think ye still need a little more muscle on ye. Let me see yer arm."

It was a game we played when we were younger, showing off our muscles. I took my coats off temporarily and rolled up my sleeve and made a hard arm muscle for Ben, who was then obliged to wrap his hand around my arm. But this time, for the first time ever, he couldn't get his fingers to close around my upper arm. Ben looked at me and grinned from ear to ear. "Glad ye're here and with me little brother," he said as he pulled me into a bear hug.

⚬◯⚬ ⚬◯⚬ ⚬◯⚬

Wrapping my coats tighter around me and my blanket over them, I collapsed into the large pile of hay that was my bed. Bone tired and finally warm, the soft mat eased me quickly into a deep sleep, only to be awaked long before dawn by Ben.

"Get ye up, lazy beast! If ye're gonna stay with us, even temporary, ye're gonna need to carry yer own weight."

"*Ja, ja,* all right," I yawned, while running a hand through my hair. "Ye said as much last night, Ben. Does it need to be at four in the morning, though?"

"Yes sir, best time ever! Come on, we've got to leave soon for duty and ye can help by making us a warm breakfast. Ye and I need to go to the spring first, though. I want to make sure ye remember its location. Don't

133

want ye disappearing on me this soon."

"*Ja,* all right," and I followed him out of the tent, stumbling over my feet for a bit while reaching for the snowshoes. Putting on the snowshoes after my boots was a habit I had developed the last couple of days.

"Ye aren't gonna need those snowshoes. The snow is packed down out there already, remember? It didn't snow that bad last night, thank God. Where'd you get them, anyway?"

"I made them. Cornplanter showed me how," I said as I settled into my boots.

"Shhhh, Daniel, don't mention that name or any other Indian name around here. Ye'll make some folk angry with it," he said as he looked to see if anyone was close.

"He saved my life."

"Is that so? Just how did he do that, little brother? Ye know he's killed as many whites as befriended?"

"*Ja,* I heard all the way here 'bout the Iroquois and the massacres at Cherry Valley and Wyoming.

"I'd not seen that side of him ever. He never did want to be involved in our war with the British. He wanted to stay neutral and tried to convince the other chiefs of the same. But when Joseph Brandt, his clan brother, spoke, he was obligated to join him or break with his clan family forever.

"A breach of this tradition would unravel the clan. Master Brandt sided with the English, and believed that they would win the war and return the Indian lands settled by the whites to the Iroquois. Besides, it was the Iroquois women who voted for war, and that was that. For the most part, no Confederation wars happen without the women authorizing it."

He looked through me for a moment, seeing something entirely other than me or the black trees in front of us. "We had about as much choice as yer friend, Daniel. I am not comforted by what I saw and what was done.

"So, tell me, little brother, how did he save yer life and when did he teach ye more about hunting, making the shoes and all that?"

"When ye and Papa were out on the trading trips. Cornplanter claimed it was important to show me the Indian ways. What I learned has been very helpful, especially learning how to speak a little of his language." We were far enough away from the encampment that I thought no one would hear Cornplanter's name unless I shouted it and that I wasn't about to do.

"He taught ye Seneca?"

"Just a little, enough to get by. I was glad to have it when I came across the Mohawk. They understood the little Seneca I had. Straight and then left to the spring, Ben?"

"*Ja,* it's over there," he replied with his arm out and pointing with his finger.

"As for saving my life, just before I left him and his warriors, he handed me his wampum belt. When the Mohawk leader pulled Cornplanter's wampum from my pack, he showed it to the others and they stopped beating me, or I would be dead. At first, they thought I had killed Cornplanter to get it, but could ye see me up against him?"

"Ah, no. Sorry, little brother."

"Anyway, they sent out scouts to see if there were other whites with me. When they found there were none as I said, they had a change of heart and decided that he had given me the wampum belt on purpose to guarantee my safe passage to my people. They asked me as much before I passed out, and I told them that Cornplanter had put the belt in my hands and that I tried to give it back, but he said no.

"The next day, they packed me up, put the wampum belt back, gave me food and medicine and sent me on my way."

"Is the wampum belt still in yer knapsack?"

"*Ja.*"

"Good. Keep it out of sight, for the sake of peace. Cornplanter didn't try to send ye back to Aletta?"

"I thought he might, but then he believed me about Boers and had seen how he behaved with me for the last three years. Ye do know that the Seneca don't spank their children?" "Na, not heard that."

"Well, they don't. Not at all.

"That's interesting. I don't think Papa would go for that though."

"Me neither."

"Ye'll be able to get to the spring in the dark tonight, right? We won't be back from guard duty until late." The creek had frozen over during the night and looked a little different in the pre-dawn light. Yet the spring still gushed through the water trough, unaffected by the cold. Ben stepped to the side and set his bucket on the flat rock and let the water from the piping tumble into the bucket.

"*Ja*, think so. I came all this way to get to ye. Don't think I am going to lose my bearings now.

"Good. When ye are up here waiting for the bucket to fill, take this axe to chip away the ice that forms on the mouth of the trough—and do it gently," he said, showing me how. "We need to keep the water flowing through the trough, so we don't have to find another log to hollow out anytime soon. Goodness, it's cold! I think it's gonna get a whole lot colder soon, too."

"*Ja*, ye may be right about that, brother. Heard that from the Duttons as well."

We talked a little on the return and when we got back to the campfire, Ben went right to work, stoking up the fire and showing me how to make the porridge so that it was edible and make the coffee we got from Master Vanderveer so that it was drinkable.

"Ye think ye can cook what breakfast we have for thirteen of us, little brother?"

"*Ja*, Aletta taught me how to cook some foods. Those were harder than porridge and coffee, though."

"Good, ye can make breakfast then, as part of yer up-keep. Though there might not be much to fix after yer saddle bags are empty," he said, nodding at the bags. "This is the first real food we've had in several days. General Wayne brought a few cattle to us from a raid some days ago, but that's been long gone. We hear that our store houses are nearly empty; getting flour to make fire cakes has been darn near impossible. So ye'll need to dole out what ye have in small amounts to make it last for a while."

"Fire cakes, raids? Isn't raiding thievery?"

"*Ja.* Fire cakes are made from flour, salt, and water and if ye're lucky, maybe some cornmeal. Cook them on a rock that sets over a fire until they're brown. They're not the best, but ye'll eat anything if ye're hungry enough.

"As for the raid, no, it wasn't thievery. The cattle were taken from the British regulars. They were getting them ready to ship them somewhere else when General Wayne snatched them up.

"Congress and the state governments have been slow on feeding the Continental regiments and any state militias that may be with us. In the meantime, we're expected to protect Patriots' lives and homes from the British. The Redcoats have the tendency to pull people out of their homes in the middle of the night and send them away. Very rarely are they seen again. The Brits take what they want out of the home and burn the rest. We're supposed to keep that from happening if we can; but we can't protect anyone if we're half-starved to death.

"Mind ye, we still hunt and forage, but with this many men in one place, food in the wilderness gets scarce fast."

"Maybe I can remedy that a bit. Cornplanter showed me how to eat off the land and in the woods. When fixed properly, those foods aren't so bad, and they'll fill ye up. They won't replace meat, though."

"All right, little brother, maybe ye could show me too. Ah, here come the lads, they'll be surprised. No breakfast at all the last couple of days."

"There's breakfast? Where?"

"Sit yerself down, Joseph, and the rest of ye, too. Ye're welcome to what is here. Not much, but it's something, and it isn't gonna last long with all of us. So, enjoy it while ye can," Ben replied.

"If ye forage for us Daniel, do not go south or south-east at all, stay within sight of the camp, and don't go beyond the checkpoints around the camp," he said as he sat down by the fire. "The Redcoats and Loyalists are out and about. Ye never know when ye might run into a group of them. Did ye bring yer fife?" Ben asked as he swallowed a heaping spoonful of steaming porridge. I nodded yes, busy slurping my own off my spoon.

"I think we may be needing a fifer or two. Some of the musicians just walked away, deserted the other day. Look for the musicians that are wondering around entertaining the troops, and see if they'll let ye play with them," he said, taking a sip of the coffee. "Ahhh, that's good. Likely the warmest thing we'll have all day.

"Go see Corporal Johnson after cleaning up. He may have something ye can do too; keep ye out of mischief.

"Again, under *no* circumstances are ye to leave this camp on yer own, save foraging where I told ye. Ye hear me? Ye do and ye'll have more than me a tarring yer hide," he said as he looked at the other men. They all stopped shoveling the oatmeal into their mouths and stared at me, measuring me up and bobbing their heads in agreement.

"I hear ye. I hear ye all. I'll be here when ye get back."

"Better be, little brother," he whispered in my ear as he gave me a hug and a pat on my back and went back to what was left of his porridge.

Ben and his motley crew took all of five more minutes to finish eating and drinking the coffee. Looking mighty fierce, toting ten-pound muskets, with hunting knives and axes in their belts, they doffed their raggedy, dirty gloves with finger holes, woolen caps and were off to guard the camp. The group strode silently out of the tent village, looking more like backwoods hunters than colonial soldiers, yet their faces were those of warriors, all stern and determined, ready to take on anything that would bring harm to them or the men in the camp.

Chores finished, I headed to see Corporal Johnson. Warmth had finally returned to my hands after cleaning the morning dishes and I felt streaks of sunlight warm my face as I walked past the tents that lined the walkway. The entire camp had been roused and a few soldiers had taken to walking around aimlessly in their ragged blankets, trying to get warm.

I stood still and watched them for a moment, wondering just how life would be to be one of them. I thought I may have imagined all that I saw when I arrived. After all, I had been very tired and cold. I could see clearly now that I hadn't imagined a single thing, but I wished that I had. There was little I could do for them, though.

Johnson had nothing for me to do, so he sent me on to Captain Weatherby. The captain's tent seemed to be a little smaller than Ben's, but then, he was the only one housed in it. It was warm and a little smoky inside from the brazier set near the middle of the tent.

Weatherby looked up from reading a letter and pointed to a chair, then went back to his letter for a few more minutes. When he was done, he meticulously folded the letter, opened his battered trunk, and laid the letter on a neatly folded shirt. He stroked it gently with his index finger and then closed the trunk lid.

"It was a letter from my wife. I've tried three times in the last twenty-four hours to read it all the way through. I am sorry to keep you waiting, son. So, you must be Daniel? I heard about you last night from Corporal Johnson. He said you some distance to get here, to find your brother or father. I know you found your brother. What about your father?"

"He's not here, sir. Ben said he left him a week ago to catch me up at my sister's. I must have just missed him. As for the walking, I did what I needed to do to get here. Everyone is making it out to be more than it is, sir."

"I think one boy walking by himself, eighty miles through the wilderness to find his family is quite an achievement."

"Thank ye, sir. I did have some help, though."

"Doesn't matter."

"Thank you, sir."

"Are you hungry? I've got some eggs and toast here, a bit of coffee if you like."

"No, sir. I ate with my brother this morning. Abby, the horse Master Dutton let me borrow, was laden with food from the Duttons and Vanderveers. Not enough for the whole regiment, but enough for Ben's mess for several days, anyway. Corporal Johnson said to share the food amongst us and anyone else that was hungry, and we have."

"Good. I need to pen a short note here for Colonel Shreve and if you would, I'll have you take it to him. Do you read and write, young man?"

"Yes, a little bit, sir."

"I understand your brother does not. Odd that you do. No matter. There's a newspaper over there on the table to read if you like, while you're waiting."

"Thank you, sir. Might just have a look, then."

The paper was dated November 5th 1779, and it had the article about the rebel General Anthony Wayne, who had absconded with a 100 head of cattle and grain on November 2nd. Ben had briefly explained this to me last night and said that Wayne had taken the animals right out from under their noses. The newspaper didn't write about that, though. They called it outright thievery, though. It must have been a Loyalist paper.

"All right, Daniel. Normally, I would have you take this note to Colonel Spencer, but he is not here at the moment, so please deliver it to Colonel Shreve," Weatherby said as he handed me a bit of crumpled paper that was folded and sealed by wax. "Do you know where his tent is?"

"*Ja,* Ben told me where ye all were before he left. I'll get it there safely."

"Good. Wait to see if he will make a reply or if he would like you to run another errand for him. In either case, return here and we'll talk about continuing your schooling with what I have here, at least until your father comes back to get you. I agree with the corporal—it simply isn't safe to send you home."

"Sir, I promised my brother that I would have dinner ready when he and his platoon returned."

"Do not worry, Daniel. I'll have you back in time to cook dinner and if you are late, tell your brother that I kept you. You'll have no argument from him."

"Thank ye, sir," I said as I secured the letter in my coat and reached for my fife.

"You know how to play that, Daniel?" he asked as he nodded his head to the fife in my hand.

"I do. Thought I'd keep company with it while walking to Colonel Shreve's tent. I've not played badly in quite some time, captain. I shouldn't bother anyone with it."

"I'm sure you won't, Daniel; play something cheerful as you walk. I'll see you back here in a little while."

❧❧❧ ❧❧❧ ❧❧❧

Colonel Shreve's tent was guarded by a rather tall and husky private who came to attention from his relaxed state when he saw I was not going to pass by. He grimaced at me and put out his hand for the letter I carried. He must have been used to boys bringing messages to the Colonel.

"Captain Weatherby requested that I bring this to the colonel," I said, as he turned it over to look at it.

"All right, boy. Got any knifes, axes, that sort of thing?" His voice was deep and raspy.

"No sir. Just the fife. That's all."

"Let me see if the colonel is ready for visitors. If not, ye will have to wait here until he is."

He left me standing by myself outside, waiting for the response. The officers' quartering was by far cleaner than the soldiers' quarters. Maybe that was because there were far fewer men trampling the mud and snow. Regardless, the whole officers' area was set in a strict grid formation, with tents set in straight lines one after the other; there was no two or three feet offsetting between the front of the tents as there was in the enlisted area.

Behind me and through the tent door flap, I heard the movement of dishes and paper, along with conversation that was just above a whisper.

"Sir, a boy by the name of Dan'l Applegate is here to see ye. Comes from Captain Weatherby with a letter, he says. Do ye wish me to send him in, now or later?"

"Send him in, Jesse. I've been waiting for a response from Weatherby. Thank thee."

"Ye, can go in, Dan'l. Mind yer manners, boy."

"Thank ye, sir." I responded and turned to enter the tent.

"Would thou like some tea, young man? Well, what we call tea anyway, it's not that good, but it is warm," he said, holding his hand out for the letter.

"Here, help thyself while I read this. I might need thee to take a letter back. There's some tea on the table over there along with some biscuits if thou art hungry."

"Thank ye, sir," I responded, bowing to him and then leaving him to his reading. I poured the tea and took a small swallow. He was right. It was not very good at all, bitter with an aftertaste of sweetness that was likely from the honey pot sitting on the table beside the biscuits. I sipped on it nonetheless. The tea was still hot and felt good when I wrapped my fingers around the mug. The biscuits were better, smothered in butter and honey.

I watched Colonel Shreve pausing mid-bite of a biscuit as he read what Weatherby had written. Shreve was a rather portly fellow with chubby cheeks that rolled downhill from the upper bridge of his nose, that then formed a thick downward crease from each of his nostrils to his jaw. I wouldn't say he had jowls just yet, but he was getting there.

His nose had been broken long ago, leaving a hump in the middle of an otherwise straight piece of bone. His protruding lips moved silently with the words as he read and then suddenly curved into a slight smirk accompanied by "Well, is that so," as he pushed his graying long hair out of his twinkling light blue eyes and put it back behind his ears to read more.

He shoveled another biscuit drenched in honey into his mouth and licked his fingers after. I didn't blame him. Those honied biscuits were what I always thought mana would taste like after wandering through a desert. He downed several more in the time that I had waited.

"Daniel, thee are Richard's son?"

"Yes, sir. I am the youngest."

"Thought so. That means thou art Benjamin's brother. I agree with Captain Weatherby that thou should stay with thy brother, that is, in his tent, with the other enlisted, so that he can keep an eye on thee."

"Thank ye, sir."

"Thou art welcome, son. Good man, thy father. I am sorry that thou missed him. He brought some grain and other supplies from the Lanterman farms to feed the men not too long ago. Hopefully, he will return soon and gather thee up. I am not sure I can get a letter to thy sister, to let her know thou art safe, but I will try."

"Thank ye, Sir. But I do not want to return there."

"I understand. I will not send thee back to thy sister. Captain Weatherby told me of thy situation. We will keep thee until thy father comes and I suspect he will be here before too long.

"In the meantime, do thy lessons with Captain Weatherby; he has already agreed to do them. He also says thou plays the fife. We may be able to use that skill in our fife and drum corps around the camp."

"Here's the note back to Captain Weatherby. See it safe to him. Thank thee, Daniel."

"At yer service, sir."

᙭᙭᙭

Within a week or so of my arrival, Abby had been sent back to Mr. Dutton. Thank God for that. I feared that the men would kill and butcher her for her meat. Ben's platoon was pretty good at teasing me about doing just that thing, but I didn't think that they would go that far, even if there was a hint of truth in what they said.

I gave my second coat, cap, and mittens to a messmate who had none, soon after my first full day at the encampment. It sure would have been nice to have that second layer though when foraging, but it was better to have something rather than nothing like so many of the men.

The food I brought lasted only a few days between all of us and then after that we ate fire cakes and whatever I could bring back from the woods and fields nearby. By Providence, Ben and I managed to take a down a rather large eight-point buck, providing fresh meat for our company the last week of November just before the first of the heavy snows came in December.

The days went by quickly and moved into weeks as I established a routine with the platoon, Weatherby, and Shreve. I would cook and do laundry for my mess, run messages between the officers' tents and, on occasion, even take a message or two to Brigadier General Maxwell when he was in the camp. He was a fiery individual when he got his dander up for sure.

I always left the officers' quarters with some biscuits, breads, and the like, stuffed in my knapsack. The officers had little for themselves, but still insisted I take something to eat. So, I took the food and shared it mostly with my brother privately. There simply wasn't enough for everyone.

I made friends with the other drummer and fifers. They taught me the regimental music, and the popular songs that everyone knew. In my free time, I would roam the camp with them, playing for the soldiers and officers. I was told our job was to help keep their spirits high, regardless of the circumstances they found themselves in. There were days where this was a nearly impossible task, but eventually they would come 'round. We even played for General Maxwell, who rewarded us with the coin he had on him at the time. Unfortunately, there was no outpost nearby where we could spend it.

Papa never made it to the Scotch Plains encampment, the weather such as it was. Storms with heavy snow and cold began between late November and early December, even making travel within the camp difficult. I couldn't imagine what it would be like getting through the passes from Pennsylvania. I hoped Papa would remain where he was until they cleared.

We got the deer hide curing before the December storm hit, so that at some point we could repair my boots and make a few moccasins for those who had no shoes, that is, if their feet lasted that long. Likely we were going to have to use the hide half cured to save those few feet and mine. A messy business, for sure. There was always the off chance that the New Jersey Legislature would come through with provisions of food, clothing, shoes, and blankets, as promised, but it wasn't too likely, according to Ben.

When the weather made my other chores impossible, I'd help clean and oil the muskets, make their cartridges and practice loading Ben's musket, a Brown Bess. Ben had said that soldiers were required to be able to load a musket and fire it within twenty seconds or less. He thought it might be a good idea for me to learn to load the gun quickly; then I'd be prepared if an emergency required it. Shooting it with any accuracy would have to wait for better weather.

On the Road

"Daniel, pack it all up. Everything but yer bed roll, that is, and the dishes we'll cook with and eat on tonight. The rest will go on the wagon," Ben said as he came into the tent in a rush of cold wind. I was in the tent getting a pot and a pan to start the evening meal. The sun had begun to set with twilight and full dark not far behind.

"We're going somewhere?"

"*Ja*. Word just came that General Parsons had made it to the Sound, and we were ordered to pack all we have and walk to Morristown tomorrow. Well, actually to the Wick's farm and more precisely his backyard," he added while rustling around his belongings, seemingly to organize them. "The other brigades are already there. This Mr. Wick is taking a great risk in letting the entire northern Continental army make its winter quarters there. Oh, and I heard that the men that need it most will be supplied coats and the like. Finally!" he said as he rushed from the tent, then suddenly turned around and stuck his head through the flaps. "I left ye a present outside. Did a bit of ice fishing on the pond at the crossroads with a spear while out on the line. It was quiet . . . today," he explained as he shrugged his shoulders and then he was gone.

"Dinner in a half an hour, then!" I shouted as he stomped away outside. I looked in the bucket and it was filled with several large-mouth bass. It likely took a few hours on the ice to get that much. He took a great risk getting them. I didn't think the ice was as thick as it should have been. You'd need about three to four inches and then pray that the floating surface doesn't tip. In this cold, falling in the water would be fatal. I'd have to ask him later how he managed to not be frozen or dead.

ℓ◯ℓ ℓ◯ℓ ℓ◯ℓ

Spirits seemed higher this night, more so than any of the others since I came to the camp. I thought it was just due to the prospect of travel tomorrow. After all the walking the men did through Pennsylvania and New York this past summer; they still seemed eager to be going somewhere, anywhere again, especially if it meant an actual cabin with a fireplace in it.

The aroma of the fish and sliced potatoes fried with a bit of bacon grease and seasoned with the last of the thyme wafted out from the cooking fire, drawing the men of our mess slowly back into our campsite. I had purposely built the fire up on the other side of the fire pit from the cooking coals in the hopes that they would meander in that direction and leave me unhindered with the task of cooking. It worked. They followed the wave of warmth, leaving me to cook with no interference.

"I am sore hungry, little brother. Is it gonna be ready soon? Ben inquired as he walked towards me.

"*Ja,* I think so. Maybe five minutes?"

"There ye are, Ben. I've been look'n for ye."

"Well, ye found me, Samuel. Ready for dinner? Daniel says it will be done soon."

"That's good. Boy, ye're mak'n my mouth water," Samuel said as he turned to me. "Just bid'n my time here Ben, tell'n Oliver here about our adventure this afternoon. How ye took up the hunters on a dare to cross that-half frozen pond to fish, even after we argued ye against it," he said with a nod of his head in Oliver's direction.

"Ye know yer crazy for having done it, right?" Oliver responded. "And if ye fell in, there'd be hell to pay for both Samuel and John, regardless of whether ye lived or died? And once ye were well, if ye survived the falling in, ye'd have to pay for ye're poor judgment too? Army property and all that?"

147

"*Ja,* I knew Oliver. I believed I could do it though. If I hadn't, I wouldn't have tried. Sides, we needed a proper meal to walk to Mr. Wick's farm at Jockey Hollow. Long ago, Papa showed both me and Daniel how to make sure the ice was safe for fishing, and I thought it was, that's all. I was careful about the patch I chose; the ice sheet was nearly three inches thick when I cut through it with my knife. It was risky to be sure, especially if the sheet tilted in any way; but I reasoned through it and tested a couple of places. It seemed solid enough, so I prayed, and figured I should try it. I did get a little cold when it was done," Ben replied, shrugging his shoulders.

"Little *cold! Ye come back ta us, barely stand'n up, and with yer hair hang'n out from the bottom of yer cap in frozen icicles, yer eyebrows, eyelashes, and beard frosted with white, and yer right hand look'n ta be a block of ice from pull'n the line out of the water!*" Samuel shouted, releasing a few hours of pent-up frustration and concern. He took a deep breath and closed his eyes, letting go of the emotions of the last few hours. "Ye scared us witless Ben, with the ice mak'n crack'n noises every time ye moved and just know'n how cold ye were get'n and how much colder ye would be before mak'n it back to us. Glad we insisted on the rope around yer chest, in case ye lost yer foot'n," his voice showing deep concern. He said no more, but grabbed Ben in a bear hug for a second or two and then let go.

"I had wondered if that rope wasn't gonna be the death of me as I backed out. I got twisted up in it more than once between my feet, the spear, and the bucket. I had visions of being tangled in it under the ice," Ben said with a smile on his face. "Ye're right though, maybe it was a bit foolish, but truly, I believed it would all be well, especially with ye and John there to warm me back up. I promise I won't try it again for a while. See all my parts work, including my right hand," he said while grinning and waving the hand in the cold air, "cause ye had a fire and warm blankets to wrap me in. I couldn't have done it without the both of ye."

"I am sure the whiskey we dumped into ye certainly helped," John added as he strolled up to the fire. "That stuff would thaw anyone out.

Did ye get in a nice nap? I dare say ye needed it."

"*Ja,* I did John. Just a half hour or so, I did need it, hard work ice fishing."

"So, where's this whiskey?" asked Oliver.

"I got it," replied John. "Not only is there whiskey, but applejack too. We'll partake some after dinner.

"*Ja,* that was part of the deal," Samuel replied. "Ben was ta catch six large fish for each of the hunters in return for the whiskey and applejack. They said they had no luck find'n any game for their families, though they hunted much of the day. Animals must just be hunker'n down. Anyway, the hunters didn't want ta go home empty-handed, and they certainly didn't want ta get on the ice ta fish, thus the deal that Ben agreed ta catch the fish for whiskey and applejack. The hunters made good on their promise and Ben took all that they had with them in return for the fish."

"Dinner!" I hollered.

"Ben brought up a total of twenty fish in no time using the spear and the little wooden fishy tied to a string that he dropped in the water after making the hole with his knife. He wasn't out there too long, but long enough," John added.

"Ah well, there *is* something to be said of prayer. I really was praying the whole time that wouldn't fall in and I would catch as many as I could," Ben said as he bent to get his plate and held it for me to add his ration of fish and potatoes. "Where'd ye get the potatoes, Daniel? There are no root vegetables in the camp to be found."

"I ran a letter from one officer to another, and both wanted to pay me in coin for the delivery, but I talked them into giving me the potatoes and bacon grease," I responded, dumping the mix on Ben's plate. "What was I gonna do with coin out here, anyway?"

"Thank ye, little brother," he said with a bit of a laugh, laying his hand on my shoulder and squeezing it lightly. "There will come a time when getting paid in coin will be the better thing. But for now, being paid in potatoes and bacon grease was the better choice."

"Ah, Daniel, that smells wonderful! How'd ye learn ta cook like this?" Samuel asked as he stood behind Ben, waiting for his turn.

"Through experimentation mostly." Samuel looked at me quizzically. "Ye know, trying something until ye find what ye like?"

"Oh, so ye mean ye kept practic'n until ye got it, right?"

"Something like that; and I watched my mama and sister. Mama let me help with the cooking when I was near seven years old." I had also learned from Cornplanter, but it wouldn't do for me to mention that.

"I am glad ta be the beneficiary of yer successful experiments son," Samuel responded and then turned to the men behind him waiting in line and bellowed, "There be no wolf'n down this meal, gentlemen. Tisn't fire cakes!"

Fire cakes were all that we had for the last couple of weeks and by themselves kept hunger pangs away for the most part. They just tasted like fancy parchment. We had the habit of eating them quickly to avoid the taste of crunchy, dry bread. Tonight though, after Samuel's reminder, we all would be very conscious of every bite of food, savoring each fork of fish and fried potatoes as if it would be our last, because it could very well be our last for some time.

Plates all filled; the men stood around the fire waiting for me to get mine. Then Oliver, since he was the most learned religious person among us, bowed his head. "Let us pray," he said, and all bustle stopped so that only the crackle and hissing of the logs could be heard. "Lord, thank ye for this day, but maybe not so much for the cold. Thank ye for keeping Ben safe as he laid and moved on the ice and thank ye that the others were there to get him warm, so no harm would come to him. Thank ye for this meal that ye have provided and for the one who cooked it and see to our safety tomorrow as we walk to the winter camp. Amen."

◉◯◉ ◉◯◉ ◉◯◉

The food gone and dishes done, there was little else to do but while away the evening around the fire and staying warm. "Feel up to playing a bit little brother, maybe bring that fiddle out to try"? Ben asked, as I made my way to sit beside him.

"Sure, I'll be back in a second." Fife I could play, but the fiddle I was just learning. It was a very different instrument and required a more determined touch between the bow and the strings. A fiddle played wrong sounded much like a keener; a woman who was paid to scream and wail at the top of her lungs to lament the dead. The very last thing I needed to do was remind them of keeners or funerals. I hadn't thought I was that bad, though, and Ben wouldn't have asked if I was.

I had gotten the fiddle from Captain Weatherby. A long-time friend of his had died in the past year, but before he died, he gave the captain his fiddle. His friend, Alexander Thompson, told him that if he didn't play the instrument, to pass it on to a young lad who would. Alexander loved that fiddle more than life itself and entertained family, friends, and of late, the New Jersey Battalion when he visited, with his passion for music and song.

From our conversation, I gathered that Alexander was more like a brother to Captain Weatherby than a friend. After Alexander's death, the captain had traveled everywhere with the fiddle, packing and unpacking it carefully each time the regiment moved, but he told me couldn't bare to make himself play it once it was unpacked.

"Alexander would have been honored for you to play his fiddle" he had said before he handed me the fiddle. "A musical instrument should be played, not stored, or carried from place to place forever, as I have done. You know, instruments have a life of their own when they are mastered, and a well-played instrument is a gift from God and is as food to a hungry soul," he said.

"You are so like him; he was as adventurous, courageous, and as talented as you are Daniel," he said as his eyes were looking at the tent wall, thinking of times past possibly. He soon focused them back on me and continued, "But Alex's love of adventure and his possession of courage caused him to lose his life much too early.

"I noticed you had an ear for music some time ago and gave it some thought after hearing improvement on your fife these last few days," he said, nodding at my fife that was sticking out of my coat pocket. "It would honor Alex and me if you tried your hand at his fiddle."

It had been well cared for and glowed, with a deep brownish red color. I was sure the glow was from the light coat of bees' wax that I could smell when I placed it under my chin. I drew the bow slowly over the strings; made it squawk and about jumped out of my boots. Captain Weatherby laughed at the mishap and said with a hand on my shoulder, "Don't worry, Alex did the same when he first played it; I was there and saw him. You'll learn, just as he did, if you work at it. There are plenty of fiddlers in the brigade, just find one to teach you."

"I will, and thank ye sir," I said, bowing low with my lips nearly reaching my ears in a grin.

"I know you will, Daniel, and you are welcome."

I smiled at the memory as I walked back to the fire with the fiddle in hand and inserted myself between Ben and Oliver. John had gone back to the tent just before me to bring back the hidden whiskey and applejack. He was long in returning and must have taken a side expedition because he arrived back at the firepit a half an hour after I left to retrieve the fiddle. Likely he hadn't hidden the spirits in the tent, but placed them where they would be safe elsewhere in the camp. If there was anything in the whole encampment that found legs and walked, it would be the liquor; it seemed to disappear right under its owners' noses.

"Here it is, boys! The finest that New England has to offer," John said, taking a swig and passing a flask on to the next person to his right, which was Ben.

"Oh, that applejack is good. *Ja,* it's all right Daniel, ye can have some too and maybe one more, but that's it for the night," Ben said as he passed it to me. I managed a small gulp before he grabbed it back from my hand and then passed it on to Oliver. It did warm the insides a bit.

I began to tune the fiddle while listening to a bit of a song that Oliver was humming under his breath. "Mad Anthony Wayne" it was called, and if I was lucky, I might just be able to play something resembling it well enough that the others could sing along. That was, if my hands kept warm enough by the fire.

Ben had told me the story of "Mad" Anthony a week or two ago. "Mad" Anthony was Brigadier General Anthony Wayne. The same general that took the cattle and grain right out under the noses of the British. He got the name "Mad" Anthony because of some usual strategy he used in storming Stony Point, a British stronghold of land that jutted out a quarter mile in the Hudson.

This summer past, with a sliver of the moon and just after midnight on the sixteenth of July, General Wayne's light infantry of a thousand men attacked the Point. They walked soundlessly through the marshes that surrounded the Point at high tide, recognizing each other only by the white paper patches that were attached to their hats. Their destination was the promontory, a piece of land one hundred and fifty feet above the level of the water. The climb itself was made treacherous with the rocky terrain and the barricades of tree limbs that hid thirteen pieces of British artillery that were ready to be used at a moment's notice.

General Wayne ordered two-thirds of his men to use bayonets only, the other third became a diversionary force that could fire their muskets at will. That diversionary force succeeded in confusing the British so much that the Brits mostly shot at each other. As for the cannon, only two of the cannons were used and only one did any harm. Within twenty-five minutes, the battle was over and "Mad" Anthony succeeded in taking Stony Point, its cannon, supplies, and a little over four hundred men as prisoners.

His scheme was very dangerous, but just 'mad' enough that it worked. General Wayne's men followed him through the insane attack, and many lived to tell the story. They were all brave men and a little crazy themselves for staring down thirteen cannons. I am not sure I would be that brave, but on the other hand, I would be hard pressed not to help when help was needed. Maybe that is part of what it means to be courageous, standing together, or alone for that matter, for a righteous cause, even if it means losing it all.

The men here were just as brave and determined as those at Stony Point, surviving all sorts of trials and mishaps. I hoped they would all make it through this season. For now, they were all relaxed, smiling and laughing around the fire. Andrew, Phillip, Henry, and Thomas were seriously involved with a game of whist, gambling away the trinkets they possessed from their travels this summer as part of the Sullivan expedition. Samuel, George, James, and Ludlow sat comfortably around the fire, sharing cheroots of tobacco and discussing further the merits of having winter huts once we arrived at Mr. Wick's farm and the Jockey Hollow encampment. They concluded that staying warm in a hut and starving would be better than the situation at Valley Forge two years ago, where they were starved and were with no shelter against the cold.

"Ye ready, little brother?" Ben asked, distracting me from my thoughts while I warmed up.

"*Ja.* Fiddle tuned and hands warmed. I am good." I put the fiddle under my chin, played an entire stanza of music and then nodded to Oliver, who bellowed in his deep tenor:

> *His sword blade gleams and his eye-light beams, and*
> *And never glance either in vain;*
> *Like the ocean tides at our head he rides,*
> *The fearless Mad Anthony Wayne.*
> *Bang! Bang! The rifles go, down falls the startled foe.*
> *And many Redcoat here tonight, the Continentals scorning,*
> *Shall never meet the blaze of the broad sunlight That shines on the*
> *morrow morning!*

Was e'er a chief of his speech so brief,
Who utters his wishes so plain?
Ere he speaks a word the orders are heard,
From the eyes of Mad Anthony Wayne.
Aim! Fire! Exclaim his eyes; Bang! Bang! each gun replies,
And many a Redcoat here tonight, the Continentals scorning,
Shall never meet the blaze of the broad sunlight That shines on the
morrow morning!
It is best to fall at our country's call, If we must leave this lifetime of
pain;
And who would shrink from the perilous brink, When led by Mad
Anthony Wayne?
Ran! Tan! The bugles sound, our forces fill the ground,
And many a Redcoat here tonight, the Continentals scorning,
Shall never meet the blaze of the broad sunlight That shines on the
morrow morning!
Let them form their ranks in firm phalanx, It will melt at our rifle-
ball rain,
Every shot must tell on a Redcoat well, or we anger Mad Anthony
Wayne.
Tramp! Tramp! Away we go, now retreats the beaten foe,
And many a Redcoat here tonight, the Continentals scorning,
Shall never meet the blaze of the broad sunlight That shines on the
morrow morning!

By the time we were done, we had not only our camp singing with us, but the ones on either side as well.

"Well done, Daniel! Ready for another?" Oliver shouted over the voices that were still singing another chorus while I still played. "Cause if we don't come up with another, there'll be the devil to pay," he added with an ear-to-ear grin. "How, 'bout *Battle of the Kegs?*"

"Sure! Give me a moment to retune."

After a minute, Oliver gave up his patience and stood up, putting his fingers in his mouth and letting out the loudest whistle I had ever heard. Silence ensued immediately all around the campfire and all eyes were on Oliver. "Sorry. Just trying to hear what Daniel was saying, and I can't. We're working on the next one."

"Ye heard of *Maggie Lawder?*" he said to me as he turned from the others. "The music for it is used for *Battle of the Kegs.*"

"*Maggie Lawder*, goes something like this?"

"Aye, there ye have it, Master Applegate. Play," and so I lightly played another stanza while Oliver continued his discourse with the men.

"What ye think, boys? *Battle of the Kegs*, next?" Oliver yelled over top of me as I continued. The men picked up their cue, and in response shouted in song:

"*Oh, these kegs hold now the rebels bold, Packed up like pickled herring;*

And they've come down t'attack the town in this new way of ferrying."

Oliver raised his hand to quell the onslaught, and in turn looked at each of them with a finger to his lips, when all was quiet again, he began:

"*Gallants attend, and hear a friend, Trill forth harmonious ditty,*

Strange things I'll tell, which late befell in Philadelphia City."

One by one they joined him in an expanded joyous choir of harmonized voice eased by the passing of rum, applejack and whiskey.

"*'Twas early day, as poets say, Just when the sun was rising,*

A soldier stood, on a log of wood, And saw a thing surprising.

As in amaze he stood to gaze, The truth can't be denied, sir,

He spied a score of kegs or more, Come floating down the tide, sir.

A sailor too, in jerkin blue, This strange appearance viewing,

First damn'd his eyes, in great surprise, Then said, "Some mischief's brewing"

These kegs now hold the rebels bold, Pack'd up like pickled herring;

And they're come down t'attack the town, in this new way of ferrying.

The soldier flew, the sailor too, and scar'd almost to death, sir,
Wore out their shoes to spread the news, And ran til out of breath, sir.

Now up and down, throughout the town, Most frantic scenes were acted:
And some ran here, and some ran there Like men almost distracted.
Some fire cry'd, which some deny'd, But said the earth had quaked:
And girls and boys, with hideous noise, Ran through the town half naked.

Sir William he, snug as a flea, Lay all this time a snoring,
Nor dreamt of harm as he lay warm In bed with Mrs. Loring.
Now in affright, he starts upright, Awaked by such a clatter;
He rubs both eyes, and boldly dries, "For God's sake what's the matter?"

At his bedside, he then espy'd Sir Erskine at command, sir,
Upon one foot he had one boot, and t'other in his hand, sir.
Arise! Arise! Sir Erskine cries: The rebels—more's the pity —
Without a boat, are all on float, and rang'd before the city.
The motley crew, in vessels new, With satan for their guide, sir
Pack'd up in bags or wooden kegs, Come driving down the tide, sire.

Therefore prepare for bloody war; These kegs must all be routed;
Or surely we despis'd shall be, And British courage doubted.
The royal band now ready stand, All rang'd in dread array, sir,
With stomach stout, to see it out, and make a bloody day, sir.
The cannons roar, from shore to shore: The small arms make a rattle:
Since wars began, I'm sure no man E're saw so strange a battle.
The rebel dales, the rebel vales, With rebel trees surrounded.
The distant woods, the hills and floods, With rebel echoes sounded.

The fish below swam to and fro, Attack'd from every quarter;
Why sure, thought they, the devil's to pay, 'Mongst folks above the water.

These kegs, 'tis said, thought strongly made, Of rebel staves and hoops, sir,

Could not oppose their powerful foes, The conquering British troops, sir.

From morn till night, these men of might Display'd amazing courage;

And when the sun was fairly down, Retir'd to sup their porridge.

An hundred men, with each a pen, Or more, upon my word, sir,

It is most true would be too few, Their valor to record, sir.

Such feats did they perform that day, against those wicked kegs, sir,

That years to come, if they get home, They'll make their boasts and brags, sir.

They ended the song with a great shout of "*Rebels!*"

Ben walked over and patted me on the back, and crouched down to hand me a steaming cup of cider. I had no idea where he got it, but I welcomed it like I welcomed Christmas. I had been sitting facing the fire for both songs to keep my fingers and the fiddle warm, but not hot. "Ye earned it Daniel, yer sounding pretty good for having that fiddle only a couple of weeks. How are the fingers holding up? It's getting colder out here. Think ye can play one more after?"

"This is good," I replied as I sipped the hot cider and let the wooden cup warm my fingers. "*Ja,* let me finish this a bit and I'll try *Fish and Tea.* Papa liked that one. I'll have to play it on the fife, though." Looking up at him, I could see no stars overhead. That was likely a good thing. The clouds would hold back some of the cold, but bad in that we would likely wake up to snow.

"*Fish and Tea* is a good one, little brother. Whenever yer ready, just start playing again. Don't think we'll have much more singing, though.

Some of the boys from the other campfires have already moved back to their own. It's getting late and we've a bit to go tomorrow," he said as he started to walk back to his log.

"Hey Ben, ye know, I've never really understood the lyrics to 'Battle of the Kegs'. Who was this Sir William and this Mistress Lowery, and why were they in the same bed?" Ben turned back around and looked at me, then at Oliver, who was desperately trying not to laugh.

"Ah, well, Sir William is Major General William Howe, Commander-in-Chief in America for the British, and Mistress Lowery accompanied him everywhere in Philadelphia when he stayed there."

"Even at night; in his bed? Why would she go to his bed if she wasn't his wife?"

"Well, that's just the point. It was likely a made-up story; don't ye worry about it."

"Nice scrambling there, Ben," Oliver said, grinning from ear to ear.

"Scrambling what?" I asked.

"Never ye mind!" both of them said loudly.

"Why?" I got a very fierce 'don't ask me again' look from them both, and then changed tactics. "What about the kegs? Were they made up too?"

"Ah, no little brother. There is this gentleman, David Bushnell. He's a bit like Master Franklin; always trying to figure things out, experimenting and such. One day in January of '78, he floats a keg down the Delaware, full of black powder with a device that would make it explode when it struck another object in the water. I think his intent, though, was to see if he could damage the British ships in the water or near the docks."

"Well, the keg floated peacefully for about ten miles," Oliver said, taking a seat on the other side of me, getting closer to the fire to warm. "Then two boys in a rough canoe, who were likely fishing, saw the keg, maneuvered towards it, grabbed on to it to drag back to the riverbank and *boom!* It blew up.

"I heard Master Bushnell was pretty upset about it for some time. He followed his device at a distance and watched through a looking glass as it had happened. There was no time to warn the boys. He did find out that the powder would stay dry as the keg floated down the river, though."

Ben passed Oliver some of the whiskey and picked up the story from there. "It was a couple of days, if I remember the story correctly, before Master Bushnell tried again. This time, he sent more kegs—maybe four or five," Ben said, shrugging his shoulders. "Anyway, when the Redcoats spied them floating peacefully in the water, the entirety of the British military lined both sides of the Delaware, armed with their muskets, cannon and anything else they thought would stop the barrels from reaching the ships or the docks. It *seemed* an extraordinary amount of firepower for the five kegs.

"Mind ye, these casks are supposed to hold sixty-four gallons of liquid, and they would hold less than that in powder, when the triggering device for the explosion was added. So mebbe a keg might carry about sixty gallons of powder at most. That could do some serious damage to the ships or docks, right, Oliver?"

"*Ja,* no doubt as long as the powder stayed dry," Oliver responded as he reached for a stick and repositioned the logs in the fire. "If the powder in the barrel didn't get wet, and the if barrel rested at least halfway in the water, then the explosion could still occur, but the water would dampen any explosion regardless. If any damage was done, it would have been close to the waterline of the ship or the dock.

"So, Redcoats proceeded to shoot anything in the water that moved before it got to the ships or the docks. Any stick, log, or cask was thoroughly destroyed many times over as it meandered downriver. Thus, the British army proved their military fitness over the American rebels," Oliver said with a smile.

"General Howe was so pleased about the 'victory' that he sent a fast packet ship with a dispatch to King George and his court commending his soldiers on their prowess in the Battle of the Kegs," Ben finished up, taking another swig of whiskey, and passed it back to Oliver.

"Poor General Howe was looking for almost anything to boast about. He's had some serious lapses of judgement in the last couple of years and was not a favored soldier of the British Court. That's why the general was relieved of command soon after this incident in the spring of seventy-eight," Oliver replied and saluted Ben with the flask of whiskey and took his sip. "On second thought, Ben, I'm gonna head back to the tent," he said as he passed the whiskey on. "I might actually sleep warm tonight with all the spirits pumping through my veins. Ga' night!"

"See ye at sunlight, Oliver. Night!" Ben replied.

"Well, it looks like most of our visitors have gone. Andrew, Henry, Phillip, and Thomas are still playing that game of whist, and the others have moved on to the stories of the Sullivan Expedition of last summer. I think that might be it for music tonight, little brother. Ye probably should pack it all up."

"All right, I'll finish getting the knapsack packed with the fife and fiddle and come back. Mind if I sit and listen to those stories?"

"Na, seems to me I owe ye a story or two myself. Don't dally, I want to get to bed soon. So, we'll stay only a bit when ye return. Otherwise, the morning will come like bolt lightning tomorrow."

Battle for Wyoming

"**G**et'n back ta what we were talk'n about, I did hear the strangest story, though, James," I overheard Samuel say as I walked back to our campfire. "Someone in one of the regiments, came upon a rattler that was about twelve feet long, while he was just walk'n through the high grass search'n out rabbits for dinner."

"Did he get bit?" I asked, as I sat back down at the fire.

"Na, but I heard his pants were a wee darker in places that shouldn't be when he returned to ta camp. If ye get my mean'n," Samuel answered. We all had a good laugh at that.

"What about those old trees we heard about, Samuel? "*Ja*, it's true, we measured them, James. Most was sixteen feet 'round ta an inch, and there was a couple of twenty-two footers too," an irritated Samuel responded. "Wasn't no liquor involved neither, none ta be had in a month of Sundays. It was at least that long since we had any, right, Ben?"

"At least. I did see some of those trees ye talked about, Samuel, but didn't take the time to measure them. I was too busy keeping an 'eye' out for Indian scouts, unlike other folks." Ben said as he rolled his eyes.

"Well now, sir! Every now and then a man's gotta look around and enjoy what's around him, Ben," Samuel retorted.

"If what ye both say is true, those trees would make some mighty fine ships. Would ye remember where ye saw them, Samuel,?" James asked. James was a little older than Ben, maybe by five years. He would debate the devil himself, if given a chance when he was in one of his moods. It was best to divert him when possible with another conversation.

"Well, sure. I remember James, but pull'n a log filled wagon over that terrain might be a bit difficult, not ta mention the possibility of run'n into Indians again. I'll tell ye more tomorrow, on the way ta camp. It'll give us someth'n ta talk about then," Samuel replied as he added another log on to the fire.

"Indians? What about the Indians? Did ye see any?" I asked, wondering if Cornplanter or any of his men had followed the men of the Sullivan Expedition through the wilderness.

"Yes, there were Indians, Daniel," Ludlow responded. "Not many, just a few Indian scouts. There were more than I wanted to see as we passed through. We saw the destruction they left behind the year before as we moved north. Ye were one of the first to see Wyoming, weren't ye, Ben? Ye went up with the officers?"

"*Ja,* I did. I only got to go because I was a decent shot with my musket. It wasn't an honor or anything. We had seen a band of Indians at the edge of the meadow watching us and following our movements for several days. Where there was one, we knew there would be more. I went with the officers to help make sure everyone kept their scalps attached to their heads.

"The officers wanted to see where our Colonel Zebulon Butler stood against the Tory Colonel John Butler, his soldiers, and the Senecas led by Cornplanter and Disappearing Smoke." Ben paused at this point to take a swig of the whiskey that Samuel passed off to him, keeping his eyes on me again for a reaction to the news of Cornplanter's part in the battle.

The only answer I had for him was a noncommittal shrug of my shoulders. Cornplanter had briefly mentioned his part in the Wyoming battle, but did not tell me the whole story that night we camped together. This was no place for the two of us to talk about it, anyway; hatred for both the Indians and their British handlers ran high.

"Ahh, that is good," Ben remarked as he shut the flask to pass it on to Ludlow. "Anyway, they didn't want to go without an armed force.

As I said, we'd been followed into the Wyoming area by a small band of Indian scouts on and off over several days. So, Colonel Spencer asked that I come join him with the others in the light infantry that were in charge of protecting the officers. It was a pleasant day away from camp for the most part, not too hot, clear skies and a slow breeze across a crystal stream that would cool yer feet and make a nice bath if ye had the time. Probably not unlike the day Tory Colonel John Butler unleashed hell on a thousand families.

"With Generals Maxwell and Hand, and Colonels Proctor, Butler, Shreve, and our own Colonel Spencer, we rode up to Colonel Courlandts' encampment to meet up with Generals Poor and Fisk. From there, we followed Colonel Zebulon Butler to the battlegrounds to hear his story about the fight on July third of seventy-eight.

"All told, there were about five hundred and seventy-four men including British regulars, Loyalist fighters and Seneca-Iroquois warriors with the British Colonel, John Butler when he took Fort Wintermoot on June thirtieth. Colonel John didn't really take Fort Wintermoot, it was given to him. The Wintermoot family welcomed him; opening the fort's gates to him, his soldiers, and the Seneca, to partake of their hospitality. In the early evening, Colonel John sent a smaller force about a mile north to Fort Jenkins. That force took three men prisoners and killed the several others, but his real goal was Forty Fort, a little south of Fort Wintermoot.

"Colonel Zebulon Butler was furloughed at the time from the Continental army and visiting Forty Fort. Forty Fort got word of what happened at Forts Wintermoot and Jenkins and by the agreement of the citizens of Forty Fort, he assumed command of the militia, which included about three hundred and eighty–six men.

"At daybreak Colonel Zeb sent Colonel Dennison and Lieutenant Colonel Dorrance from Forty Fort to Fort Jenkins. They found two Iroquois warriors. The colonel and lieutenant colonel relieved them," Ben said with a half-smile as held his hand out to Andrew for the whiskey flask.

"The warriors were standing guard over Fort Jenkins and the scalped and mutilated dead bodies of the men they had killed, leaving them for the crows. The colonels saw that the dead men were given a proper burial; and then returned to the Forty with their men." Ben took another swig and passed the flask on, then stood up, rubbed his arms, and moved a little closer to the fire, dragging his sitting log with him.

"The card game done for the night, Andrew?"

"Yes, they wanted to turn in and I wanted to hear the rest of yer story," he said, as he grabbed another log and threw it on the fire.

"Ye all right there, little brother?"

"*Ja,* just a little chilly."

"Well, move on up here. It is warmer, and I can keep an eye on ye, case ye fall asleep. Where was I?"

"Colonel's men just returned from Fort Jenkins."

"Ah, that's right.

"So, come July second, Daniel Ingersoll, a resident of Fort Wintermoot, was made to deliver Colonel John Butler's terms of surrender for Forty Fort. Master Ingersoll, you see, disagreed with the wisdom of the Wintermoots, and while he was in the process of preparing an armed revolt against the Wintermoot guests, he was discovered, overwhelmed, and immediately shackled by a loyal British subject, who then brought him to the attention of Colonel John Butler. I guess Colonel John must have reasoned that Master Ingersoll would make a good emissary to Forty Fort 'cause the men of the Forty would likely shoot him first instead of his escort.

"Master Ingersoll, with a Loyalist ranger and an Iroquois warrior in tow, did deliver Colonel John's terms of surrender to the men of Forty Fort. The ranger and Indian kept within earshot of Ingersoll, and he was unable to say much of anything else concerning the situation at Wintermoot. Colonel Zeb Butler, with Colonel Dennison by his side, replied to the demand for surrender with: 'Not this day, nor the next!' and then sent Ingersoll and his escort back to Wintermoot. By noon, additional reinforcements arrived at the Forty from the town of Hanover.

"Master Ingersoll was back on the morning of July third with another demand for surrender. He came with a little larger escort of four men, including two guides, another white man and an Indian. It seemed to the Forty Fort folks that the men of the escort were likely spying out the place. Ingersoll and his escort were sent back again to Wintermoot Fort to deliver the same message as the day before. Our Colonel Zeb didn't budge.

"Colonel Zeb called a council of war in the hopes of trying to convince the younger militia men, especially those from Hanover, that it would be best that they try to delay action with Colonel John by opening some sort of discussion with him. After all, Colonel John had the greater force, something like two to one. All the Forty Fort townspeople had to do was hold out two more days and Captain Spaulding would arrive with another sixty local men, who were trained fighters and had experience gained from the battles at Brandywine and Germantown. Waiting would better the odds. Colonel Dennison, who was second in command and Lieutenant Colonel Dorrance agreed with Colonel Zeb.

"However, Captain Lazarus Stewart, who led the contingent of men from Hanover, strongly disagreed. He argued passionately that an attack needed to be made immediately. '*It was why the men of the militia had signed their names to paper, to fight and defend their land and people, not talk the enemy to death,*' he said. He also reminded the war council about the whiskey that was stored in the fort, a very large cache of it. There was quite a bit of silver to be had in that whiskey if it ever made it to the coast."

Ben took a gulp of the applejack that Samuel handed to him, and I watched, wondering just how Ben could think and talk straight with all that alcohol in him. I might be carrying him off to bed if he drank much more. Then again, I would probably need help to do so. He had grown a lot bigger since I had seen him last April. Yet, he seemed clear-headed enough and picked back up where he left off after handing the jug back to Samuel.

"Captain Stewart also claimed that there was no certainty that Spalding would arrive in time or intact with the troops anyway, given the roaming bands of Indians, Loyalists, and British regulars. That was enough, I guess, to push the younger men to decision. They were in the majority, and they voted for an immediate attack.

"So come that afternoon, the militia walked out of Forty Fort with the intent of meeting the enemy at Fort Wintermoot. The Redcoats had Indian scouts watching the fort from the woods, so the minute the militia was out of the gate, the information was dispatched back to Colonel John.

"Around three o'clock in the afternoon, the Forty Fort men got within sight of Wintermoot, which sits high up on a bank between two plains," Ben explained, drawing a picture with one hand higher than the other, as he talked. "Wintermoot sat about right there, just under the higher plateau," he said as he wiggled a finger around where the invisible earth rose into his hand. "There's also an area directly below the fort that is filled with trees and brush.

"The militia knew something caught fire because, as they were almost halfway up the road to Wintermoot, they could smell the smoke. Sure enough, the fort had been set ablaze and was now smoking like the dickens. There was a lot of talk among the men after seeing the ruin, that Colonel John had retreated and that perhaps they should just turn around and go back. But our Colonel Zeb wasn't fooled. He knew that Colonel John was nearby.

"Colonel Zeb ordered two of his captains and their lieutenants to draw up the battle line. The officers placed the militia in a line from the sandy plateau that borders the Susquehanna River up the steep bank to the gravel covered plateau above. Those on the left flank stood on the higher plateau, keeping company with a dense forest of trees and brush in a curve around them, ending in a swamp a little farther behind them. Angled a little below them was the burning hulk of Wintermoot sitting on the bank. Our right flank stood in the bank facing the fort with the river behind them by about four hundred forty feet away, and Colonel Zeb was with them.

"The men of the militia started shooting at about six hundred feet from the Queen's Rangers, and then would advance, reload, and shoot again. The enemy rangers refused to stand up and fire back at us. They were hugging the ground on their bellies, and in all honesty, it might've been a little difficult for them to jump up quickly and shoot immediately. Several of them, though, graciously showed us their backside as they jumped up and ran faster than a jack rabbits away from the battle.

"Then when Colonel Zeb got within three hundred feet of the British line, all hell broke loose. The Iroquois warriors came hollering with blood-curdling screams, tomahawks shaking and guns blazing, running from the thick brush and woods that grew beside the fort, right through and over the Rangers in front of them. Colonel John and the Rangers were the last to erupt from the ground after the Iroquois had passed and made an attack on the militia's right flank.

"At the same time, warriors on the higher plane rushed our left flank, running through the swamp with tomahawks raised and guns firing with equal shrieks of death. The left flank was quickly overwhelmed; and the officers tried to get them to wheel back to create a wedge with the main line to face the enemy head on-to prevent being overrun. What our men of the left flank heard, through all the screaming, muzzle firing confusion, was '*retreat*,' and so they did.

"The left flank then took flight back to the road they came on, through the fog of black sulfur and thick wood smoke, hearing the bloodcurdling screams of crazed Iroquois and Loyalist British in a battle frenzy. As the right flank joined the left, we retreated past the cries of the dying.

"The combat lasted all of thirty minutes. We were outnumbered nearly two to one. The rout led immediately to a massacre of those that could not escape. It was twelve hours of hell on earth until the light of day brought a stop to the terror. Ye'all have seen a cat toy with the wee animals it catches? This massacre was much the same."

Ben got up to relieve himself a short distance from the campfire, and we waited in silence for his return. I kept an eye on him, just in case he fell or anything, but he held the liquor just fine and returned chaffing his hands together to warm them. "Any more of that apple jack, Samuel?"

"Yes, just a bit, it's yer's, son. Ye earned it today."

"Thanks." Ben took a gulp and then sat down in his place at the fire and was quiet for a moment, then took another drink and handed the flask back to Samuel for safe keeping. Andrew added another log to the fire and looked at the sky overhead. I followed his line of sight to the sky above to find it was now free of clouds, a good sign for leaving in the morning. Hopefully, there would be no snow tonight, just the bitter cold.

"The Iroquois blocked the retreat to Forty Fort and men were trapped in the crossfire between the rangers and the warriors. Men tried to escape by throwing themselves into the Susquehanna only to be speared like fish by the Indians. Others were tracked down and tomahawked where they stood. Our Colonel Butler and about seventeen of his men managed to escape the carnage by hightailing it to the mountains," Ben said as he stared into fire and became still for a few moments. Just as I was about to rouse him, thinking he had fallen asleep with his eyes open like he used to when we were little, he came back to us and began again.

"Colonel Zeb took us to the main battleground where many of the dead still lay unburied. There were bone parts of maybe a hundred men there, scattered all over the field like they were balls and sticks used in a cruel child's game. Weathered and eyeless, dirty white skulls grinned at us in the hot sun.

"Some of the heads were missing their crowns, but jagged edges of the open heads were left to witness the strike of dull tomahawks. The feet, leg, arm, and rib bones were not spared; what wasn't taken by a musket ball or tomahawk had been chewed and gnawed for the last of tendons and marrow by the animals that feasted on our dead.

"Me and a few other men volunteered to dig graves for those that Colonel Zeb and Captain Spalding had not had time to bury last year. It was that day the main battlefield was given the name 'The Place of Skulls' by the men of General Sullivan's expedition.

"Colonel Zeb then took us to another grassy area near the main battleground where he and Captain Spalding, a month after the battle, had buried seventy-five men that had fallen there. The colonel and captain had received permission from General Washington to harvest the wheat that had been planted earlier in the spring before the battle, to help the families that had returned to the area despite the continued Iroquois and British threat.

"We then walked to a much smaller piece of land for the last part of the colonel's tour. He said an individual who managed to escape the horror of this peaceful place had told him of the violent and brutal deaths of the men that now laid under our feet. The colonel didn't believe a word of it until he saw with his own eyes and found fourteen skeletons with most of their parts lying in a circle and several other individuals resting in the center of the ring where they had been burned completely to black char and brittle bone.

"The soldier that had escaped—his name was Slocum, if I remember correctly. Slocum had told the colonel that our men and colonists had surrendered to the Iroquois upon being told that they would be given mercy. They were made to sit down in a circle and watch the Iroquois celebrate their victory with wild dancing, drumming, singing, and hollering around a huge fire in the center of the ring.

"As the celebration progressed, the Iroquois took a few of our people, staked them out on log poles, and lifted them into the fire. With the scent of their charred flesh and bone in the air, the Indians turned their attention to the rest of the prisoners in the circle and by that hellish fire light they were tomahawked one by one, in front of each other.

"Slocum just laid there, hidden behind the brush and tall grasses beyond the fire. He could do nothing but listen to his neighbors and friends scream in anguish until they were no more. When there was an unexpected commotion in the opposite direction from where he was, Slocum slipped away quietly and managed to make his escape."

Ben turned his head and looked directly at me with his black eyes searching and saw the pain in mine. He knew he had destroyed any heroic image I had of Cornplanter. Cornplanter had tried to tell me when I met up with him some weeks ago, but what he said wasn't real to me, until now. I was gutted and Ben knew it, but I couldn't talk to him, not here, not now. He reached out to me and squeezed my arm and said nothing again until I lowered my eyes.

"The colonel had dug graves for each of the fourteen at the place where they had fallen. That small cemetery is now covered in grasses and wildflowers; a peaceful, holy shrine surrounded by the tall trees, the watchers of the wood. Out of nearly four hundred men, only about sixty survived," Ben said quietly and then held his hand out to Samuel for the last of the applejack.

Eyer's Forge

"Wake-up, Wake-up, Daniel!" Ben said, shoving me, trying to pull me out of a nightmare. I felt him there, but just couldn't get above the surface of a thick dark, pulling me back into the screaming slaughter in blood and hellfire. Ben's voice was insistent, and I latched on to it, pulling myself up from under the quicksand that was the dream. "Sshh, shhh, there little brother, ye are safe," Ben whispered as I sat up, shaking in his arms and wiping my hands across my eyes.

"Ye 'bout woke all the men in the tent, Daniel. Are ye all right now?" he whispered as he loosened his grip on me. "Can ye talk about it?"

"May be. Just little bits and pieces. It was dark, but I could see the dull red light of a huge forest fire, I think. There was a lot of fighting, screams, war whoops; blood was splattered everywhere and even on me, I couldn't help anyone." He listened to me as I whispered more of my dream, shedding the fear and terror, and then stayed awake with me until I fell back to sleep.

I woke again peacefully this time, just before dawn, listening to Ben's even breathing for a few minutes before I scooted out from under Ben's arm that laid across my chest. Free of the partial bear hug, I meandered to the campfire and started it back up again. Snow dusted my hair and eyelashes, and a frigid cold wind made its way through the layers of clothing and boots I wore as I walked from the tent to the fire pit. It would be a freezing walk to Master Wick's farm today.

The most I could offer the men that morning was some coffee made from roasted acorns and sweetened with a dram of honey. It was a small treat, especially the honey, it would make the fire cakes go down a little easier. The acorns and honey were payment from Colonel Shreve; he had me deliver a wooden box to General Maxwell earlier in the week. The general then sent me back with a letter to the colonel, thanking him I guess, and the colonel then insisted that I take the acorns and honey. If we had not been so food poor, I would not have taken them. As it was, there wouldn't be anything at all to eat for dinner that evening, so I had to make the most of what was here for now.

Ben woke with a bit of a headache and could not stomach even the thought of fire cakes, but he took his share of the honeyed acorn coffee, warming himself by the fire. The entire group was quiet, saying very little, sipping on coffee, and crunching on the fire cakes, seemingly getting their minds set about the journey to Master Wick's farm through the bone chipping cold. The call was given to pack up the tents and all our belongings, if we already had not done so, after we broke our fast. At the last, our campfires were smothered, and the long procession of men began walking to the northeast in the frigid cold, under a grey sky thick with clouds.

ༀ ༀ ༀ

"So, little brother, how do ye feel about *our friend* now?" The sarcasm on 'our friend' dripped from Ben's lips like the thick honey that plopped into the acorn coffee this morning. I sighed long and deep and turned my face to watch my feet while I thought. I knew I would need to choose the right words for this, and I also knew that he was likely to disagree with me. The icy wind felt like a slap across my face, but the crunch of the snow from the footfalls of the men ahead and behind brought a familiar rhythm and calm. It would be very cold again tonight; the temperature had dropped throughout the morning as we strode through the woods and meadows. Ben likely would not share his blanket with me tonight after this conversation.

I looked up at the grey clouded sky and closed my eyes, letting the snow fall on them. They melted, of course. I felt the lacy, fragile ice structure dissolve, running down my eyes like tears. "Ben, I hear ye. I know ye disapprove of our friend's actions and I sure don't like them either."

Ben slowed his pace a bit to get some distance from the group ahead. The ones behind us were far enough back that we could talk quietly without being overheard. "It is more than disapproval, Daniel. He was wrong, very wrong, for allowing this savage cruelty, ye know this."

"*Ja,* and have we not been just as barbaric? I heard a story about a lieutenant in the Newtown battle. He seemed to think skinning a couple of dead warriors from the hips down to make boots was a fitting thing to do. We are all capable of being the bogeyman, brother.

"No, I certainly did not like what I heard last night. Whether or not he helped to slaughter those people, I do not know, he didn't say, and I am not sure he could have stopped the terror given the frenzy of his warriors, but whatever happened at Wyoming, he was not proud of it and told me as much. He said he would live with it forever. As I told ye, he gave me his wampum beads so I would be under his protection from other Iroquois in this wilderness," I said, raising my hand to the dark thick woods where we stopped. "He treated me as a friend and a son. "I have no understanding of this savagery. Yet, this I know, all men are capable of both good and evil, and in that there is no difference between one man and another. Evil abounds when men make choices out of unrighteous anger, ruthless selfishness, or vanity beyond measure. Ye get a group of people like this together, then there will be trouble, lots of it. Papa taught us this."

"So, ye forgive him? Cause, I'm sure I don't."

"No. I don't forgive him for anything. He's not wronged me other than to deeply disappoint. If anything, I fear what he became in the heat of battle, and I hope I never see anything of the like of what ye described last night. I'll tell ye what though, whatever made him have his regrets, will cause him to live with it until the end of his days, that I believe.

"What do ye think Ben, how did ye behave at Newtown? I've seen ye wrestle and how fearsome ye're at it." That question stopped him dead in the middle of the dirt path. He stared at me in stunned disbelief as the cold wind blew on his chapped face and made his eyes water.

"If ye think for one second, that I could do what *they* did at Wyoming *or what that lieutenant did, for that matter, ye are wrong,*" he hissed at me, like the bobcat that hissed and growled at me when I got too close to its young near the forest trail behind Aletta's house a few years ago.

"No, I don't, but I am not sure that ye knew that for yerself until just now. I have seen ye fight brother, ye're pretty good at it too. I don't remember ye ever picking a fight, but I do remember ye putting a quick end to them. Ye've never done more than was needed."

"Thank ye Daniel. Come on, we gotta keep moving or were likely to freeze where we stand," he said softly as he watched several of the men walk around us, paying us no attention. It's way too cold out here for man or beast."

It was twilight when we arrived at Master Wick's Jockey Hollow. We walked silently to the encampment, too tired to speak to each other and all of us looking like walking snow men; the snow had built up on hats, shoulders, and pant legs, the bottom of which were now crusted and frozen from being melted by the warmth leaching from our legs.

We thought we would settle there in our tents for the night, but the corporal on duty had other orders. He told us we had about five more miles to go. South it was, to a hillside near the Eyer's iron forge. Not a one of us wanted to move another foot and I heard some grumbling from behind me, then all went silent. Oliver, with not a word, moved out of the line, moved forward ahead of us all and started down the path south towards Eyer's hillside. Ben grabbed me and we followed.

Freedom is a Right From Birth

"I'm worried about Papa, Ben. He should have been here even before this weather." It was the second week of January. Snow, cold and a wind sharp as any knife had assailed us since we arrived at Eyer's Forge. The snow was two to five feet high, where it had not been shoveled.

"Me too, little brother. As much as I would like to see him, I hope he stays put. Can ye even imagine how high the snow is between here and Easton?"

"*Ja,* yer right. No wagon or horse is gonna get through this, out there. Ye think he's close enough to home not to be taken by the Torys and the Redcoats?" We'd hear a new story every day about people being sent to the Sugar House or dying in the act of defending themselves from Tory patrols and British foraging raids.

"Daniel, worrying isn't gonna to do either of us any good. We can pray. That is all we can do until we hear something. So, focus on looking for those berries and roots ye were talking about, so we can put some food into our bellies."

"Ye're right. Just hard not to think about it." Those of us with warm clothing had left the encampment just after dawn to hunt and forage for anything that might be edible. Jockey Hollow's commissary was empty, with no promises of food from the state governments or Congress anytime soon. Even if they had provisions to send, they wouldn't be able to get it to us because of the conditions of the roads and the rivers. The rivers were mostly solid ice and no boats could make it through.

As far as clothing, a lot of the men in Jockey Hollow had their trousers and shirts torn in the rush to get their huts built, and many were still without proper shoes, coats, and blankets. Congress and the states had seemingly forgotten about the men at the forefront of the fight.

Ben, Andrew, Phillip, and Henry went with us several miles into the woods beyond our encampment, hoping to improve the odds of finding game. Game animals were very scarce in the immediate area around the encampment, having already been hunted out by the almost twelve thousand men living on the Wick's farm.

By late afternoon in the grey twilight, we were forced to come back to our small cabin. The severe chill had returned and with it, heavy falling snow. It was hard to see twenty feet in front of us, but we made out two figures ahead of us, looking very much like man-beasts that were part of a story Cornplanter told me long ago. He had said that they walked on two feet, were hairier, bigger, and taller than any man. They roamed the woods in search of mates or food. He also said I was not to cross one because it would rip me apart with its two hands if I angered it. I didn't enter the woods for months after that story.

"Samuel, Oliver?" Ben shouted as we trudged on the path to our small cabin.

"Yes, it's us, Ben. Hurry up, the snow is get'n worse. Any luck?" Samuel asked as he and Oliver stood waiting for us to catch up to them.

"Where'd ye go? I thought ye both were gonna stay with Thomas. Nurse him back to health and all," Ben said as finally met up with them.

"We did get to do some of that today, but thought I might be more help at the infirmary, and Oliver was itch'n to get out. Weren't ye?"

"That is so. Good to get out and stretch the legs. Felt like we did some good there, though. They certainly needed the help," Oliver replied as he turned to start walking again.

"'Sides Ben, Thomas is on the mend and ye know they got all those sick men at the hospital, more than they can handle. So, we volunteered to go cut wood for the hearth, feed others some broth, lift them from their beds and the like. The doctor and his helpers are exhausted, for sure. Ahh, there it is, gentlemen! I see smoke coming from the chimney. Looks like Tom managed to keep the fire go'n. Tis good news. I'm 'bout frozen!"

Thomas heard us coming and opened the door a crack to see us shaking our snowshoes and kicking the side of the hut with our boots, to lessen the tracked in snow and maybe prevent a muddy mess on our dirt floor. After being in the clean air for several hours, the air that flowed out through the cabin door was an assault to our noses; the reek of unwashed clothes, bed linens, bodies, sickness, and smoke was quite noticeable and without remedy. We each accepted it for what it was and were grateful just to know we'd be warm in the haphazard shelter despite the stench.

"Ye find anything, boys, at least enough for a broth for dinner?" Thomas asked in a scratchy voice as he peered around the corner of the open door, trying to hold back a coughing fit. We walked in as he finally gave into it. He walked to the hearth, wretched his throat, and flung yellow mucus into it, like a stone released from a slingshot.

"Thomas! That was a slapper of a spit. Not sure I could have done it any better, and I learned from the best. Ben, that is."

"What evil did I teach ye, Daniel?" Ben asked as he walked in and set the skinned squirrel carcasses on the make-shift table.

"How to spit. Look!" I said nodding my head to the hearth, "Thomas made it straight into the fire and didn't miss at all."

"Well, good there Thomas! This summer, if we can get one, we'll have a watermelon seed spitting contest and see just how good ye are against the best," Ben replied, grinning.

"Ah, well, I've got to survive this all first," Thomas replied with a wave of his hand and then sat back on his bunk to watch as Andrew expertly quarter the squirrels without taking off his hand. A feat considering how his curly black hair all fell forward over his eyes as worked. "The squirrels were out and about? I wouldn't have thought they would be."

"We didn't think so either, Tom, but we kept a lookout on the trees, and there they were. It was much warmer for the few hours we were out than it has been for a few weeks. Maybe they thought it was spring," Andrew answered while plopping pieces of the fresh meat into the kettle of boiling water that hung in the hearth. "Good of ye to keep the kettle going, Tom. Ye'll have that broth and then some. Should feel pretty good going down."

"Thank ye, Andrew. Daniel, any of that salt left on the mantle?"

"*Ja,* think so, here let me look."

Henry was the last to come in after Samuel and Oliver. He threw his knapsack on his bed, landing it with a resounding thunk, and peeled off his wet coat hat and gloves. "Daniel, get yer coat and boots off, yer dripping on the floor, little man."

"I was just looking for some salt up here on the hearth and who are ye calling little? I'm as tall as ye, Henry!"

"No, not yet, son, not until ye can think about hanging yer coat up to dry and putting yer boots near the hearth as soon as ye get in," he said, ruffling my hair.

I hung the coat and bent over to pull off the last boot when I stood up and smashed the top of my head into something solid. "Ouch!"

"Daniel! Will ye watch what ye're doing? Ye just about took my head off," yelled Phillip as he rubbed his neck and chin. "I was headed for my bunk to get out of the way. None of ye want me cooking for sure."

"I didn't see ye and this stupid boot wouldn't come off. I am sorry, Phillip."

"I know. It's this place. It's too small; it's not yer fault. Just move a little closer to the hearth and let me by. I just wanna fall into my bunk."

Our fourteen by sixteen-foot hut was built to house twelve men and with even only half of us in it at the same time, it was darn near impossible to move past one another without ending up on the dirt floor in a tangle. Most of us handled the situation with minor annoyance, but there were moments that were not pleasant.

"Ye alright there, Phillip? Ye're white as a sheet and all sweaty, too."

"Well, Oliver, compared to ye, I am always pale," Phillip replied teasingly. "As for being sweaty, I need to cool down. Ye're closer, can ye hang up my coat on the peg?" he asked as he shrugged out of his ragged hunting jacket. "Thank ye, my friend. I am just gonna lie down for a bit. Wake me when the food's ready."

"Henry, can ye and Daniel chop up those taters, carrots, and onions ye got from the farmer's cellar? It won't be long before we need them."

"Sure, Andrew. Come on kid, let's get at it." Henry plopped the knapsack on the table and reached in pulling out a potato to peel with his rather dirty knife. "I'll be willing to gamble that ye'll think it was well worth the trouble of going to down to that pitch-black cellar to get these, Daniel."

"Mebbe. All I could think of was the very big raccoon and her four babies that I nearly cornered in a burned-out cabin not too long ago. That scared the bloody hell out of me." I had found very little in the woods to eat; the deer had gotten there first, munching down on berries, bark, and stems above the snow line. We gave up after a while and left the woods from a different direction after we caught the squirrels and stopped at a farmhouse. The owner was kind enough to let me take what we needed from his cellar to make the stew; he just didn't have a candle that would light my way into the dark hole.

"Watch ye're tongue, young man," Andrew responded. "Ye've been around us too long and ye've not earned the right to swear like that."

"Ben says it all the time."

"I do not. I use it when something's amiss and I am angry, frustrated over it."

"Ben is, what, four years older than ye, Daniel?"

"True, Henry, but that's no reason he should be allowed, and I'm not."

"Well, seems to me that he's a soldier, a man and he's allowed to do as he pleases, unless an officer tells him otherwise. Ye're not a man yet. Until then, ye need to be respectful; otherwise ye might be find yerself in more trouble than ye can handle."

"I couldn't have said it better, Henry," Oliver chimed in.

"What, yer gonna to side with him, Oliver?"

"I am, Daniel. Hand me one of those carrots. I'll help ye. It will do ye well to listen to yer elders."

"I'd a thought James, William and George would be back by now," Tom said, changing the subject.

"Well, they're supposed to be. They likely got caught in a card game. Ye know how they are, Tom."

"I do Ben. Just wondering. Did any of ye see anyone else, any news of anything?"

Samuel had his back to us, looking through his pack, when he spoke up. "Well, I got word at the infirmary. Near as anyone can reckon, another fifty or so men have deserted in the last week. Worse time ta do it, though. They're gonna be damn lucky if they make it home in the cold. Ah, there they are. Here, Tom brought ye a pair of stock'ns and a bit of a shirt. Don't ask," Samuel said, holding his hand up to stop Tom from speaking. "Thought ye might be able to pull the thread from the shirt ta mend some more clothes." We had found out that early on that Tom was pretty good with a needle and thread; he had been apprenticed to a tailor when he was my age.

"Thank ye, Samuel. The stockings, where'd they come from?"

"Told ye not to ask, Thomas," he said, sighing noticeably. "We've not been able to bury anyone for darn near a week, on account of the frozen ground. The man that wore 'em didn't need 'em anymore. Ye do, and ye need to keep those feet warm, or ye'll lose yer toes. If ye don't, then yer gonna have trouble walk'n. Those stock'ns are in good shape, fairly clean, and don't smell.

"Ye're right, I guess."

"Course I am."

"Getting them from a dead man don't bother me none as much as it might have, had ye stole them off someone in a card game."

"What? Me cheat? Nay, I don't need ta 'cause I'm just that good," Sam said, reassuring Tom.

"Well, that's comforting. Means ye'll be with us a bit longer. Thank ye, Samuel."

"Are vegetables ready, Oliver?"

"Yes, they're cut and ready for the pot when ye are Andrew."

"The meat needs to cook a little more; I'll add them in a few minutes," Andrew replied as he sipped on the broth, tasting it and then adding another pinch of the salt that was payment for a quick errand I had run for Captain Weatherby.

"How long ye think 'till dinner, Andrew?" I asked.

"Ah, maybe half an hour. Why?"

"I spied a nice un-molested feathery pine back down the path a ways from the hut when we were coming home. Those rushes would make for a clean bed. Thought I might have time to get some yet before dinner. Tom could definitely use them, being sick and all."

"I'll go with ye, little brother. God knows ye need to be watched," Ben said with his lips curled in a smirk as he pulled his hunting shirt, just mended by Thomas, over his head. "Anyone else wanting a change of bedding? I'll see what I can bring back. Samuel, Andrew? Phillip has nodded off in his bunk. I'll bring some for him, for sure."

"I could do with some fresh bed'n" Samuel replied. "Thank ye."

"Andrew?" Ben asked again, not sure that he heard the first time as he was focused on the squirrel stew.

"Please Ben, if ye got enough hands for it."

"Oliver?"

"It would be nice to sleep in a cleaner bed. I'll go with ye and help, Ben. Hope the temperature hasn't dropped too much more."

The snow had stopped and the temperature outdoors hadn't dropped much more, but it was going to. The sky was clear of clouds and the air crisp. The stars lit our way, and we quickly found the pine tree I saw earlier in the evening. Between the three of us, we hauled back plenty of clean rushes and deposited them near the door and shook the snow off our snowshoes and boots for a second time in an hour.

"Hurry in, ye're letting the cold in for sure!" Andrew exclaimed as he brushed his wind-blown curls out of his eyes. "Dinner's ready! Grab your bowls and spoons, gentlemen," Andrew announced as he ushered us through the lintel.

We had just dumped our coats on the beds and the boots at the hearth. Andrew finished serving up Tom and Phillip first and patiently waited for us with his wooden spoon in hand. I was the first in line.

"What's so funny, little brother?" I had let a bit of a giggle out under my breath while watching Andrew in his pose. I didn't think anyone else had heard it.

"There was this little Dutch lady, actually she wasn't so little, that fed me very well on my way here to find ye and Papa. I think I might a mentioned her to ye at one point? Anyway, she stood and looked much the way Andrew does now."

"Ye think I'm looking like an old stout Dutch woman, kid?"

"Ah, no sir, ye're just standing with the spoon in yer hand, just like her. Her food was as delicious as your squirrel stew smells, Andrew. Thank ye kindly for making it. I am gonna enjoy every bite."

"Well thank ye, Daniel. That's about the nicest thing I've heard in a while," he said grinning. That was the best response I could hope for, given that I gave him fighting words to begin with.

Oliver gave the blessing over the stew, and all was quiet for a while as we supped. Meat and vegetables were a rarity, and few of us knew when we would have more. That farmer was a godsend to us. Several of the messes had taken to raiding Jockey Hollow neighbors' larders. Not the friendliest thing to be doing, given that folks need to feed their own. The officers were blind to it, not sure what they could've done about it, anyway. We had decided that we would find another way.

With a bit of God's help, we were able to live off what we hunted and what little I earned from the errands the officers gave me when it wasn't so cold that I could run them. There were times when we had nothing at all. As for buying any food, we could when the government had money to pay us, which didn't happen often. Regardless, even if we had the Continental dollars, a month's pay would only buy about a week's worth of food at that.

"Andrew, fine job with squirrel stew. I couldn't have done better," Oliver said after his fourth or fifth spoonful from his bowl.

"Thank ye, Oliver. There's a little more if anyone else is still hungry. There won't be enough for morning."

"Anybody up to hitching a ride to Springfield this week with General Irvine's men?" Ben asked. "I've got a couple of days of leave still and could use a bit of a change. Daniel and I are going to see if we can ride on one of Colonel Hazen's sleds. I hear the Colonel is moving some of his men there."

"I shouldn't. I think I may be getting sick," Phillip replied.

"Samuel, Henry, Oliver, Andrew, ye up for it?"

"Got line duty," Oliver replied as he stopped blowing on his spoonful of stew.

"Too darn cold out there, Ben. I've had enough for the week, if I can help it," Samuel answered, while crumbling a bit of fire cake into the stew. "What, Daniel?"

"Umm, guess ye like fire cake in everything?"

"Well, *yes*, son, makes a right fine cracker, if ye ask me."

"Andrew, Henry?"

"Na, think I'll stay here just so I can bother Samuel a bit. What 'bout ye Henry?"

"I'll stay. I am thinking Andrew's gonna need some help bothering Samuel. Maybe we can start our own day long card game."

A silence fell over the group then, except for me, as we slowly finished the last of their stew.

"Oliver, why did ye decide to sign up, join the Continental army?"

"Ye heard I was born a free man, Daniel? Not everyone like me in this country has this blessing."

"I know. They should have, though. *Freedom is a right from birth,* I read it in one of the newspapers Captain Weatherby had. I believe it as well."

"Here, here!" the others said in one voice of agreement while clanking their spoons on their bowls.

Oliver put his spoon in his bowl and lowered his head as if in prayer for a few moments, then raised it and looked straight at me, and replied solemnly, "That is the truth of it, son. I joined up to see this fight through so that all people, including the likes of me, are free to be their own masters. Slavery is most ill-natured, and its practice must end. This country, should we win this war and not quit slavery, will not endure the next century."

Why We Fight

"**A**re ye sure ye want to do this, Daniel? Corporal Johnson is such a smooth talker, wished he'd asked me first," Ben said through the neck scarf that covered half of his face. We were huddled together, shivering with the other men on a sled as the icy wind whipped through us, bending us over like a field of hay just before a thunderstorm. So many of the men were still without decent clothes, shoes, and coats, along with mittens and caps. Several would lose toes or fingers to frostbite by tomorrow, especially if this became a two-day trip instead of one.

"I don't know, Ben. I can't have ye looking after me all the time. Yer worry for me might get ye killed with all that's a going on around here and then what? Look, we got cousins, aunts and uncles in New Jersey and New York. Don't ye think I should do what I can to keep them safe, like ye? I can do that by staying with the army; working the odd jobs I have been assigned, so that the soldiers older than me can be free to do what they signed up for: the chance to protect and encourage a future without tyrannical kings and the plans they make for our lives.

"It is right lofty of ye to think that way, but I am not sure Papa will agree with that line of reasoning."

"Well then, there's Oliver, Samuel, Andrew, Phillip, Henry, and Thomas; they're like brothers to me, and then there is ye. We all are family, and it is right to be alongside my brothers when they fight, doing whatever I can do to ease them in this burden."

Ben put his arm around my shoulders, pulling me into a hug and let me go, then turned and looked to the sky. "Ah, little brother, I should have counted on ye having a good argument for staying. But here and out there," he said, lifting his head into the direction of the surrounding hills, "danger and death are everywhere. Every day there's a new fight brewing in one of the towns, or in the hills and valleys between. With the Tories, Patriots, and refugees running to and fro, and not even to mention the British regulars, ye might get yerself caught in the middle, not knowing one from the other, and be killed. I am not sure I could live with that."

"True enough, and that is always a possibility. I could've died getting here, with all the beasts in the woods and the Iroquois and me with only a bow and hunting knife. If I had died, ye'd never of found me to give me a decent burial, at least here, ye might find me," I added with a chuckle.

"Ye've been thinking about this for a while, then?"

"I have thought it was a possibility before I found ye."

"Papa's gonna have my hide for letting ye do this, ye do know? But at this point, I kind of figure that the more men watching after ye, the better.

"There is no real guarantee that ye'll get to be with my mess when ye sign up and ye're likely to do the three years at least. Ye'll be in the music corps, I suppose. But that entails more than just playing that fife. Ye'll likely be doing all yer job plus others as well. Some, ye may not like," he said, shaking his head as he looked at the ground.

"*Ja,* I know. Corporal Johnson said as much. He did tell me I'd be with the musicians, but I already am. I still get the feeling they're not wanting me to join either, but don't quite know what to do with me. They don't want to send me back on my own. It's too cold, the snow is too high, and they are still concerned about the Iroquois."

"Who's they?"

"Do ye know that Papa knows General Maxwell, Colonel Spencer, and Colonel Shreve?"

"That's not surprising. What would surprise me is if he didn't know them. I think he has done some business with the general and the colonels in the recent past."

"Corporal Johnson, Captain Weatherby, Colonel Spencer, Colonel Shreve, and General Maxwell all got together and discussed my situation and offered up the solution to me. But they said that I must decide for myself. I have been thinking on the conversation I had with them for a little while, and thought now was the time to talk to ye."

"Ye know if ye are on the battlefield and ye will be, at some point, ye are a target, ripe for shooting. Ye'll have to rely on the honor of the Tories and the Redcoats not to shoot ye on sight. After what I've seen, I am not so sure I believe in the honor of either one."

"Ben, when it is my time, there's nothing anyone can do about it. The Lord will take me when he wants, I am sure; but until then, I will not spend my life fretting about it."

"Some days it is hard to see virtue in this, whatever this is," Ben said, waving his hand over the men, many wearing rags of clothing and blankets on their feet, hands, and bodies. "Those who argue in Congress and in the state assemblies and claim the righteousness of this war seem to find it hard to provide for those men that must fight in it. Where's the justice in that? I wonder how much they value our service. I was required to join. Ye are not for the time being, anyway."

"I hear yer discontent, Ben. Remember what ye told me before ye left last year for the regiment? Ye agreed with Papa. Ye said that maybe this is the first war fought on principle alone. It's not about grabbing a piece of ground, or riches. It's about, it's about . . . "

"*The divine constitution, and government of God over his intelligent creatures. It is fixed, and it does not become men to exercise their invention or wisdom in seeking any alteration or change it: but to study the most ready and cheerful submission; as they may be assured, that whatever God requires, is fit and right for his subjects to comply with. His authority and power over us is unlimited and uncontrollable, and cannot be denied, or opposed without our being guilty of the highest crime of rebellion,"* finished the grizzled old man bundled up in a well-worn blanket and huddled beside me for warmth. "Jacob Van Wert, young sirs, at your service. Let me see if I can remember the rest of this:

"But no created being is invested with such absolute, unlimited power, nor qualified for the exercise of it. Error and imperfection belongs to every individual of the human race. The brightest character that was ever justly drawn among mortal men, has this dark shade in it: So that the will of none, is infallibly right in all things, and cannot therefore be complied with in all instances, consistent with a good conscience, and the superior obligations we are under to the sovereign Ruler of the world; who still maintains this rightful authority over us, and has not given it by delegation to any one among created beings: all of whom were originally made free-agents; and considered as in a state of nature, previous to their uniting as members of society, have their liberty and free choice to agree upon such a form of government, and mode of administration in their civil and temporal affairs, as the judge most conducive to their happiness and good: any one of which has no more claim than another to be of divine right on any other principle, than its being more conformable to right reason and equity, by the eternal rules of which, God has manifested it to be his will, that is rational creatures be governed."

"Right smart man, Samuel Sherwood. He wrote this sermon, Scriptural Instructions to Civil Rulers, in 1774 in New Haven, Connecticut. You understand what this part means, gentlemen?"

"I do," Ben replied, as I shook my head in agreement. "It means God is the only sovereign ruler, that His government is fixed, just, and cannot be opposed by any other power, human or otherwise. No created being has absolute, unlimited power over another and lacks the morality to wield such power, because he is not God. The government provided by God, the laws and Commandments given to us, are superior and above all other man-made laws and ordinances. God remains the sovereign ruler of this world, no matter how many times man has tried to make it otherwise. Daniel, what do ye think?"

"I agree, but I also think Reverend Sherwood says that because we were originally made to be free within the bounds of God's law, that He also desires that we form a governed rational society based on His law, to look after our own happiness and good."

"You are both right. You must have listened to your teachers. My students had a little bit of trouble with this high language, but we did manage to get through it, eventually. Now for the second part."

"Ye're a teacher?"

"Yes Daniel, I have been for the better part of twenty years. I believe it is my duty to serve this cause. For the first time in the history of man, we are fighting to create a new kind of government, free from the whims of an individual. Now for the second part.:

"*As societies and communities have their beginning and origin in voluntary compact and agreement; when persons have entered by consent and free choice, into society, they must acknowledge themselves under strict and sacred obligations to act toward one another agreeable to the laws and constitution of that society whereof they are members. There are certain duties required of rulers, as well as of subjects; and their obligations faithfully and punctually to fulfil them, rise in proportion to the dignity and importance of their high and elevated stations; and the effect and influence which their conduct has on the rest of the body.*

"*Subjects have rights, privileges, and properties; and are countenanced and supported by the law of nature, the laws of society, and the law of God; in demanding full protection in the enjoyment of these rights, and the impartial distribution of justice, from their rulers. And when rulers refuse these, and will not comply with such a reasonable and equitable demand from the subjects; the society is dissolved; and its fundamental laws violated and broken; and the relation between the ruler and the subject ceases, with all the duties and obligations that arose from it.*"

"What do you think, Ben, Daniel?"

"I think what he is saying, is that when the governed society finds that their rights, privileges and property, given to them by nature, and the laws of that society based in the laws of God, are consistently violated by those that govern, that any relationship between the governed and the government ceases," Ben answered.

"Yes, you are correct. Elisha Williams of Boston in 1744 said this—it is only part of the whole essay:

"*For which purpose God was pleased to make a grant of the earth in common to the children of men, first to Adam and afterwards to Noah and his sons: as the Psalmist says in Psalms, Chapter one hundred fifteen, verse sixteen.*

"*And altho' no one has originally a private dominion exclusive of the rest of mankind in the earth or its products, as they are consider'd in this their natural state; yet since God has given these things for the use of men and given them reason also to make use thereof to the best advantage of life; there must of necessity be a means to appropriate them some way or other, before they can be of any use to any particular person.*

"*And every man having a property in his own person, the labour of his body and the work of his hands are properly his own, to which no one has right but himself; it will therefore follow that when he removes any thing out of the state that nature has provided and left it in, he has mixed his labour with it and joined something to it that is his own, and thereby makes it his property.*

"*He having removed it out of the common state nature placed it in, it hath by this labour something annexed to it that excludes the common right of others; because this labour being the unquestionable property of the labourer, no man but he can have a right to what that is once joined to, at least where there is enough and as good left in common for others.*

"*Thus every man having a natural right to (or being the proprietor of) his own person and his own actions and labour and to what he can honestly* acquire by his labour, which we call property; it certainly follows, that no man can have a right to the person or property of another: And if every man has a right to his person and property; he has also a right to defend them, and a right to all the necessary means of defence, and so has a right of punishing all insults upon his person and property.

" Hence then the fountain and original of all civil power is from the people, and is certainly instituted for their sakes; or in other words, which was the second thing proposed, The great end of civil government, is the preservation of their persons, their liberties and estates, or their property. Most certain it is, that it must be for their own sakes, the rendering their condition better than it was in what is called a state of nature (a state without such establish'd laws as before mentioned, or without any common power) that men would willingly put themselves out of that state.

" That and that only can then be the true reason of their uniting together in some form or other they judge best for the obtaining that greater security. That greater security therefore of life, liberty, money, lands, houses, family, and the like, which may be all comprehended under that of person and property, is the sole end of all civil government."

"This sounds so much like the Declaration of Independence: *Life, Liberty and the Pursuit of Happiness.*"

"Doesn't it though, Daniel," Master Van Wert replied with a smile in his eyes as he re-adjusted his neck scarf over his nose and cheeks in the attempt to keep them warm. "Civil government is supposed to protect these things. The government of the King George has not done well in this area."

"No, he hasn't. Daniel and I are fourth generation Americans, Master Van Wert. Our family, for all those generations, has not had the protection of the King in all that time. He took little interest in us, and we got along just fine without him. We followed God's laws as best we could, found ourselves in a bit of trouble every now and then, but survived in this wilderness on our own, with nothing but our Christian faith, the strength of our minds, and hands. We are in no need of a government other than what is provided by God and our community."

"Ben, why then after all this time has he imposed his government and his soldiers on us, forcing us to feed and house those soldiers, restrict our trade and pay his unjust taxes? It is simple, he needs to pay for all the British wars of this century. Wars that we had no say in because we were not allowed to be represented in Parliament.

"Not to mention all the other abuse we suffer because of his standing army. It is unjust and we have no need for a government like his.

"So, I would say that the Reverends Williams and Sherwood have the right of it: first no man is above God; and second, no man is above another. All men were created equally and born free; and third, all men are entitled to the fruits of their labor and security of their property and family. When any of those are threatened, it is right and proper to defend them. All of this has been ordained by God," Master Van Wert responded.

"Well, tat's why me and me friend here signed up," said the man next to Ben, "tay burnt us out. We had ta do someth'n. They took tha food right out of our we'ens mouths."

"Many of the men that are with us are here because the British tax us unjustly for the work of our hands. They impress our boys into their military, burn us out of our homes and farms while stealing our grain, produce, and animals; and they force us to house and feed their soldiers. Cruelty and lawlessness. This is why we put up with a lack of decent clothes, shoes, and food. We believe in the promise of our own government. "The pledge of land grants in place of pay are not worth all we suffer as part of this ragged and starved army, but the prospect of our children free from British tyranny, yes that is worth fighting for," Master Van Wert added.

"Hear, hear!" several others around us responded.

"Well then, I believe we are all agreed," Master Van Wert said with a grin as he rubbed his hands together for warmth.

"Thank ye, Master Van Wert. I needed to hear all of that again, to reset my purpose. It's just that there is much despair with the cold and the state of living in camp."

"Ben, think of the purpose and have faith. God is with us in this. I am convinced of it. Several times this army has faced impossible odds, but with divine providence, we have managed to go on and not be overwhelmed by the enemy."

"I will do my best, sir. Thank ye.

"Daniel?"

"*Ja?*"

"Are ye sure ye want to do this?"

"*Ja.* I do."

"Ye must do what they say, all the time and not make a fuss. Can ye do that?"

"I do it now, big brother. There's not been a fuss I made that has come back to haunt ye, has there?"

"No, that's true. Once this is done, it's done and there's no going back, ye hear? Disobeying orders is mutiny. That'll have ye hung quick."

"I'll be all right, Ben. I know how to behave myself.

"Oh, I've heard that one before!" he said as he punched me in the arm.

"Ouuuuuch! What ye do that for?"

"For lying, I know how ye are," Ben said, smirking at me.

"I just need some practice, that's all."

"Ye'll get it, that's for sure, or they'll make ye."

Bottle Hill Tavern

By early afternoon, the sledges all came to rest in a place called Bottle Hill. It was a rather small village with several dark brown clapboard buildings, all of which looked as if they dropped out of the sky and slid perfectly, right into large piles of snow. Every building was buried to the first-floor windows, and the snow was still higher around the south and west sides of some of the homes. Grand swirls of frost covered most of the windows, spinning out to the jambs where thick ice would be until the first warm day in spring, and smoke poured out from the chimneys in vain to keep the residents warm.

Bottle Hill was familiar territory to the Continental army. Master Van Wert had said that "Mad" Anthony Wayne had stayed in the little town at Sayer's house and Colonel Ogden at the Millers around the winter of 1777. He pointed them out to us as we slid past the homes to the town center where the tavern was. He said that the foot soldiers had stayed at the Loantaka encampment nearby.

Once stopped, we disentangled ourselves and left the sleds in a flurry. We hoped to stay here the night if we could find a barn to sleep in. The other men were to continue their journey on to a camp in Springfield and were allowed only a few moments to get their blood flowing, relieve themselves, buy food, and drink at the tavern, if they had any coin. Many would go hungry and thirsty this night unless vittles were available when they arrived in the encampment.

We said our goodbyes to Master Van Wert and sent our prayers with him and all the good men of Hazen's regiment, then walked to the far end of the main street to stay warm as we waited for the tavern to empty and the last sledge of men to leave town.

The tavern tap room was overly warm with the smell of wood smoke, sweat, unwashed bodies, and the very welcoming aroma of beef stew. Ben ordered the stew and biscuits, and added two pints of the local brew to our bill. Carrying the pints, we grabbed a table near the hearth fire to warm ourselves and waited for our food with our bellies grumbling impatiently.

"Hmmm, that smells absolutely delicious," Ben said to the tavern maid as she laid full bowls of the stew and butter dripping biscuits before us.

"Tastes even better, gentlemen. Oh, the man in the corner, over there, paid for yer drinks. Ye might want to thank him," she responded.

We turned to look and, sitting in a corner, was Corporal John Johnson. We raised our glasses and nodded to him, thanking him for the gift of the beer.

"He must have come in after us. I didn't see him when we first came in. Slow down, little brother, don't inhale the stew, savor it. We may not see the likes of this until Papa finds us and even then, we might not 'cause of the cost of everything is so high."

"I'm sorry. I was just so hungry, and this is better than anything we've had in a very long time. Thank ye."

"Welcome. Just enjoy it, slowly. Did ye talk to Reverend Caldwell about signing up? I saw ye standing off in the corner a bit with him at the service last Sunday."

"*Ja*, I did. He pretty much told me the same thing that Master Van Wert said, or rather what the other two ministers, Williams and Sherwood, said. He did think I was a bit young to enlist, but said the same thing as the other officers – it's just not safe to go back."

"Ye know, it is likely ye won't even be assigned to my regiment. Are ye all right with that too?"

"I will have to be. Think we'll see each other at all?"

"*Ja*, there will be a time and place. I'll see to it little brother. Ye'll still be in the Jersey Brigade, that won't change. Ye already know Colonel Shreve and my Colonel Spencer.

"Look," Ben said under his breath. "Promise me one thing though, if this all turns for the worse, like we are overrun by the British and I can't get to ye immediately, strip everything off ye that makes ye a look like a rebel and head back to the Scotch Plains campsite. Wait for two nights. If I've not come by the afternoon of the third day, head back to Peter's farm, the way ye came and I'll catch ye up."

"Ye think it will come to that?" I whispered back.

"No. I pray not, but I've a feeling that there's a real rough spell coming. We just must be prepared for all things. When I get time and the weather's good, we'll practice running with the musket, turning, and taking aim. Ye need to keep up with yer loading skills too, even if the plan is to keep ye from battle."

"Gentlemen, we have some apple pie, if ye'd like some?"

"Thank ye, no mistress," Ben replied.

"It's on the house. We've got more than we can eat or give away. Are ye sure?"

"I'd like some, if that is all right, Ma'am?"

"Well, with that toothy smile and those mischievous green eyes, how can I not bring it to ye, young man?" I'll bring ye the whole pie then, ye can share it with yer big brother here. Milk?" I nodded my head and continued to smile at her. "I'll be right back, then."

"*Ouch!* That hurt, Ben!" Ben had kicked me in the shin under the table, trying to restrain me from asking more of the mistress. We had no more money and couldn't pay for the pie or milk and Ben wasn't one who liked to take charity.

"It's not right to accept handouts when ye're able bodied to work. Ye must learn to live within ye're means, little brother."

"But she offered."

"*Ja,* she did. She was being kind and generous. We look a little worse for the wear and maybe a bit like we're starving. I guess we are sort of starving, but we're not nearly as much as some others. Maybe some hungry child in town could use that pie instead of us."

"Oh, I'd not thought of that, but surely she wouldn't have offered it if she knew a child needed some food and this was all she could offer?"

"I wouldn't think so, but ye never can tell, can ye? Sometimes folks do things for others in the hopes of gaining a benefit for themselves in doing the kind act, but I don't think this is the case with the lady. Anyway, it is embarrassing, but it's done now. Here she comes."

"Let's see, one warm apple pie fresh from the oven, two plates, forks and two mugs of milk. Keep yourselves safe out there. We've heard stories from neighboring towns about combined British and Tory raids on townspeople and farmers alike. Do take care, boys."

"We will do our best, ma'am; and thank ye very kindly for everything. The pie smells so much like home, cinnamon, sugar molasses and apples," Ben said as he breathed in the aroma. He was right, it did, and it brought a rush of good memories. "Our Mama would make the pies for us early in the morning and we'd have to wait until dinner for a slice."

"I bet the wait was well worth it."

"It was. Thank ye again, ma'am."

"Ye are most welcome," she said as she left the table.

"Ready for me to cut the first slice, Daniel?"

"*Ja,* Ben, but how 'bout we take the pie over to Corporal Johnson and share it with him? He's just sitting by his lonesome reading."

"Ye sure ye're ready to do that? Ye know he's gonna ask ye to sign."

"*Ja,* I am ready, I think.

"Grab the milk then. I got the pie."

"I was wondering if you were going to stroll on over here, gentlemen," Corporal Johnson said as he stood in greeting us. "Glad you both got out of camp for a bit. Are you ready to sign papers and swear in, Daniel?"

"Not before pie, sir. Thought we'd share some with ye, if ye like apple pie, that is. The mistress gave us the whole thing."

"Absolutely not before pie, Daniel. Sort of your last real supper - aye?" he asked with a crack of smile, fully knowing the truth of it.

"There is no doubt. The military is not the best place to count on to get a meal and, least of all, a decent one," I replied with a smirk.

"I'll take that slice there, Daniel. It is mighty kind of you and your brother to share it. When I was your age, I'm not so sure I would. Thank you both," he said as he raised his cup for the mistress to come with more acorn coffee. "It sure would be nice to have real coffee or tea to wash down the pie, but there is none to be had in town. Hmmm, that is good," he said as he stuffed his fork full of crusted apples dripping with cinnamon sugar sauce into his mouth.

"So ye'll still be able to work with me on the fife, sir? I mean, ye said playing the fife would be one of my duties."

"Yes, I will teach you the commands for the battlefield. I've heard you play reveille - nothing really to be taught there and you will continue to play for the camp. It was decided the other day that you would remain with the Jersey Brigade. That's where they need you most. You'll also be expected to help with the sick and run errands for the officers, as you have been. You'll train like every other soldier by learning the steps, marches, and movements on the field, how to load, and shoot while on the run, and . . ." he said as noticed the frown on my face and stopped. "I take it you know something about shooting, Daniel?."

"He does. I've been working with him a bit. Daniel's got the rhythm, just needs to work at speed," Ben replied for me.

"That'll make things easier. Just need practice then. Did Ben show you how to clean the gun?"

"Yes, I can tear it down, clean it, and put it back together. Learned long ago how to do that."

"All right then. But your main duties will be to learn the fife signals for the battlefield, since you are already familiar with regimental music," he said as he lifted his fork with more pie.

The mistress came and poured the coffee into his cup, and all was quiet while we ate our pie and sipped on milk and coffee. I turned my head to the window to gage the time and weather. The sun had disappeared behind thick clouds, making the late afternoon much darker outside than it was this morning. I hoped that wasn't a sign of more snow. Snow would make a tougher walk back to Eyer's Forge, which we would do if we couldn't find a barn to sleep in. I was gonna miss the tavern hearth and fire for sure.

"Your milk's about to run out. Want more? I'll buy," Corporal Johnson said as he got the tavern mistress's attention by waving his hand. "What'll you have Daniel, Ben?"

"Coffee with a bit of sugar if ye have it and cream?" Ben responded. "Ye want the same Daniel?"

"Sure."

"I think we might have some left, corporal," she responded with a smile and made her way back to the kitchen.

"You read, don't you, Daniel?" Corporal Johnson asked. He pulled his old leather satchel out from under his chair and pulled out a bunch of paper.

"I do, sir."

"Ah, here they are. The enlistment papers. Take time and read it while you're finishing your pie. Don't be afraid to ask questions. This is serious business we're talking here, son."

"Yes, sir." I read through the short document and was done by the time the mistress came back with the coffee.

"So, what does it say? I want to make sure you know what all you're getting into and all of that."

"It says that my life belongs to the Continental army for the next three years or so. That they'll feed me and clothe me, for the time during. Little luck with that, though, from what I've seen."

"That's true. If we win this war, there is a promise of land, one hundred acres to each soldier."

"Where is this land, and how did we come by it?"

"There were treaties made with the Indians long ago and we continue to make treaties with them for more. There's land in western Pennsylvania, Virginia and near the Ohio River."

"Hmmm. That may not bode well." At this point, Ben kicked my shin under the table again and glared at me over his cup of acorn coffee. "I'm not much of a farmer, anyway".

"That may be so, but the hundred acres will be there if you want it."

"All right. How much will I earn each month?"

"Well, there's the two hundred dollar starting bonus," Corporal Johnson said as he scooped another bite of pie with his fork. "You'll receive six dollars a month that you can collect as pay, but know that the paymaster is slow to pay because Congress is slow to fund it. What do you think, Daniel? Do you want to sign your name?"

I looked at Ben one last time before I wrote my name on the paper. He shrugged and then turned his head to the window to watch the snow fall in earnest.

"All right then," I whispered, and reached out for quill and ink that had been waiting for me. Ben then turned from the window and made his mark next to my name. It was done.

"Daniel, please stand, raise your right hand and say these words after me:"

"*I, Daniel Applegate, do acknowledge the United States of America to be free, independent and sovereign states, and declare that the people thereof owe no allegiance or obedience, to George the third, king of Great*

Britain; and I renounce, refuse and abjure any allegiance or obedience to him: and I do swear (or affirm) that I will, to the utmost of my power, support, maintain and defend the said United States, against the said king George the third and his heirs and successors, and his and their abettors, assistants and adherents, and will serve the said United States in the office of Private which I now hold, with fidelity, according to the best of my skill and understanding. So help me God."

"You're a soldier now Daniel, how does it feel?"

"No different from five minutes ago, but give me a year with experience and I'm sure I'll say different."

"Just how old are you?"

"I turned twelve a few months back, sir. Feels like a lifetime ago."

"I thought you were older, near Ben's age."

"I've heard that a lot recently. Guessing my height has something to do with it."

"All right, then. For now, you will report to Captain Weatherby. When you return to camp, give him this paper. I'll try to see you for a fife lesson or two next week. Keep up with the fiddle and the book learning, too."

"Yes, sir."

"Thank you, Daniel and thank you both for sharing the pie. I talked to the owner here and he has said that if there were any soldiers that needed a place to sleep for the night, that they would be welcome to stay in the barn loft behind the tavern at no charge. There should be a sled back to camp in the morning around eight, I don't know if there will be another later. So unless you want to walk the distance back to camp, be on the one at eight."

Bobby

"Slowly drag the line, ye ninny or ye'll scare them!" I said under hushed breath. The ninny wasn't one, but I had lost my patience. Time was running away too fast; the sun had climbed above the horizon, turning the light ground frost into sparkling water droplets and with the warmth of the sun, a swirling ethereal mist arose on the meadow behind us that competed with the river mist in front of us. All was a place of ghosts and magic. It was about six o'clock and I would need to be back at camp soon to work in the infirmary.

Bobby and I left before dawn to fish, and he had yet to get the knack of it. He could shoot game well enough, but fishing was beyond his abilities for some reason. That was all right. I had already caught enough for him and the men of my mess, but I thought it best to work with Bobby, so he would have an alternative should a gun not be at hand.

"I think I got one," he said, whispering, not looking at me but watching the line bob as the fish tugged on it.

"I think ye do. That's it, slowly draw it to ye. 'Member, don't move anything else but yer arms and do that slowly. There, ye got him, quick now tug him out and grab him! There he is! Hurry, throw him in the bucket, 'fore he slips out of yer hands."

"Sun's up. We gotta go, don't we?"

"*Ja,* I do and fast. I'll get these fried up at the hut, we'll eat, and then I need to be off to help Dr. Campfield with the sick. Ye can go with me if ye like. We can always use one more person. Be good for ye to see the dark side of the army. Maybe it'll knock some sense into ye about staying,"

I said as purposefully bumped into him to emphasize the point.

"Ye're here, aren't ye, to help? That's all I want to do."

"Yes, but that was not my intention. I left my home because of being beaten by the factor that worked there. I came looking for my father and brother because I knew I would be safe with them. Living on my own was no longer a choice after all I went through to get here. If Papa had come before I enlisted, I would not be here now.

"My oath to the United States and the Continental army cannot be broken unless I die. I have no plans of dying anytime soon so, I am with the New Jersey Brigade for this year and the next two.

"Do ye really want to give up three years of yer life for little pay and no food for a good portion of those years? I mean, I understand ye want to help, but running from a loving family that can feed ye and keep ye in clothes and shoes is running in the wrong direction. Ye need to go back home, help with the spring planting. "This is no place to be. Ben and the other men believe there will be a real battle here soon, mebbe, when it gets closer to summer. With the British so close across the Hudson, everyone's just itching to pick a fight and it's getting worse.

"In January, Tories took it upon themselves to abduct Master Hedden in Newark, after bayoneting his wife and leaving her to die in her bed. He was fever sick and could do little to stop them and save her. The Loyalists walked him barefoot, dressed in his nightshirt in the frigid cold across the Hudson River. It was solid ice then. They left him at the Sugar House. We've not heard from him since. He's likely missing some feet by now, if he survived it at all.

"On the same night in Elizabeth Town, other Tories took exception to the Presbyterian meeting house, burning it to the ground. The firing of the church was a message to our own Reverend Caldwell. It was his church. Anyway, I could be talking to ye about this for days. There have been many, many acts of violence against Patriots since I got here in January. Ye do remember Reverend Caldwell from last week?"

"I do. He came in with a bunch of men, went to the lectern, put his Bible on it and then took his two pistols and sat one on either side of the Bible. Never thought I'd see a man of God carry guns."

"The Loyalists call him the 'rebel high priest' because he preaches against the king and talks of freedom for the colonies, encouraging folks to fight for our independence. Just like General Washington, there's a price on his head, dead or alive. Those men with him are his bodyguard, assigned to that duty by the general, I heard.

"Then there are Patriot refugees from New York and Long Island roaming throughout New Jersey. They've lost their homes and livelihoods to the British. They are unpredictable and retaliate against anyone they believe is in their way. Since I've been here, they've attacked Tories, destroying their lives and property, something not appreciated by us much. They've not been all that friendly directly with the Continental army either.

"This is like no game I've ever played before; I don't know who the enemy is, often enough," I said as I came to an abrupt stop, setting down the bucket and opened my fingers slowly to uncramp them. I looked at him, expecting some sort of retort, but he was deep in thought. I had hoped that he was taking what I said to heart. The boy was thirteen, a year older than me. He should understand. Ah well, ye can lead a horse to water, but it is up to him to drink.

"Want me to carry the bucket for a while, Daniel?"

"*Ja,* sure. It is just a bit heavy. Thank ye." He picked up the fish bucket and started to walk ahead of me. "Give me a minute. I want to dump this water out of my boot." Cold water from the pond and the dew on the grass had been pulled in through the holes on the sides of my boots. "I thought I could go on without doing it, but I can't. Papa better come soon, or I'll be walking bare foot before long."

"Ye know, ye needn't get caught up in this Bobby, ye have both parents, younger brothers, and sisters. Be with them. Go home, live yer life. I'd leave if I'd the choice," I said as I poured a trickle of water from the boot.

"All right, I'll give it some thought. I promise."

Something Lost is Found

"**W**ho goes there?" one of the two sentries standing on the road inquired of the teamster as they both pointed their guns at him while he slowed his horses upon entering the crossroads.

"Richard Applegate, gentlemen," he replied as he brought the horses to a stop, leaving the reins drop on the bench beside him. Richard unbuttoned his coat at the waist and kept his hands on his knees. "I have supplies for the quartermaster general and the commissary." His rifle was primed and was sitting on the floor, just behind his feet, and his hunting knife lay securely tied to his calf. The primed pistols on his hips were still hidden under his coat and were readily available if he needed them. The next few moments would see him robbed and in a battle for his life or sent on his way with an escort to Morristown.

He knew he had been followed at a distance from the woods the last mile by two additional not so quiet men in shabby, worn-out clothes. Now, they were on the road directly behind him. That made a total of four men guarding the crossroads, but he scanned the woods for more that he might have missed, anyway. He could easily handle the four, but really hoped he would not have to.

"What's under the tarp?" the same disheveled sentry asked, walking around to the back of the wagon and using the barrel of his musket to lift the heavy canvas covering the bed. "Do I smell jerky and dried fish? I guess fish is better than nutt'n. We're gonna have ta lighten yer load a bit, Master Applegate," he said as smirked and nodded his head at the other sentry standing on Richard's left who then raised his rifle at Richard. The other two men from behind sauntered up and stood on the right side of the wagon. The taller of the two followed suit with his compatriot, and raised his musket too.

"Who ye got there, Nate?" asked the shorter man on Richard's right. He at least had the decency not to raise his musket. Nate, his musket now slung over his shoulder, was the man who made himself busy rustling through the goods in the back of the wagon. "His name's Richard, Richard Applegate, John," he replied, holding up a small box and turning it and shaking it.

"Barney, relax, put yer musket down and yer's too George, and Nate put the box back," John requested. "If Master Applegate wanted to leave, he could've run right over ye while shooting his way out before ye knew what had happened. He's got his hand on one of his pistols, probably aimed right at ye, ye old fool. He knew a mile back we were tracking him and never made a move to stop us.

"What's yer business here, sir?" John asked, lifting his chin in a challenge.

"Well, John," Richard said as he removed his hands from his knees and reached for the handhold to step down from the wagon. The muskets came back up to their former positions and Richard raised his empty hands, leaving the pistols quite visible under his coat. It seemed that John might not have things in hand after all, and he waited to see what the group of them were going to do next.

"Gawd, he's a bigg'un, ye think 'e's as big as tha general?" Barney asked no one in particular. "Look'n like he'd be a brother, or at least a cousin. What ye think?" Barney said as he turned to his cohorts.

"Well, yer never gonna find out are ye, ye big lout, unless ye put yer muskets down. All of ye do it. *Do it now!*"

It was quiet for a few seconds, only the sound of the cool spring wind could be heard. Its freshness turned sour though, as it now carried the scent of long unwashed men with it.

"All right, all right John. None of us have tha will ta fight that behemoth. Are ye related to General Washington, sur? Really, ye do look like 'im a bit," George asked, eyeing him up and down.

Richard lowered his hands and made to come down to the ground. "No, George, can't say that I am. Just tall, that's all, and my hair is nearly the same color as his. I've met our general in passing a couple of times. He's a friendly fellow and I am no less the same," Richard replied as he walked to the back of the wagon. "Come, I'll show ye what's in the wagon. We'll get some of that jerky for ye and yer friends. Looks like ye all might be a bit hungry." They were nothing but skin and bones dressed in rags, all four of them, caused by the hard winter and the machinations of politics. All were signs that war effort could be trouble just because of the lack of food and proper clothing. He prayed again that Benjamin had fared better, and that Daniel was with him.

"Where'd all this come from, Master Applegate?" asked John.

"Hopefully, supplies will be more regular with the weather breaking a bit. It can't be winter forever, can it?" Richard replied with a smile, pulling out a canister that contained the jerky and made to open the lid. "Here, grab a handful and save some for yer knapsacks, there. Ye can thank the Maxwells of New Jersey and the Lantermans of Pennsylvania for what's in the wagon. There's milled flour, milled corn, jerky, lard, salt pork, clothes, blankets, boots, beans, and some other things."

"Ye mean, our General Maxwell?" John asked.

"Yes, that's the one. Ye know him?"

"Scotch Willie, yes sur! We'ins heard he wrote a scath'n letter to Congress about the situation 'round here. Little good it did, but he tried and I, for one, appreciate the try'n. He's a good'un," Barney said, replying for all four of them.

"Well, gentlemen, I need to be on my way. John, can ye spare one of the men to show me the way to the commissary and then on to Scotch

Willie?"

"Yes sir, we can manage that. George, ye go, because ye won't talk the poor man to his death. But ye come right back, ye here. There are enough men that go missing these days. I don't want to have to report ye gone."

"Thank ye, John. I'll pass on yer best to Scotch Willie," Richard replied, grinning from ear to ear. "He'll like to hear about it. Come on George, times a wasting and I need to be a couple of places yet before dark."

Scotch Willie—
<u>The Promise</u>

If a man makes a vow to the Lord or swears an oath to bind himself by some agreement, he shall not break his word; he shall do according to all that proceeds out of his mouth.

Mosaic Law: Numbers, Chapter 30, verse 2.

"**S**ir, I have a backwoodsman here to see ye. Says it's important. His name is Applegate, sir."

"Which one? Oh, never mind. Let him in," the general said with a hand waving in dismissal. What he was reading wasn't all that important, anyway; reports on things he could not even begin to try to control. Little good it did to write a letter to Congress about the conditions of the men. The lack of food and clothing supplies was taking a toll on the general morale of the encampment. Congress had no idea and didn't really care to listen. It was frustrating. Visitors were a welcome distraction.

Richard pulled back the patched tent flap and stuck his head inside, and wished that he had gotten there earlier in the morning. The muggy, humid air was stale with the smells of unwashed bodies, smokey dead coals from the brazier, some cooked sausage that should have been buried from the smell of it, and the effects of eating the sausage—a sour stomach, which had produced a particular bad scent of flatulence.

The general hadn't changed much since he'd last seen him. On second thought, maybe there were a few more streaks of white in that unruly coal black hair; a whole section of which refused to be locked down by the queue and thus hung over his cheek. William didn't bother to look up, he was trying to look as if he were studiously reading a dispatch, But Richard knew better and played the game his way. Completely violating military propriety, he busied himself by tying back the tent flaps to let in as much fresh air as could be found from outside. "Uh, umm, ye know, *general,* ye really should allow yer aide to do things for ye, like tidy up a bit?"

"Who the hell are ye, that yer telling me what to do, sir?" the general asked as he leveled his dark blue eyes at Richard. "Richard? Richard? Is that ye?" Ye're, ye're alive!" he said as he pushed himself out of the chair with such force that it fell over while rushing to pull Richard in a rough bear hug complete with an open hand pummel on the back. "Yer not dead, I, we, the boys, thought we lost ye. Damn good to see ye!"

"Not dead yet, by the good Lord's grace, my friend. Ye said the boys? My sons?"

"They are both here, safe. For the moment anyway."

"Oh, thank God!" Leaving all other protocol at the tent entrance, Richard strode over to a chair at the general's table and dropped into it like a thick cooked German egg noodle that had lost all its rigidness in boiling water and was dumped into a dry bowl. All the worry that he had carried with him for so long was gone. "Do ye have a couple of glasses?" He asked as he pulled his satchel off his shoulder and pulled out a flask.

"Is that what I think it is?" the general questioned as he passed the water rinsed glasses to Richard.

"It is, and it is ten times better than what ye've been drinking from the smell of the swill ye just rinsed out of those glasses."

"Ah, well, we can't be choosy, Richard. Supplies are hard to come by, ye know. Oh, that is good. Yer's?"

"Yes, the whiskey was not aged as long as it should have been. It's only eight years old. I brought it with me as a sample for trading; but I've not found anything worth trading my barrels for. Seems like the perfect time to share a bit of it though," he said with a smile and raising his glass.

"The boys, how are they? I heard Benjamin was with the Sullivan Expedition. There was a fierce battle last summer, was there not?"

"Ben is fine, and he did well at Newtown. He may be a bit hungry and raggedy at this point; but then we all are. He is in one piece like most of us, and he's not one to talk about the battle. He's done good in caring for Daniel. Ye'll be proud of him."

"And, Daniel, how's he doing?"

"Ye did well training up yer boys, Richard. Daniel, he's holding his own with this lot of ruffians. He continues his schooling for an hour or two each day. We made sure of that. The boy plays his fife like no other for the troops. He even has learned the battle signals to get our boys to move from one side of the field to the other. He helps the doctors with the sick, builds latrines, and otherwise he runs errands for our officers inside the camp. We won't let him outside of it."

"Now that's wise. That rascal does have a way of taking off when ye don't want him to."

"Ye know, he said he walked eighty miles to find us, to find ye. Unbelievable!" the general replied, sipping the last of the whiskey in his glass and then poured himself and Richard another.

"It's no lie, William. He likely came straight from Aletta's to here wherever here was at the time."

"Scotch Plains, it was Scotch Plains. Eighty miles then. He left at the right time, for sure. Made it just before the first heavy snow in November. Brave lad. He can tell ye all about it when he sees ye."

"At this point, I am of a mind to be tanning that hide for leaving in the first place. He knows better. Thank ye, William, for taking him, keeping him." Richard said as he raised his glass again, this time in salute to his friend.

"Well, don't thank me too soon. Ye see, we thought ye were dead—all of us. Ye were late even before the storms occurred in November and then the ones in December. No one, but ye could've made it through and ye didn't.

"There's been increasing tussles between us and the British pawns lately and, if not the pawns, the British themselves. Then there's, the refugees and Indians all running amuck on roads and through the forests. All of their activities are leading to battle, and it will happen soon.

"We couldn't send him back home because of the combatants or the weather. We waited and we just couldn't wait anymore. Ben needed to be free to move with Spencer's Regiment and, as ye can imagine, keeping an eye on Daniel was not an easy task for him."

Richard held his glass in mid-air and held the general's eyes in a fierce look of his own. "Tell me you didn't."

"I did. I saw no other alternative, Richard."

"Yes, but enlisting him, William? He's only twelve years old."

"He is, and he's proved himself to have a cool head and strong wit with the men many times over. Something I would expect from someone much older and, as such, the men don't see a twelve-year-old child, but a young man. Settled some arguments he has, and not with his fists. He's exceeded in every task we set before him, totally unexpected. I think ye'll find that he's grown quite a bit.

"I put him with Israel, in the Second. His studies have continued under Israel, mostly, but Captain Weatherby—Ben's captain under Colonel Spencer—has been there as well. Corporal Johnson has taken him on as a student for the fife. He's earned his pay. He's good with that fife, lightens the mood around here and the Lord knows we need it. He has been a blessing. Oh, and he's got a fiddle too, not bad on it either.

"He's made a new friend, one near his age. He's another runaway, brought his own drum and everything. Thought he would make the Rhode Island regiment his home since he's from there. He came, he says, to serve in whatever way he might. Robert is his name. His parents live on a prosperous farm there. The regiment's colonel is in the process of finding a way to send him back to his family; he received a letter from his mother not too long ago. I hope they do it soon, before things heat up. He and Daniel are the best of friends and have become the wandering minstrels in the camp."

"So why take on Daniel, if yer' so opposed to the other boy being here, William? It makes no sense. Ye should've sent him home."

"No, I could not; not in good conscience, that is. I knew ye were out on our business to bring supplies and information to us. When ye didn't come, like I said, we'd no alternative but bind him to us.

"Ye weren't here to see the scars on his back, bumps, bruises and the beating his face took. I was. We found out about the broken ribs when Dr. Campfield looked at him. There's a line that should not be crossed when whooping a child. The people that did this went far beyond that line. He told us that a Master Boer and some Mohawk all had a hand in the beatings over a couple of days."

Richard was quiet for a time, staring at the back of the tent, organizing his thoughts. Both anger and remorse were tangled in his emotions. He should have been there for Daniel instead of wandering around the country, buying and selling goods and sometimes playing spy for this fledgling government. If he had, this whole mess would never have happened. This was his fault; and he knew it. He shouldn't have left him in the hands of Aletta and Boer without Peter there.

"This is my fault."

"Ye didn't pound Daniel and break his ribs."

"No, I did not. Now that I look back, there were signs, and he tried to tell me about Boer. I just thought he was just being overly dramatic when he told me. I dismissed his stories and took Boer's side. That is how it is my fault. Boer is Peter and Aletta's factor. Aletta told me Daniel ran the night of the harvest supper and offered me no other information."

"Well, when ye get back, ye might want to personally see that *'gentleman'* off their farm."

"I'll do more than see him off the farm," he said as he wiped the sweat from his brow with the kerchief he carried. "Is there any chance of getting Daniel out from under this?"

"I don't know how too, to tell ye the truth. He signed the papers and understood completely what they were about, Corporal Johnson made sure of that. Ben signed them as well. He had to since he was next of kin. Might be best to talk to Daniel first to see what he's about at this point. If he wants out, I'll see what I can do.

"General Washington and Lord Stirling are sticklers about discipline in matters of commitments, though. If they let Daniel go, there might be issues with the other rank and file. Allowing one man as they see him to leave because his father has shown up would be difficult for us. I'll do my best if ye come back to me to tell me he wants out, but I can't guarantee the outcome."

"I hear ye. All right then; I'll sort it out, but first I think I'll see Benjamin. One more dram, before I go?" Richard responded while pouring out the golden liquid for himself. It was the equivalent of gold and maybe worth more than the same weight as the metal itself. It was money well spent, he figured, as a thank you for watching out for his sons, namely Daniel.

"Just a dram, and no more. Don't want to be accused of not being able to perform my office by reason of drunkenness again."

"Politics, William. I've not seen ye drunk in some time and when I did, ye were at home, having a bit of fun like the rest of us," Richard smiled as he spoke. "What of other news?"

"*Morris?*" the general hollered abruptly to the man outside the tent flap. Morris, a tall and gangly red-headed boy complete with a good set of freckles, stuck his head inside. "Sir?"

"Grab that teapot, Morris, and get some fresh water for my tea. Thank ye."

"But, sir, I was told to stay, to guar—to make sure no one enters the tent without yer permission."

"Richard, do ye think anyone is going to enter this tent without my permission?"

"Ah, no sir, General. I'll keep ye safe if I must while Morris is gone, sir," Richard responded with a great, toothy grin.

"Well, the last time ye said that, we both got a little bruised for it. I'll take my chances, anyway. *Go, Morris.*"

"Sir? Yes, *sir.*" With that, Morris moved out of the tent as if his back side were on fire.

"We have about ten minutes without being overheard. Keep an eye on the entryway."

"I will. So, tell me."

"Do ye know we have Hessians breathing down our neck, just across from the Hudson? They are ready to move at any time, and they are likely to take us. My brigade is down to about a thousand men, due to discharges, deserters, and lack of recruits.

"Continental enlistments are way down. The incentives of money and land are no longer an enticement. We can't get the men to sign on. The Continental coin is worthless; ye have to take a basket of money to buy a loaf of bread. Land is promised, but who knows if ye'll survive the war to work it.

"Given the lack of follow-through with the state legislatures and Congress, it is no wonder we can't get the men. They lack food, pay, clothing, and shoes. Mutiny and desertion are no longer rumors; they are facts.

"A few of the deserters have been caught and returned, those not getting a reprieve from General Washington meet the noose with resolve and bravery; for the most part. Hanging, though, is an ugly thing. Men were chosen from the officers and the rank and file to watch the hangings to make them think twice about leaving without permission. Military discipline is a cruel master.

"If anything happens, we're going to have to rely on the militia.

Time and again, we've all seen them break ranks and run. There's not much we can do about it, that's for sure. Ye know just how much training they get—ye participated in a militia out of Northampton, right?"

"I did. There is no real training, but the men know how to hunt, and the officers expect that the skills from hunting easily transfer to shooting in a battle. They are good shots, but when faced with an organized army with bayonets fixed and cannons firing, all bets are off."

"Aye, that's what I've seen. We might have 3,000 men between all the regiments and the militia. It's not enough. The Hessians are supported by British troops, which include Queen's Rangers and Skinner's Greens. We've had estimates of up to 15,000 British in the near vicinity—not here just yet, but they may come. We're outnumbered, out trained, and outgunned," the general replied before he swallowed the last sip of his whiskey and slammed to glass against his table, then reached around for a fan to cool himself. The temperature in the tent had risen considerably in the last hour. It was going to be a sweltering day for sure. William turned back to Richard only to find him deep in thought and decided to let him be for a moment. This war was never a game, and the chances of the boys' survival would drop, even if a fraction of the Hessians and their supporters came across the Hudson.

Richard raised his glass to his lips and held it there, looking at the back wall of the tent, listening beyond it. The camp was busy with the stuff of military life; shouts from the sergeants trying to keep men in formation, drums beating, horses baying and, of all things, singing and a bit of laughter. His sons were here in this, and likely soon to battle. He had thought of this moment often enough, shelving his feelings about it, but he couldn't this time; the reality of it was clear.

"Will, I've raised my sons in constant danger. How could I not in the backwoods? Between living in the wild and trying to tame it, unfriendly Indians, and poor decisions about either of those or anything else could easily result in death, but war is entirely different. War is intentional, and the result leaves lots of dead and maimed men, all for the desire of material goods or land.

"Yet sir, this war with the British isn't about land or wealth, it's about freedom, freedom to follow your heart, provide for your family and their security without the fear of it being taken by the whim of a king and his government thousands of miles away. The only way to *pursue this happiness* is the willingness to risk it all. Benjamin understands, and I think Daniel does as well. The odds of going through this Revolution unscathed have always been grim, my friend.

"Both of my sons know the meaning of an oath, a bond; I had made sure of that, by holding them accountable when they were old enough to understand. They are mindful that an oath—of any kind—is as sure as black iron shackles made to fit the wrists, holding the vow maker prisoner until the completion of the promise. They are men in this, regardless of their age. To go back on their word now would shame them for the rest of their lives. I cannot and will not have that. To do so would make those shackles become the noose around their necks, killing who they are truly meant to be. Shame has a way of making a man feel uncertain and worthless. These, in this life, will find ye dead quick." Richard threw back the last bit of the whiskey and turned his eyes back on William.

"Aye, Richard. I feel no less anxiety than ye do. I will do everything in within my power for Daniel and Benjamin, all the sons, brothers, and fathers here; ye know that."

"I do, Will. What can I do? Can I come back and fight with the line, but not enlist?"

"Aye, I don't think anyone in their right mind will turn ye down if ye want to add yerself to the line. If the battle comes, yer a rifleman. I'd give it a few weeks, early summer maybe, so don't take too long to return to us.

"Go see to yer boys. It will give me time to find out if we can release Daniel—mind ye, I don't think we can."

"No, Will, don't bother. I stand by what I just said. I'd like to help keep them safe. If I can, getting on the line will allow that opportunity. Is there anything else I might do to help?"

"Talk to folks in yer travels back and forth. Mind ye don't say much of what I told ye. Let them know a fight is coming, and let them know the truth as ye see it. Maybe we'll get more men than we expect when General Washington calls for the militias."

"I can do that. Anything else?"

"No, not that I can think of for now. Let's see, Benjamin is encamped on the northwest side of Elizabeth Town with Colonels Dayton and Spencer. Benjamin as I said is in Captain Weatherby's company and Daniel's entrusted to Colonel Shreve at the moment, but he's likely to be running from one mess to another playing that fife or maybe his fiddle. Just follow the music. If ye hear nothing and can't find Shreve, then locate Oliver Cromwell, under Captain Bowman with Shreve's regiment—folks will know who he is. Oliver usually keeps an eye on Daniel when Ben in is not the vicinity. He'll likely know where he's at and what he's up to."

"All right. What about this fiddle?"

"Aye, Captain Weatherby had been carrying it everywhere with him. It belonged to a childhood friend that had died some time ago in one of the battles, I think. Anyway, Daniel's put it to good use—he's not too bad either. He does manage to skreetch it every-once-in-a-while though, enough to make yer ears hurt a bit."

"Well, let's hope he doesn't get that nervous about it when he sees me. That sort of thing is truly sore on the ears," Richard laughed as he riffled through his satchel. "Oh, here's the rest of the whiskey. Make it last, general. I'll have more in a few weeks when I return. Hopefully, I'll have some food and clothing for the commissary, too."

"Those are most needed, although that could be said for the whiskey, given the times. Safe travels, my friend."

"Thank ye, Will. Yer servant, general," Richard said as he bowed deeply and left William Maxwell standing alone in his patched tent.

Music

"It goes like this: tat, tat, ta, tat, tat," I said to Bobby, slapping my hands together to show the rhythm of a song we were preparing for the camp. "Ye got it?"

"*Ja,* think so. Let me tap it out for a bit here, Daniel."

"All right." I turned to my fiddle to re-tune it a bit as I looked at the innards of the camp while Bobby practiced. It was a buzz with movement, like ants at an ant hill moving every which way, trying to get chores done quickly before the real heat of the day set in. It was going to be a scorcher, I thought, and tempers would be short.

A couple of men walked past us and toward the camp carrying wooden buckets full of water, a few of those bucket would need a visit to a cooper for repairs before long. Small streams of water fell from the underside of several buckets, watering the already muddy path. What water was left was poured into a large laundry caldron warming on the fire. The laundry itself was piled into misshapen heaps on dry ground and that were getting larger as women came from around the camp bringing their dirty clothes to wash. I watched the laundresses work to keep the fire going under the caldron and simultaneously use a paddle to swirl a load of clothes in the hot water. I had wondered if the water got too dark with dirt and grime, if they'd dump the caldron, but wasn't sure exactly how they would do that without getting burned by the fire heating it.

Food was cooking too, everything from fire cakes to fried bacon and sausage. I wondered how they had gotten a hold of the bacon and sausage, but let the thought go because it did no good to think about it.

My day would be made easier if folks shared what they had with us, as they generally did most days. There had been no meat to speak of in the camp for some time. Leaving the camp to hunt alone was not safe, not because of other animal predators, but because of who you might run into in the woods. Just as well, I suppose. The nearby wood had been hunted out in January. Ye still had to go much farther into the forest to find anything.

I turned back around, waiting patiently for Bobby to finish the rhythm practice. My enlistment required me to give our audience what they wanted and needed, a respite from their circumstances and the war. Today, my only task was to bring music and song to lighten their hearts. Bobby, though still not enlisted, helped me in that cause, while the elder drummers were involved in other camp duties. If we were lucky today, we would make at least two rounds of the entire camp and get fed in between breaks.

"Ready, Bobby?"

"*Ja,* let's try it one more time, then go in."

"All right, a 1 and a 2 and a 3 and—" and we were off playing *American Taxation.* Bobby kept the rhythm tight this time and before we were done, a small crowd had gathered around us singing the last of the stanzas, out of order, of course. That didn't matter in the slightest when they shouted over one another for more music. I looked at Bobby to see if he was up to playing more; he shrugged his shoulders and smiled. I returned it, bent over, and stuffed the fiddle in the haversack, throwing it all on my back. With the fife back to my lips, we started to play again and walked back into the immediate camp confines with the crowd in tow, just like those stories of the pied piper.

We played our last song by early afternoon; the heat of an early summer's day was taking its toll on us all. We were covered in sweat and grime from walking through the camp. Most everyone else had departed for the shade of a tall maple or oak by noon—it was way too hot to do anything else. Rather than lay on a grassy hill with shade, we wanted to do nothing but splash in a deep brook covered by overhanging trees that was a short distance from the main encampment, and fill our mouths and canteens to the brim with its sweet, cool water.

"Taking yer pole and bucket, Daniel?"

"*Ja.* I doubt the fish will be biting this time of day, though. Likely they're all hiding in the darker, deeper pools. Too hot even for fish!" I replied as I stood up, looking off in the distance, and seeing the heat waves down the dirt lane that separated the tents on one side or the other. There was a tall man in the distance riding through the camp on a large pack horse; an unusual sight, given that the few horses in camp were held under guard, for fear of them ending up on someone's dinner plate. "Are ye ready there, Bobby? The afternoon is a wasting, and I'll need to be back in camp way too soon."

"*Ja,* I got everything with me so I can return to the 2nd Rhode Island after we go to the stream. I can't stay long." The New Jersey Brigade had marched from Eyers Forge to Elizabeth Town last week, so Bobby hopped on a wagon and rode down here in the early hours of the morning to see me. Rather than spend the night, he planned to return to the Rhode Island Regiment at Jockey Hollow in the late afternoon.

"All right, we'll practice a bit more if we have time, after we've had a wash. One of the laundry ladies handed me a piece of soap this morning. I think there's enough for both of us to use. The officers say a good bath will keep ye healthy. I heard the same from my sister. I've not had a decent bath all winter. I threw in Robinson Crusoe in the pack too, thought we might have a go at reading it?"

"Sounds good. I got some biscuits and cheese from one of the camp cooks that we could share too if we get hungry. I think we're gonna have a rare feast if we catch any fish!"

"Well, let's go then. Keep yer eyes and ears about ye in this tall grass. Saw a rattler slithering through it a few days back when it was not as hot as today."

<u>*Papa*</u>

Richard had followed them keeping his distance, observing Daniel's every movement, memorizing it for the time when he wouldn't see him. His son's gait was light; somewhere between a skip and jump every six feet or so through the high meadow. There would be a lot of picking ticks off those long legs of his, once he got around to it. He was much taller now than when he last seen him, he had to be maybe five foot ten, and that curly strawberry blond hair was as wild as ever under his cocked hat.

"Ah, Catherine . . . what a wonderful gift ye bestowed on me with this last child in the beginnings of our old age. I promised to keep him safe, but I fear that may no longer be possible," as he spoke softly to his dead wife.

The boys found their creek, still singing that bawdy song they had sung since he had gotten close enough to hear them. He thought he should really have a talk with Daniel about it, but then thought better of it after considering where and who Daniel had been living with these almost eight months.

" Yet on the other hand, I can't let him think about women that way. Well, if the opportunity presents itself, I'll say something, I promise Catherine," he said as he looked to the sky this time.

Letting the horse graze behind him, Richard went to a thicket of soft white pines and crawled under their skirts into the spicy coolness. He lay on his belly to watch the boys at the creek and could do nothing but laugh. The boys were playing like six-year-olds; whooping and hollering, picking each other up only to dump the other back into the water with a great splash.

"*Well, that is one way to get their clothes clean,*" he heard Catherine say in his mind and smiled at the memory of them watching a younger Benjamin and Daniel doing much the same.

"*No doubt they'll smell better, too,*" he replied under his breath.

It was rather comfortable under the pines and Richard regretted leaving the soft bed of needles, but it was time to sneak up on them in fun and maybe teach another lesson about being vigilant in the woods.

The Brook

We passed the time walking to our brook playing *Maggie Lawder* and diligently watched for those snakes. The water was cool and after we thoroughly washed our clothes and our bodies with the soap, we started our own war, dunking and throwing each other in the water, trying to make bigger and bigger splashes each time. Until a deep male voice from behind the pine trees stopped us dead.

"I could kill ye where ye both stand. Ye need to pay attention to yer surroundings. Never underestimate the element of surprise, and never feel comfortable out here alone, especially with war brewing," he said as he came out from the pines, throwing down his rifle and running like a wild beast and sounding like one at the same time.

We just stood in the water, stunned as we watched the madman gallop towards us. He ran completely past Bobby, making a beeline towards me, screaming and hollering with no intention of stopping, then picked me up and threw me back into the water. The man doubled over in laughter while watching me thrash as I tried to get my bearings. I stood and charged at him as I simultaneously pulled my hair from my eyes. I realized too late who the man was. I skidded into him, tackling him, and almost ended up drowning the both of us.

"Papa? It is ye? Are ye hurt?" I asked as I grabbed my father's forearm and hauled him up out of the water. "I'm so sorry. Ye just about the scared us both to death."

"Well, that was my intention, and yer greeting has made me feel every one of my forty-five years simultaneously. Ah, that's better. Here, let me look at ye," Papa said as he stood up and pushed me back a little. "Ye've gotten much bigger since I saw ye last; how'd ye manage that?"

"Not with the amount of food here, that's for sure. I come from good stock, that's all," I responded with a grin.

"That just may be. And ye got some light reddish fuzz coming on yer face," he said as he turned my chin back and forth to get a better look. "No need to shave it yet," he said with a twinkle in his eye.

"Well, that's good. I've no razor, anyway."

"I'll see if I can remedy that situation here soon, 'cause ye'll need one soon anyway."

"Oh Papa, Ben and I thought ye might be dead when ye didn't come." I said as I wrapped my arms around his frame to make sure he was as solid and unbroken as when I saw him last. My head no longer rested under his chin, but way over his shoulder, very soon I would be as tall as he was.

"I'm a little whiter, maybe, and a few more lines in my face I think, but no, I am not dead yet," he said, holding me and patting my back as he had always done. "I am sorry I wasn't here sooner, son. I managed to get to Peter and Aletta's two weeks after ye left. By then, the snow was falling, and the passes were blocked. Aletta gave me yer letter and not a day went by that I didn't pray to find ye."

"I had to leave Papa."

"I know, and I am grateful to God that ye made it here in one piece. I am proud of ye, and amazed that ye walked the distance and are alive to tell about it. I saw General Maxwell not an hour ago and he told me about what Boer and the Mohawk had done to ye. I can't do much about the Mohawk, but I will take care of Boer when I go back to the Lanterman's. Let's get out of the water before we both sink in the mud."

"When you go back? Ye just got here!" I said, as I followed him to the bank. Bobby was still fussing with his clothes to get the rest of the soap out and trying to ignore us both.

"There's something I gotta do for General Maxwell. I'll be gone just a few weeks. We'll talk about it over supper when yer brother gets here. Whose ye friend, Daniel?" he asked, raising his chin towards Bobby.

I lowered my voice a bit, so only Papa would hear: "Robert Vandersloot, but I call him Bobby. He arrived here mid-March looking for glory and adventure after running from his family farm in Rhode Island. He seems to think he will find both with the 2nd Rhode Island Regiment. He wants to help, and he does, which is honorable, but I've told him more than once he'll find nothing adventurous or glorious about cleaning up a sick man's bed or digging a new latrine, which is what I have done a lot of recently. Ye see how he listens, because he's still here."

"Well, his stubbornness reminds me of someone else I know," Papa said, smiling and ruffling my hair. "Ye, however, were given a good reason to leave, and I can't fault ye for that. Does Robert see the difference? Let's head towards those flat rocks over there, under the shade of the trees, after I get my rifle and the saddlebags that I threw on the ground."

"No, he doesn't. Early on I thought about the possibility of joining, but put it out of my mind because I knew ye would come eventually. When ye didn't, it seemed the only way to keep my sanctuary. Ben was furious about it, but we could see no other way around the enlistment in January. He couldn't keep an eye on me all the time; he had his duties, and those were the priority. So now I have more than one brother to keep me out of trouble and they make sure that I am busy most of the time, that is for sure. "That is good, the more eyes the better. General Maxwell says that yer doing well with those responsibilities."

"I think so. The camp hasn't thrown any rotten food at me for playing music, yet, but then there might not be any rotten food to throw, anyway. The men do always appreciate a new latrine, and they thank me for that. I hope ye're not angry with me, Father?"

"No," Papa left out a heavy sigh as he stopped to turn to face me. "How could I be angry when this is all my fault to begin with? No, son,

I am very proud of ye," he said as pulled me into another hug. "I am so sorry. I should have been there. I should have believed ye the first time ye told me about Boers," he told me in a softer voice as he released me to look into my eyes.

"I forgive ye, Papa. Yer here, ye came," I replied and gave him one more hug before we broke apart laughing as my belly rumbled rather loudly for food.

"Hmmm, I can fix that, Daniel. I have some beef jerky and dried apples in the bags, if ye'd like some. I'll work on pulling it all out. Go call yer friend. I'm sure he's hungry, too."

I walked back down to the creek, gathered up Bobby and our things, and together we ran up to the rocks where Papa was sitting.

"At yer service sir," Bobby said to Papa as he fought to even out his breathing. "I am Robert Vandersloot, Master Applegate," he said as he stooped low in a bow, dripping water all over the ground.

"I am honored, Robert," Papa responded by bending at the waist too. "Well, Masters Vandersloot and Applegate, step up on the flat rock here and I'll share what I have with ye, but we might just have to go fishing in the creek for our supper later."

ᎨᎣᎨ ᎨᎣᎨ ᎨᎣᎨ

"I've not had dried apples since I left Letta's and I ate the last bit of jerky we put up at the farm long before I made it to Scotch Plains, Papa. This feels like a Christmas feast, given what we've had these last several months."

"I have no doubt. What do ye think, Robert? These dried apples aren't too bad, are they now?"

"No, sir!" he said, stuffing several more slices in his mouth, which made Papa grin even more.

"They are from lines that were in my family long before we arrived in this country more than a hundred years ago; with the secret to growing them passed from one generation to another. What good is an Applegate if

229

they can't grow a grove of apple trees?"

Bobby and I both chuckled as we sucked on the fruit, getting as much of the sweetness on our tongues as we could before chewing and swallowing the rest.

"We've got apple trees on our farm."

"Ye do, Robert? What kind?"

"Red sweet ones mostly. They'll be in bloom here soon with the bees buzzing 'round them. A real treat to eat a freshly picked apple, sir."

"I would agree with ye. Who'll pick the apples at yer family farm this year, if ye're not there?"

"I don't rightly know. Mama has her hands full with my younger brothers and sisters. My papa is always busy with one thing or another on the farm. I guess he'll need to make time for it," he said with a shrug of his shoulders.

"Ever thought of going back? I am sure they miss ye."

"I have. But it is important to be here too, with so few men, I think I can be a help. Besides, there is nothing like being on yer own."

"That I understand, son, but ye really should think about going back. I am willing to bet that ye're Mama and Papa could use yer help more than ye're willing to believe. I am sure yer Papa could use yer hands to mend fences, plant the garden, hunt, and chop wood. The other boys might just be too small to do that yet. Besides, who'll train up those brothers to catch crawdads and fish and hunt frogs when yer not working with yer Papa?"

"I really hadn't thought about it sir, I am not much of a fisherman, but ye have a point. Thank ye. I'll think on it for a bit, Master Applegate. What about Daniel? Shouldn't it be the same for him?"

"*Ja*, it should, but it cannot be. That Daniel is here at all is completely my fault. I will have to live with it for the rest of my days. He has joined the army and there is no changing it, but I am going to do what I can to keep him safe and so will his brother, regardless.

We all sat quietly on the rock for a few moments, listening to the babble of the brook and frogs in the short distance. I stretched out and laid down on the cool smooth surface of the boulder to watch the hawks from under the small canopy of leaves, as they flew their circles on the warm breeze in search of small ground animals. Papa did the same for a bit and then drifted off. Bobby, I could tell, was still lost in thought, staring at the creek.

"Daniel, think I'm gonna head back to the regiment. I have much to ponder about. See ye tomorrow at the regular time and place, if I can get a ride back down?"

"*Ja*. I think so. If I am not there, then I got waylaid by some officer."

"Are ye leaving so soon?" Papa asked, holding himself up with one elbow.

"*Ja*, I'd better get back. Thank ye, sir, for the jerky and apples; best food I've had in some time."

"Ye are most welcome, son. Think 'bout what I said and do take care of yerself."

I watched as Bobby took his leave from our rock and the shade. "Not sure ye got through, Papa, but ye gave him pause. And Papa?"

"*Ja?*"

"I love ye."

"I know. I love ye too, Daniel, and I want what's best for ye. Don't ye forget it. Doesn't matter if ye're twelve or a hundred and twelve."

I laughed at that and laid down, watching the hawks as they continued their circles on the warm waves of the wind and let the cooler air under the shade tree drift me to sleep.

Reunion

"There he is!" Papa said shouting, as he stood up and turned around to see Ben.

Ben was running towards us like he was being chased by a wild animal. He slammed into Papa and about knocked him over, while grabbing him in a bear hug. They held each other tight for a few moments, then Ben reluctantly pulled himself away. Ben's eyes were flowing with tears, a sight I didn't think I'd see again after he left home.

"When ye didn't make it, we'd feared ye dead, Papa," he said softly, looking at him as if trying to mesh his memory of Papa with the man who stood before him all while trying to snuffle back his tears.

"No, son, I'm here and no ghost," he responded softly as he raised Ben's chin so that he could look into his eyes. "Though I am pretty good at finding my way around the wilderness, this is true. But that skill was nothing against this past winter and there was little I could do about it until now. I can see ye are no worse for the wear either, thank God," he said as he moved his hand to Ben's shoulder. "Come Ben, we have a log here to sit on where we can catch up while Daniel cooks the rabbit he took with his bow. I take it ye had no issue with finding us?"

"Captain Weatherby said he'd gotten a message from Colonel Spencer that said I was to find ye and ye'd be with Daniel. I knew where Daniel's favorite spot was, so I headed this way. Then I saw Oliver, and he said he'd talked to ye, that ye had been looking for Daniel and pointed ye here. I tried to get Oliver to come with me, but he'd not have it. He thought it best if we ate as a family with no meddling from any others."

"That Oliver is a good man. I made the offer too, but he thanked me and said no."

"He's been like an older brother and father rolled into one. We've no friend any better than Oliver, that is for sure."

"I can see why. I heard ye were in a couple of battles last summer. Had me a bit of a worry over it."

"*Ja,* we were at Newtown. I held my own and am mostly whole now, I think. Had to be, for Daniel's sake."

"How are ye mostly whole, Ben?"

"Newtown was an honorable battle; there we fought against Butler's Rangers, Loyalists, the Iroquois and their leader Joseph Brant, Papa.

"Before we reached Newtown, though, we were given orders to burn Iroquois crops and homes, and take or destroy anything else in our way during our expedition. There was little resistance from the Iroquois villages. What could old men, women, and children do against an army? There were no young men, no warriors to defend them. They all seemed to have disappeared.

"The destruction just didn't feel right to me. It was not honorable. We left the women, children and old standing there in tears as they watched their fields burn. I knew they'd starve this winter, and I prayed that their warriors would return soon and leave with everyone. Ye reared me with a bit of a conscience, Father. I've found the army a hard taskmaster," he said with his head hanging low, looking to the ground.

"It is, and I have no regrets about ye're conscience," Papa said as he moved close enough to wrap an arm around him if he needed it. "Your conscience will lead ye true, Ben, if ye listen. It is God's way of bringing us back on the right path, son," he said quietly as he touched Ben's forearm.

"As for the army, ye had no choice but to do as ye were told. Anything less would have been mutiny and a hanging. I am for one, and yer brother for another, glad ye took heed. If this is a just war, and I believe it is, then Providence will see to the needs of the women, children, the old, and the warriors. I have seen such in my lifetime."

"I want to believe it so," Ben replied, raising his head and searching Papa's eyes for confirmation.

"It will come to pass, son. I did hear that a good many of those left in the villages made their way to Canada soon after the Continental army went through.

"Ye know this Revolution, this war, cannot be won by fighting it on two fronts. Many more lives will be lost, and not only in terms of solders if we continue to combat the Iroquois and British coalition on the frontier and the British in the east. There are colonists in both places to think about.

"The Redcoats want to spread us thin like butter on bread, then rip the bread slice into pieces, throwing it to the crows to pick at and leaving nothing for any of us. The same strategy has been used time and again. They know we don't have enough men, supplies, or munitions to fight in two places. The George Washington I knew long ago would only have sent General Sullivan on this course because he had no other choice. From what I've seen and heard as I traveled, there was no other choice to be had."

"Knowing that doesn't take the feeling of guilt away."

"No, it doesn't. If it did, ye would not be the son I raised. It is the God given responsibility of every man to keep his family and people safe, fed, and housed. He must see threats before they become acts of aggression, and engage in discussion by all other peaceful means before turning to violence.

"We exhausted those possibilities with the Crown long ago and when the Iroquois Confederation aligned itself with the British, they became our enemy as well. British payment for the first colonial scalps taken by the Confederation sealed their arrangement in innocent blood; they are the enemy as much as the Brits are.

"The most we can hope for under these circumstances is to be just in what we do—that is to be slow to anger, quick to listen, and pray for forgiveness, for grace; and put it all in the hands of God and try to move on."

Bye For Now

Papa gently shook us awake before dawn, handing us each a mug of warm coffee. "There's eggs and bacon on the fire, if ye'll have some," he said quietly as he left to tend to breakfast.

Ben and I inhaled the coffee aroma simultaneously, giggled at each other over the timing and each took a small sip from our cups, savoring the taste. Carefully carrying the mugs, we made our way to the fire, smelling the efforts of Papa's work that made our mouths water.

"Where'd ye get all of this, Papa?" Ben asked as between bites of bacon and eggs. "And the coffee, let alone sugar for it."

"Here and there—mostly as a trade for something else before I arrived here. I managed to bargain for the eggs from one of the camp followers. We got lucky. They weren't spoiled," Papa responded as he sipped his steaming coffee. "I wanted to send ye both off with a good breakfast. Something ye likely not had in sometime."

"Yer right about that. Thank ye, Papa."

"Ye all right there Daniel? Ye're awfully quiet."

"*Ja,*" I yawned. "Just waking up; slept much better than I have in a while."

"Ah, well, sleep is a treasure to have in the army. I think ye probably needed it."

"That I did, Papa. The real treasure is this breakfast. It is very good." I helped myself to more and looked up when I saw a flash of light to the east, sheet lightning it was, and I heard the rumble of thunder that came soon after. It was going to be another hot, muggy day.

We ate the rest of the meal slowly, enjoying it in silence, and let the coffee do its work, waking us to the present world. None of the three of us wanted to rush the time. I wanted to hold on to this moment, for the future remained uncertain for all three of us.

"Boys, I debated with myself on what I am about to say, but in the end, I thought it best to tell ye my perspective about the realities of the situation with the army. I kind of figure, though, ye already know ye're in for a fight soon?"

"*Ja,* there's been quite a few skirmishes recently, if not outright small battles, and building burnings in and around New Jersey," Ben replied between sips of his coffee. "Reverend Caldwell's church in Elizabeth Town was burned down in January and some of our men were taken prisoner. The Reverend managed to move his wife and their children to Connecticut Farms and, hopefully, out of range of the British and the Loyalists. In February, a party of fifty men invaded Newark, stole some cattle, and took two prisoners," Ben replied.

"In March, four hundred British soldiers and Hessians invaded Paramus, plundering homes, and taking prisoners. Then, in early April, worst of all, Colonel Shreve lost men to desertion before a British attack on the garrison at Paramus. Not only that, but then deserters turned their coats and joined the enemy in the assault. Our regiment was defeated," I added.

"Then ye both can see what this is leading up to. Good. Heads are getting hot, maybe too hot, and it won't be too much longer. We didn't have the chance to talk about this last night, but now's the time.

"Keep this to yerselves; Maxwell has charged me with talking to folks, recruiting them if I can in my travels the next few weeks and getting them to come here should the army send for help. I'll do my best; the Lord knows we need them. Lastly, should it come to an all-out battle, ye'll likely will be outnumbered. Yet, bear in mind, this army has been outnumbered before and survived to see another day. I want ye to stand fast.

"I am coming back to be with ye, God willing, and we will fight together. If I am not there with ye, and should all fall to the wayside around ye, escape by any means. Ye'll know when it is time. Find each other, and Benjamin, get yerself and yer brother away silently, quickly into the woods, head west towards Pennsylvania. Ye will survive to live and fight another day. I will not be too far behind ye.

"Ben told me about yer visit with the Duttons, late last night while ye were sleeping, Daniel. They are good people. I want ye both to make yer way to Abe and Bessie's farm. That should get ye far enough out of harm's way. Ye remember the way, Daniel?"

"I remember. Oh! I nearly forgot. Master Dutton says ye have long been missing from their hearth and would enjoy yer company for a while when ye have the time, and he gave me this letter. I've kept it in my knapsack since early November last year."

"Thank ye, son. I'll read it at my next stop. All right, should everything go bad, I'll meet ye at the Dutton's and we'll work out what to do next."

The Dark Day

"**I** thought for sure we'd get some rain from the lightning and thunder we heard earlier this morning, but there is none; just this fog and these dense dark clouds above us," Ben said with some concern in his voice as we both took a break from walking to look at the sky. "There, see just there, the brown tinge?"

"*Ja,* I do barely. Ye think the there's a field on fire near Elizabeth?"

"I hope not. What a way to use our furlough time, putting out a brush fire." Papa had written permission from General Maxwell to keep both of us for the night, but we had to report back for duty by six o'clock in the evening the next day.

"We need to pick up the pace, Daniel. They might be needing our help." Going faster would have been all well and fine, if we hadn't been ladened with musket balls, cartridges, and extra food in our knapsacks, which tripled the weight we had to carry on our backs. We silenced our conversation and concentrated on moving our feet faster and stayed within our own thoughts.

Before Papa left, he had thoroughly emptied his saddlebags, providing us with things the army could not, including a pair of new moccasin boots for both of us and a musket that he gave to me.

"It is time ye had one of these Daniel," he said, showing me the new musket with its gleaming red stock and burnished barrel. "Ye need it. Do ye remember that conversation we had a couple of years back?"

"Yes sir, I do. Ye told me that a weapon is not a toy. It is not to be used in anger or in vengeance against anyone. It is only to be used to protect family, property and put meat on the table."

"It is yer's," he said as he put the gun in my hands. The musket was much heavier than I thought it would be.

"Ben said that he had ye practice loading and shooting his musket. That is good, keep practicing. The faster ye are, the safer ye'll be. Use yer bow for hunting and save the balls and cartridges for saving yer life." He stepped back then and took a long look at us.

"Both of ye have changed so much," he said as he walked forward then and gathered us in his arms as he had done when we were children. "I love ye both," he whispered softly, patting us on the back. Those were his last words before he put his foot in the stirrup, swung the other leg over his horse, and was off on his quest for General Maxwell. We watched him until he disappeared into the thick morning fog.

We arrived at Elizabeth Town to find the village intact and not on fire, but enshrouded in a brown - grey cloud. The birds and insects were quiet; and we thought perhaps it was just dark enough for them to think it was night. The bustle of daytime activity was nearly non-existent, as people had moved indoors and went about lighting their candles. Those folks not inside scanned the murky sky above in amazement, whispering fears of the world's end, of Armageddon, to each other or no one in particular.

"Smell that, Ben? The smoke is thicker here." We were just past town a bit. Ben and I were getting ready to say our goodbyes. Our camps were in different directions.

"*Ja,* it is, and don't look-up, ye'll get soot in yer eyes. It's in yer hair and mine too," he said as he pulled a hand through his greasy loose locks, that left his hand black and grey with soot. "Must be one huge fire up north to bring ash down on us like this. When ye get back to yer camp, that is, if ye can find it in this muck, if ye read or hear anything about this, let me know when I see ye next. I am curious. It may be a while 'til I see ye again, though. Love ye, little brother, stay out of trouble with that gun and do as Papa said, practice reloading."

"I will do my best. Love ye too, Ben, and ye be safe," I said as I gave him a bear hug and then watched him walk off into the foggy dark.

The Mutiny

"Ye know, yer Papa was right, Daniel."

"What do ye mean, Bobby?" The grassy knoll under a shade tree was perfect for eating the bread and cheese we had earned on our musical tour of the Jersey Brigade camp. Bobby had caught up with me just before noon as I walked the circuit playing the fife or fiddle with a drummer named James, who had not been required by the corps to return to Morristown the day before.

James was a little new to drumming, so he was not well practiced. Bobby, with the patience of a saint, took him through the rhythms and we managed to do a couple more circuits of the camp and by early evening earned both praise and food for our efforts. James was older, so he let us be, while he trotted off somewhere else to visit friends with his share of bread, butter, and cheese that we had been given.

"I should go back home," Bobby said as he buttered another slice of bread.

"I've been telling ye that for a while, this really is no place to be. If I leave, and I get caught, I'd hang for it."

"I know. Speaking 'bout hanging, there was one yesterday."

"Why?"

"Well, eleven men were charged with desertion. General Washington pardoned ten after the mutiny and hung one man for forging over a hundred discharge papers."

"What mutiny? I've heard nothing 'bout any mutiny!"

"I'll get to that, Daniel. The eleven men abandoned their posts because they were hungry. They were all caught and charged with desertion.

"The mutineers decided that charging the eleven with desertion was unjust given the circumstances and decided to do something about it.

"I heard the talk in whispers 'bout the fairness of it all in the morning after the graves were dug, before the deserters were to be hung, and it continued until the entire 8th Connecticut Regiment decided that they had enough. After mustering for the evening parade, they refused to disperse and go back to their huts. They just want to go home to provide for their families and themselves.

"A hanging is a gruesome thing. I certainly don't want to see the likes of one ever again and I really wished I hadn't this time. It will stay with me until I die, for sure."

"I believe ye, Bobby. So, what about the mutiny? What happened next?" I split the rest of the bread, butter, and cheese between us and handed his half to him.

"The typical stuff, when one is looking for a fight, I guess. Good bread, Daniel, and fresh too!" he responded as he munched on some of it and drank his fill of water. "There was evil talk before. The men of the 8th Connecticut were not wanting to be part of the 'camp color,' those doing the chores and the like. Then the shouting match began between the adjutant and the men, and some name calling -comparing the men to dogs. Before it got too much more out of control, the adjutant ran off to get the other officers.

"Meanwhile, the mutineer leader of the 8th Connecticut that argued with the adjutant yelled: 'Who will parade with me?.' The whole 8th regiment stepped up. Then shortly thereafter, the 4th Connecticut joined in. Both the 8th and the 4th regiments are part of the 2nd Connecticut Brigade. The officers just watched the goings on as the men shouldered their guns, faced, and began to march to the sounds of the drums and fifes towards the 1st Connecticut Brigade, made up of the 3rd and 6th regiments.

"Finally, some officers, rather than watch the 2nd Connecticut

Brigade leave the grounds, decided it would be best to involve Colonel Return Jonathon Meigs before things got much worse. They ran across Primrose Brook to the 1st Connecticut Brigade ahead of the mutineers and informed Colonel Meigs what was what. If ye remember, Colonel Meigs oversees both brigades. Unusual name Return Jonathon Meigs," he said as he paused, sipping from his canteen to wash down the rest of his bread and cheese in his mouth and then took the last bite of both.

I waited for him to finish the last of his meal, closing my eyes as I relished in the evening breeze stirring from the coast. The clouds were gathering, and it would rain tonight. I opened my eyes just as he had swallowed the last of his food and I started the conversation back up again.

"*Ja,* that name is unusual. I heard it came from a direct ancestor that had rejected her suitor and then later begged for him to return to her. Thus the 'Return Jonathon.' So, what happened then, Bobby?"

"The men of the 2nd Brigade finally made it to the 1st Brigade, then they shouted above the din of the drums and fifes for the 1st to come join them. Their plan was simple: they would march on the camp commissary, take what was there and then leave for Connecticut doing what they needed to do to survive the trip back. A grim prospect, to be sure.

"The 1st Brigade rather liked that idea and made their way to their huts to retrieve the possessions that they had, including any weapons that were stored inside. When the 1st Brigade got to their huts, they found a blockade of muskets pointed directly at their bellies. Colonel Meigs had ordered that if anyone tried to enter the huts, they were to be shot.

"The 1st and 2nd Connecticut Brigades then turned on the colonel and his officers. With all the shouting of angry words, pushing, and shoving, one man got past the hut guards. Colonel Meigs grabbed him one handed and threw him back in with his fellow mutineers, in front of the muskets. That man then turned around and punched Meigs in the chest. Then all went dead silent.

"Colonel Meigs didn't lose his temper and didn't return the punch.

He put his hand over the place where he was pummeled, and looking at the crowd, he told them that he thought of himself as their friend and thought that they had treated him in the same way. He wanted to know if he was mistaken.

"Silence reigned for a few more minutes and then the men of the 1st Brigade removed themselves, grumbling words to the 2nd Brigade; that they wanted no part of the revolt. The 2nd Brigade, still as angry, eventually left, crossed the brook, and returned to their parade grounds.

"That wasn't the end of it, though. The 2nd Brigade refused to stand down, even after several officers tried to talk them into it again. Then, this officer comes out of the woods and tells the men that there is a good number of cattle just arrived and ready for butcher if they would like to have at it. The shortest way to the pens, though, was through the woods.

"Then Colonel Sumner, he's with the 4th Connecticut Regiment, walks on the parade grounds. He had a somewhat friendly conversation with the 2nd Brigade and tried to persuade them again to return to their huts. They would not move. Then he told them about the Pennsylvania troops with loaded muskets in the woods between them and the cattle pens. The 2nd Brigade didn't believe him, so when he shouted for them to shoulder arms, they did nothing. In the end, he ended up screaming at them and then left disgusted and dismayed.

"A few brave men from the 2nd Brigade went into the woods to check Colonel Sumner's story about the Pennsylvania troops. It turns out that there were Pennsylvania troops mucking around silently in the woods. Those men were told they were on a secret mission.

"The men of the 2nd Brigade told the few Pennsylvania men they saw in the woods what their likely mission was: to control the mutiny. However, the Pennsylvanians thought the mutiny was a good idea as well and were prepared to join in with the 2nd Brigade.

"Colonel Stewart, who was in charge of the Pennsylvania troops, got word that perhaps those Pennsylvanians in the woods would join the

2nd Brigade in their rebellion. He called the Pennsylvanians back to their quarters. Then he went to see the men of the 2nd Brigade.

"Surprisingly, the 2nd Brigade listened to Colonel Stewart. They believed him when he said he and the other officers had no money to buy supplies and there was nothing in the public store to be found. He didn't even have the sixpence to pay for a partridge that had been offered to him. If I remember correctly, he said: ' *You know how much you injure your own character by such conduct. You Connecticut troops have won immortal honor to yourselves the winter past, by your perseverance, patience, and bravery, and now you are shaking it off at your heels. I will go and see your officers and talk with them myself.'* Most of the men then went calmly to their huts after that. It was after nine o'clock before the parade were grounds finally emptied."

"They came very, very close, didn't they? This doesn't bode well."

"No, it doesn't, Daniel. If not for Meigs, Sumner, and Stewart, I am not sure we would be here talking about it. As much as I should go home, I think being here right now is maybe more important. We need all the men we can muster, and I can do as much as ye do, maybe more. I believe in liberty, and should I pay the ultimate cost, so be it," he said with conviction.

I was quiet for a time, with my eyes lowered to the ground, evaluating the full meaning of the emotion behind his words. I decided to take it for what it always had been, a heart-felt desire to be of service to this raggedy army. "It may be so, Bobby. The butcher is coming to collect soon. We all see the signs. There was another incident yesterday with our soldiers. Thirty-three were taken prisoner and four killed. So, ye may yet have yer chance to serve."

"What, yer not arguing with me about it this time?"

"No, wouldn't do any good anyway, now would it?"

"Na. A man must do what he must."

"*Ja.* I'd still rather ye go home, so that while I am out there on the field, I'll know that I can come visit ye one day in Rhode Island."

"Ye'll be able to do that and stay for a week or two, maybe a month. Mama won't let ye out of her sight. She'll put some meat on those bones for sure," he said as he grabbed my upper arm, pinching the muscle with a grin.

I punched him in the chest and then we were off play fighting, wrestling, and giggling. Drained of energy we lay on the grass, enjoying the cooler air and watching the sky as the sun descended below the western horizon. "Let's head back to my camp, ye can stay with me the night and leave at daylight for the 2nd Rhode Island. Safer that way 'cause of the camp picket lines."

Invasion

Ensign Moses Ogden and twelve of his men bent over, trying to catch their breath at the crossroads of De Hart's Point and Elizabeth Town Point; after a vigorous one mile run from their camp near Elizabeth Town, with only a crescent moon and the light from the milky way to guide their footsteps. It was a true blessing that the ocean breeze had cooled the late evening considerably, otherwise some of them might not have made it.

They stood on high ground at the crossroads, surrounded by tall grass, where the spring hay had not yet been scythed. Elizabeth Town was cast in a dim shadow that grew darker when a cloud would cover the moon. The enemy was coming. Moses' men could see their lanterns move with their steps as they climbed out of their boats and rafts at the shore.

"There, over there, men. That's as good a place as any," Moses said under his breath, pointing to the northwest corner of the field behind them. Almost silently, as if they were on a hunt, they made their way on to the pasture and then crouched low into the grass, hiding themselves as much as possible.

"Remember, we are to shoot one volley, that is all. Then run like the dickens, because your life depends upon it, the enemy will follow us. Get to Jelf's Hill in the center of the Elizabeth Town where Colonels Dayton and Spencer will be waiting," Ensign Ogden said as he crouched in front of the men.

"How many Redcoats, ye think, sir?" Ben asked.

"Not sure. Enough, Applegate, I won't lie to ye," he responded.

Colonel Dayton had told Moses that there were five thousand men, maybe more, of the enemy coming across from Staten Island. He said that the British force was almost ten times the size of the combined 3rd New Jersey and Spencer's Additional Regiments at Elizabeth Town. The rest of the New Jersey Brigade was with General Maxwell at West Farms; too far for the brigade to reach Elizabeth Town in time. "No sense in worrying about this now. We can only do what was put before us and pray that ye all make it back alive," the Colonel Dayton said to Moses.

"All of you were chosen because you know each other. You all watch out for each other and me; and you are the most able to run and run fast," Moses said to encourage them. We'll do this thing and then be gone before the enemy knows what has happened. Oh, and Johnson, hide that white cloth ye got in yer hand. If anyone else has anything white on them, get rid of it so it's not seen.

"They're likely to use dark lanterns. Keep ye're eyes at belt height to see anything that might reflect the light and listen for the troops walking and their whispers, then wait for me to give the order."

"Sir, whose property are we on anyway? Will we have any problems with the owners?"

Moses chuckled. "No, Johnson, we won't have any issues with the property owner. The owner is my uncle." There was a bit of quiet mirth over that, then the men hunkered down to watch, just as if they were waiting for game at a salt lick.

"Ye hear that?" someone said in a whisper.

"*Ja,* there's a large group coming from the sounds of the footfalls, horses and all."

"I hear the clinking of metal," whispered another.

"Can ye see any light reflecting from the metal?" Moses asked. They were all closer to the ground now, trying to make themselves smaller.

"Yes," said a third man.

"All right, get ready, men. We'll shoot on my mark, then fly swiftly and silently like owls after their prey," Moses whispered back. The men moved as one into an upright position, with a knee to the ground and heads just above the grass, holding their muskets tight to their shoulders and all barrels pointed at the enemy force. "Just a few more seconds. Wait until they are at the crossroads."

"Fire!"

Breaking Camp

"Wha, what's going on? Oliver? Is it raining? Heard some thunder. There's lots of water on my head. Just, let me sleep," I said as I rolled over away from him and throwing my arm over my eyes and ignoring the rain.

"*Can not. Move it, boy! I threw water on ye!* Get yerself up, Daniel, we gotta go. We're leaving camp, get yer things."

"All right, all right! I'm soaked! What ye mean we're leaving?" I asked, as I wiped the water from my face and scratched at the fine fur lining my jaw. I was going to need to do something about that soon. "It's the middle of the night!"

"Tis so son, it is a little half past midnight, in fact. This is the army. We go when they tell us to go," he responded as he threw what clothes I had in my backpack along with my books, fife, fiddle, and any other possessions of mine that he could readily see. "Get yer boots on, use the latrine and hurry."

My messmates had already packed what little they had; and had begun to tear down the tent around me. I escaped to the outside before the roof collapsed in a heap on top of my head and headed to the privy. Frothy clouds drifted through the night sky, reflecting the dim glow of the crescent moon, and the milky way was as bright as polished silver. I said a word of thanks for the cooler night air; it would make travel more bearable for all of us.

I returned to find Oliver waiting, as promised. The others had already left. "Here, yer fife is on top in the sack, ye might need it later and grab yer musket. Hurry, we've gotta go; catch us up with the others."

"They've not done roll call, have they?"

"Not yet, as far as I know, I don't think the officers took the time to do it. Ye know what happens if we're not there anyway, and we don't answer. I, for one, don't want to face a noose."

At that point, there was no talking, just running the length of road as fast as we could to catch up with the other men. Both Oliver and I stumbled several times over ruts, rocks, and holes in the road, some hidden in deep shadow. We managed to stay upright, not landing in the mud or manure left by the horses and their wagons.

"There they are, ye see um, Daniel?" Oliver said between breaths as he slowed his pace. "As soon as we get close enough, I'll find out about the roll."

"Ja! I see a bunch of them, and Henry, too. He'll know something."

"Henry?"

"Oliver, that ye? What ye doing back here? Thought ye'd be up front." Henry wedged his way between the men immediately behind him to meet up with us.

"Well, sleeping beauty here didn't want to wake for me either, even after ye tried. I was a little more persuasive."

"*Ja,* ye dumped a whole bucked of water on my head."

"I tried, Daniel, I really did, but ye just weren't moving at all for me. That's when I ran to Oliver. Thought ye might listen to his deeper voice."

"Why are we moving a perfectly good camp site from one place to another in the dark, anyway?"

"I take it ye didn't hear the all the noise while ye were sleeping, Daniel?"

"No, Oliver, I was dead to the world. A hard, hot day yesterday."

"I suppose yer right, playing that fiddle and fife can be very tiring, no doubt?"

"Ye're right. I shouldn't complain. I do have it a bit easier than most."

"I'll let ye off this time, but mind ye, tis not easy for anyone."

"Yes, sir. So why are we leaving camp?"

"While ye were resting young'n, Oliver and I heard the musket fire, a lot of it, all of it in the direction of Elizabeth Town. Woke the camp, it did. Oliver met me outside the tent to listen for more and figure out what had happened when we saw Major Ogden, Aaron that is, take off towards Elizabeth Town riding his horse as if he were being chased by demons from hell and now, we're headed the same direction," Henry replied.

"Papa was supposed to be here before this, said he felt this coming. Ben! what about Ben, Oliver?"

"Don't know. But don't ye worry none, yer Papa will be here. I only met him for a few minutes. He's not likely to forget his promises to his sons, Daniel. As for Ben, he can hold his own. I've watched him at Newtown."

"Ye're right. I . . . I shouldn't worry." We marched in silence for a few paces, with Oliver and Henry giving me a little more time to get a hold of myself. "All right then, so ye think we're headed to a fight at Elizabeth Town?"

"We might just be headed to a fight, but we won't know 'till we get there. I doubt the officers know much at this point, either. It will be all right," Henry said in a softer voice as he patted my shoulder. "Just stick with the captain as ye should and ye'll do just fine. Ye might try passing that gun to someone else. Ye shouldn't be on the field with it. I think ye'll be safer without it."

"Why's that?"

"The Brits won't care how old ye are if ye have a gun that's pointed at them. They'll shoot ye on sight. I guess in a way, though, it don't matter much, ye're still a target with that fife. They'll shoot ye if ye signal and are in range."

"I'd thank ye, Henry, not to scare the boy much more. He's had enough to think about for the moment," Oliver scolded Henry. "Henry's right about Captain Weatherby, though. Ye stick with him or Colonel Shreve. Ye'll be safer that way."

"All right. Like a bee to a flower. Where are we do ye think, Oliver? Looks like the line has slowed up ahead," I responded, hoping to change the subject. The less I thought about what might happen in the next few hours, the better I would feel.

"Don't know. We've been double timing it maybe a little more than an hour. Whose home is that, Henry?" Oliver inquired.

"Why it's Governor Livingston's. They named the manor house Liberty Hall. General Maxwell must be meeting with him to talk over the commotion we heard earlier. Yep, look, they've paused the line."

"All right, since we're stopped, might be best if ye find yer company up ahead, gentlemen. I know I'd better be off to find mine."

"You both will vouch for me, and say that I was with you all this time?"

"Well, ye were at least with Oliver, all the time Daniel."

"We will, won't we Henry?"

"Sure. Since it was really my job to haul yer backside out of yer bed," Henry said in agreement. "I'm just not nearly as good as Oliver at waking the dead."

"That's true and I thank ye both," I said as I made a slight bow and then turned to leave with Henry.

"No, wait, Daniel!" Oliver rustled around in his pack for a minute and pulled a small, folded cloth bundle out of the top of it. "Here Daniel, I saved some biscuits from my dinner last night, want some?" "Sorry, it's not more. Oh, I got an apple for ye too," he said as he reached back into the pack and tossed it to me. "That might stop that belly of yer's from grumbling so loudly," he said with a nod to my mid-section.

"Are ye sure?"

"*Ja,* go ahead. We should be setting up a camp before long, whether it be here or another place close. If we've the time, we'll be able to cook some food then."

"Thank ye, Oliver. If ye see Ben, tell him to get word to me as soon as he can," I replied and ran to catch up with Henry.

๏๏๏ ๏๏๏ ๏๏๏

"Does any of this look familiar to ye, Henry? Do you have an idea where we're headed?" I asked him under my breath. We were still under orders to keep talking at a minimum and in whispers. Our stay at Liberty Hall was short-lived, maybe fifteen minutes or so, and then we began another leg of the march heading to the northwest, I thought.

"Well, we're not going to Elizabeth Town, that's for sure. The scent of the ocean would be lot stronger. I think maybe we're headed back almost to where we were, a little place called Connecticut Farms. Is that musket of yer's primed?"

"Ye just told me about an hour ago not to even think about using it!"

"That was different. We were talking about ye not being seen with it in a battle. Here in the dark, we've no idea what might jump out at us, and we just might need yer help a bit," he said as he scanned his side of the road for any sign of movement. I looked in the same direction but saw nothing but trees and leaves moving to a light breeze.

"*Ja,* it's primed. I'd prefer to shoot a deer."

"Me too, could use the meat," he said as he kept his head roving up and down the side of the road like a nervous hen. Most of the men on either side were doing the same, so I couldn't really fault him.

"I can load the gun in about three seconds. Ben had me work on that skill and Papa helped me refine it when he was here," I said, just trying to keep my voice low, calming and to a drone. I thought Henry might just jump out of his skin if he heard anything too loud.

"That's good, kid. We might be need'n ye're help then, switch'n out one musket for another already primed," Samuel said as he placed a hand

255

on my shoulder and moved a bit closer to both of us. "Ye alright there, Henry?"

"I think so, just can't see much of anything out there," he said with a nod to the tree line to the south side of us.

"Have ye tried look'n out at the sides of yer eyeballs?"

"What on earth are ye talking about, o'l man?"

"Ye know, ye have vision out the sides of yer eyes? I read 'bout it sometime ago. Ye probably already do it anyway and don't know it."

Henry, being younger than Samuel, was not nearly as well read as Samuel and Samuel was always one to have, and give tidbits of advice from his book learning. "Do this, Henry: look straight ahead, don't move yer eyeballs, and see if ye can see anyth'n moving ta the left of your left eye or ta the right side of yer right eyeball. See anyth'n?"

"I see Daniel on one side of me and ye on the other, almost clear as day, without moving either eye."

"There ye have it. Now, try that for the tree line. Just point yer eyes straight ahead. Daniel, move back a bit. Likely ye'll just see the tree line, but a little clearer."

"Ye're right Samuel, it's clearer."

"What do ye see?"

"Trees, and that owl that's been hooting."

"Good. Look up ahead. The road is widen'n a bit. I think we might just be near Connecticut Farms. We made pretty good time, not too long before we can set up camp and make some breakfast! Ye get ta cook Daniel."

"Ah, really Samuel?"

"I traded some flour for bacon; fire cakes are not suit'n my fancy this morn'n. Sure, ye don't want ta cook?"

"Oh, I'll cook and do it with a smile on my face for bacon."

"I knew ye were a good boy, there," Samuel said, roughing up my loose hair.

"Hey! Why's the 1st New Jersey splitting off from us? See them over there. They're leaving."

"I see them, Henry. My best guess is that they are gather'n up with the 3rd New Jersey. I had overheard that Colonel Dayton was bring'n those regiments together at Connecticut Farms near a meet'n house," Samuel replied.

Connecticut Farms

"**A**re we there yet, Samuel?" I asked after we walked a bit more west, but still in sight of the meeting house. "The brigade officers are headed off towards the meeting house as well," I said as squatted in front of him, taking in the reds and pinks of the early dawn sky. Samuel sat on the boulder near the road and watched the barely lit meeting house in the distance. He took his pipe bowl and knocked it against the boulder to loosen the old tobacco. I thought for sure this would wake Henry, who was sleeping with his back to the boulder, but it didn't. Samuel refilled the bowl and lit the pipe, drawing in a deep breath and made the tobacco within glow a soft red.

"We may just be. This is a place of higher ground. We'll see them com'n, if they decide ta try us again. We'll know for sure that this is the place if the officers ever get done with their confer'n over at that house," Samuel said after drawing on his pipe

"I wonder if I have time to fish before they get done. I think Oliver packed my string." Oliver hadn't forgotten it. I found the string buried in the bottom of the pack and pulled it out.

"If ye do, ye'll likely need to be quick about it, 'cause Captain Weatherby is now heading this way. The meet'n for the captains just broke up."

⊕⊕⊕ ⊕⊕⊕ ⊕⊕⊕

"Gentlemen, gather round. Some of you may know the enemy made their incursion into Elizabeth Town Point last night, just before midnight. A detachment of twelve men, including a few of our men are in that detachment, fired their muskets simultaneously at the enemy, and gravely wounded a British general while he sat upon his horse. All twelve ran immediately to Jelf's Hill, just outside of Elizabeth Town. For now, the enemy has stopped, but the feeling is that they will be on the move again, and soon. We believe that they will attack again when the day breaks.

"The 1st New Jersey and the detachment from Spencer's Regiment will remain under Colonel Dayton and Lieutenant Colonel Smith's command, since Colonel Spencer is occupied elsewhere. Most of my platoon will stay with the 2nd New Jersey. Colonel Ogden is still ill and will not be able to command the 1st.

"The 2nd New Jersey will stay here until we are told to move. As you know, Colonel Shreve has detached Captain Bowman's company at the fork in the road to defend anything that might come up Galloping Hill Road. We are to stand firm just north of the fork until further orders.

"After we are settled into our defensive positions, cook what rations you have. If the battle begins, there will be little time for cooking. I am told that there will be a supply wagon arriving soon. Get as much rest as you can in between. I doubt you will get any when the battle begins. Any questions? Oh! Private Applegate?"

"Yes, sir?"

"You're with me," and then he turned back to the men and their questions. I stood beside Samuel instead and didn't want to move.

"Go on there, son. I'll see ye soon wonder'n around with the fiddle or that fife," Samuel said as he pushed me forward. I didn't move.

"It'll be alright."

"But Samuel, now ye too?"

"It'll be all right. I'll be fine and I've done this before too. Now go, not proper ta hold up the captain," he said softly in my ear.

"Have I answered all your questions?" Colonel Weatherby asked, looking at his troops, but there was just silence. "All right then gentlemen, we've got a lot a work to do in the next two hours, if we have that. The sun's not going to wait for us. Let's get to it."

ᖇᖇᖇ ᖇᖇᖇ ᖇᖇᖇ

The men were now resting as well as they could under a thick leafy maple, and only a few were still enough to be asleep. Most knew what was coming. I had no clue as I prepared what breakfast we had.

"Daniel?" I turned from watching the men of my mess to the soft voice that had just called my name.

"Yes, captain?"

"Do I smell bacon?"

"Yes, Sir. Samuel got it from somewhere. I thought I'd fry it up with the fish I caught."

"Well then, I have part of a smoked ham in this sack. It will help supplement the fish and the bacon ye've got in that pan. Good catch, by the way. All that fish, not bad for a few minutes' work."

"Where'd ye get the ham, captain? No supply wagons here."

"Your father, he's been here, and he's gone looking for Ben. He stopped to drop this off first."

"Then he's not coming to see me?"

"No, not yet. Maybe later. He's agreed to help us harass the British troops. He also wanted me to remind you of the conversation that you had with him when he came to camp a few weeks ago, but he wouldn't say what it was about, so I can't help you remember if you don't."

"I remember."

"Good—don't you tell me either, I don't want to know. Then let me help ye slice up this ham and fry it for breakfast while I talk. I am way past hungry. I am sure you are and the others as well. If we engage the enemy, I want you to hightail it to Colonel Shreve, farther up on the road on the hill," he said as he deftly sliced the ham with his hunting knife and added the slice to the frying pan. "He will be expecting you. In the interim, you are to stay close to my side. Got that? No excursions to the woods or otherwise, unless I say you can."

"Yes, sir. Those fires lit on the hills are those signals for the militia?"

"They are, and we need their help. If they don't come because they aren't keeping watch, the 'old sow' will get them out of their beds."

"Old sow?"

"A very loud fat bottomed cannon, up higher on that hill over there. See it? General Knox brought it back with the other cannons from Ticonderoga in the winter of '76."

"I heard about that story. All those cannons pulled on skids in the dead of winter across the snow to New York. That was a feat to behold."

"It was, and they came at the right time and undamaged. Oh! Here's a loaf of bread and some butter to go with the meat. It was buried in the pack. Ahh, this smells so good, that alone will bring the boys out of their slumber with their mouths watering. We've not had anything like this in a while."

"Will I relay yer commands for the men?"

"I don't know, likely not, with the way battle strategy laid out. You know how to use that musket?" he asked, nodding at where it lay on my right side.

"Yes, sir. I learned from Papa when I was nine. He took me hunting and told me we wouldn't eat that night if I didn't catch a deer and it was a long way home to get dinner, so I shot the first deer I saw, and we had dinner." Captain Weatherby grinned as he flipped pieces of ham over.

"Then keep it with you. Do you think you could shoot a man to save your life or another's?"

"If I felt threatened, I would do what I could do to stop the man from hurting me or another."

"If it happens, don't think about it too long, or he'll kill you first, then whoever you are trying to protect."

"Sir, how am I going to tell our men from theirs? I mean, if they are wearing uniform colors other than ours, I'll know. But what about the ones that don't have uniforms, that are with the Loyalists. Many of ours don't have uniforms either."

"Simple, ask them for the watchword and countersign, if you have time. The watchword for today is 'tomorrow' and the countersign for it is 'look sharp'. That would be the best any of us could do. Regardless of who they are, or how they are dressed, if they threaten you, don't hesitate. Unfortunately, there are real villains in both armies."

"All right. I will remember. Tomorrow and look sharp."

"That's right. Don't forget them. You know most of the men in camp, so that should not be much of a problem, and I am pretty sure all our men know who you are, even if you don't know them. You've played enough around camp to be recognized." He said nothing more for a few minutes and cut the last pieces of the ham for the frying pan. "Here son, eat what's on the plate, then I want you to find a place under that tree and sleep for as long as you can, soldier. I'll get the men up to break their fast and we'll do clean up, if we have time."

"Where will I find ye, sir when I wake?" I asked between large bites of ham and yawns.

"I'll be right here with the men, Daniel. I guess you were hungry; that's the fastest I've ever seen anyone eat their food. Do you want more?"

"Na but, wouldn't mind some later if there is any left. I'm heading to that maple over there, where there's more room. I don't think I can sit up straight anymore. Night, Captain Weatherby."

e◯e e◯e e◯e

"Shhhh, shhh; Daniel, it is all right. Wake-up, wake up, I got ye son," Samuel was right beside me, holding me in a bear hug as he sat on the ground. "Ye're all right."

"I am fine? I hear muskets." I broke away from Samuel to make sure all my parts were there.

"I'd be hold'n ye down if ye were miss'n anything. The muskets ye hear are in that cherry orchard we walked past last night. Here, drink this."

"What's in the cup, Samuel?"

"Watered down-applejack in a bit of acorn coffee. Drink, it will help set ye right." Another loud boom sounded, and I jumped; almost spilling the concoction all over myself.

"What the devil was that?"

"That would be the 'old sow'. Ye slept through two of her sound'ns and musket fire. She's not much use as a cannon, but she certainly makes a lot of noise."

"That she does," I said, rubbing my ears and scratching my head.

"The sun's just barely up and the British are mov'n toward us. Ye can see them off in the distance just there, with their red and green coats. The green coats, those are the Loyalists, remember? Now if they've got funny hats and green coats, then they're the Hessian mercenaries. More precisely, the Jägers. Ye see them?"

"*Ja,* I do." The enemy soldiers looked like little red and green ants running through the cherry orchard as it glowed in the glory of the early morning sun until the smoke from the musket fire came between the trees and the sun, muting all colors. I could barely make out our men, even in the golden light. Most of them wore their own tattered clothing, from hunting shirts to homespun and leather that readily hid them in their surroundings.

"Take another sip." I drank a little and then turned the cup back over to him. The watered-down applejack and acorn coffee was making me feel much warmer than I wanted to be.

"Feeling better?"

"Think so. Had a nightmare. I don't quite remember it except we were running in a dark wood trying to get away from a mad boar with tusks dripping in blood. There was a lot of shooting, but everyone missed. The boar didn't miss, and he skewered all men that were in front of him. My turn came next, and I screamed, running as fast as I could. That's when ye woke me."

"Had ta, ye were scream'n. Just like a girl," he said with a chuckle as he ruffled my hair. "No shame in it. Most of us have had nightmares on the eve of a battle, come to think of it. After that, we learn not to sleep the night before."

"I believe ye, remind me not to lay my head if there is a next time. How many men do ye think they have, yonder?"

"I don't quite know. I won't lie ta ye son, there are quite a few more of them than there are of us," Samuel said as he pulled a small stick out from under his leg and threw it in the direction of the meadow below filled with spring hay and sprinkled with wildflowers and a few cows that boarded the orchard. "Sure is pretty over there, isn't? Those milk cows might do better in the woods just beyond, though.

"That aside, don't worry none. By Providence, we've made it this far and by Providence we will hold until General Washington gets here with the other regiments ta send the British and the Hessians back the way they came." Samuel said as he downed the applejack acorn coffee that was left in the cup and then turned to face me again. "Get yer water flask filled from up-stream over there before the day catches ye. It's already warm'n up and it will be a lot worse by afternoon. Make sure Captain Weatherby knows where ye're off ta first. He might want ye ta fill some others too. Go quickly now."

ᗣᗣᗣ ᗣᗣᗣ ᗣᗣᗣ

"So that is what they call harassment. Looks almost like hide'n'seek," Henry said as he stood beside me on the top of the creek embankment, watching the movement between the puffs of smoke coming from the musket fire in the cherry orchard below.

"How many balls was everyone issued?"

"I think I heard we all have enough cartridges and balls for maybe 30 shots."

"That doesn't seem like it would be quite enough for the number of the British and Hessians, does it?"

"Enough for the British, anyway," he said, smiling. "We're better at shooting them than they are at us. It's the Jägers we must keep an eye on. They are huntsmen. Come on, the captain said I should gather ye up and bring ye back. Doesn't want any of us to stray too far."

"I've gotta go back down and fetch a water flask downstream and finish filling the rest. Then I'll leave with ye."

"I'll come help."

"Thank ye, Henry."

"Did ye get much rest under yer tree?"

"Just a bit. I managed to sleep before that 'old sow' woke me out of a solid sleep."

"She was just a tad bit loud, even for my ears. Louder than a bunch of drummers that we played with, for sure."

"Hear that?"

"*Ja*, it sounds like it is closer to us, and they are firing more than they should." We knew the strategy. The men were to attack in twos and threes and then retreat behind whatever they could find: trees, bushes, tall grasses, homes, barns and the like. Then reposition themselves, reload, fire, and run for their lives again. It was the only way to fight a battle where we were outnumbered six men to one. "Let's get a look when we're done."

We filled the flasks as quickly as possible while the noise of the fight grew louder and the volley from the muskets grew faster. *Help Papa, Ben, Oliver and all the others, Lord. I don't want to lose any of them*, I prayed quietly as I worked.

"Ready, Daniel?" Henry asked as I secured the last canteen and walked up the embankment.

"Right behind ye. What do ye see?"

"We've moved back. They are following us, so they are closer to this position, and Captain Bowman's company is now engaged as well. That's why it is louder now. Bowman is beginning to move back," Henry shouted above the din as he crested the embankment. In the short time we finished up the flasks, the battle had shifted. The enemy had cleared the woods and part of the village of our men. Our men were now in retreat towards the Rahway.

"There are men on the ground, not moving."

"Daniel, *Daniel!* We gotta go. Samuel is calling us. They are leaving," Henry said as he grabbed my arm and attention away from the battle.

"We can't leave the men on the field. It's not right. I can help bring them back."

"*No!* No, ye can't. We have our orders. We must go, Daniel. The others on the field will pull them back as they retreat if they're able to, and if not, we'll get to them when the fighting stops for the night. We can't help them now. Come on, we gotta go!"

"All right, but I don't like it, Henry."

"Neither do I. But it won't do any good for anyone if we get in the way down here."

ᎾᎾᎾ ᎾᎾᎾ ᎾᎾᎾ

"Captain Weatherby, I passed out all the other water flasks. This last one is yers," I said as I caught up with him. He brought up the rear of the company as we moved a little closer to Captain Bowman's company. "Do ye want me to get more waterskins from the men and fill them? I mean, the British have paused for a time, and it might be a while yet before they start shooting again and the men could really use the water." I asked as I handed him his water pouch. He watched the field below between two large gulps of water.

"This heat makes me think we are on hell's doorstep in more ways than one," he said as he wiped the sweat off his face. "Not a cloud in the sky. No, Daniel. There's no time. Things are about to change very quickly, I think. The rest of them will have to go without if they don't have water already. See there, General Maxwell is having a word with Lieutenant Colonel Smith. It may be that some more of the 2nd New Jersey besides Captain Bowman's company has been pushed back on the bridge. They are fighting hard to maintain it. We will engage the enemy soon. It's time for you to report to Colonel Shreve."

"Surely there is something I could do to help here? I can stay in the back and reload at the very least."

"No. I will not pay the price of freedom with the blood of our children if I have a choice. Right now, I have that choice. Now, Go."

"Sir, I am as big as any man here and just as fast. I can help."

"I know, but not in this."

"But sir, I--"

"I'll brook no argument on this with you," he said, raising the flat of his hand stopping me. "I want you with the colonel. Besides, I am selfish. I want you to be able to play for the troops later tonight if all stops at dark, as I suspect. They will need what comfort you can bring them."

Battle of Connecticut Farms

It only took me a few minutes to reach Colonel Shreve. He was up higher on the hill and keenly watching the movements on the field below. Captain Bowman's company was fully engaged at the first bridge on Galloping Hill Road with the enemy. Captain Weatherby's platoon and the rest of the 2nd New Jersey had moved in position between us and Captain Bowman's men to safeguard the way to Morristown and our provisions.

"Will ye look at that, Colonel? I don't think I've seen them all in one place before," I shouted over the booming musket fire.

"It is a sight, Daniel. The whole New Jersey Brigade is there, including most of Spencer's regiment. We will do what we can to hold the enemy off until General Washington arrives, and if we are blessed, we will push them back. They are good men, all of them, the bravest," he yelled back.

"Papa is here, sir."

"Is he? Thou has seen him?"

"No, not yet colonel, sir."

"Then he's with Spencer's detachment and with thy brother. They'll be safe. Richard will see to it. He's a good man, and he keeps his head."

"Thank ye, sir. Doesn't do much to dispel the worry, though."

"No, it does not, but I thought it might help thee to be reminded of thy father's skill. Did thou manage to bring thy fife in all the rush? General Maxwell may need thee and the drummers to direct the troops shortly."

"Yes sir, I have it."

"Very well, then. Take some rest under that shade tree with the drummers and cool down for a bit. I'll call for thee if anything changes."

"Thank ye, sir, but no. I won't rest. May I stay here, with ye, colonel?"

"Thou may, but come up in the wagon. Thou will see better from up here."

"Thank ye, sir," I said as I climbed into the wagon. "I see a few men still in the cherry orchard over there, but there's so much smoke I don't see the rest." I took a moment to wipe my face on my sleeve to remove the sweat stinging my eyes, hoping that would make some difference.

"Ahhh, they are there, retiring to the defile. There's some protection there, but not much. At least there is some water there to cool them. Soon they will be near Captain Bowman's troops," he said as he pulled his kerchief out of his coat pocket and wiped his face as well. Though it was not quite mid-morning, the sun and humid air blanketed us in a swelter.

Something on the field caught his attention, and he leaped to his feet, rocking the wagon. "We need to move back and *now!*" he bellowed in frustration as he shielded the hot sun from his eyes. The colonel was not one to get overly excited at most things, and when he yelled, the young drummers found their feet and ran to the wagon to have a look-see themselves. Observing protocol once again, I jumped from the wagon to be with my fellows but stayed within earshot of the colonel.

"Good. Dayton and Smith are retiring the men to the Springfield bridge; they see the British moving forward. Who is that covering Bowman's Company? Can thou see, Daniel?"

"Don't know, sir. I think it is a combination of the 1st and 3rd New Jersey laying down suppressing fire as they get past the Springfield Bridge."

"And the militia has moved into place at the Springfield bridge. At least I think it is the militia, one of the drummers chimed in. Whoever it is, they brought a cannon with them."

"Yes, I see them, Obadiah. It is the militia. Thank thee, Generals

Sterling, and Maxwell. The militia and their cannon are most welcome."

The five of us stood, eyes locked on the battle as it played out in front of us. The fight raged for nearly two hours in a repeated rhythm of our troops driving forward only to fall back while men on both sides of the field fell. At the last, we were pushed to the north side of the Springfield bridge and then the militia cannon thundered to life. The enemy responded in kind with their cannon, but then, for an unknown reason, abruptly broke off the engagement and headed back the way they came.

I didn't wait for an order or get permission; I ran down the hill with fear fueling my feet, wanting only to find my brother, my father, and my friends safe in the field. The drummers followed after me, scattering in all directions toward the injured men At the bottom, I bent over, trying to catch my breath while my face dripped in sweat and my sopped salty hair fell across my face.

"Ye all right there, boy?"

"*Ja,* yes, sir," I slowly stood upright, wiping the wet my hair away from my eyes. The man was with two others, and they all looked worse than I felt. "Wanting to find my father, my brother," I said between breaths. "Last name, Applegate."

"I know quite of few Applegates son; what would be their first names?"

"Richard and Benjamin—Ben."

"I know them. Last I saw, they were fine. They're just over there," he said as in pointed to the east. "Ye got any water left in that bag?"

"*Ja,* sure. It's yours." The three of them drained the contents and handed my leather canteen back.

"We're just gonna rest up there in the shade of that tree for a bit. Just a little tired."

"All right."

"Daniel! *Daniel!* need yer help, *now!*' I turned towards the voice and ran to Obadiah, who was trying to walk back up the hill with a man twice his size with a bandaged leg. I grabbed the man's waist and lifted him as he swung his arm around my shoulders. "I think I saw a doctor sitting up there by the colonel, before I came down. It's all right, sir, we got ye now, we'll get ye to the top and the shade tree. More help should be up there."

"Don'tcha be bump'n that leg. I might just swoon on ye if ye do and I, for one, would like to stay awake while I'll be see'n the physician. Don't trust them, they're too friendly with their bone saws. Ye two are but boys, whatcha do'n out here?"

"We're musicians, sir. We watched ye from up on the hill and waited with the colonel in case commands were given for the field. Ye all were doing so good on yer own that we weren't needed at all," Obadiah said, trying to be encouraging.

"Don't like retreating and all, but not sure what else we coulda done," he said as he winced to lift his leg, trying to help us keep his bad leg off the ground. "Way too many of them. We were enough though, 'cause they left. Did either of ye lay eyes on the general yet?"

"Na, not seen General Washington yet, but word is that he'll be here soon, with the rest of the troops," I chimed in. "What's yer name, sir?"

"Zebulon Johnson. Call me Zeb."

"Well Zeb, ye kept Morristown safe for today," I replied.

"For today," he repeated. "I am about done, boys. We better hurry."

"There's the tree and the doctor. See them Zeb? Not too much farther. We'll set ye down under it right here and have a word with Doctor Campfield," I responded.

"All right. I'll just rest a bit then."

"Obadiah, ye doing all right?". Obadiah had begun to sway a bit where he stood.

"I'm good. Just hot, that's all, Daniel."

"Then sit for a minute with Zeb. I'll be back after talking to Campfield." No sooner than I said this, the doctor yelled my name, and I ran the few feet to him.

"Daniel, carry this man over by Obadiah, have Obadiah put pressure on the man's leg wound, show him how. The bleeding has stopped, but it could go again with the movement. I'll be over there in a minute to take care of the rest." The doctor yelled, taking his attention just a moment from an arm he was bandaging. "Then come back here for the water buckets, fill them up and start ladling out water to the men under the tree. They're gonna die from the lack of water if we don't get some into them soon. You're going to need to make several rounds with those buckets, so make sure you drink, too. Feels like we're at the gates of hell with this heat," he said as he focused his attention back on the man in front of him.

"Yes, sir." I said as I turned to the man with the wounded leg. "What's your name, sir?" I asked, as I bent over him.

"Ephraim. Ahhh, that hurts."

"All right Ephraim, I am going to be yer crutch. Ye ready?"

"Do I have a choice?"

"Don't think so. Ready, on the count of three. One, two, three, up ye go." He screamed as I lifted him. I did my best not to flinch at the howl. We stood there for a moment while he caught his breath. "Let's go. Might be twenty steps as most. I'll count them down. Ready?" Ephraim shook his head, 'yes' and clenched his jaws shut, determined not to shriek in pain again. "All right, nineteen to go. Where you from Ephraim?"

"Nut Swamp."

"I got family around Nut Swamp, by the name of Applegate. Fifteen steps."

"I've heard of some Applegates. Old William Applegate comes to mind at the moment."

"Ye're doing good there, Ephraim; 10 more steps. *Ja*, that's my Uncle Bill, not seen him in a long time."

"Bill sold me one of his draft horses. Good strong, healthy beast."

"I'll let Uncle Bill know ye are pleased with the horse when I see him next. All right, we're here. Obadiah, can ye help me get him to the ground?"

"Sure." We set him down as gently as we could, but he still squealed in pain. "I got him, Daniel."

"Press on his leg here and keep it there until Campfield comes."

"All right, Daniel. I can see that Doctor Campfield is about done. Go get the water," he said as he maneuvered around to Ephraim's injured leg and began to apply pressure as I showed him. The leg didn't bleed at all in moving Ephraim. I prayed it would stay that way.

༄ ༄ ༄

I set the buckets of water on the dry, crunchy grass. I had sloshed more of the precious liquid to the ground than all the other buckets I had carried so far; I was getting tired. *Well, even the grass needs a drink every now and then.* I slowly stood, feeling a little dizzy, as I massaged my upper arms and shoulders. I turned my head because I thought I heard Papa's voice calling my name when all went sideways and dark.

"Daniel, Daniel! I got ye, I got ye. Here, drink this, son," he said as he propped me up against the trunk of the tree that I had been standing under. "*Ja*, that's it, drink. There is plenty more." It wasn't just water; it was cold honey water. I drank deeply from his canteen.

"Yer here," I croaked.

"Of course, I'm here lad. Been here since this morning. Came in with the militia, as promised. They were none pleased that the British came through Elizabeth Point. I ran into a few problems getting back and couldn't return as soon as I had planned. I am sorry."

"That's all right. Yer here now. Ye look to be in one piece."

"I am, thankfully."

"Is Ben, all right? Have ye seen Oliver?" I asked after another swallow.

"Ye brother is fine, as far as I know. Saw him not too long ago, although by now he might be chasing the rest of those Jägers back to the Point with the other men. Saw Oliver too. He's back up here, resting under

273

another shade tree. He was helping to take some of the injured to the doctor.

"Are ye up to walking a bit, to a more comfortable place, ye think? Doctor Campfield says it's time for ye to rest. I think he's right. Here, drink more," he said as he filled the cup again. "Yer regiment has been ordered to that meadow over yonder, to set up the camp. Captain Weatherby's already there. I'll walk ye over and then get ye some food. Then ye can sleep. I don't think there'll be a need for music tonight; besides it's gonna rain soon, the air is too heavy for it not too."

ꟼ○ꟼ ꟼ○ꟼ ꟼ○ꟼ

I woke out of a dead sleep hearing musket fire and sat up very quickly, knocking my head against a wooden board. "Ow! That hurts," I said under my breath as I rubbed my crown, getting my hand wet in the process. It must have rained while I slept under Papa's wagon. I barely remembered crawling under it in the early evening. Thunderous noise boomed to life over top of me, making me jump where I sat. At first, I thought it was musket fire, but after a few minutes of silence, I realized it was just thunder overhead.

"Be careful, there son, ye'll cause more water to fall on us," Papa whispered in an annoyed tone, laying on the ground near me. "Thunderstorm after thunderstorm last night. Did ye not hear any of it?"

"No. Slept right through them," I responded as started rooting around for my musket and cartridges that I had made. If they had gotten wet, I'd not be able to fire the musket; ye can't shoot with wet powder. We were commanded to sleep on them, to be at the ready and keep them dry. I wasn't quite sure how we were supposed to get any rest sleeping on what amounted to a rock underneath ye, so I laid them beside me and slept.

"Settle down, son. The musket, balls, and cartridges are safe. I laid them under the best part of the wagon floor and put a blanket over them, after ye fell asleep. They are but an arms-length away from ye."

"They are. I just found them. Thank ye, Papa."

"Get some more sleep if ye can. Dawn is just a few hours off."

Connecticut Farms Aftermath

"Wake up, little brother! Times a wasting and so is breakfast, if ye don't get yer feet under ye quick!" he said as he shook me, hard.

I grabbed his hand to make him stop. "Ben?"

"Who else would I be?" he said as he yanked me up onto my feet, causing me to nearly thump my head again on the wagon bottom and fall on my knees in the wet grass.

"Maybe yer ghost?" I replied as I rubbed my face with the flat of my hands.

"I'm no ghost and I don't think ghosts can pull ye off yer feet, anyway. More importantly, I'm hungry and if ye don't get moving, I'm carrying ye."

"All right, all right. Can ye wait a minute while I relieve myself?"

"Hurry, Papa got special permission to have me here, so I can't stay too long. Mmmmm, smell that? I'd like to eat it before I leave."

"*Ja,* I do. It's making my belly growl," I said as I walked the short distance to the tree line. "Been a while since I had sausages," I hollered behind my back. The trees were still dripping rainwater from last night and splattering on my head and running under my shirt, giving me goose bumps.

"Where did Papa find the sausage?" I asked as I walked up to Ben.

"Don't know, and not gonna ask."

"Sit, boys," Papa commanded as he shoveled eggs and sausages onto wooden plates, handing us one each. "I wish we had more time this morning, but I'll take what I can get. I'll come back to this spot in the early evening, if not sooner."

"Where ye going, Papa?" Ben asked, stopping his spoon in front of his mouth.

"I need to locate William, General Maxwell, that is. I want to make sure I'm still welcome to be here. I am not officially part of the militia, or the Continental army. The general may have had his mind changed for him since I last saw him when he said he would not refuse me if I joined in the melee."

"Ye sure were part of us yesterday down in that defile."

"Got too much practice in my younger years, Benjamin," he said as he forked another piece of sausage from the pan and added it to his plate. "By the way, ye handled yerself very well yesterday. There was a lot going on in that small space of creek bed."

"I was just doing what I supposed to do."

"Don't dismiss it. It's called courage when everything in ye tells ye to run away, but instead ye decide to stand and face the overwhelming odds presented to ye. Ye showed a lot of courage son, as did all the other men with us in that defile."

"I hadn't thought of it that way though, Papa. Thank ye."

"Is that coffee ready ye think, Daniel?" Papa asked.

"Think so," I replied as I poured the coffee and handed him the hot cup. He closed his eyes and sniffed the steam.

"Not bad for acorn coffee, I guess. What were ye up to before I found ye with the water buckets yesterday?"

"Not nearly as much as Ben. Captain Weatherby sent me to Colonel Shreve to keep me out of harm's way."

"I thought I saw ye up on the hill with Israel. Ye were as safe as ye could be, I guess. Anyway, it kept me from worrying about ye in the battle. Yer time will come, but not just yet.

"Doctor Campfield said ye helped save soldiers' lives by bringing the wounded men to him quickly and then went to hauling up the buckets of clean drinking water from the river to drink. Those men were comforted by yer service to them. That's a lot more than could be said of some pastors I've met.

"Thank ye, Papa."

"Don't leave those eggs to waste, boys eat up."

Papa and Ben ate in silence while the sun made its way above the horizon. I could eat no more and picked up my cup of black acorn coffee as I looked over the field where we held the line yesterday, remembering all those tense moments. Most of us made it through, but not all.

The dead must have been gathered up after I had fallen asleep last night. I could see the crushed grass where they had fallen, the only testament of their sacrifice. The surrounding blades were sprinkled with raindrops that sparkled with the light of the sun. A gentle wind came and bent the wet tall grass towards the blunted empty spaces to pay homage to those that died, those whose blood had been returned to the ground. It would always remain holy ground to me.

Papa and Ben were gone by 6 o'clock after they finished their coffee, and I was left with the cleanup. My plan was to find Captain Weatherby to see what he wanted me to do for the day, but he found me instead as I cleaned the rest of the dishes in a nearby creek.

"Ahh, there you are, Daniel. Did you have a good visit with your father this morning?"

"I did, sir. He's gone to see General Maxwell."

"Well, he's likely not to be back soon then. General Maxwell does like to talk."

"Yes sir. I've seen it."

"Well then, the men are still recovering from yesterday and the New Jersey Brigade has been ordered to maintain its position with arms at the ready. So, if you are up to it, I'd like you to play with the drummers in the camp. We could use some light-hearted music, but keep your wits about you and stay near the camp; do not cross the picket lines to go fishing, hunting or anything else. It's too dangerous to be wondering about."

"Yes sir. I didn't get a chance to ask you last night Captain, were any of the men in the platoon hurt?"

"No, they all made it back to camp in good health."

"That's the best news of the day so far. And Oliver, any word on Oliver? I heard he was all right, but I wanted to make sure."

"He's well. I saw him very late last night. All right, go find the drummers and other fifers in the regiment and make some music for the camp. You might take that fiddle with you as well. Check in with me at noon and before dinnertime. Oh, and be aware, General Washington might be about camp. He arrived late yesterday. Be mindful of your manners."

We did as the captain asked and kept the music light, but very few had the heart for it. They were solemn men, still hot, tired, and wondering what the next day would bring. So, we played quietly as we roamed the camp and listened to their stories of the day before, if they wanted to talk a bit. I wasn't quite sure what to make of some of the events as they described them, but I thought I'd get it all sorted out at some point.

♀○♀ ♀○♀ ♀○♀

The evening came slower than I wanted, but eventually I was back at Papa's camp and among family, with a decent supper and companionship that was a salve to this melancholy day.

"Ben, why would they burn Connecticut Farms down? What purpose would it serve?" I asked as I stirred up the embers in the dinner campfire and added a log. It had been another hot day, but the evening brought in a cooler breeze off the ocean, and we had all moved closer to the fire for warmth after eating our supper.

"No purpose, son, other than to encourage us to lose our heads the next time we meet," Papa interjected. "More beer or something stronger, Oliver?"

"Beer's fine, Richard. Thank ye," he said as he held his long arm out with his mug, giving it to Papa, and then stretched out his long legs beside the fire, leaning his back against a log on the ground. "That British departure was marked by pure vengeance. They plundered the little settlement, then lit it on fire and ravaged the women as they left, but that's not all."

"No, that's not all," Ben responded, holding his cup out to Papa for more beer. "Reverend Caldwell's wife is dead. The Reverend is beside himself with grief, as ye might expect. I offered what condolences I could from our family, Papa. I saw him as he had made his way through the regiments soon after roll call this morning."

"Thank ye, Ben. I did not see the Reverend while running my errands today and General Maxwell said nothing to me this morning of her death. He must not have known at that time, or he'd a said something. Mistress Caldwell was a pearl beyond price. Did ye know her well?"

"She always had a smile for me and Ben after church," I chimed in, "and would send me back to camp with some bread or sweets if she had any. She was kind to us all and reminded me a lot of Mama. I just can't believe she is gone."

"Me neither, little brother," Ben said as he wrapped his arms around my shoulders, giving me a short hug.

"How'd she die, Ben, Oliver? Do ye know? I've heard stories today, not sure what to believe at this point," Papa asked.

"Ye tell the story, Ben. Ye got it firsthand from one of the men that went with officers to talk to the ladies that were in the house with Mistress Caldwell," Oliver responded, as he shifted himself to sit up on the log that he had been leaning against.

"All right," Ben replied before he swallowed a mouthful of beer, giving himself a moment to order his thoughts. "All right, this is what I heard from Sergeant Brittin. Mistress Caldwell and two other women took sanctuary in a room at the rear of the house. The room had three stone walls and one window. It should have been safer than any other room in the home; musket balls don't go through stone.

"Anyway, a British foot soldier shot her through the window while she was sitting on a bed with one of the women who held the Caldwells' eight-month-old child. The child's brother, ye know, the three-year-old, was right there playing on the floor in front of his mother. The British soldier shot her twice, the sergeant said. The children saw all of it. They'll have nightmares for a long time, I expect," he said as he set his mug on the ground and looked into the fire.

"The British didn't waste any time getting into the house at that point. They kicked the door in and destroyed all that they couldn't carry as they moved through the rooms and hallways. They found nothing of value, so they came for Mistress Caldwell and the others in that back corner room. As Mistress Caldwell lay in her own blood, either dead or dying - I really hope she was dead by then - they ripped open her bodice, looking for jewels. She had no jewels, of course.

"When the British officers arrived, they ordered all the men out of the house, and determined that it should burn with the rest of the village. They allowed the women to leave with the children, and Mistress Caldwell was to be buried by the fire and the crumbling walls.

"The women then begged the officers to bring her body out of the house. They granted their wish by ordering two soldiers to remove her body. The foot soldiers removed her only to dump her on the side of the road before lighting the house afire." Ben picked up his cup and drank the last of his beer, and set the mug back on the ground.

"There was no reason to attack that house with only the women and children in it. There were no Continentals or militia hidden in the building. We all left for the defile long before the foot soldiers arrived," he said in a low, dark voice. He continued to stare into the fire, as if it would burn him free from the anger and guilt that were not his to bear, but lived within him anyway.

"It is not yer fault, son."

"Is it not mine and all the others' as well?" Ben answered, his eyes boring into his father's. "We should have stayed near."

"No, it is not yer fault or anyone else's. Staying to watch the home would have gotten more of ye killed. The right thing was to move back as ye did. No one expected the British to be so dishonorable as to attack unarmed women and children in their home.

"Our time will come to bring justice to the British for what was done."

"Then let us pray, Richard, that our justice remains on the side of righteousness and honor. Anything less would make us like the British and dishonor her memory and her beliefs. She was a good woman, always a kind word to me and anyone else she met," Oliver said before he took his last sip of beer.

Bobby Returns

"**B**obby? Ye're here? I thought I saw ye dancing and walking all at the same time towards me. Ye were quite a sight," I said with a smile as I wiped the sweat from my face with the handkerchief Papa had given me. I had just finished playing a new jig with the other musicians for a small group of camp followers and soldiers. Even in this heat, they felt the need to make merry and for a few short moments we made them forget about everything but where their feet were supposed to go. "Good to see ye, my friend, but I had hoped ye'd gone home."

"No, not yet. Anyways, I came down with Colonel Angell's Regiment. I couldn't roam around much until today, or I would a come sooner to see ye."

"I know, none of us can, it's too dangerous. Been itching to fish a bit, but it will violate orders if I do. I might ask the captain, anyway. Ye up for it?" I asked as he followed me to the where my band mates were resting. "We could use the food."

"Ja sure. Yer Papa here?"

"He's here. He arrived just before the battle."

"Well, if we catch fish, ye think he'll cook it for us? It was so good the last time."

"Don't think that will be a problem," I said as we sat down a little away from the others under a large shady oak. "Ye said 'not yet,' have ye had a change of heart?"

"Not yet? Oh! Ye mean about going home? *Ja,* I think so. I mean, I do want to help here, do my part, but I've been thinking more about what yer Pa said when I last saw him; and others in the regiment that have been saying the same thing. All of it has worn down my resolve."

"That's not such a bad thing, is it, going home to family? Anyway, mine is here. I am home, for the most part."

"I suppose ye already heard about Mistress Caldwell?"

"*Ja,* it's been two weeks, old news, but it still feels like it happened yesterday," I said as I dropped my chin to my chest, remembering her. "I caught Reverend Caldwell out of the corner of my eye the other day, as he walked through the camp talking to the men. I turned to look past him, expecting to see Mistress Caldwell hanging on his arm, and she wasn't there. It is still sad. He's holding up, but he looks a lot like Papa did when we lost Mama."

"Daniel, it's time. We gotta move on or we'll have the devil to pay."

"Coming! Wanna make use of that drum Bobby, and play with us today?"

"Sure."

"Daniel, ye ready?"

"Yes, sir. Can my friend drum with us?"

"That depends. Can he drum?"

"I can, sir," Bobby responded.

"Then on the count of four: One. Two. Three, and—"

Battle of Springfield

"Wake-up, wake-up, Daniel!"

"Wha, what Henry?" I said, grabbing his arm so that he'd stop shaking me. "Let me sleep. I was up late playing and in the middle of Christmas dinner and besides, it's still dark." I went back to my mess the day before, since Papa had been sent on an errand for the army. There was no telling when he'd be back.

"Christmas dinner? It's June. Have ye gone daft from too much sleep? Didn't ye hear the alarms?" he said as he threw my shirt at me.

"No, there were alarms?" I said through a yawn while trying to find the top of my shirt and pull it over my head. "What's to do?"

Henry looked at me, shaking his head, "The captain wants ye. Get yer arse moving, pack what ye have, and get to Weatherby."

"I sure wish this man's army would decide to stay in one place just for a bit."

"Can't. The enemy is on the move, and so should ye be, now git. Don't ye hear the musket fire?" Then he was off to help the others bring the tent down for packing on the wagon.

I stumbled out of the tent with my knapsack, musket, and boots in hand, feeling the dew-covered grass beneath my bare feet. The sun was shimmering just above the horizon, weaving an edge of golden light between tree trunks beyond the meadow and bringing with it the promise of another very hot day. I decided the first order of business was boots on my feet and then the necessary; it seemed safe enough while the 2nd New Jersey was busy swarming our tent village.

I squinted my eyes against the rising sun as I walked towards the Captain Weatherby's tent looking over the heads of the men rushing to assemble for orders. I found him standing alone, fussing with dispatches in his hands and sweat already dripping down his face.

"There you are! Glad you decided to join me, private!"

"My apologies, sir. The necessary was my first stop. I had to go."

"All right Daniel, not to worry. You're here soon enough. You and Joseph are with me," he said, nodding in Joseph's direction. Joseph was a gentleman older than Papa and he was very good at drumming, but not so much at shooting. He had a better chance of hitting one of us with a musket ball than the enemy, so they took his musket from him and gave it to another. He hadn't been bitter about it, but took it in stride and served as he wanted.

"Sir?"

"Remember, I said I wouldn't have you out here unless I really needed you? Well now, I need you. You will relay the commands to the company with Joseph. Can you do that?"

"Yes, sir!"

"Then both of you follow me. I need to speak to the rest of the men." He strode over to the gathered soldiers and motioned them to come closer.

"We've not much time, gentlemen. The musket fire you hear is from Colonel Dayton's men and that of the enemy. Dayton's regiment and some of the New Jersey militia are coming back to us by the way of the woods and orchards along the same defile they were stuck in two weeks ago. The men of the 2nd Rhode Island under Colonel Angell are moving to meet them, near the village. Our job is to provide cover for both regiments and the militia, bringing them to a place of safety across the Springfield bridge and beyond our lines. We *must* hold that ground for our brothers, men!"

"Are there any questions?"

"Do we know how many of the enemy there are, sir?" Henry

asked.

"Plenty. We'll have a long day ahead of us." He then turned to put his foot in the stirrup, lifting himself on his horse at the head of the column. "To the left - wheel!" he yelled as he raised his sword, leading the company to the left, following Colonel Shreve's lead. Joseph and I followed with the appropriate signal and fell in step beside Captain Weatherby.

"Look at that. Where's Colonel Shreve off to, I wonder? He's needed here, I'd think," Joseph said quietly in my ear as the muskets went silent for a moment.

I turned my head and watched Colonel Shreve ride his horse up the hill as the muskets began to fire again. "He must have a reason," I shouted to Joseph. *Shreve, who bravely fought at Brandywine, Germantown, and Monmouth, who never seemed to be afraid of anything, was leaving us? Why would he do that when we needed him most, when the British and Hessian forces down the road were weighing, measuring, studying us like a beast after its prey? We are outnumbered five to one.* I felt like I was going to be sick.

"Looks like Lieutenant Colonel Smith is in charge now. Are ye all right there, Daniel? Ye look a little peaked. Get some water into ye son, ye can't play if ye are half dead of thirst!"

I wasn't going to be half dead from thirst, but from fear. I didn't argue the point, but did as I was told and raised my face to the sky, hiding my panic as I quickly downed the tepid water. Joseph raised his own canteen to his mouth, gulping whatever liquid he had in there. "Gonna be a hot one today for sure," he said as he wiped his shirt sleeve across his mouth. "Shreve's headed to the barn with the tree up there, ye see him?"

"*Ja.* It must be cooler up there," I replied, trying to maintain calm by pulling my hair from my face and tying it back for the second time that morning.

"That is odd, him leaving like that. Doesn't feel right. That Lieutenant Colonel is a young and ambitious, but he does have the knack of handling men. Oh, come here Daniel! Quit fussing with it. I'll get yer hair tied back and it'll stay."

"Ye see the bits of the Queen's Rangers through the trees? Angell and Dayton's men are in the thick of it. Some of our men are back in the defile, I think." Joseph shouted in my ear as the muskets fired intermittently with their booms echoing through the hills.

"I see them. They are rapidly chasing our troops out of the woods."

Directly in front of us, the combined British and Hessian troops lumbered slowly up Galloping Hill Road. General Knyphausen was in no hurry to engage us; but left all that work for the Queen's Rangers while he watched our resolve, or so I thought.

"It's all right, Daniel. Won't be too long now. The Rhode Island detachment is about their business and Lieutenant Colonel Forrest's artillery is now place in front of us," Joseph yelled back. No sooner had he finished his statement that Captain Thompson of the Rhode Island detachment fired his cannon in the direction of the Loyalists, trying to scatter them. Another handful of our men came scrambling in and around the artillery crew while other troops came across the bridge and through the creek.

"I hope Bobby had the sense to leave," I said to Joseph in a few seconds of quiet between the musket fire and artillery. I didn't see him on the field at all, thank goodness.

"He better be gone. There's gonna be a serious argument down there before much longer; we put a bee in Knyphausen's bonnet at Connecticut Farms. Knyphausen has moved his cannon and men into place down at the bottom of the hill. Very soon those six pieces of artillery will be pointed at Rhode Island's one and the boys operating it." He paused for a moment and then looked back at me. "Ye shouldn't be here either, son."

"Well, maybe. I don't regret the choice I made." I replied, feeling the weight of my musket, the pinch of its strap, and the promise I made to

Papa and Ben. The time was not yet. *God willing, let it not come, and Lord, please let me see them again.*

I watched as Lieutenant Colonel Smith responded to Knyphausen's approach by ordering two whole platoons to fire at the British as they tested the range and trajectory of each of their six cannon against the men of the Rhode Island artillery. The Red coats aimed short, just missing our Rhode Island men.

In utter defiance, the Rhode Island cannon cockers turned their only cannon to face those of the British and answered their fire.

Meanwhile, the 2nd New Jersey covered Dayton's men and militia as they withdrew behind our line from the woods and cherry orchard. Surprisingly, the Loyalists and Queens Rangers that had been chasing our men through the orchard and woods, disappeared back into the forest and were not seen again. Moments later, we heard the sounds of a battle to the northwest. We were being flanked.

Then all hell was let loose, bringing smoke, fire and the searing heat of musket balls and grape shot from cannons that ripped and burned the flesh of men caught on both sides. I heard no screaming; nothing could be heard above the booms of the repartee of the British cannon and American cannon and our own musket volleys. The enemy fired and fired and fired until there was no Rhode Island cannon left, and its men lay dying in pieces, pouring their life's blood into the ground.

The Rhode Island and Lieutenant Colonel Forrest's cannon cockers bought us time, we brought most of Dayton and Angells' men in from the woods, orchard, and the defile, and the village back behind our lines and then we all had to pull back beyond Springfield bridge, near General Green, out of range, waiting for the enemy to overrun us. There were twice as many of them as us, with more firepower than I could even imagine, and coming at us very fast.

Then suddenly the British stopped abruptly, like they had done at Connecticut Farms, and retreated going back the way they came.

Broken Pieces

"**A**pplegate!"

"Sir?" I was busy ladling out water to the men that managed to make it to the shade. Many just laid down once they got there and went straight to sleep in the cooler grass. I had instructions from the doctor to wake them and force water down their throats, if need be. Fortunately, there was no forcing anyone, and they drank the water without reservation, which was unusual given that whiskey was the beverage of choice.

"I need yer help! I need to get this musket ball out of this man and sew him up. Bring that water."

I brought the water and stared at the damaged leg that looked like a piece of raw meat. The man was screaming at the top of his lungs from pain and fear; there was no laudanum to quell either. "Don't you even think about throwing up now, private." I did as I was told and managed to keep what little there was in my belly. "Here, I need you to hold him down. Sit on him if you must. If we're lucky, he'll go unconscious. *Watch him*, not me, for heaven's sake. I don't need you swooning, and . . . breathe through your mouth." The man had vomited down the front of his shirt. In this heat, I felt like I was swimming in it. "Ready?"

I hadn't even answered when the Doctor Campfield dug into the man's leg to get the bullet out. The man did swoon. Thank God, and the doctor was able to clean and sew the wound together. Hopefully, he had saved the leg, but there was no telling. We placed him on the wagon with the others to go to the hospital.

In my absence, Henry had taken up my bucket of water and ladle continuing to bring water to the tired and very hot men. So, I walked down to the field of battle to find more wounded. The cool ocean breeze had deserted us, and the field below had turned into hell's caldron: it shimmered with waves of heat, and reeked of dirty bodies, vomit, blood, sweat and stank like a latrine. The crows that had been comforting companions to me on my previous journeys now sounded like harpies to my ears as they flew over the broken men, waiting for them to die. Crows weren't the only evil there. Black flies infested the field in the afternoon sun, biting everything dead and stinging everything alive.

I hauled one injured man back to the doctor and then another and another, clearing the field one at a time until more help came.

"Ben?"

"Drink, little brother." Ben came out of nowhere and handed me a canteen filled with water that was clean, fresh, and cold going down my throat. "Slowly, now or ye'll be sick." I had just stopped for a moment and plopped down cross-legged on the meadow under a small tree to cool down when he found me. "Ye're not hurt anywhere? I least I don't see that ye are bleeding."

"Na, all I had to do was fife and stay out of the way. The men, I need to get them."

"And ye shall, but ye won't be any good for them unless ye get some more water in ye and rest a bit."

"Where were ye?"

"My company was stuck up there with General Green. We were there to keep the enemy from getting access to the road to Morristown, this time. I came as soon as the officers felt it was safe for us to come to help."

"Papa?"

"He's all right. He's using the wagon to bring more wounded back from the village. Oliver is fine too. I just saw him off to the hospital. I don't know about any of the others just yet."

"Oliver? What happened to him?"

"Got himself shot in the leg, no damage to the bone, missed an artery, hit just the fleshy part. He'll be fine."

"Bobby? Ye know if he's still here? He'd be with Rhode Island. I hope he wasn't with them in this."

"Don't know. I've not seen him. What I do know is that most of the Dayton's men made it back uninjured and some of Angell's men covering them did too. There, ye're looking better. Ye ready to get back at it, ye think?"

"*Ja,* I'm ready. Probably should fill my water bag back up first, though."

"Ye do that and splash some of the water on yer face. Ye'll feel better if ye do. I'll head on down and see who I can bring back. Love ye, little brother."

"Holler for me if ye need help. Love ye Ben."

ᴥ◯ᴥ ᴥ◯ᴥ ᴥ◯ᴥ

We worked into the late afternoon in that field, bringing in the wounded, the dead, and pieces of the dead that we could find. I saw that Ben was by himself where Angell's artillery attachment had been obliterated and headed his direction. The field was now empty of the brave Rhode Island men who with one cannon had done battle against six and greatest army in the world. They fought with unbridled courage and with the knowledge of certain death, as they provided cover for our men.

"This, too, is holy ground, Daniel. Sanctified by the blood of mere men," Ben whispered as I approached his side. He reached out for my hand as we stood together in silence. "Let us and our cause be worthy of this great sacrifice, Lord," he said. We closed our eyes and let the peace of the place fill us. Neither of us wanted to leave, but as the sun started to make its slow descent, we needed to be on our way. "Let's go find Papa. I think I saw him up on the hill a few minutes ago."

As we turned, my eye caught sight of a splash of blue nestled in the tall grasses near the border of the woods. "Ben, I'm gonna head over there a bit. I think we have another man down," I said as I nodded my head in the general direction. "If I need help to bring him back, I'll holler."

"Na, I'll come with ye, then we'll look for Papa. Maybe he'll have a camp set and be ready to cook by the time we find him. I have some water left, ye want some?"

"Thanks. Not sure I'll be able to eat, but I am ready to sleep. I am so tired." I said, as I passed the water back to him.

Ben walked out ahead of me, breaking the trail of tall grass, and I followed in his footsteps. He handed the water bag over to me for one last sip, as he bent over the splotch of blue that I couldn't see from behind him. "Well, that's not a man. It's a perfectly good drum. Blue with a red rim."

I stood still, frozen in place. *No! That can't be. There are a lot of blue drums with red rims.*

"Daniel? Are ye all right, little brother?" he asked as turned to look at me.

"*Ja,* it's just been a long day," I said as wiped the sweat from my face and eyes. "Is there a fresh slanted 'X' mark carved in the top rim near one of the ropes?" I held my breath as I watched Ben pick up the drum and turn it. About halfway through the rotation, he stopped and walked towards me.

"Is this the mark?"

"*Ja* . . . it is." Tears formed in my eyes and dripped down my face. "It's Bobby's drum."

"Maybe not. I have seen others with 'X's' scratched in the rims. The drummer may have thrown it away so that he could run faster from the British. We need to find him," he said as he squeezed my shoulder. "Look over there, where the grass is trampled. That seems the place to start. Do ye want to carry the drum, or should I?"

"Na, I'll carry it. If it's Bobby's, he wouldn't want anyone but me to touch it, anyway; tuning drumheads is a little tricky," I said as wiped the last of the tears while holding on to the hope that we would find him alive.

We didn't have to walk too far, maybe a hundred yards or so, before Ben turned, blocking my view. I had my eyes to the ground for much of that short walk, just making sure I put one foot in front of the other. "He's here, Daniel."

"Who's here, Bobby? Let me see."

"No. Ye don't need to see this, little brother," he said as he pulled me in closer to him, and away from what lay down the grassy path.

"It's Bobby?"

"Boys!"

Ben raised head and hand to Papa's voice, and I made my escape from his arms, dropping the drum and running towards the place where Bobby laid. I had to see him for myself.

"*Noooooooo!*" I screamed as I fell to my knees in a flood of tears. "Nooooo!" I shrieked again while swiping at the flies that covered his body once I was on the ground. Then Papa and Ben were both there, both trying to hold me, to move me back, to turn my eyes around. Bobby was long dead. There was no doctor's skill that could have mended his mangled body. A well-aimed cannon ball had taken his life.

⚈◯⚈ ⚈◯⚈ ⚈◯⚈

I woke to Papa and Ben talking in subdued tones and wasn't really understanding what they were saying. Barely awake, I turned to the side and put my forearm down, lifting myself off the ground gently, not wanting to add to my distress by hitting my head again on the wagon bed above me. I was still tired and the sadness that I had felt was still there but seemed not to be ripping at my soul as much.

"Papa?" He came and squatted down directly in front of me. Night had fallen, and I could only see him as a dark outline edged by a halo of red and orange firelight. The crackle of the fire was comforting, and all I wanted was to go back to sleep.

"I am here," he said as he handed me something in a cup.

"What is it?"

"It's chamomile tea from the doctor. He said it would do ye some good."

I was hesitant to try it. It was well known that when a doctor gave ye something to drink, it usually tasted like dung. I sipped it and found the tea filled with the taste of berries and something else. "Whiskey?"

"*Ja,* just a tad, not much more than that, thought it might help. Think ye can eat?"

Before I could answer, my belly growled loudly.

"I'd say that was a definite yes. Crawl out from there and we'll get ye a plate of dinner then."

We walked together in companionable silence. I sat slowly to the ground, with Papa there to catch me if I fell. Ben handed me a plate of potatoes, ham and beans, and a canteen full of fresh water. The food was not from the military stores, and as before, I was not inclined to ask how Papa came by it. I ate my fill and leaned back against the log as I sat on the ground gazing into the fire, not wanting to talk, yet needing to all the same. Papa and Ben were quiet too, with their own thoughts, watching the fire.

The whole day had been a nightmare for me that only got worse as time moved on. I just wanted it to be over. I thought I would wake up from the nap and realize that this day hadn't happened. It was just a bad dream, and that everything was fine, but everything wasn't fine. I had been broken, it hurt, and I felt the pain of Bobby's death close, again.

"Papa, I remember how I felt when Mama passed, when ye came to tell me. I think I had expected it. She was so sickly for so long, but it still hurt deep inside when she passed. I didn't have the words then, but I do now. I think we all died a little bit that day. I remember the dark days afterwards, each of us missing her in different ways. I kept looking for her, listening for her voice and then remembered she was not here, not with us."

"Ahh, but she is with us, son. She's here and here," he said as he touched his hand to my chest and my head, looking into my eyes to make sure I understood. "Bobby is there too, if ye look for him," he said, as I nodded in response.

"There was nothing ye could do to change Bobby's mind. Ye bear no fault. Ye know this in yer heart, little brother. He wanted to be here, he thought it was important to be here, and no matter what ye, Papa or I have counseled."

"Know that ye made his days better while he was here. Spending with him many an off hour from your duties to fish, hunt,swim and to play that drum. Ye made good memories with him. Lean on those, they are a rare treasure indeed. Just like yer mama, I don't think ye'll ever get over this, but the pain will ease with time," Papa added.

"How do I move forward, Papa?"

"Keep yerself busy. The regiment should be able to help with that. Keep yer brother and friends close when I cannot be here. Lastly, live yer life. Bobby would want that."

"We will bury him tomorrow, in town. One of the town's people gave us a plot in the churchyard for his burial and the men of the Rhode Island and New Jersey regiments have had a new maple coffin made for him. He will be laid to rest with full honors."

"That is good, Ben. Ye both will go with me?"

"We will stand with ye tomorrow Daniel," Papa replied.

"I am feeling pretty sleepy at this point. I am going to head back to the wagon," I said as I stood up. "I think that chamomile tea is more potent than ye thought, Papa."

"Don't know, might be. Ye need some help?" Papa responded when he rose from his log.

"Na, I'll do, but a hug from both of ye would be nice, though."

Acknowledgments

Many thanks to the following folks:

Tim Abbott, who wanted to believe and cared enough to contact John U. Rees for confirmation of Daniel's identity in history.

John U. Rees, who has a penchant for historical statistics and reading very bad cursive writing. Without his work and ability to share it, this novel may have never been written.

Lars Hedbor, who took a chance with this novice and stayed the course with knowledge, patience and perseverance.

Lawrence Schmidt, for his knowledge and wisdom.

2nd New Jersey, Helms Company Re-enactors – The American Revolution, for questions answered and knowledge gained.

Susan McLaughlin for reading with a teacher's eyes.

James Sission for making himself available as a secondary reviewer and editor.

Andrea, Amy, Becky, Bill, Lois, Lorrain, Pam, Salina, Sue, Shannon, and Susan for their encouragement.

Ernie, for our discussions on little known pieces of American history.

My son for making sure no research materials were lost during this ten-year project.

My husband, for listening, reading, and encouraging me through the tough spots of this project.

Bibliography

Applegate, Charles. *Let Buck Get His Fiddle.* 1870.

Applegate, Shannon. *Skookum: An Oregon Pioneer Family's History and Lore.* First Edition ed., Oregon State University Press, 2005.

Applegate, Susan. *Family Party in Winter.* Yoncalla, Oregon, 1983.

"Before West Point Military Academy (USMCA) There Was Pluckemin." *Mrlocalhistory.Org*, Mr. Local History Project, www.mrlocalhistory.org/pluckeminwestpoint/. Last date accessed: 28 January 2025

Boekmann, Catherine. "Ice Thickness Safety Chart." *Almanac.Com*, The Old Farmer's Almanac, www.almanac.com/ice-thickness-safety-chart. Last date accessed 27 January 2025.

"Bottle Hill, 1710 - 1834." *Madisonhistoricalsociety.Org*, Madison Historical Society, www.madisonnjhistoricalsociety.org/1710-1834-bottle-hill?rq=Bottle%20Hill. Last date accessed: 27 January 2025.

Brown, Zachary. "The Rhetoric and Practice of Scalping." *Allthingsliberty.Com*, Journal of the American Revolution, 2016, allthingsliberty.com/2016/09/rhetoric-practice-scalping/. Last date accessed: 27 January 2025.

Bubis, Dan, and Jax Bubis. "On This Day in History, January 25, 1780, The Court House and Presbyterian Church Burned at Elizabethtown, New Jersey." *Revolutionary War and Beyond*, Facebook.com, www.facebook.com/profile/100063443187186/search/?q=The%20 Court%20House%20and%20Presbyterian%20Church%20 Burned%20at%20Elizabethtown%2C%20New%20Jersey. Last date accessed: 31 January 2025.

Campbell, Mike. "Mohawk Names." *Behind the Name*, 1996-2023, www. behindthename.com/submit/names/gender/masculine/usage/ mohawk. Last date accessed: 27 January 2025.

Continental Congress. *Oaths of Enlistment and Oaths of Office, Voted 3 February 1778*, history.army.mil/Research/Reference-Topics/ Oaths/. Last date accessed: 27 January 2025.

Cox, Caroline. *Boy Soldiers of the American Revolution*. University of North Carolina, 2016.

"Dark Day-Today in History, May 19." *Connecticut History.Org*, Connecticut History.org, 19 May 2020, connecticuthistory.org/ dark-day-today-in-history-may-19/. Last date accessed: 27 January 2025.

"Dragging Cannon from Fort Ticonderoga to Boston 1775." *Gilder Lehrman Institute of American History*, 2012, www.gilderlehrman. org/history-resources/spotlight-primary-source/dragging-cannon- fort-ticonderoga-boston-1775. Last date accessed: 27 January 2025.

Federal Reserve Bank of Philadelphia. "Money in Colonial Times." *Philadelphiafed.Org*, www.philadelphiafed.org/education/ teachers/resources/money-in-colonial-times. Last date accessed: 27 January 2025.

"The Fighting Man in the Continental Army, Daily Life As A Soldier." *Battlefields.Org*, American Battlefield Trust, 2017, www.battlefields.org/learn/articles/fighting-man-continental-army. Last date accessed 27 January 2025.

Gelber, Ben. *Pennsylvania Weather Book*, Rutgers University Press, New Brunswick, New Jersey, 2002, p. 34.

Gerard, Paul. "History of the Sweet Potato." *Many Eats*, manyeats.com, 2 Apr. 2012, manyeats.com/history-of-the-sweet-potato. Last date accessed: 27 January 2025.

Godbout, Andrea. "John Locke's Ideas about Child Development." *Hellomotherhood.Com*, Hello Motherhood, 13 June 2017, www.hellomotherhood.com/article/1004884-john-lockes-ideas-child-development/. Last date accessed: 27 January 2025.

Hart, Hugh. "Collectors Are Hooked on Vintage Ice Fishing Decoys with Their Intricate Detailing." *Special to the Tribune*, Chicago Tribune, 4 May 1994, www.chicagotribune.com/news/ct-xpm-1994-05-08-9405080382-story.html. Last date accessed: 27 January 2025.

Headle, Lura E. "Grants of Land by the United States to Our Soldiers of Past Wars." *Jstor.Org*, Advocate of Peace through Justice, www.jstor.org/stable/20660002?seq=1#metadata_info_tab_contents. Advocate of Peace through Justice, Vol. 84, No. 5 (MAY, 1922), pp. 176-178 (3 pages), Last date accessed: 27 January 2025.

Herwick, Edgar B. "New England's Dark Day Time, That Time in 1780 When It Was Night before Noon." *Wgbhnews.Org*, GBH, 26 May 2015, www.wgbh.org/news/post/new-englands-dark-day-time-1780-when-it-was-night-noon. Last date accessed: 27 January 2025.

"Ice Fishing Safety." *Takemefishing.Org*, Take me Fishing, www. takemefishing.org/ice-fishing/. Last date accessed: 27 January 2025.

J., Christina. "The Lard That Binds (or My First 18th Century Pomatum)." *Onlivinghistory.Blogspot.Com*, 11 Aug. 2014, http:// onlivinghistory.blogspot.com/2014/08/the-lard-that-binds-or-my-first-18th-c.html. Last date accessed: 27 January 2025.

"The Killing of Hanna Caldwell." *Njstatelib.Org*, New Jersey Journal, 14 June 1780, www.njstatelib.org/wp-content/uploads/ slic_files/imported/NJ_Information/Digital_Collections/ NJInTheAmericanRevolution1763-1783/9.9.pdf. Last date accessed: 27 January 2025.

MacWelch, Tim. "Survival Cooking: How to Cook with Sticks." *Outdoorlife.Com*, 2019, www.outdoorlife.com/survival-cooking-how-to-cook-with-sticks/. Last date accessed: 27 January 2025.

"Martin Luther's Table Prayers." *Redbrickparsonage.Wordpress.Com*, Redbrick Parsonage, 4 Nov. 2014, redbrickparsonage.wordpress. com/2014/11/04/martin-luthers-table-prayers/. Last date accessed: 27 January 2025.

Matchett, William H. "Western Friend, Some Notes on Quaker Speech." *Westernfriend.Org*, July 2016, westernfriend.org/magazine/on-heritage/some-notes-on-quaker-speech/. Last date accessed: 27 January 2025.

McKee, Samuel, 4th Circuit Judge for the State of Kentucky. "Daniel Applegate Pension Request." National Archives through Fold 3, 21 June 1819.

Mckee, Samuel, 4th Circuit Judge for the State of Kentucky. "Daniel Applegate Pension Redetermination." National Archives through Fold 3, 11 December1819

Moon Giant. "Moon Phase Calendar." *Moongiant.Com*, www.moongiant.com/. Last date accessed: 27 January 27, 2025.

A new and accurate map of New Jersey, from the best authorities. [London, 1780] Map. Retrieved from the Library of Congress, <www.loc.gov/item/97683600/>. Last date accessed 27 January 2025.

"The New England Dark Day, May 19, 1780." *Newenglandhistoricalsociety.Com*, New England Historical Society, 2023, newenglandhistoricalsociety.com/new-england-dark-day-may-19-1780/. Last date accessed: 27 January 2025.

"Punching Bag." *How Products Are Made*, www.madehow.com/Volume-7/Punching-Bag.html. Last date accessed: 27 January 2025.

Rees, John U. "One of the Best in the Army, An Overview of the New Jersey Brigade, 1775-1783." *Revwar75.Com*, John U. Rees, 2002, revwar75.com/library/rees/njbrigade.htm. Last date accessed: 27 January 2025.

Rees, John U. "Supply Shortages, Suffering Soldiers and a Secret Mission During the Hard Winter of 1780." *Revwar75.Com*, 2002, revwar75.com/library/rees/blanketts.htm. Last date accessed: 27 January 2025.

Rodriguez, Sarah. "10 Most Powerful Medicinal Plants Used by Cherokees." *Askaprepper.Com,* 24 Sept. 2019, www.askaprepper.com/10-most-powerful-medicinal-plants-used-by-cherokees/. Last date accessed: 27 January 2025.

Roth, Steven M. "Stage Operations and the Mails in New Jersey." *Docs. Lib.Org*, 2013, docslib.org/doc/673169/stage-operations-and-the-mails-in-new-jersey. Last Date accessed: 27 January 2025.

Sandoz, Ellis, and Samuel Sherwood "Scriptural Instructions to Civil Rulers." *Political Sermons of the American Founding Era: 1730-1805, 2 Vols, Foreword by Ellis Sandoz (2nd Ed. Indianapolis: Liberty Fund, 1998)*, vol. 1, The Online Library of Liberty, Carmel, Indiana, 1998, https://oll.libertyfund.org/titles/sandoz-political-sermons-of-the-american-founding-era-vol-1-1730-1788--5. Last date accessed: 31 January 2025.

Sandoz, Ellis, and Elisha Williams. "The Essential Rights and Liberties of Protestants." *Political Sermons of the American Founding Era: 1730-1805, 2 Vols, Foreword by Ellis Sandoz (2nd Ed. Indianapolis: Liberty Fund, 1998)*, vol. 1, The Online Library of Liberty, Carmel, Indiana, 1998, https://oll.libertyfund.org/titles/sandoz-political-sermons-of-the-american-founding-era-vol-1-1730-1788--5. Last date accessed: 31 January 2025.

Schenawolf, Harry. "Loading and Firing a Brown Bess Musket in the Eighteenth Century." *Revolutionarywarjournal. Com*, Revolutionary War Journal, 1 Oct. 2014, www.revolutionarywarjournal.com/brown-bess/. Last date accessed: 27 January 2025.

Stryker, William S. "Official Register of the Officers and Men of New Jersey." *Njstatelib.Org*, WM. T, Nicholson & Co., Printers 1914, www.njstatelib.org/wp-content/uploads/slic_files/searchable_publications/reg/NJREGIntro.html. Last date accessed: 27 January 2025.

Struzinski, Steven. "The Tavern in Colonial America." *Cupola.Gettysburg. Edu*, The Gettysburg Historical Journal, 2003, cupola.gettysburg. edu/ghj/vol1/iss1/7/. Last date accessed: 27 January 2025.

"The Vanderveer Family and Farmstead." *Jvanderveerhouse.Org*, jvanderveerhouse.org/vanderveers. Last date accessed: 27 January 2025.

"Vanderveer Family Tree." *Jvanderveerhouse.Org*, img1.wsimg.com/ blobby/go/256b6e48-6328-41df-a432-a5dd4cd95e0f/downloads/ Vanderveer Family Tree.pdf?ver=1733366191273. Last date accessed: 27 January 2025.

"Vanderveer, Knox and the Pluckemin Cantonment." *Njskylands*, Skylands Visitor, 2013, www.njskylands.com/history-vanderveer-pluckemin-cantonment. Last date accessed: 27 January 2025.

"Vocabulary in Native American Languages: Seneca Words." *Native-Languages.Org*, Native Languages of the Americas, 1998, www. native-languages.org/seneca_animals.htm. Last date accessed: 27 January 2025.

Wallace, Anthony F.C. *The Death and Rebirth of the Seneca*. Vintage Books, 1969.

Wier, Stuart. "Biscuits, Hard Tack, and Crackers in Early America." 8 July 2014; www.westernexplorers.us/Biscuits_Crackers_Hard_ Tack_2010_SKWier.pdf. Last date accessed: 27 January 2025.

"William Howe, Commander in Chief - America." *Battlefields. Org*, American Battlefield Trust, www.battlefields.org/learn/ biographies/william-howe. Last date accessed: 27 January 2025.

Yarborough, Mike. "How to Make Acorn Coffee." *Wolf and Iron*, 7 Oct. 2015, wolfandiron.com/blogs/feedthewolf/how-to-make-acorn-coffee . Last date accessed: 27 January 2025.

Battles

"06/23/1780 Battles, Battle of Springfield in New Jersey." *Revwartalk. Com*, Rev War Talk, American Revolutionary War History, www. revwartalk.com/06-23-1780-battles-battle-of-springfield-in-new-jersey/. Last date accessed: 28 January 2025.

"The Battle of Springfield." *Revolutionarywar.Us*, American Revolutionary War 1775-1783, revolutionarywar.us/year-1780/battle-of-springfield/. Last date accessed: 28 January 2025.

"The Battle of Stoney Point." *Revolutionarywar.Us*, American Revolutionary War 1775-1783, revolutionarywar.us/year-1779/battle-stoney-point/. Last date accessed: 28 January 2025.

Fleming, Thomas. *The Forgotten Victory, The Battle for New Jersey-1780*. First Edition ed., Reader's Digest Press, Distributed by E. P. Dutton & Co., Inc., 1973. Last date accessed: 28 January 2025.

Grant, Larry. "Siege of Savannah." *Mountvernon.Org*, George Washington Presidential Library at Mount Vernon, www.mountvernon. org/library/digitalhistory/digital-encyclopedia/article/siege-of-savannah/. Last date accessed: 28 January 2025.

Lengle, Edward G. *The Battles of Connecticut Farms and Springfield*. Westhome Publishing, 2020.

Munn, David C. "The Battles and Skirmishes of the American Revolution in New Jersey." *Nj.Gov/Dep/Njgs/Enviroed,* Bureau of Geology and Typography, Department of Environmental Protection, www. state.nj.us/dep/njgs/enviroed/oldpubs/battles.pdf . Last date accessed: 28 January 2025.

"Newtown." *Battlefields.Org,* American Battlefield Trust, www. battlefields.org/learn/revolutionary-war/battles/newtown. Last date accessed: 28 January 2025.

Sheehan, Michael J. "Battle of Stoney Point." *Mountvernon.Org,* The George Washington Presidential Library at Mount Vernon, www. mountvernon.org/library/digitalhistory/digital-encyclopedia/ article/battle-of-stony-point. Last date accessed: 28 January 2025.

"Siege of Savannah." *Battlefields.Org,* American Battlefield Trust, www. battlefields.org/learn/revolutionary-war/battles/savannah. Last date accessed: 28 January 2025.

"Tyron's Raid." *Revolutionarywar.Us,* American Revolutionary War, 1775 to 1783, revolutionarywar.us/year-1779/tryons-raid/. Last date accessed: 28 January 2025.

Oliver Cromwell

Korfhage, Matthew. "Black Soldier Who Crossed Delaware with Washington to Be Honored in New Jersey." *Courierpostonling. Com,* Courier Post, USA Today Network, 9 Feb. 2022, www. courierpostonline.com/in-depth/life/2022/02/09/oliver-cromwell-nj-revolutionary-war-soldier-honored-black-history-month/6646926001/. Last date accessed: 28 January 2025.

Oliver Cromwell, Oliver Cromwell Black History Society, Burlington, New Jersey, 2019.

"Oliver Cromwell." *Web.Archive.Org,* Burlington County, New Jersey, Cultural Affairs and Tourism, web.archive.org/web/20130129032716/ www.co.burlington.nj.us/pages/pages.aspx?cid=504 . Last date accessed: 28 January 2025

Rees, John U. "Nineteenth Century Remembrances of Black Revolutionary Veterans: New Jersey Soldier Oliver Cromwell." *Allthingsliberty. Com,* Journal of the American Revolution, 25 Feb. 2021, allthingsliberty.com/2021/02/nineteenth-century-remembrances-of-black-revolutionary-veterans-new-jersey-soldier-oliver-cromwell/. Last date accessed: 28 January 2025.

Schenawolf, Harry. "African Americans in the American Revolution: Oliver Cromwell." *Revolutionarywarjournal.Com,* Revolutionary War Journal, 15 May 2013, www.revolutionarywarjournal.com/ oliver-cromwell/. Last date accessed: 28 January 2025.

Captain Johnathon Dayton

Dayton, Jonathon. "I. To George Washington from Captain Jonathan Dayton." *Founders.Archives.Gov,* Founders Online, National Archives, founders.archives.gov/documents/ Washington/03-26-02-0233-0002. . Last date accessed: 28 January 2025

Brigadier General William Irvine

Irvine, William. "To George Washington from Brigadier General William Irvine." *Founders Online*, National Archives, founders.archives. gov/documents/Washington/03-24-02-0082. Last date accessed: 28 January 2025.

General Henry Knox

Heathcote, Charles William. "General Henry Knox, Adapted from The Picket Post." *Ushistory.Org*, Valley Forge Historical Society, www. ushistory.org/valleyforge/served/knox.html. Last date accessed: 28 January 2025.

Makos, Issac. "The Guns of Ticonderoga." *Battlefields.Org*, American Battlefield Trust, 8 Dec. 2020, www.battlefields.org/learn/articles/ guns-ticonderoga. Last date accessed 28 January 2025.

Brigadier General William Maxwell

Sobol, Thomas Thorleifur. "William Maxwell, New Jersey's Hard Fighting General." *Allthingsliberty.Com*, Journal of the American Revolution, 15 Aug. 2016, allthingsliberty.com/2016/08/william-maxwell-new-jerseys-hard-fighting-general/. Last date accessed: 28 January 2025.

Maxwell, William. "To George Washington from Brigadier General William Maxwell." *Founders Online*, National Archives, founders. archives.gov/documents/Washington/03-26-02-0030.

Colonel Israel Shreve

Shreve, Israel. "Battle of Connecticut Farms, 12 June 1780." Letter addressed to Polly Shreve, *Israel Shreve Letters*, University Archives and Special Collections, Prescott Memorial Library, Louisiana Tech University, 1780, Ruston, Louisiana.

Shreve, Israel. "Colonel Israel Shreve, Letter to Wife Polly, Camp at Scotch Plains, 6 November 1779." Received by Polly Shreve, *Special Collections and University Archives*, Rutgers University, New Brunswick, New Jersey.

Lieutenant Colonel William Stephens Smith

Smith, William Stephens. "To George Washington from William Stephens Smith, 10 November 1780." *Founders Online*, National Archives, founders.archives.gov/documents/Washington   /99-01-02-03889. Last date accessed 29 Sept. 2022.

Colonel John Taylor

Frazza, Al. "Taylor's Mill Historic District, Colonel Taylor's Grist Mill." *Revolutionarywarnewjersey.Com,* www. revolutionarywarnewjersey.com/new_jersey_revolutionary_war_ sites/towns/readington_township_nj_revolutionary_war_sites. htm#s2. Last date accessed: 29 January 2025.

George Washington

Washington, George. "Circular to the Brigade Commanders, 6 January 1780." *Founders Online*, National Archives, founders.archives. gov/documents/Washington/03-24-02-0034. Last date accessed: 29 January 2025.

Washington, George. "The Diaries of George Washington, Diary Entry 10 January 1780." *Founders Online*, National Archives, founders. archives.gov/?q=%20Author%3A%22Washington%2C%20 George%22%20Period%3A%22Revolutionary%20War%22%20 Dates-From%3A1780-01-10%20Dates-To%3A1780-01- 11&s=1111311111&r=1. Last date accessed: 31 January 2025.

Washington, George. "From George Washington to Brigadier General William Irvine, 4 January 1780." *Founders Online*, National Archives, founders.archives.gov/documents/Washington/03-24-02-0022. Last date accessed: 29 January 2025.

Washington, George. "From George Washington to Brigadier General William Irvine, 6 January 1780." *Founders Online*, National Archives, founders.archives.gov/documents/Washington/03-24-02-0034. Last date accessed: 29 January 2025.

Washington, George. "From George Washington to Brigadier General William Irvine, 9 January 1780." *Founders Online*, National Archives, founders.archives.gov/documents/Washington/03-24-02-0051. Last date accessed: 29 January 2025.

Washington, George. "From George Washington to Brigadier General William Irvine, 12 January 1780." *Founders Online*, National Archives, founders.archives.gov/documents/Washington/03-24-02-0081. Last date accessed: 29 January 2025.

Washington, George. "From George Washington to Brigadier General William Maxwell, 1 November 1779." *Founders Online*, National Archives, founders.archives.gov/documents/Washington/03-23-02-0112. Last date accessed: 29 January 2025.

Washington, George. "From George Washington to Brigadier General William Maxwell, 28 May 1780." *Founders Online*, National Archives, founders.archives.gov/documents/Washington/03-26-02-0148. Last date accessed: 28 January 2025.

Washington, George. "From George Washington to Major General Stirling, 13 January 1780." *Founders Online*, National Archives, founders.archives.gov/documents/Washington/03-24-02-0091-0001. Last date accessed: 29 January 2025.

Washington, George. "General Orders, 4 November 1777." *Founders Online*, National Archives, founders.archives.gov/documents/Washington/03-12-02-0100. Last date accessed: 28 January 2025.

Washington, George. "General Orders, 10 June 1780." *Founders Online*, National Archives, founders.archives.gov/documents/Washington/03-26-02-0247. Last date accessed: 29 January 2025.

Washington, George. "George Washington to the Board of War, 27 May 1780." *Founders Online*, National Archives, founders.archives.gov/documents/Washington/03-26-02-0137. Last date accessed: 29 January 2025.

Brigadier General Anthony Wayne

Wayne, Anthony. "To George Washington from Brigadier General Anthony Wayne, 4 November 1779." *Founders Online*, National Archives, founders.archives.gov/documents/Washington/03-23-02-0146. Last date accessed: 29 January 2025.

Music

St. John, Peter. "The Music of the 1770s: A Directory; American Taxation." *Motherbedford.Com*, Mother Bedford, www.motherbedford. com/Music062.htm. Last date accessed: 29 January 2025.

"The Music of the 1770s: A Directory; Anthony Wayne." *Motherbedford. Com*, Mother Bedford, www.motherbedford.com/Music064.htm. Last date accessed: 29 January 2025.

Tait, John. "The Music of the 1770s: A Directory; Banks of the Dee." *Motherbedford.Com*, Mother Bedford, www.motherbedford. com/Music067.htm. Last date accessed: 29 January 2025.

Moore, Frank. "Banks of the Dee – American Revolution War Song." *Americanrevolution.Org*, www.americanrevolution.org/war_ songs/warsongs17.php. Last date accessed: 30 January 2025.

Hopkinson, Francis. "The Music of the 1770s: A Directory - The Battle of the Kegs." *Motherbedford.Com*, www.motherbedford.com/ Music004.htm. Last date accessed: 30 January 2025.

More, Frank. "Battle of the Kegs - American Revolution War Song." *AmericanRevolution.Org*, www.americanrevolution.org/war_ songs/warsongs55.php. Last date accessed: 30 January 2025.

"The Music of the 1770s: A Directory - Fish and Tea." *Motherbedford. Com*, www.motherbedford.com/Music093.htm. Last date accessed: 30 January 2025.

"The Music of the 1770s: A Directory - Maggie Lawder." *Motherbedford. Com*, www.motherbedford.com/Music034.htm. Last date accessed: 30 January 2025.

Wyoming Massacre/Sullivan Expedition

"The Battle of the Wyoming Valley (Massacre)." *Revolutionarywar. Us*, American Revolutionary War 1775-1783, revolutionarywar.us/year-1778/battle-wyomimg-valley-massacre/. Last date accessed: 30 January 2025.

Bishop, Morris. "The End Of the Iroquois." *Americanheritage.Com*, American Heritage Magazine, www.americanheritage.com/end-iroquois. Last date accessed: 28 January 2025.

Beyond the Marker. "Battle of Wyoming Historical Marker." *Explorepahistory.Com*, Explore Pa History, explorepahistory.com/hmarker.php?markerId=1-A-17B. Lasts date accessed: 30 January 2025.

Hardenbergh, John L., et al. *Narratives of Sullivan's Expedition 1779*. First ed., Leonaur, an Imprint Oakpast Ltd., 2010.

"History of Luzerne County Pennslyvania." Edited by H. C. Bradsby, *Usarchives.Net*, Us Archives, www.usgwarchives.net/pa/luzerne/1893hist/ch4.htm. Last date accessed: 30 January 2025.

Lossing, Benson J. "Position of the Wyoming Forts, 1770s." *Pictorial Field-Book of the Revolution*, I, Harper and Brothers, 1851, https://etc. usf.edu/maps/pages/8100/8176/8176.htm. Last date accessed: 30 January 2025.

Lubinsky, Mary Ann, et al. "The Battle of Wyoming." *Pagenweb. Org*, PAGen Web Project, www.pagenweb.org/~luzerne/patk/ wyoming.html. Last date accessed: 30 January 2025.

"Map of the Battle of Wyoming." *Wikimeida.Org*, Pittson Gazette Centennial Handbook 1778-1878, upload.wikimedia.org/ wikipedia/commons/5/5c/Pittston_gazette_centennial_ hand-book%2C_1778-1878_-_one_hundredth_anniversary_ of_the_battle_and_massacre_of_Wyoming%2C_July_3_ and_4%2C_1878_-_containing_a_complete_historical_sketch_ of_Wyoming_Valley_%281459667996
7%29.jpg. Last date accessed: 30 January 2025.

McGinnis, Richard. "Richard McGinnis' Account on the Battle of Wyoming on July 3, 1778." Edited by Henry Steel Commanger and Richard B. Morris, *Explorepahistory.Com*, Explore PA History, explorepahistory.com/odocument.php?docId=1-4-B6. Last date accessed: 30 January 2025.

Schenawolf, Henry. "Battle of Wyoming Valley and Massacre." *Revolutionarywarjournal.Com*, Revolutionary War Journal, revolutionarywarjournal.com/battle-of-wyoming-american- defeat-or-massacre/. Last date accessed: 30 January 2025.

Soodalter, Ron. "Massacre and Retribution, the 1779-1780 Sullivan Expedition." *Historynet.Com*, Historynet, www.historynet.com/ massacre-retribution-the-1779-80-sullivan-expedition/?f. Last date accessed: 30 January 2025.

Speigleman, Robert. "Sullivan-Clinton Campaign, Then and Now." *Sullivan-Clinton Campaign*, www.sullivanclinton.com/. Last date accessed: 30 January 2025.

Stryker, William S. *General Maxwell's Brigade of New Jersey Continental Line in the Expedition Against the Indians in the Year 1779*. Franklin Classics, *openlibrary.org*, https://openlibrary.org/books/ OL39015748M/General_Maxwell's_Brigade_of_the_New_ Jersey_Contintental_Line_in_the_Expedition_Against_the_ Indians_. Last date accessed: 30 January 2025.

"Wyoming Massacre." *Britannica.Com*, Britannica, www.britannica. com/event/Wyoming-Massacre. Last date accessed: 30 January 2025.

Diaries from the Men of the Sullivan Expedition

Cook, Frederick. "Journals of the Military Expedition of Major General John Sullivan Against the Six Nations of Indians in 1779 with Records of Centennial Celebrations." *Usgwarchives.Net*, US Genweb Archives Pennsylvania, www.usgwarchives.net/pa/1pa/1picts/ sullivan/booktoc.html. Date Last Accessed: 30 January 2025.

Lee, Michael. "Lieutenant Colonel Adam Hubley, 11th Pennsylvania Regiment Diary of July 11th 1779." *Clinton-Sullivan Expedition Daily Diary*, https://www.facebook.com/groups/122416607846399/ permalink/2293611897393515/.

Lee, Michael. "Lieutenant James Norris, 3rd New Hampshire Regiment, July 3, 1779 July 2nd, 1779." *Clinton-Sullivan Expedition Daily Diary*, https://www.facebook.com/groups/122416607846399/ permalink/2280174308737274/.

Lee, Michael. "Reverend William Rogers, Hand's Brigade; Diary of July 8th 1779." *Clinton-Sullivan Expedition Daily Diary*, https://www.facebook.com/groups/122416607846399/ permalink/2288575961230442/.

French and Indian War, James Burd

Bryon, Matthew A. "Battle of the Monogahela." *Mountvernon.Org*, George Washington Presidential Library at Mount Vernon, www. mountvernon.org/library/digitalhistory/digital-encyclopedia/ article/battle-of-the-monongahela/. Last date accessed: 30 January 2025.

"Colonel James A. Burd Historical Marker." *Explorepahistory. Com*, Explore PA History, explorepahistory.com/hmarker. php?markerId=1-A-75. Last date accessed: 30 January 2025.

Cubbison, Douglas R. "'I Have Done Everything in My Power to Facilitate Their March to the Allegany Mountains': Organization of the Movement to Fort Cumberland, January - March 1755." *On Campaign Against Fort Duquesne: The Braddock and Forbes Expeditions, 1755-1758, through the Experiences of Quartermaster Sr. John St. Clair*, McFarland and Company, Inc., Jefferson, North Carolina, 2015, pp. 55–57, https://books.google.com/books ?id=qIfeCQAAQBAJ&lpg=PA48&ots=qcXbosTwPF&dq=Capt ain%20Rutherford%27s%20company%20of%20NY%20Foot%20 Soldiers&pg=PA56#v=onepage&q=Captain%20Rutherford's%20 company%20of%20NY%20Foot%20Soldiers&f=false. Last date accessed: 30 January 2025.

"Forts of the French and Indian War." *Weebly.Com*, frenchandindianwarforts. weebly.com/james-burd.html. Last date accessed: 30 January 2025.

"French and Indian War - Battle of Monogahela - 1775 Braddock's Defeat." *Britishbattles.Com*, www.britishbattles.com/french-indian-war/ battle-of-monongahela-1755-braddocks-defeat/. Last date accessed: 30 January 2025.

Hickman, Kennedy. "French and Indian War - Battle of Monongahela." *Thoughtcompany.Com*, 1 Sept. 2018, www.thoughtco.com/french-indian-war-battle-of-monongahela-2360798. Last date accessed: 30 January 2025.

Nixon, Lilly Lee. "Colonel James Burd in the Braddock Campaign." *The Western Pennsylvania Historical Magazine*, vol. 17, no. 4, 17 Dec. 1934, pp. 235–246, https://journals.psu.edu/wph/article/ viewFile/1703/1551. Last date accessed: 30 January 2025.

"Ten Facts about George Washington and the French and Indian War." *Mountvernon.Org*, George Washington Presidential Library at Mount Vernon, www.mountvernon.org/george-washington/ french-indian-war/ten-facts-about-george-washington-and-the-french-indian-war/. Last date accessed: 30 January 2025.

Morristown Encampment

"Jockey Hollow - Morristown National Historic Park, New Jersey." *Nps.Gov*, National Park Service, www.nps.gov/morr/learn/ historyculture/jockey-hollow.htm. Last date accessed: 31 January 2025.

"New Jersey Brigade Area and Cross Estate." *Nps.Gov*, National Park Service, www.nps.gov/morr/learn/historyculture/new-jersey-brigade-area-and-cross-estate. Last date accessed: 31 January 2025.

Thatcher, James. "Diaries of Doctor James Thatcher, Winter of 1779 - 1780." *Trent University Library, Journal of the American Revolution*, vol. 1862, Hurlbut, Williams & Co., pp. 180–191, archive.org/details/militaryjournal01862thac/page/180/mode/2up. Last date accessed: 29 January 2025.

"Washington's Encampment at Morristown, New Jersey and the 'Hard Winter' of 1779-1780." *Battlefields.Org*, American Battlefield Trust, www.battlefields.org/learn/articles/washingtons-encampment-morristown-new-jersey-and-hard-winter-1779-1780. Last date accessed: 31 January 2025.

Winslow, Thomas J. *Continental Army Winter Encampments, Morristown, New Jersey and Vicinity*, National Park Service, Morristown, New Jersey, 2019.

Winslow, Thomas J. *Morristown Encampment 1779-80 - A Chronology*, National Park Service, Morristown, New Jersey, 2019.